CROW
MOUNTAIN

lucy inglis

Chicken House

2 Palmer Street, Frome, Somerset BA11 1DS
www.doublecluck.com

Text © Lucy Inglis 2015

First published in Great Britain in 2015
Chicken House
2 Palmer Street
Frome, Somerset BA11 1DS
United Kingdom
www.doublecluck.com

Cover and interior design by Helen Crawford-White
Horse illustration by AmyLyn Bihrle
Typeset by Dorchester Typesetting Group Ltd
Printed and bound in Great Britain by CPI Group (UK) Ltd, Croydon CR0 4YY

The paper used in this Chicken House book is made from wood grown in
sustainable forests.

1 3 5 7 9 10 8 6 4 2

British Library Cataloguing in Publication data available.

PB ISBN 978-1-910002-35-3
eISBN 978-1-910002-85-8

This is a beautiful and thrilling love story. One that stretches across time to link two couples who have to survive the wilderness to find their true selves, and the secrets that they share. It made me angry on their behalf, fiercely hopeful for their survival and awed by Lucy Inglis's ability to create two such powerful worlds of love in such a singularly beautiful setting. Maybe hope can lead to happiness after all.

BARRY CUNNINGHAM
Publisher
Chicken House

For Charlie, Ruth and Jack Tweddle.
With love.

Also by Lucy Inglis
City of Halves

You already possess everything necessary to become great.

APSÁALOOKE PROVERB

'Hope! The taxi's here!' Meredith shouted.

Hope rammed the last of her stuff into her black nylon holdall. 'Coming!'

She clumped down the stairs lugging her heavy bags, as her mother stood in the hall, looking at the clock.

'He's cutting it fine.'

'We've got hours, Mum.' *And hours of hanging around in airports for the next day.*

'Do you have everything you need? Where we're going is very remote.'

'Where we go is always very remote. And yes, I have everything. I think.'

The black-cab driver beeped his horn. Meredith threw open the door, letting in London's pale spring sunshine. 'Then let's go.'

The driver rolled his window down. 'Taxi for West?'

'That's us.'

When they were loaded into the cab, he checked their destination. 'Heathrow, Terminal Five, ladies?'

'Yes, please,' Meredith said curtly, clearly annoyed with his familiar tone.

As they left the end of their road, he began to make conversation. 'Going on holiday?'

'No, work.'

'What's your work then?' he asked, with the typical bluntness of a London cabbie.

'I'm an environmental and forest ecosystem scientist specializing in sub-alpine microclimates.'

Hope squashed a sigh. Meredith was more than usually on edge when they had to make a flight.

'A sub . . . righto.' The driver continued undeterred. 'Where are you working then?'

'Montana. On the edge of the Glacier National Park. For a month.'

He whistled, pulling into the traffic heading for the North Circular. 'Had a man from Montana in my cab once. Know what they say about it?'

'No,' Meredith said.

'They call it The Last Best Place.'

'Because of its remarkable ecology?'

'No. Because of how it's one of the least populated places in America. You can lose yourself in the wilderness there and never be found. The Unabomber, outlaws, people like that. Go off grid in Montana and you're never seen again.' He glanced at Hope in the rear-view mirror. 'The real Wild West.'

CHAPTER 1

'YOUTH IS THE SEASON
OF IMPRESSION.'

Montana, 1867. The camp was a jumble, full of rough men and women, animals, dirt and noise. I stood aside, out of the thoroughfare, waiting for the others. The street, the only main street in Helena, was full of clapboard frontages with painted signs. At the edges, plots were still pegged out with string and stakes. Between the buildings, undergarments hung on washing lines in alleyways. Not far away, in a side street, someone had made a pigpen and the stench was in the air. Helena, it seemed, was to be like every other camp we had visited on our long and arduous journey. My heart sank.

Miss Adams stood with me as Mr Goldsmith climbed down, stiff-limbed, from the roof of the coach and began to fetch our overnight boxes. Mr Goldsmith had told me interesting stories about the history of America as we crossed the varied landscapes of the Great Plains. Or at least he had until Miss Adams made him sit outside on the roof with the teamsters who were escorting us, deeming his many nuggets of information unnecessary for my ears.

'Come, you cannot stand out here,' Miss Adams said, pushing through the doors of the hotel.

Like all those on the trail, it was busy and accommodated a bar. I had never been exposed to working, drinking men in England, and found their bold stares and filth terrifying.

'Don't look, Miss Forsythe. It only encourages them.'

The hotel owner appeared: he wore, like so many American men, an unattractive droopy moustache, greasy from lip-licking. There was a pair of spectacles with green lenses resting on the top of his balding head.

'Good afternoon, ladies,' he said cheerfully. 'Spencer party?'

We were travelling under the name of Spencer for more than one reason. The first was that Papa thought it prudent I, whilst travelling with so small a party, remain anonymous. The second was that with the displacement from the Sioux Wars, and so many people coming to the Montana gold fields, even the meanest places were full. Making multiple reservations in more than one name was somewhat dishonest, to my way of thinking, but had, on two occasions so far, secured us rooms when otherwise we would have been sleeping in the nearest pigpen. Still, we had perhaps only another three weeks of this before arriving at our destination, Portland.

There, I would meet the man I was engaged to marry – Anthony Howard Stanton from the family of the biggest railway constructors in America. Presently they were engaged in building a west-coast infrastructure, hence our rendezvous in Portland, where he was working on the branch line. We were to live in San Francisco, on Larkin Street, opposite Yerba Buena Park. The house was newly finished and already had a full staff, waiting for our arrival.

Miss Adams allowed the hotel keeper's wife to show us to our accommodation as I trailed behind them, lost in thought.

Married life. I was not quite sixteen. Very young for marriage; I knew it. It wasn't that I didn't know how to run a household, for I did, but the idea of being a wife kept me awake in the small hours. What if he could not love *me*, or found me lacking in some way? But Mama and Papa were convinced it was the best match I could make. Two of the finest families in the two greatest countries in the world, united.

When the photographs of Anthony Howard Stanton had arrived, Mama and Papa had expressed their approval whilst showing them to me: 'Darling, we think he looks most handsome and civilized.'

I had taken them, barely able to keep my hands from shaking. Quickly I had placed them on my sewing table, so that the tremor might not be detected. Aged twenty-two, Mr Stanton was a good height, slim and, yes, he was handsome, remarkably so.

The rooms were small, but they looked clean. I waited by

the door until Miss Adams confirmed her satisfaction and dismissed the proprietress. Miss Adams, I knew, was being paid handsomely to accompany me. A serious woman in her late twenties, she seemed to take no pleasure in anything. Her dress was plain to the point of severity and her hair so tight as to be unflattering. She also had a long nose, which, coupled with her all-seeing eyes, made her seem like a malevolent field mouse. I hoped I should be allowed to let her go once the wedding was over.

As our boxes were delivered, Miss Adams busied herself with unpacking the things we might need for the night. I washed my hands and face, drying off on the hard towel on the washstand, catching my pale reflection in the spotted glass hanging above it.

What had Mr Stanton thought of my portraits? I had loathed sitting for the photographer, my head in a carefully concealed brace to keep it still, but Mama and Papa seemed very pleased with the result. He had captured my pale skin and large eyes so well, everyone said.

I stared at the mirror, turning my head slowly left and right. My abundant hair was black like night and shone as if it had been varnished. Piled up as it was, it gave the overall impression that my head was too heavy for my neck. Mama thought this appearance artful, along with some very tight corset lacing. All of it conspired to make me appear the merest slip of a thing, particularly at parties, where she often had my stays tightened by an extra two inches. And perhaps it had been worth it, for Mr Stanton's proposal had come so soon after his receipt of the photographs. He had telegraphed my father the following day, and over the next hours my future had been tapped out in Morse Code across thousands of miles at the cost of one dollar a letter. At the memory, my chest tightened and the walls suddenly seemed to be closing in on me.

'Miss Adams, would you be kind enough to loosen these stays, please? The room is not hot, I know, but it is so very airless.'

Her mousey face sharpened but she unfastened the back of my dress and let out the stays, just a little. I took a deep, inelegant breath, dragging at the collar to free my throat and shoulders.

'And might we open the window a little?'

The manner in which she threw up the sash indicated she did not approve of this either. And perhaps she was right, as the air that came into the room was scarcely that of the purest kind. Still, it was cool and there was a tang of the fresh wind we had experienced on our long journey over the Great Plains, first by rail, then by stagecoach.

Papa and Mama were travelling separately, and had departed earlier in order to get to San Francisco early and finalize the wedding plans. The journey through Montana was our final leg, but the coming weeks were probably to be the most arduous – or so Mr Goldsmith had warned me. The Indians were attacking all along the Bozeman Trail and no one was safe, but on this route he told me they were mostly unthreatening. And on the Oregon Trail people were dying of a terrible disease and that must be avoided at all costs. It was so bad they were being buried under the trail itself, so that the wagons passing over them might break down their bodies very quickly and stop the wolves eating their bones.

I looked over at the window, wanting to feel the breeze on my skin. After all day in the coach I felt horribly trapped in the small room, but it would be indecorous to stand any closer to the window, where I might be seen, my pale shoulders exposed.

It was then that I saw you.

You were riding a white horse spattered with large tan splotches, your feet kicked out of the stirrups as you approached the hotel. Behind you trailed another horse on a rope. I had never seen anyone so at ease on horseback, and moved closer to the window. I hadn't yet seen your limp, nor your pale eyes, but I could see your longish brown hair and your unshaven jaw. Around your neck was a leather lace, from which dangled assorted objects. There seemed to be a knife, some feathers, with a few spent cartridges amongst them. You were squinting with fatigue, for the early evening spring sunshine was not bright. I hadn't noticed I'd taken another step further towards the open window, fingers touching the frame. A rifle sat behind your right leg, stock sticking out of its sling, though I had become used to guns in my short time in America. I had seen more guns in the month since we arrived in New York than I had thought to exist in the entire world. You were dressed in long, soft Indian boots that laced around your legs, trousers, and a shirt with a battered suede waistcoat over it.

I forgot about the strictures of my stays, captivated. You pulled the horses to a halt in the rutted dust by the hotel's hitching post, and swung yourself down in the most graceful manner possible. As you slung the reins over the horses' heads and caressing them, I could see you were speaking to them but in the noise leaking from the hotel and the clamour on the street there was no way for me to hear what you were saying. As you moved to tie them to the rail I saw the difficulty you had when out of the saddle: you were lame in the right leg.

I watched as you handed the waiting hotel urchin a coin to keep an eye on the animals, and I was still standing there, staring, when you looked up, your expression unreadable. My breath caught and my heart began to thump as if it would jump out of my chest. From the window frame, my fingers lifted, then hesitated, uncertain. How long we stood there I, to this day, have no idea.

Miss Adams's cry of dismay pierced me. She ran forward, pulling me away and flinging the window down. Turning on me, her tirade was impressive. 'Miss Forsythe! How could you expose yourself to such a man? To the whole street, undressed!'

I put out my hands, pleading, yet I couldn't help but glance back at the window again. 'I wished only for a moment or two of air. I had thought there was no harm in it. Please, do not tell Mama. I shall not behave in such a fashion again.' I stood, dress hanging from my shoulders. If Miss Adams did tell of what I had done, then I would be in considerable trouble, and

Mama's disapproval was so hard to endure. I thought quickly. 'But if you were to write to Mama, of course, she would wonder why I had been left to my own devices.'

Miss Adams's mouth closed like a man-trap. I said nothing more, but went over to the bed, fetching the travelling photograph frame containing my two photographs of the handsome, immaculately suited Mr Stanton. Going to my nightstand, I opened the frame with a snap, like a book, and placed it where I should see it when I went to sleep and when I awoke, as had become my custom.

'I should like to change before we eat. These clothes feel travel-stained,' I said, presenting my back to her. She unfastened my dress, hands crueller than necessary. I made a mental note that, as a married woman, I should very much like a lady's maid who did not pull me about, and was considerate with the hairbrush. Worthy Miss Adams may have been; gentle she was not.

'Might we eat downstairs, do you think?' I asked, as she finished buttoning my evening gown.

'Amongst his kind of rabble? I think not,' she sniffed.

I bit my lips together. Was I so transparent? Had I even admitted to myself I should like to catch a glimpse of you again? What was it about you that made me brave enough to request eating in a room full of men who terrified me? You were older than me, that much I guessed. It was hard to say how much older. Your tan, though undesirable in a civilized man, suited you. But you did look wild, and dusty. The horses were still hitched to the post. You were down there, somewhere.

We ate in the room. The food was dreadful. Some sort of leathery pork steak with the obligatory beans. Owing to father's entertaining duties for the embassy, our meals at home in London had frequently featured caviar, champagne jellies and spun sugar confections, but I loved best Cook's little treats of an apple and cheese or a biscuit slipped on to my tray when Mama wasn't in the room. I placed my knife and fork together in silence. Miss Adams said nothing. Eating very little was ladylike, and she approved of ladylike behaviour. My travelling companion wasn't one for conversation, but as all she would have done would be to remind me of my lapse I was grateful for the silence.

So, the interminable wait for the moment of retirement began. I had read all my books, and there were no more to be had at the hotel. Some had a small stock laid by, but Miss Adams had yet to find something suitable. The coach was to depart at dawn the following morning, so we were going to be up early. I stifled a feigned yawn. I doubted I would sleep: the wilder the territory became, the more fear crowded my thoughts and it was worse at night.

'I shall prepare to retire, I think.'

I managed to snatch a glance out of the window as I passed. The white and brown horse was still there, waiting patiently. But alone.

The next morning, we were up and dressed before the sunrise. The stagecoach team were keen to cover the miles.

We would be travelling long distances over the coming days and stopping only at staging posts. It was the remotest part of our journey, and not without its perils. Our guards were armed and taking no chances, as there were deserters and road agents to be found in the foothills of the mountains.

When hearing of our plan to avoid the Oregon Trail, Mr Stanton had written to tell me that his family's railway company were planning to scout our route for a new branch of the Pacific Railroad. He asked me if I would be so kind and such a help to him as to make notes on the terrain, and any large bodies of water or mountains. Perhaps I might even sketch them? I ordered new pencils, water colours and sketchbooks so that I might be of use to my future husband.

Outside at dawn, waiting to climb into the coach, I looked at the hitching post. The horse was gone. The street empty.

Mr Goldsmith, huge and forbidding in his great overcoat, appeared and opened the coach door, handing me in. 'Morning, miss,' he said in his gruff manner, smelling somewhat of whiskey.

'Good day.' I settled into my seat, stays already digging into my hip bones.

We left Helena, and set out on a trail towards a place called Fort Shaw, hurrying because soon the glacier high up in the mountains would experience the spring melt, which would make crossing all the rivers far more dangerous. Fort Shaw, according to the men I had heard talking when we stopped to water the horses, was little more than a military camp to keep the trail open, but there we would take on provisions and fresh horses. After that, we would branch west into the mountains.

Indian territory.

CHAPTER 2

'I can't believe we forgot the tea bags,' Meredith said.

I didn't forget them. I told you I didn't have room in my case.

'And you should eat something.'

'Please, Mum, I'm OK.'

Far beneath them, the Great Plains were spread out in the midday sun. Hope took the water bottle from the back of the seat pocket in front of her and chugged a gulp. The silence between them stretched out. Meredith hated it when Hope called her 'Mum'. So Hope did it quite a lot. Meredith's idea of equality and feminism was that all women were on first-name terms. Hope's idea was that having a mum meant you got to call her 'Mum'.

The pilot announced that they would soon be starting their descent into Helena. Hope grabbed her wash bag and went to the back of the small aircraft. Inside the cramped space, the fluorescent light flickered as she threw the lock. She eyed her scruffy reflection, like a wary stork. After a slow start, the last couple of years had added inches to her height, and Hope was still settling into being considerably taller than her neat little mother. A pair of khaki shorts, a white singlet and a thin grey cardigan all hung from her, crumpled. There were violet smudges beneath her green eyes and her freckled skin was washed out in the harsh light. Only her long fair hair was full of life, streaming over her shoulders. The flush sucked out with a noisy whoosh and a blast of cold. She washed her face, brushed her teeth and her hair and applied some lip balm. Then she was back in her seat as the seat-belt sign came on and the little plane lurched into its final descent.

On the tarmac, the terminal building came into view. Long, low buildings in a solid grey surrounded a green, barn-like building with a pitched roof. The airport was tiny. Behind it, huge mountains rose up in the distance, almost lost in the haze of the spring day.

'Well, we're here,' Meredith said brightly, as the cabin crew mobilized and the aircraft rolled to a halt.

'Great,' Hope murmured under her breath.

Her mother shot her a look. 'At least give it a chance. How many people of your age get to travel like you?'

Hope gestured towards the window. 'A ranch? What am I going to do for a month, on a ranch?' She stood up and opened the overhead locker, pulling down her rucksack and shoving her wash bag inside it. 'If they don't have proper WiFi, and the movie channel, I'm going to die.'

Meredith stood. 'They told me they do. In the emails they sent me,' she said. 'I asked especially. Though why you would want to fly five thousand miles to one of the last great ecosystems in the world and spend your time watching Hollywood films, I just don't know.'

'I didn't ask to come.'

'You're sixteen. And you always come. It's one of the great advantages of home-schooling,' Meredith said, tucking her short, sleek dark hair behind her ears. 'And what are other girls your age doing? Hanging around in a park, drinking? Taking drugs? Messaging boys naked pictures of themselves?'

'I've never done that and I won't.'

'Men only take advantage if you let them. You must use your personal agency as a woman to stop that happening.' Her mother tugged her handbag out of her cabin luggage, taking out a comb and running it over her head. Meredith disapproved of make-up.

Hope slung her rucksack over her shoulder and looked down the gangway to where the few other passengers on the tin-can plane were pulling on sweaters and retrieving their bags. The cabin door opened and sunshine flooded in. She gnawed her lip, arms folded.

'Will you just try and appreciate the time here? For me?' her mum added. 'Who knows, it could be a real adventure.'

They crossed the tarmac into the green terminal building. Inside, it was lofty and utilitarian, smelling vaguely of cinnamon-scented cleaning products.

They queued for passport control and then waited in silence for their bags with the dozen other passengers, the carousel squeaking. Theirs was almost the last stuff to come through. Hope grabbed her large, black nylon holdall, struggling with the weight. Meredith lifted her rolling case and popped up the handle efficiently. They went towards the exit, and emerged into the terminal building. There was a seating area and a bar called Captain Jack's. Meredith came to a halt, Hope just behind her.

'He said he'd be here . . .' she said slowly, scanning the terminal.

'Who?'

'Caleb Crow.'

Hope raised an eyebrow. 'Caleb? Sounds like a Mormon.'

'No, he's a hugely respected rancher. And he has no religious affiliations as far as I know. I told him what we looked like.'

Hope wasn't listening. She was staring at a tall boy wearing jeans, plain brown leather boots and a chequered shirt with the sleeves rolled above his elbows. He was on his phone with his weight slightly on one leg, shrugging as he talked and scanned the stragglers. Everything about him was narrow and angular, his hips, his chest, his throat. He had bright blue eyes, shiny brown hair pushed off his face, a sharp jaw and tanned skin that looked slightly dusty. Hope had never seen anything like him. She knew she was staring as she began to revise her expectations of Montana very sharply upwards. He caught her gaze and stopped talking. There was a long second before the person on the other end of the line gained his attention again, as Hope and the young cowboy stared at each other. He ended the call and walked towards them.

Hope looked away, embarrassed to have been caught gawping and hoping he wasn't going to try and talk to her, while wanting more than anything in the world for him to come over. But it always went badly if a boy tried to talk to her in front of Meredith. She looked at the floor, just as a pair of well-worn leather boots appeared.

'Mrs West?' asked a clear and very American voice.

He's here for us? Oh God. Please please let him be here for us. Maybe he works for the ranch. Oh God.

'It's Dr West, actually.' Meredith's voice was cool.

'Ah, sorry, ma'am. Of course. Dr West,' he said seriously.

She raised an eyebrow. 'We were expecting Caleb Crow?'

He offered a tanned hand. 'You've got him, ma'am. We're both Caleb. Me and Dad. I'm Cal, for the sake of all our sanities.'

They shook. 'This is my daughter, Hope.'

Cal turned to her. He radiated health and athleticism. Hope felt even more exhausted. His dry, calloused grip enveloped her hand. He shook once, then let her go. 'Hey there,' he said, not quite meeting her eyes. 'Let me take your bag.' He stooped and put his hand on the black strap of her holdall.

'We only bring what we can carry ourselves,' Meredith said. 'We can manage.'

Cal removed the bag from Hope's hands without trying, straightening up. 'Sure you can. But now you don't have to.'

20

Turning, he took the handle of Meredith's case and began to drag it behind him, loping off towards the bright glass doors of the terminal.

Meredith took a deep breath. 'Well. He seems very nice,' she said, 'chauvinism aside. But this is the Midwest, I suppose. Still living in a different century.'

They followed him out into the fresh air. Hope took a deep breath and looked around. Cal was stowing their bags in the flatbed of a vintage white Ford pick-up. It was huge. He walked to the passenger door and opened it.

Hope looked at him, and he gestured inside. There was room for three. A rifle was strapped into the rear window. She held back, looking at it and the spartan interior. Meredith climbed in, busying herself with fastening the lap belt. Hope sighed, not wanting to be cramped up again. Her limbs hadn't started to loosen from a day's flying and waiting around in JFK, then Salt Lake City.

'It's really not too far to home,' Cal said in his steady, light drawl, as if reading her mind.

Hope looked at him. He met her gaze, his eyes an even brighter blue in the sunshine. She bit her lip on a smile. Somewhere nearby a bird was singing. It swooped low above them, its wings a stunning blue. He watched it whip through the air, disappearing over the long-term car park, song fading out.

'Was that a Montana bluebird?' Meredith called from inside the pick-up, startling them out of their shared moment. 'Astonishing to see one so close to an airport.'

'Yes, Dr West,' Cal replied. 'Must've heard you were coming.'

Hope swore he shot her the ghost of a wink. She got into the pick-up, pushing her holdall into the footwell, and he closed the door behind her.

They skirted the edges of Helena, driving down a long boulevard with low buildings on either side. Traffic lights hung on arched gantries over the tarmac junctions. Gaudy signs for stores and restaurants clustered by the side of the road. There were the golden arches, and a huge plastic pig was advertising a ribs shack. A drab motel had only a few cars outside. Hope stared out of the window, as Meredith attempted to make conversation.

'So, Cal, how far are we going?'

They were at a stop signal. He shifted in the seat a little, his elbow out of the window and long body lax in the seat. 'Not too far. It's just a few hours.'

Hope's heart sank, but she stayed looking out of the window.

'We need to swing by Fort Shaw and collect a few things from the store.'

Meredith nodded. 'Well, thank you for meeting us. It's very kind. It would have been such a nuisance to hire a car just to get to the ranch and back.'

He shrugged. 'A pleasure. And like I said in the email, there's plenty of vehicles you can use back at home so pointless to get a rental for one journey.' The light changed and they moved forwards. Hope wound down her window, wanting the breeze on her face.

'I thought it was your father in the emails,' Meredith admitted.

'Did you?' He sounded surprised. 'No, it was always me. Dad's not big on email. Not even sure he would know how to use it. The only thing he looks at on the computer is the weather forecast and the price of feed.'

'I'm very much looking forward to seeing the ranch. I've heard a great deal about the ecosystem you've managed to maintain. I think it will be invaluable for my research.'

He nodded. 'The ranch goes back a long way in the family. The first deeded acres we have are from 1871. We've worked hard over the years to keep everything as natural as we can. We don't use any pesticides and we cultivate as little as possible. It's a working ranch though,' he said after a pause. 'Not much glamour about it.' The way he spoke was slow compared to Londoners.

Hope carried on looking out of the window, breathing in the fresh air. The buildings were thinning out.

'I respect that and thank you for letting us stay with you. We don't need glamour, do we, Hope?' Meredith said.

Hope shook her head, looking at her hands.

'Hope's rather shy, as you can see.'

Great, thanks, Mum. The hottest boy ever, and you're making me out to be a massive loser already.

He said nothing, just indicated to turn on to a different road, a two-lane highway stretching into the distance, dead straight. On one side were the mountains, on the other, the plains stretched away.

As they drove, Meredith questioned him. His answers were economical, but not unfriendly.

'Yes, I'm nineteen.'

'Which college are you attending?'

'I'm not at college, Dr West.'

'Oh, are you taking a gap year?'

Hope sighed internally and let her head rest against the doorframe.

There was a long pause. 'I didn't graduate high school.' Hope sensed, rather than saw, him look sideways at her mother. She also sensed the judgement coming from Meredith, who thought that higher education was the meaning of life. Hope leant against the ribbed white enamel of the door and stared out at the landscape.

Ahead of them by the side of the road was a tall, metal-clad building, almost like a tower with no windows. Around it were other towers, but round. They looked ghostly and abandoned. Parts of the metal cladding were falling away.

'What's that, please?' Hope asked, trying to lighten the atmosphere.

He looked across at her for a moment, surprised by the sound of her voice. 'Grain elevator. Storage. That one's not been used in a while.'

'It looks like a lot around here hasn't been used in a while,' Hope said, feeling the colour rise in her cheeks, unsure of why she was even still speaking.

'Yeah, we've suffered a little with the economy, depopulation, stuff like that.'

Coming up on their left was a small fenced-off square. Inside, old wooden crosses mingled with the odd headstone. In front of one were artificial flowers in a jam jar. Hope leant a little to keep it in view, and realized as the square passed behind the driver's side window that she was looking straight at Cal. She sat back, letting her hair fall in her face.

'Do you study, Hope?'

Hope looked at her hands in her lap, thumbs locked together around her empty water bottle, as her mother answered for her.

'Hope is home-schooled, and we're still discussing what she will study at university. A vocational or science degree is best. It's very difficult for Arts graduates to find work in the UK at the moment.'

He drove one-handed, putting his free hand on the roof rail at the top of the door outside. 'Well, our vocation's ranching. What's your vocation, Hope?'

Writing, I want to be a writer. More than anything. Hope took a breath to speak, the words seemingly stuck in her throat.

'Hope will study a science, probably chemistry,' Meredith said, and no one spoke much after that.

They drove on. At one point they passed a low, dirty house with smoke coming from the single chimney. Scattered around it were more than a dozen old buses and trucks, their shapes familiar to Hope from old movies. Rusting and collapsing into the scrubby prairie, they looked like a herd of decrepit animals.

A phone buzzed somewhere. Cal pulled it out of his pocket and looked at it for a second before putting it back. Hope was annoyed at herself for wanting to know who was getting in touch with him. She pulled out her own phone and checked her text messages.

'Is the roaming turned off?' Meredith asked for the tenth time.

Hope stared out of the window. The landscape was changing again, with bigger dips and rolls, and to the right was a group of old wooden buildings. The land around them was cultivated and there was a group of women working in a field, weeding with long-handled hoes. Their clothes were brightly coloured, consisting of a pinafore dress and flat leather shoes. On their heads were black, white-spotted kerchiefs.

Cal saw her watching them with interest. 'They're the Hutterites. Kind of like Amish. No cars, no electricity, nothing modern. Came from Germany in the nineteenth century, settled all over these parts and up into Canada. Folks round here call them the Hoots. They farm, mostly.'

'This terrain is rather inhospitable to traditional arable agriculture, isn't it?' Meredith asked, gesturing out to the scrubby plant covering the miles of untended land. 'That's sagebrush, I think. Very hardy.'

'Yeah, we got about sixteen types. It grows where other things won't. And yeah, the land isn't great. Lot of failed homesteaders around here back in the last century. Ranchers generally aren't keen on little farms breaking up the land and farmers tend not to like waking up to a load of cattle trampling their fields. But the Hutterites, they work crazy-hard. And land is all they have.'

A red sign on the side of the road informed them they had arrived in Fort Shaw. It was a small town, with one main street. There was an old military cemetery with a white sign proclaiming it dated from 1867. Cal halted the pick-up outside a white wooden shack with an ancient Pepsi sign sticking out of it, next to a faded silver convertible. Sitting under the shaded porch, humming, was a white refrigerator as ancient as the sign, with a glass front containing beers and sodas, and a large mongrel dog. A sign on the door behind the dog read 'Open'.

'I'll be just a moment.' Cal got out and went to the door, stepping over the dog and going inside.

Meredith and Hope sat in silence.

'Apparently lots of young Americans don't graduate high school. It's a shame, but we mustn't let that affect our judgement of him.'

Hope resisted the urge to say that she hadn't judged him at all.

'Look,' Meredith's tone softened, 'I know you're shy, but it would be nice if you tried just a little harder. I'm going to take this opportunity to use the loo. Coming?'

Hope shook her head. Meredith got out of the pick-up on the driver's side and went through a door that said 'Restroom, Patrons Only' just next to the shop. Hope watched the street.

Cal reappeared, a case of wine under each arm. He hooked the door open with his foot and stepped back over the dog.

27

He put the wine in the flatbed and disappeared again, coming out a few seconds later with a vast bag of something slung over his shoulder. The pick-up bounced a little as he dropped it into the back. He went back to the store, pulling money from the rear pocket of his jeans, elbow sharp behind him. He stood in the doorway, talking to a bulky American Indian man as he handed over the money. Hope listened to him as they talked.

'Nah, thanks anyway though. Two fifty, right?'

'Yep. Two twenty for the wine and thirty for the dog food. I swear Buddy is sponsored by the pet-food people, the amount he eats. Thanks.' He took the cash. 'Send my best to your parents.'

'Will do. Thanks, Joe. You guys coming up next weekend?'

The store owner grinned as he tucked the money away. 'Wouldn't miss a Crow barbecue after all this time. And we're looking forward to meeting your visitors.' He waved towards the pick-up. Hope lifted her hand and smiled.

Coming towards the pick-up on the quiet street was another truck, newer and shinier. It sped up as it got closer, engine loud and music pumping. The driver's window was down, and as it passed shouts and jeers came from the blacked-out interior, and a large plastic cup smashed against Hope's side of the pick-up, exploding in a spray of ice and watery Coke. She recoiled as the truck drove away, music fading as it turned the corner.

Cal jumped down, leaning in the driver's side window. 'You OK?'

Hope brushed a couple of splashes from her shoulder. 'Yes. Thanks. Friendly locals.'

He was scowling, looking after the truck.

'Local idiots,' the man called Joe said. 'Sorry about that, miss.'

Hope shrugged, unsettled, as a tall American Indian woman in jeans, a tight T-shirt, and a gun in a shoulder holster walked out of the store, letting the door bang behind her. On her belt was a police badge. Her narrow eyes were focused down the street, where the truck had disappeared.

Cal took a bottle of water from the noisy refrigerator, just as a police cruiser slid to a halt right in front of the pick-up's nose. Two men got out. Both were large and intimidating. Their belts bristled with batons, handcuffs and firearms. Cal's pace, returning to the vehicle, slowed. 'What *now*?' Hope heard him say under his breath.

'Well well, young Caleb Crow,' the older man said. He wore mirrored sunglasses on his craggy face and his uniform looked more senior than the young man's. He had muscular arms he folded over his chest. Joe came back on to the porch of the shop, and the dog lifted its head, suddenly alert. The tall woman stuck her hands in her back pockets and watched, her glossy shoulder-length hair caught by the breeze.

'Chief Hart, Officer Jones,' Cal said politely, with a slight nod.

Despite the man's sunglasses, Hope knew his gaze had shifted to her. She ducked her head.

'What have we got here?' The chief sauntered over to the

rolled-down driver's window and stooped to look in at Hope. 'Hello, miss. You from out of town?'

'Hello. Yes, I am.'

'Listen to that pretty accent. You English?'

'Yes.'

He straightened up, speaking to Cal again. The other officer was standing intimidatingly close. 'You gotta go some distance these days to make sure they ain't heard your reputation, don't you, son?'

Cal's face was impassive, but Hope saw his hand tighten around the water bottle. The chief saw it too.

'Ah now, boy, don't get riled. I ain't gonna tell her what a no-good piece a-shit you really are.' He bent to the window again, looking in at Hope. 'Now, miss, you take real good care of yourself around this boy, OK? He ain't to be trusted. Enjoy your stay here in our fine county.' He slapped the door of the pick-up, then his eyes shifted to the flatbed in the back, seeing the wine. A triumphant smirk spread across his face. 'Now, would that there be alcohol I see you just purchased from our upstanding ethnic storekeeper here in town?'

Cal said nothing and Hope suddenly remembered that the legal age for drinking in America was twenty-one. Cal was underage. Joe's expression was unreadable, but Hope could feel the tension in the air.

The policeman walked back to where his fellow officer was standing, almost toe to toe with Cal.

'Looks like I got me an open and shut case. Shame to close down these fine stores, but I ain't got no choice. Can't

30

condone the selling of alcohol to Montana's minors.'

Cal didn't move, his jaw set. Joe said nothing.

'Knew I'd get you in the end, Black. Just a matter of time. Your kind just ain't good around liquor, are you—?'

'He was collecting an order,' the tall woman interrupted, knocking a cigarette out of a soft packet. 'That's all.' She and the policeman stared at each other for a long time, his eyes unreadable behind the glasses.

'No one asked you . . . Officer,' he said. 'So I suggest you get along to the rez and do whatever it is you do there.'

The woman lit the cigarette. 'No business there today. Business here,' she said around it.

His face hardened further. 'This place is under my care, you remember that.'

'I remember,' she said placidly.

Meredith came out of the restroom. 'Is there a problem, Officers? We've only parked here for a few moments so I could use the conveniences. I'm sorry, we've just come from the airport and I was quite insistent.'

The police chief nodded in her direction. 'Ma'am, I'm afraid we have an incident of the sale of alcohol by Mr Black to young Mr Crow here. There are serious penalties for that in this state.'

Meredith didn't even blink. 'Alcohol? Do you mean the wine?'

'Yes, ma'am, I do.'

'Oh, but I purchased it. We're here for a month, you see, and I do like a glass of wine at the end of the day.'

31

Hope breathed a sigh of relief. The police chief looked seriously disappointed, almost as if he was grinding his teeth. The tall woman was trying not to smile.

'You got a receipt?'

'I'm afraid not. I paid in cash so I didn't take one. Two hundred and twenty dollars.'

After a pause the police chief spoke again. 'Then there's no problem at all, ma'am. I'd like to welcome you and your daughter to Montana. You take good care of her out at that ranch.'

There was a silence. Meredith refused to fill it, her face hardening at the mention of Hope.

'Because, you know, anything could happen,' he finished. With that, both men turned, got back into the police cruiser, taking their time, and the car lumbered off. Hope looked down, wishing she were as brave as her mother. Meredith got back into the pick-up through Cal's door, sliding across the seat and buckling her belt.

Cal eased back into the pick-up and turned the key. 'I'm obliged to you, Dr West.' He looked out of the window. 'You too, Officer.' The tall woman threw down the end of her cigarette and stamped on the stub, then turned and left with a small nod in his direction.

Meredith clicked the seat-belt fastener. 'Not at all. I loathe men throwing their weight around.'

'How did you know how much it cost?' Cal looked genuinely bemused.

Meredith shook her head. 'Have you heard the acoustics in

that bathroom? You can hear every word that's said right outside the store. Dreadful. I hope it doesn't work the other way round.'

Hope hid a smile.

As did Cal. 'Still, thanks again. Joe could have been in real trouble.'

'Yes, so I imagine. As could you. But we'll say no more about it. And I'd far rather have the wine than not.'

Hope sat listening in silence.

'It's not far now, I promise,' Cal said, leaning across and holding out the bottle of water to Hope. 'We live off Highway 89.' She looked at the water, surprised, before taking it. He said nothing about what had just happened, but there were stripes of red high on his brown cheekbones.

He turned off on to a single-track road and stopped the pick-up, jumping out and checking a sturdy white mailbox on a post, emblazoned on the front with 'Broken Bit' and beneath, the words '*Oro y plata*'.

Gold and silver. Montana's state motto, Hope had learnt from a cursory check of Wikipedia when Meredith had announced the tickets were booked.

A bundle of envelopes in his hand, Cal got back into the vehicle and drove on, heading for the mountain range to the west. The land rose in waves. Stands of trees clumped here and there and rocks dotted the landscape. After a short while, they passed beneath a huge wooden arch, seemingly fashioned from massive, scavenged, tree branches, burnt repeatedly with a motif Hope hadn't seen before. The sign that hung from it held only one word in rusted iron letters: CROW.

'What does the burnt symbol mean, please?' Hope asked.

'It's our brand, for the livestock and the horses. Broken Bit ranch. Everyone puts theirs on their gatepost round here, if they're ranching. Ours is a little unusual – it's a broken D-ring snaffle bit, hence the name of the ranch. But it's also two Cs turned to face each other.' He curled his thumbs and fore-fingers to face each other in the shape of two letter Cs on top of the steering wheel. 'Crow. And Caleb. We're all Caleb. I'm the fifth.'

Post and rail fencing appeared. Cattle dotted the landscape.

'I thought your ranch was horses,' Meredith said.

'It is. The finest American horses,' he said, matter-of-factly, glancing across at Hope. 'But we also raise pedigree cattle. Rare breeds that are under threat. It's a family thing. We have buffalo here too. We're one of the original five families who saved them from extinction back in the nineteenth century. We've been here for almost a hundred and fifty years, kept the ranch intact through the fence wars, the Depression. My great-grandma kept it going while my great-grandaddy was a prisoner in the Pacific during World War Two. All the time we've been working on bringing back the buffalo. Still trying to even out the gene pool with them.'

'Cattle are detrimental to the delicate environmental balance you've got here.' There was a note of accusation in Meredith's voice.

'We keep an eye on it,' he said mildly. 'We have to manage

the cattle and the buffalo separately on the land anyway, because of the disease risk.'

The pick-up raised a dust cloud behind it as they headed further up the track. When they had been driving for some time, a group of red-roofed buildings appeared, nestling into the edge of a forest. In front of them were corrals, where groups of horses gathered in the corners, quiet in the afternoon sun.

They arrived at the cluster of buildings. Hope looked up at the house. The central building was huge, constructed from timber and stone, and looked like a cross between a barn and a cathedral with a wide porch wrapped around all sides. The bleached boards had long since faded to silvery grey and it had a timeless, frontier feeling about it. Above the vast front door was the skull of a cow or a bull, with gigantic horns.

A tall, lean man came out of a large and much-repaired stable barn, and walked towards them. He was almost exactly like Cal, just older.

'Meredith? Hope?' He held out his hand. 'Caleb Crow. Hope the drive wasn't too long after your journey.'

Meredith shook. 'Not at all, Mr Crow, thank you.'

Caleb shook Hope's hand too. 'Well, Miss Hope, this is a real pleasure.' Caleb Crow Snr had a stronger accent than his son. 'A real treat to have your pretty face around the place.'

Meredith's expression cooled. Cal hauled their bags out of the pick-up.

'You going to show these girls to their quarters?'

'Yep.'

Caleb gestured for them to follow his son. They walked up the steps, on to the porch and then into the cool, wooden house. Beyond the door was a huge room, right up into the roof. More horned cattle skulls adorned the rafters. Battered leather sofas were covered with throws in Indian patterns. Hung on one wall was a flat TV. Through a wooden archway beyond was a bright, clean kitchen.

'This way.' Cal tipped his head towards an exposed spiral staircase, all wood and glass. At that moment, a leggy bundle of grey and white fur hurtled into the room, banging into Cal's leg. 'Hey, Buddy.'

Hope started back. There was what appeared to be a grey wolf in the room.

Cal pushed the creature away affectionately. 'We'll get you something to eat in a minute.'

The wolf bounded up to Hope, planting both his huge paws on her chest. She stumbled back, clutching the strap of her holdall.

'Buddy,' Cal snapped. 'Where are your manners?'

The animal retreated instantly, tail wagging.

'Sorry,' Cal said, rubbing the side of the wolf's head against his thigh. 'He's just a baby.'

'A baby wolf?' Hope asked uncertainly.

'Nah. Well, half. He's a cross with some kind of domestic breed. Probably a stray. They call them wolfdogs. I found him last year, near a dumpster on the edge of Fort Shaw, when he was just a few days old.'

Meredith moved closer, fascinated. 'He seems more wolf

than dog, but very tractable. Is his behaviour consistent?'

Cal shrugged. 'We've never had any problems with him. I'll show you your accommodation.'

Upstairs, he walked along a balcony which overlooked the huge sitting room. Pushing open a door with his toe, he put Meredith's bag inside.

'Dr West, you're in here.'

Hope's mother turned, frowning. 'We're not in the same room?'

Cal hesitated. 'We . . . thought you'd like your own space.'

'We would. We do,' Hope said quickly.

Meredith backed away and walked into her brightly decorated room, saying nothing. On a trip away they had never slept separately before. Cal led Hope to another door along the balcony. The room behind it was massive, like everything in the house. The back wall was all glass, looking out over the bluff and forest at the back of the house. A white cowhide covered the wooden floor. On a table was a television and a computer. The door was open to a shower room.

He put her bag on the bed. 'I didn't know if you were bringing your own laptop, or—'

'Yes. But thank you,' Hope said, grateful.

'Is there anything you need? More water or anything?' He stuck a hand in his back pocket and gestured over his shoulder with the other thumb in the vague direction of downstairs.

She shook her head.

They watched each other for a few moments. Hope struggled to breathe normally.

'OK. We eat around seven.' He closed the door behind him.

CHAPTER 3

'TO LOVE AND TO HATE, THEN,
SEEM TO BE THE TWO THINGS
WHICH IT IS MOST NATURAL AND
MOST EASY FOR WOMEN TO DO.
HOW IMPORTANT IS IT,
THEREFORE, THAT THEY SHOULD
LEARN EARLY IN LIFE TO
LOVE AND HATE ARIGHT.'

It had taken us another three days to do what did not seem like so very many miles. The staging posts had been tolerable, although I hadn't been able to manage much sleep and the arrangements often left a lot to be desired. Still, we were making progress. Mostly, the track that passed for a road was hard and reliable.

In Fort Shaw we slept in a military tent, but I had managed to find some new books and newspapers to pass the time, given to me by an Army captain's wife who had proved very kind and a welcome change from Miss Adams. There had also been a large family there, intending to settle in the area. Their clothing was plain but brightly coloured and the women wore pretty handkerchiefs on their hair, covered with dots. There were two girls around my age and I attempted to speak to them; they would not talk to me, only turned away in silence without meeting my eyes. I learnt later that they were very religious and do not speak to people who are not like them.

As we set out from yet another staging post that morning, I opened my book, already vetted by my companion, and began to read. The day passed, sunny and fine. When I wasn't reading, I looked out of the window at the ever more dramatic scenery and attempted to draw in my sketchbook.

The air was thin and cool and I breathed in as much as I could. The ends of the steel stays of my long corsets, even though they were covered with padded material, were wearing red welts on my hip bones and the ribs of my back. I had worn, for most of my life, corsets stiffened with cane or whalebone, but Mama had taken a notion that a steel-strengthened corset was the way to proper posture. Underneath one shoulder blade, it had broken the skin. Miss Adams had applied a stinging salve to it the previous evening. I knew she could not fail to notice the other marks, but she said nothing and had laced me up just as tightly that morning. When I asked if I might travel in a looser, shorter set she refused. Apparently, Mama had told her that upon my arrival I should be straight into the smartest of San Franciscan society and I must not let myself down with a sloppy figure. Accustomed as I was to being constrained, the days had become very painful and more than once I had had to hide a tear whilst waiting to dress in the mornings, facing yet another day of imprisonment.

We met few people on the trail and the team had seen or

heard little regarding the whereabouts of the Indian tribes. Supposedly, it was common for bands of the young men, sometimes as few as two but other times as many as two dozen, to roam the country whilst the others stayed in one place. According to Mr Goldsmith, who had travelled this trail more than once, some of the local Indians were even farmers and did not use horses much, although others lived almost their entire lives on horseback.

The horseback tribes, Mr Goldsmith told me, were great hunters of the buffalo, of which we had seen so many on the plains on the way here. Thousands, in such multitudes it was hard to imagine before seeing them. I had smelt them from the train window. The bulls, as they were called, were gigantic, far more massive than even the largest of the London dray horses. Abundance seemed to be everywhere, here in America: once, the train had followed an astonishing migration of birds, pigeon Mr Goldsmith said, so many we were with them for hours and they darkened the sky above us.

And it was not only the animals that caught my attention: here and there, we had seen Indians, all on horseback, usually sitting stock-still and watching the train passing. Now we were heading through the country of the southern tribe whose name I could not spell towards the Blackfoot territory, before skirting the edge of the Flatheads' land. Part of me quaked in fear at the idea that we would encounter Indians, but now I know another part of me wanted an adventure before we reached San Francisco. I did not know at that moment, of course, what an adventure I would have.

My eyes stayed on the page but lost their focus as I thought about my new life. Before we had separated at Portsmouth, Mama had given Miss Adams a pamphlet that I was to read on the crossing, about wifely duties. I suspect she thought that, had I read it before leaving Portman Square, I may not have boarded that steamship.

It spoke only of duty and tolerance. *My* tolerance, that is. Tolerance towards what was expressed as my marital duties and my husband's natural physical needs. I had no knowledge of what form this 'tolerance' was to take, or what 'physical' part I might play in it. I regretted that Mama had not given me the pamphlet herself, so that I might have been able to ask her, but I also guessed that this was precisely what she had been trying to avoid. There were, I knew, issues of some delicacy surrounding private married life. I just wished I knew what they were. Mama and I had shared a bedroom all my life. Papa had suggested the year before that I might take one of the other six bedrooms, but Mama had refused, saying she required my company. He lived in a different wing of the house and the only 'physical' thing I had ever seen my parents do together was walk into dinner, my mother's hand on my father's arm. Miss Adams proved herself, once again, no great help, by staunchly refusing to discuss the pamphlet's existence after handing it over to me.

The coach slowed. Mr Goldsmith leant down from his perch on the roof. 'Bridge, ladies,' his disembodied voice said somewhere above the open window.

It was customary for the driver to halt the coach before a

bridge, whilst one of the team jumped down and inspected it for soundness. Then we would proceed, with some caution. Many of the bridges on this remote trail were over a decade old, and were wanting repair. I tried to see out of the window, but Miss Adams's look of reproach meant I sat back again in my seat and turned my eyes to my book. I listened though as the teamster returned and spoke to the driver in his American brogue.

'Looks fine. Few planks out further along, but doesn't look like it'll cause any trouble. It's just a gulch. Run-off for the glacier.'

The man retook his position next to the driver and the coach lumbered forward. I studied my book. Despite my vague longing for adventure, the bridges often frightened me. Crossing them was perilous; most of them were only just wide enough for the coach and took all the skill of the driver to keep them on the rails. Fortunately, our team had come out of Chicago, and had over twenty years' experience – a Mr Pinkerton had recommended them to Papa personally.

My thoughts returned to you, and the long moment we had seen each other at the hotel. Your image remained fixed in my mind. The day had turned somewhat warm. I found my fan and opened it, directing cooler air on to my face as I read and drew, trying to ignore my aching hip bones and my sore back.

'I do not know what you read that makes you so over-heated,' Miss Adams said sarcastically.

I looked at her, unable to keep the colour rising in my face. She knew well, after all, what I was reading. 'It is some poetry, of Mr Dryden's.'

'Poetry is a waste of time, which no wife-to-be should meddle with.'

I thought about that, as the coach hauled itself on to the bridge and began the slow crawl forwards. 'Mr Stanton has written to me particularly kindly regarding my own interests, which he is keen I should keep up,' I said at last.

Miss Adams raised an eyebrow. 'You will learn, soon enough, Miss Forsythe, that what men say and what they intend, are two different things.'

'What do you mean, please?' I asked, curiosity getting the better of me.

Indiscretion, or passion, had clearly got the better of her: she was florid, her nose positively agitated. 'Men are jades, Miss Forsythe. They will say and do anything to have their will satisfied. Liars and cheats all. You should no more expect to love than to hate your husband.'

'Have you ever been married?' My voice was small, the fever in her voice was so hot.

'No, and no more would I marry than I would fly to the moon,' she said, angry.

The coach came to a halt, and the silence hung heavily between us. The men were having a discussion.

'Why not?' I asked at last.

'Because I see no reason to put myself in harm's way more than absolutely necessary. And I prefer to get my own bread, than to put myself under a man's control. With their disgusting lechery and filthy habits.'

Papa was not a man of filthy habits. He was always immaculately dressed with a boiled and starched collar; a man came to shave him and make his hands elegant each weekday. And I wasn't sure what 'lechery' meant – I had a dictionary, but Mama had inked out many words.

There was a huge bang. The coach lurched to one side, throwing us across the interior. The horses began to scream. I struggled into a sitting position on what had been the left-hand wall of the coach. Out of the window, I saw, far below us, the dry river bed. I could see the dusty boulders and stones there, in perfect detail. I could also see both teamsters lying broken amongst the rubble. From one of their heads, that of the younger one, spread a darkening pool.

The driver was still on board, cradled in his sturdy seat. Mr Goldsmith too, it seemed, had managed to cling on to the roof rail.

'Ladies, brace yourselves as best you can, and hang on tight. Driver's going to try and whip us out of this.'

There was another enormous bang and the coach slid sideways again. The horses were still screaming and their voices mixed with my own as the coach, with deafening creaking and cracking, began to fall towards the river bed. Reaching up, I grabbed on to the other door, wanting to put as much space between myself and the ground as possible. I heard an inhuman howl, and saw Miss Adams clawing at her face as, through the opposite window, the river bed rushed up to meet us. Filling my compressed lungs as best I could, I screamed at the injustice of the world.

CHAPTER 4

Hope took a long shower. When she came out, wrapped in a towel, hair hanging in damp straps over her shoulders, the puppy was on her bed, tongue lolling in its sharp face. She halted. From somewhere in the house, Cal's voice bellowed, 'Buddy! Where are you, you loser? Get down here.'

The dog scrambled over Hope's pile of dirty clothes and shot out of the door, a scrap of white cotton in his mouth.

Hope hurtled after him, out to the landing.

He was already down the stairs, crossing the huge room to where Cal stood, staring up at Hope as she clutched the towel to her chest. The dog sat obediently, and presented his gift.

'Whatcha got there, hey, pal?' Cal tore his gaze from Hope, reached down and took the offering. Before realizing what it was. He looked at his hand, brows drawing together as he tried to think of something to say. He opened his mouth to speak, just as Meredith's door opened. Cal snatched his hand behind his back. 'Hey, Dr West! How you doing up there?'

Meredith looked between them. 'Perfectly well, thank you. Hope, is there something you need?'

'No, I, er, just. Nothing.' She went back into her room, kicked the door shut and leant against it, closing her eyes and biting back a groan of despair.

Fifteen minutes later, she was getting dressed in another pair of shorts, another vest and a Gap hoodie.

'Hope?' her mother said through the door.

'Yes?'

'I thought I'd take a look around. Would you like to come with me?'

Hope bit her lips together. *Not really, no. I'd like a convenient hole to crawl into.* But she knew from Meredith's tone she was telling, not asking. 'OK. Just a second, I need shoes.' She ducked back into the room and shoved her feet into some canvas espadrilles. Coming back to the landing, she tugged the door shut.

They went through the house and outside to the front. There was no one to be seen but there was a sense of constant, low-level activity in the air. From a large, plain building behind the barn, voices drifted. Meredith and Hope went to investigate. Caleb Crow was standing, hands on his hips and hat pulled over his eyes, watching as his son rode a glossy black horse in a tight figure of eight on the sawdust floor of the building. Cal wore a pair of suede coverings over his jeans, tight around his lower legs and fastening just beneath the knee, and a pair of battered leather gloves with gaping cuffs, showing off his tanned wrists. Concentrating on the horse, he didn't even seem aware of their arrival.

'Hey, ladies,' Caleb Crow said. 'Settling in?'

Meredith nodded. 'Thank you.'

He watched the horse, distracted. 'That's great. We're not used to paying guests here. You'll have to cut us some slack.'

'Everything is perfect, so far. Thank you. It's very kind of you to put us up at all.'

'Couldn't hardly refuse when you said we had all these things you need to study, could we?' He put his head on one side. 'Cal, he looks tight in the hocks to me. Could just be the time he spent in the trailer. Back him up, feel him out a little?'

Cal brought the horse to an instant halt and bumped his heels gently as he lifted the reins a notch. The horse began to walk backwards towards them. 'He's just stiff, nothing a stretch won't cure.'

'Speaking of which, we'd like to take a walk too,' Meredith said. 'Is there a particular direction we should go?'

'Well, you can go in any direction you like, for a long time, but if you head on up there' – he pointed to the trees – 'you'll hit a forest trail. Your feet might not be up to going too far in those shoes though, Miss Hope.' He looked at her Toms.

'Hope should eat something,' Meredith said. 'Before we go anywhere.'

'Cal!'

'Yeah?'

'The little lady's hungry.'

'No problem.' He jumped down and drew the reins over the horse's head.

'Please, it's fine, really,' Hope said quickly.

Cal halted, glove on the bridle. 'You want something or not?' His tone was blunt, but not unfriendly.

'Can't we just go for a walk, please, Mum?' Hope pleaded.

Meredith's lips thinned. She stalked out of the barn, up towards the forest between the stable barn and the house. Hope followed, ducking past Cal, who was still holding on to the black horse's bridle, watching her.

As soon as they entered the cool green of the forest, her mother slowed. 'I'm going to pretend I didn't see what I saw in the house. He seems a nice young man and I must admit he's remarkably handsome, but—'

'Nothing happened! I was standing on the landing six metres away from him.'

'Barely covered. Why?'

'New craze. Shower burlesque.'

'Don't be smart. As much as you don't want to hear it, I've experienced sexual attraction too.'

Oh. My. God. Hope wrapped her hands in her hair. *Please, please stop talking.*

'Just because I'm your mother doesn't mean I've never had a sex life.'

'In the car you told me to try harder,' Hope said, her feet crunching on the pine needles.

'Trying harder doesn't mean parading around their house in a towel!'

'I wasn't *parading*.'

'I've raised you to make good, sensible choices, Hope, and that wasn't one of them.'

Hope said nothing. Above them, the forest was alive with birdsong and the occasional flutter of wings. As sunlight shot through the canopy, softening in the late afternoon, it lit up insects and the odd butterfly. The trail turned back towards the ranch and suddenly spilt them out on to the meadow at the back of the house.

'I have some work I should get on with,' her mother said, suddenly seeming weary, as they headed into the kitchen through open sliding-glass doors. 'What are you going to do?'

'Check my emails, maybe.'

'Do it sitting in a chair so you don't fall asleep. We need to make it through until at least ten tonight. Try that chemistry project.'

Back in her bedroom, Hope unpacked her laptop and put it next to the router, taking the password from the sticker on top of the blue plastic. Her emails downloaded and she sent a message to her friend Lauren to let her know they had arrived. It was after midnight back at home. Clicking through Facebook, she hesitated, before updating her status with, 'In Montana'. Because of the travelling and being so shy, her social life wasn't exactly anything to shout about. At least on Facebook she didn't get tongue-tied.

Curious, she searched for Cal's unusual name, but with no

luck. Then she felt weird and stalky, and blinked, tired. Putting the computer to sleep, she got to her feet and stretched. Heading down the stairs, she crossed to the front door and went back out into the sunshine.

The horses had shifted further away now, tails swishing as they lazed. The pick-up had moved over to a cluster of buildings to her left, but the only sounds were coming from the stable barn to the right.

Hope wandered over to it and went in through the gigantic hangar-like doors. Her eyes took a few seconds to adjust to the dimness. Down each side were stalls and some contained horses. One large dark-brown animal had its head hanging over the door. It watched Hope as she approached, its liquid brown eye on her. Its head shifted slightly and Hope held up her hand and very carefully touched the horse's face. It allowed the caress, so Hope's fingers slid to its nose. The skin was like velvet and prickled with thick whiskers. She stroked cautiously down its face again. Then, suddenly, it dipped its head and butted her, hard, in the chest, sending her stumbling backwards into something solid. A pair of arms closed around her and she yelped in surprise.

'Fleet, that's no way to treat a lady.' Cal set Hope on her feet.

The horse nodded wildly, as if laughing, and Cal tutted at his lack of remorse.

'He's a joker.' He ran his hand down the horse's neck and gave him an affectionate slap. 'But he'd never hurt you.'

Hope rubbed her breastbone, over her clattering heart.

Cal scratched beneath the horse's mane. 'I need to apologize, for the fact my dog's a deviant. It's a puppy thing. I stuck your, er . . . stuff in with a load of laundry.'

She nodded, face still flushed.

'What did your mom say?'

Hope huffed and folded her arms. 'She thinks I've turned into a raging slut.'

'Raging, huh?' He was genuinely amused. His rare smiles were infectious and Hope couldn't help but smile back. 'You should talk more,' he added. 'Wasn't sure you could at first.'

They watched each other.

'Tired?'

'A bit. But I need to stay awake.'

'Then let me show you something.' He led her over to a stall and pointed over the door. Inside was a beautiful black and white horse and at its feet, folded up on the straw, a tiny white spindle-legged foal with bright blue eyes.

'This is Zach. Our newest edition. I was up most of the night with Gypsy.' Cal let himself into the stall. 'Hey, girl, how y'doing?' He pulled her pricked ears. 'Want to come in?'

Hope crept in cautiously and crouched by the foal with Cal.

'Hey, little guy.' Cal stroked the foal's head. Gypsy looked over Cal's shoulder, unconcerned. 'See his eyes? He's a throwback. They used to say horses with glass eyes were crazy, could never be tamed. Not true, is it, little guy?'

The tiny foal snorted.

'Yeah, exactly,' Cal agreed. 'Not crazy at all. And every couple of generations the pale eyes come round again.' He stood. 'Want to help me finish up with the hay?'

'Yes, please. Well, if you like.'

He looked at her. 'You want to or not?'

She nodded.

At the back of the barn, he had been shaking out clods of packed hay freed from a large bale and pushing them into net bags. About ten already sat on the floor around them. He passed Hope a net, then took another. She copied him, shaking out handfuls and stuffing the hay into the nets. It was a while before he spoke.

'So you want to be a scientist?'

'No. I'm rubbish at it . . . I want . . . to be a writer.' She waited for the usual reaction, a smirk or a joke, but he just nodded and carried on working.

When they had filled the last hay nets, they went out into the sunshine and Hope watched as Cal dunked them all in a large rain butt standing up against the barn.

'So the dust doesn't make them cough.' Then he hung them over the doors of each stall, speaking to the horses as he went. Done, he came back to Hope and checked his watch. He was covered in hay dust and his face was dirty. 'OK, it's after six but you should come and meet Chuck.'

He led her outside to a series of pens made out of dense posts and rails. Cal drew her forward, indicating she should climb up next to him on the planks. He hung over the top rail, long arms dangling a net towards a fully grown buffalo bull standing in the middle of the pen. Hope climbed up another plank from Cal and stood up tall, looking at the huge animal.

'Why Chuck?'

'As in steak?'

Hope stared at the massive hulk of the buffalo blowing softly through his nostrils as he contemplated the hay net. She looked at his dark coat and the lighter coloured curly mop between his horns. 'You don't mean . . . ?'

Cal nudged her shoulder with his. 'Nah, of course I don't mean that . . . he's one of the best breeding bulls in the States. Charles Mayweather Austin is his real name. Chuck for short, but this guy will never be beef. Dad is like totally in love with him. You should see it. Chuck? Come on, you big flirt, come and play.'

Chuck lumbered towards Cal's outstretched hand and the hay. He blew on the net for a few seconds before snatching a few strands and munching as Cal rubbed his head. Hope kept her hands well away, until Cal took one and placed it on Chuck's curls, his fingers sending little sparks up her wrist. Chuck carried on pulling at the net with his long purple tongue, snatching out wisps of hay.

'See? Harmless.'

'If he's harmless, why have you got him in this tiny pen?'

Cal's head tipped to one side. 'Ah, well. Most of the buffalo stuff is artificial insemination, genetics and all that. But Dad's big on keeping them as naturally as possible so . . . Chuck here gets to pay a few house calls over the summer. But first, it helps if you keep him here for a few hours each day and feed him up a little. Er, power nutrition, that kind of thing. And frustration. They think that helps too.'

Hope began to laugh. 'You *so* have to talk to my mother

about this. She'll have a whole view about how Chuck is representative of the worst of modern male society.' She realized their hands were still touching and pulled away, letting her hair fall into her face. 'Mention the house calls and we may have an international diplomatic incident on our hands.'

He was laughing. 'I think I've caught on to the fact your mom's into women's rights. This is modern Montana, not the Old West.'

'You wouldn't know it from that policeman. What did he mean? About you?'

Cal stopped laughing and jumped down from the edge of the corral. 'Nothing.' He walked away.

Back in the house, Hope wrestled with the remote to turn on the television. The huge screen finally came to life, showing unfamiliar American news. She went to the kitchen and opened the fridge in search of a bottle of water.

'What do you want?' Cal asked from behind her, Buddy at his heels.

She jumped. 'Oh, just water, please.'

He reached over her shoulder, tugging a water out of a drawer half filled with beer stamped 'Moose Drool', cracking the top and handing it to her. He was wearing a fresh shirt and jeans. His hair was damp and pushed away from his face, and his feet were bare. He smelt like washing powder and sun-warmed skin as he pushed the door closed.

Hope took a sip of water.

'Where's your dad if you and your mom travel like this?'

Cal asked.

'Not around.'

'See him much?'

She twisted the cap back on. 'Never met.'

He cocked an eyebrow. 'Come and sit outside?'

Hope followed him out to the seating on the terrace. The house was on the side of a rolling hill, which terminated abruptly in a steep drop. Beyond it was a plain rising into the mountains to the west towards which the sun was dropping. He collapsed into a chair, gesturing for her to do the same.

'You've never met your dad?'

She hesitated for a second. 'Dad left us for his pregnant girlfriend when I was six weeks old.'

Cal raised an eyebrow.

Hope nodded. 'Yeah, I know. Mum hadn't meant to get pregnant – she was right at the end of her PhD. And my dad was this rising star in the theatre. He's loads older and he and the other woman, they were starring in the same play. They have two boys, James and Tom. Mum got sole custody of me but she'd already filled out my birth certificate with his name, that's why I'm a Cooper, not a West. It needles her like crazy. The not seeing each other ever, me and him – legally, that only lasted until I was sixteen. So now we could meet up . . .'

'And what does your mom think of that?'

Hope blew out a long breath. 'What do you think?'

He was silent for a few seconds. 'Tricky.'

Taking a sip from her water, Hope nodded. 'He sends me tickets for everything he's in. Sent an email asking me if I wanted to visit the set of his new TV series. He seems nice, apart from the abandoning.'

'So why not?'

'Why not what?'

'See him? He's your father. You should, if you ask me, which you didn't.' His phone rang. He pulled it out of his jeans pocket with a bit of difficulty and answered it. 'Excuse me for a second – hey, Matty.'

Hope could hear the voice on the end of the line, but not what they were saying. Cal's eyes flicked to her. 'Yeah, got in this afternoon. Thirty minutes late but no big deal. Picked up the stuff from the store. I'll call you later. Dude, be quiet. Gotta go.' He clicked the phone off without another word. 'That's Joe's son. He's my best friend, but man, can he talk.' He shoved his phone on the table.

It buzzed with a text message almost instantly, lighting up the screen.

Hot or not?

Cal snatched up the phone and killed it. 'Did I also mention he's an asshole?'

Hope stifled a laugh.

He stood. 'Could use some help with dinner if you're up to it.'

Cal made cooking fun, even when he laughed at Hope for not being able to reach the rice on the top shelf in the walk-in pantry.

'Sorry. It's too high,' she called. 'Look at all this stuff!' She stared around her at the groaning, orderly shelves.

He reached over her head and grabbed the bag. 'We order most of our stuff in bulk through the Black Eagle Stores. The guys cook for themselves in the bunkhouse.'

She chopped as instructed and handed over each ingredient as they talked, shyness fading as the minutes ticked by. They were standing over the stove when she smothered a sudden series of yawns.

'If you just make it through dinner, maybe you should crash then.'

'Mum says I have to stay up until ten.' Hope yawned again.

'Not sure you'll make eight.'

He was right. Hope was so exhausted she could barely eat anything. Meredith questioned Caleb Crow about the ranch as Cal served the food. Once, as his father took a long pause before answering one of Meredith's more pointed questions, Cal caught Hope's eye and winked. She hid a smile.

'And I believe this area is remarkable for the diversity of the Native American tribes,' Meredith went on.

Caleb Crow nodded. 'Yep. Lots of different peoples up here, different reservations.'

'I've read about the social conditions on reservations. There is a high incidence of domestic abuse and addiction.'

So help me God. Hope stared at her plate. *Here we go.*

'They got all the ordinary human problems, I guess. Biggest one probably was being rounded up a hundred and fifty years ago and told to live a certain way.' Caleb Crow carried on eating.

'It's a touchy subject,' Cal said, refilling the glasses. 'There's still a lot of racism.'

'Social conditioning is very powerful,' Meredith said.

'Treating other folks with dignity and respect is powerful too,' Cal's father said, to no one in particular.

Afterwards, Hope helped Cal clear up while Caleb and Meredith moved next door. Her head ached and she rubbed her temples as she finished loading the dishwasher. A few seconds later she heard something rattle and Cal stood before her with a glass of water.

'You look done in.'

She took it gratefully. He gestured to the stairs with a tilt of his head. 'Go on, I'll finish up here.'

Conscious she was disobeying her mother's instructions, Hope climbed the stairs to her bedroom. Soon she was washed and changed and slipping into the cool white bed. The stars shone through the uncurtained windows, and above the black of the treeline and the line of the bluff, the moon was a huge white disc in the sky.

She woke with a start, feeling both very awake and seriously headachy. There was a grey pre-dawn light outside. She looked at her watch, saw it wasn't quite five, and groaned. Getting up, she splashed water on her face and pulled on her dressing gown, deciding she needed some coffee. Heading downstairs, she could smell that someone had beaten her to it. Just then, the front door opened and Cal came in with his father.

'Morning, Miss Hope,' the older man said.

Cal closed the door, toeing off his boots. 'We made some coffee before checking on the horses. Want some?'

'Yes, please.' She rubbed her eyes.

'How'd you sleep?' his father asked her.

'Good, thank you. But it's toooo early.'

'Yeah, I hear jet lag's a kicker.' Cal poured out three mugs of coffee. 'How do you take it?'

'Like that.' She took the mug from him. 'Thanks.'

They all sat at the counter. Hope gestured around them. 'Your house is amazing.'

Caleb Crow nodded. 'It's the original homestead, but we just opened it out this year, put in the big staircase.'

'It's very beautiful.'

He looked pleased. 'So, what are you gonna to do today?'

She shrugged. 'Get on with my projects, I guess.'

He frowned. 'Can't come all this way just to sit inside. Do you ride?'

She shook her head.

'Why doesn't Cal give you a lesson?'

Hope didn't miss the sharp look Cal shot his father. 'Oh no,' she said, shy again, 'it's fine. I don't need entertaining. I'm used to this. But thank you.'

He was looking not at her, but at his son. 'Misty's almost thirty years old. She loves to take care of a newbie.'

'Dad.'

'What? That old girl needs something to do with her days.'

Cal's jaw was set. 'Yeah, fine, sure. Whatever.' Picking up his mug he went outside into the pre-dawn through the large glass doors, Buddy loping on to the deck from the corner of the house. Hope examined her coffee cup.

A large hand settled on her shoulder. 'Pay him no mind, sweetie. It's not you.'

'Why—'

Cal threw his coffee on to the grass and strode back into the house. Caleb and Hope stood in conspicuous silence.

'If you want this lesson you'll have to earn it. Thirty horses to feed, all the water troughs to check before sunup. Gypsy and Zach to look in on. Chuck, the girls. What shoe size are you?'

'Er, five.'

'English five? Fine. Get dressed. Jeans, and a shirt or something. It's cool out there this time in the morning. Don't bother showering, you can do that later.'

In the flurry of orders, Hope stood, a little taken aback. Cal walked out, stamping into his boots on the porch. It was only then that she saw Caleb Crow grinning into his mug.

Ten minutes later, Hope reported for duty by the front door. Cal was standing on the porch, looking out to where the horses gathered in the corrals and a slight mist rolled along the edge of the trees off to the right beyond the barn. The damp crept over the ground towards the house and tiny needles of drizzle swarmed in the air.

'Here.' He passed her a pair of worn leather knee boots with heavy, reinforced toes. 'Most of the horses aren't shod at the moment, but don't want you getting your toes crushed.'

An hour later it was only six thirty and they had fed nearly thirty horses, tipping feed mixture into steel dispensers outside, or into the barn's mangers inside the stalls, as Buddy trailed at their heels. They went out again to check the water troughs, then walked back into the barn. One stall at the end was set aside, amongst the many, to store feed. Cal removed the top of what looked like a large, plastic oil drum. Digging the bucket inside, he checked the contents. Bulking it out with a little bran he added a shredded mixture, water and, from a catering-size tin, some molasses.

'Gypsy's feed is for moms. High calorie, supplements. She loves molasses. Real sweet tooth. And I figure she deserves a treat for giving us little Zach.'

Taking the bucket in to Gypsy, Cal tipped it into the manger. Zach was on his feet, watching them. As his mother began to munch her food noisily, he ducked his head beneath her belly and started to suckle, his fluffy white tail wriggling with joy.

'Too sweet,' Hope said, leaning on the stall with her chin in her hand.

'And he already knows it,' Cal agreed. 'He's going to be a real character, that one.'

They fed Chuck, who stood as stoic as ever in his pen, then loaded hay bales and feed mix into the back of the pick-up. Buddy bounded into the flatbed, Cal banged it shut and they drove a short distance to a different set of corrals. A small herd of buffalo grazed. They got out of the pick-up, Hope stepping straight into a pile of dung.

Cal laughed. 'Montana shoeshine. The others are further

out, so Rich'll take care of them.' He opened the gate. 'Can you just stay here while I back the rig through, then close the gate? They won't try to come through if you're here.'

Hope looked dubious, eyeing the huge animals. 'What if they do?'

'Holler. And walk towards them with your arms out. But they won't. They know breakfast's coming.'

She looked at the nearest buffalo, which stood looking back at her. It took a step forward as the vehicle started up and reversed through. As the animal took another step Hope grabbed the gate and slammed the steel closure shut. Cal was hanging out of the window, backing up to the feed hopper, and she followed as quickly as she could without appearing totally uncool and breaking into a terrified sprint. The buffalo all began to move towards the pick-up, aware of the routine. By the time Hope reached it, jogging, Cal was already standing in the flatbed, pulling a small, wicked-looking knife from his pocket and cutting all the twine on the bales.

'Just a second and I'll be done.' He pushed the knife into his hip pocket and leant down, holding out both hands for hers. 'Put your boot on the tyre.' Hope tried. 'OK, put one on the wheel rim, now the tyre, and—' He hauled her up.

They threw the hay into the hopper, then distributed the feed across the ground. The buffalo snaffled it up, noses in the dust. Hope and Cal sat on the side of the pick-up and watched, ruffling Buddy's fur. The sun was coming up. Hope saw it lighting the gently rolling hills dotted with pine trees and sagebrush, then illuminating the vast mountains to the west. Snow was clearly visible high on the peaks.

'Like the view?' Cal asked.

'It's nothing like London.'

'Nah,' he said. 'Guess not.'

'You do this on your own every day?'

'Since I was fourteen. Gives Dad a break.'

'Fourteen? But how, without this?' Hope patted the roof of the pick-up.

He glanced down at the truck, with affection. 'I learnt to drive in this old 250 when I was about twelve. She was my grandfather's farm truck, bought her new in '69. I inherited her at thirteen when Pops and my grandmother died. Their town car got hit by a truck outside Great Falls.'

'I'm really sorry.'

'Yeah, me too.' He jumped from the pick-up bed and opened the passenger door. 'Breakfast?'

Back at the ranch, they ate breakfast with Cal's father in the kitchen. Meredith had already gone for the day. After that, Cal led Hope out to the barn, where outside one of the hands was checking the saddle on a small, grey horse. Cal took over and pulled Hope to stand in front of him. 'Don't stand behind them, it makes them nervous. And I'll be to blame if you get a kick in the chest.'

'Right.'

'Stirrup.' He held up the piece of iron. 'And leather.' His fingers shifted to the strap.

'Yes, sir.' She saluted.

'Put your fingers where it fastens to the saddle, arm straight.' He took the stirrup and measured it against her arm, then down, against her ribs a little. Then he bumped her to one side and began adjusting the leathers. Moments later, he led the horse to a section of tree stump and handed her on to it. 'Meet Misty,' he said. 'Now, swing your leg over, that's it. American saddles aren't like English ones. You sit *in* them not *on* them.' He set her foot into the near-side stirrup. 'Heels down.' Gathering the reins, he put them in her hand, his fingers folding around hers to show her how to hold them. 'Misty's a good girl. Just trust her. Put your heels against her sides to go forward and then relax your legs and pull back a little to stop and tell her to whoa. OK?'

'OK.'

Two hours later, Cal helped Hope down from Misty, catching her as she slid to the ground on legs clumsy with being in the saddle.

'Oops!'

'Go easy, the blood can rush to your feet.'

She laughed, giddy with the riding and being held. 'That was such fun, thank you! She's so lovely.'

They shifted apart, self-conscious.

Cal cleared his throat. 'You look a little peaked. Maybe you should go back to the house and have some tea or a nap or something.'

'I have a chemistry project. And Mum will be annoyed if she catches me sleeping in the day.'

He gestured with his chin without meeting her eyes. 'In the barn, if you head to this end, there are some stairs to the loft. You can crash out there if you like and no one will know. You'll have to ignore all the crates of junk Mom's cleared from the attic though. She wants me to go through it and see if there's anything I want before it goes to the incinerator. Take a look if you like.'

'OK, thanks. And thanks for this.' She patted Misty. 'It was great.'

He nodded, walking away, the horse trailing in his wake. Hope found the stairs to the barn loft. It was far bigger than their flat in East London. It was all one space, with a sink and a kitchen counter, a two-burner gas ring and a few shelves at one end, with jars of coffee and sugar. The rest was taken up with a big bed and two broken sofas facing an old TV.

All along one side were crates and boxes filled with typical attic contents. Hope began to look inside. Some of them contained a large collection of fairly recent football trophies, an athletics medal, a pile of school exercise books and a sketchbook of drawings, all of horses. Another of the boxes contained cookery books from the 1960s and another held all sorts of old treasures, including a little black beadwork bag, a sewing kit, a pair of silver-framed spectacles, and a pretty shawl.

She sat cross-legged on the floor and examined each item. Hope loved old things. At the bottom of the crate was a box decorated with different kinds of wood, some of which had chipped off. She lifted it out and opened it. It looked like a small writing set. The lid folded out to make a sloping surface, and inside was a dried-up inkpot and a steel pen. It felt strangely heavy. Something moved inside. Hope frowned and lifted it up to look underneath. Nothing. Then she looked at the sides. One side had a seam in the wood not apparent on the other, but nothing she did made a difference. She got up and put it on the table, fetching a knife to try and dislodge the seamed side. It wouldn't budge.

She yawned, suddenly tired. She eyed the bed for a few seconds before collapsing on to one of the dusty-smelling sofas, pulled the knitted throw over her and was asleep almost instantly.

When she woke it was past two o'clock and time to get on with her schoolwork. The box still sat on the table but the side was now open. Inside was a worn black leather-bound book. Hope opened it and saw thin, almost onionskin pages covered in flowing lines of handwritten script. At the tops of some of the pages were printed mottoes about the duties of married women. She turned to the title page.

THE YOUNG BRIDE-TO-BE'S COMPANION

Flipping to where the writing started, she read, *Montana, 1867*. Down in the yard, a loud, outside bell signalled a phone was ringing somewhere, making her jump. She pocketed the book and headed back to the house, intending to continue when she'd got some homework done.

*

67

Immersed in her school projects, Hope's afternoon passed quickly. Languages, sciences – all of her subjects had strict tasks and timetables meant to replace ordinary school classes. Her best friend Lauren thought Hope's schedule was crazy and told her so, frequently, as she sat on Hope's bed and looked at the colour-coded wallchart over the desk.

Now, Hope sighed. She was just finishing a chemistry equation when the sun came through the window and hit the diary on the edge of the desk, making the worn black leather cover shine. Putting down her pen, she opened it again, resting her chin on her hand.

Married life. I was not quite sixteen . . .

There was a knock on her door and it opened. Meredith came in.

'How has your day been?'

'Good, thanks,' Hope said, meaning it. 'Yours?'

'Excellent. It really is everything I expected and more. The place is totally unspoilt. I'm going to start writing up my notes. Dinner is in an hour, apparently.'

Hope nodded, stomach rumbling. She really did want something to eat, and went down to the kitchen just before the hour was up. There, Caleb was looking freshened up and had a beer wrapped in his hand. Meredith was sitting at a stool at the counter, holding a glass of white wine. Dinner was spread out on the dining table.

'I'm afraid this is it, as Mom's still with my aunt in Kalispell,' Cal said.

'This looks perfect, thank you,' said Meredith.

'Some cook, my son here. He'll make someone a great wife one day,' Caleb joked.

Cal rolled his eyes while Meredith's mouth set like a steel trap.

'I made you some pasta to go along with it,' he said to Hope, 'because vegetarians get short-changed.'

'As I said in my email, Hope's a picky eater,' Meredith said.

Hope gripped her fork, white-knuckled, but said nothing. In front of them was a meatloaf, buttered jacket potatoes, a salad and a bowl of pasta with what looked like pesto. Hope took a jacket potato and some salad. And some pasta.

'You usually like just pasta,' Meredith said, looking at her plate.

Hope put the spoon back in the bowl, slowly. 'I can have seconds if I want to.'

'You sure can,' Cal's father said. 'Get the little lady a glass of wine, son. If she wants one.'

'Yes pl—'

'No. Hope won't have any. And Mr Crow, Caleb, might I insist that just as you have a name, my daughter, Hope, also has a name.'

Cal had already stood up. Hope's eyes flickered to his, and held. He hesitated, then sat back down, still looking at her.

'Oh well, sure. Didn't mean nothing by it.' His father began to make stilted conversation about Meredith's research.

Hope picked miserably at her food, appetite gone. The Crows ate a lot, helping themselves to more, listening attentively to Meredith.

'Considering how vast swathes of Montana have suffered so terribly with the pollution from mining, the ranch is a remarkable survival story.'

Cal's father nodded. 'The problems are more down Butte way, but yes, this state has got more than its fair share of troubles because of mining. Then again, a lot of Montana was built on mining, so that's a snake eating its own tail.'

Hope's phone chimed in her pocket. She pulled it out, wondering who would be texting her in the early hours from England. The message displayed on the screen. She shoved the phone back into her jeans.

'Who was that?' Meredith's voice was sharp.

'No one.'

'No one doesn't text you at three in the morning.'

Hope studied her plate. 'It's just one of those welcome to a foreign country messages.'

Meredith stood up and held out her hand. 'Give it to me.'

'Honestly. They're just reminding me to make sure my data roaming is turned off. Which it is.'

'Give.'

Hope put the phone into her mother's hand. When Meredith finally spoke, her voice was thick with emotion.

'You *told* me you didn't have any contact with him.'

'I don't. Much. He's having a break on a night shoot and was trying to make sure we got here safely.'

Meredith's voice rose. 'A night shoot? For this ridiculous detective thing? And you told him we were coming here? When?'

'He emailed.'

'*Emailed*? How does he have your address?'

Hope hesitated. 'James messaged me.' James was the eldest of Hope's half-brothers. There was only three months between them. The row was escalating, and there seemed to be nothing at all Hope could do about it.

'Messaged you how?'

Biting her lip, Hope cringed. 'On Facebook.'

'Facebook? We agreed social media wasn't healthy.'

Hope's fingers tightened around her fork, white-knuckled. 'No. You *told* me it wasn't. The way you *tell* me what to do all the time.'

Meredith's volume rose again. 'Only to protect you. That's all.'

'I don't need protecting from *your* problems with what *he* did to us. I need a life of my own,' Hope flat-out yelled back.

'How could you? After everything? How could you betray me like this?' Tears glittered in Meredith's eyes.

Hope pushed up from the table and headed for the door to the terrace, almost blinded by her own tears. She felt sick and dizzy. The bluff in front of her spun as her knees gave out and the hard wooden decking came up to meet her.

CHAPTER 5

'THERE IS NO SUBJECT ON WHICH
YOUNG WOMEN ARE APT TO MAKE SO
MANY AND SUCH FATAL MISTAKES
AS IN THE REGULATION OF THEIR
EMOTIONS OF ATTRACTION
AND REPULSION.'

I have no idea for how long I was unconscious. The carriage had shattered on impact, leaving me lying upon a large piece of padded seating, which had apparently saved my life. The only thing I could see clearly were the four huge brown mounds of the horses, nearby. Flies were already gathering over their corpses. A crow perched on the head of the closest one, and began to feast on the animal's eye. Bile rose in my throat. That would soon be my fate, if I didn't get up.

I tried. Part of the coach siding was pinning me across the chest. Every bone in my body felt broken and the back of my head was a sticky mess of agony. Even lifting my hands to push at the weight on my chest hurt beyond bearing. I lay back on the dusty stones, which pushed the stay-bones into my ribs to the point of breaking. From the corner of my eye,

I could see a deathly still mass of crumpled skirt and crino-line, the dull mauve colour of Miss Adams's dress. There was an intolerable roaring in my ears. I shook my head a little to clear it, wincing at the pain in my neck.

The wind had picked up, blowing dust over me. At the edge of my vision, I could see the trees on the unreached side of the bridge stirring. The crows began to gather. The one pecking at the horse's face now had strings of gore hanging from its beak. Tears clouded my vision. Was I to die out here? No one would miss me for weeks, possibly longer, for we weren't to reach a telegraph station allowing Mr Goldsmith to advise of our progress until we had left Montana and got to Spokane. Panic rose in my chest and I felt suffocated by the weight of the wreckage and my tight stays. A tear leaked from the corner of my eye, cutting a track in the grit on my face.

I pushed again at the debris but it wouldn't shift. Another tear.

My voice wouldn't work. And who would hear me? We hadn't seen a living soul since last night's trading post. The roaring in my ears was becoming louder. I swallowed repeat-edly to try and lessen it. Then stopped. The roaring wasn't in my ears; it was coming, seemingly, from miles away. My side was suddenly chilled. The cold spread beneath my hips, under my legs and into my shoes. Water was swirling through my hair . . .

The glacier spring melt! I was going to drown. The racket of the crows increased as they saw the possibility that their opportunistic meal might be lost. More gathered on the

73

corpses of the horses. From another part of the wreckage, I saw one land on the sleeve of Mr Goldsmith's greatcoat, his dusty hand lying palm up. There came a groan from somewhere.

'Hello?' My voice was scarcely a whisper. 'Are you there? I'm so sorry but I can't move.' No answer. I found my voice suddenly, raising it for the first time in my life; it tore out of me in desperate horror and panic.

'HELP. Somebody, please!' My scream echoed around the gulch, dying out slowly.

The crows, which had taken to the wing at my cries, began to settle. One landed perhaps ten feet away, near where I lay. We watched each other, its beady eye upon my wet ones. It hopped closer, wings spreading for balance, like an old lawyer in a black gown. It was no more than a couple of feet away now. I scrabbled a handful of tiny pebbles and flung them at it. The bird lifted two feet into the air, then came down fractionally closer. I threw more stones. It repeated the action. My movements were weakening. The cold was dulling me. And everything hurt so much. The crow hopped on to a boulder by my head. I tried to push it away. Instead, my hand fell with a splash into the water. It lifted into the air and landed on my chest, wings spread; its beak opened and closed with a clack. It dipped towards my eye.

And exploded in a cloud of feathers, splattering my face with blood.

Through the ringing in my ears I heard hooves picking their way through the water. Gun in hand, you swung yourself down in the graceful vault I had witnessed days ago in Helena, landing with a splash, weight on your left leg, then stooped and lifted the piece of coach siding from me, casting it to one side and surveying the wreckage.

'Please, I . . . will you help me?'

You just watched.

'The others . . .'

You looked around, at the horses first. Further away, I could see now, one of them was still alive and struggling feebly, legs horribly broken. You ran a hand over its wet face, steadying it, speaking to it for a few seconds before standing and shooting it in the head. Its broken legs jerked frantically, then were still. Only then did you look for the other travellers.

Water trickled over my neck in an icy thread. It was rising fast and your trousers were soaked up to the knees as you walked around, soft boots sodden. Panic was compressing my chest worse than the wreckage. I began to wonder if perhaps you were one of the road agents Mr Goldsmith had told me about, and if you were more interested in our belongings, now scattered over a wide area and rapidly washing away. You walked past me to the place where I thought the teamster lay. Nudging him with your boot, you watched for a reaction. You turned his face from side to side and pressed your hand to his neck. Straightening, you clicked something on the rifle and shot him, right there on the river bed. I tried to rise and run. How had I been saved from the fall only to die at the hands of a looter? My legs gave out and I fell clumsily into the shallow water on my back.

You came back and crouched next to me, elbows on your thighs, hands hanging slack in between. My teeth were chattering with fear and the glacial meltwater. I tried to push myself upwards, but the agony, and the strictures of the corset, sent me splashing back into the wet. You were still looking at me, your strange pale eyes unreadable. I felt the beginnings of a faint coming on. My vision darkening, my chest tight, I couldn't hear anything at all. I reached up, trying to take your hand, but your fingers slipped out of mine and I knew no more.

Sometime later, I woke. Behind my eyes, a pulse thudded. I blinked, things taking time to come into focus. Above me, faded whitewashed planks formed a pitched roof. My left thigh hurt and a cool breeze washed over my body, smelling of pine and flowers. I shivered. Beneath my back was a soft mattress, and my hands rested on my ribs over the thin linen chemise I'd put on in Fort Shaw.

I thought back, brain fumbling, trying to piece together the jumbled memories in my mind. Row upon row of tents in Fort Shaw. Indians. Soldiers. Campfires. Miss Adams in my room. Mr Goldsmith's rough hand on my elbow. The rumble of the wheels. The bridge giving way, the coach slipping, smashing, everything tumbling around inside. Black.

I tried to look around. The room was made of the same whitewashed wood. Beyond the open window, I could see blue studded with fluffy white and the smell of green, but only that. A noise somewhere: wind through the trees or maybe water rushing. I swallowed, summoning moisture to my mouth, making my head spin. I breathed in and out slowly. How long had it been? Where was I?

A fly landed on my cheek and I tried to lift a hand to brush it away, but couldn't. I turned my head, wincing, and saw a canvas strap tied around each wrist. I panicked. Incoherent pleading crowded my throat.

A door banged and someone walked into the room.

'Hey.' You pushed the dirty hair from my face.

'Cold,' I stuttered, not really sure I was cold. Was it just that I was wearing only a thin underdress? With relief, I realized the stays had gone and I could breathe freely for what felt like the first time in many months.

You took a blanket, laying it over me. I strained against the straps around my wrists, drawing my knees up. You put a hand on the bed to one side of my waist, the other testing the heat of my forehead, face and throat, lifting an eyelid. It was the closest I'd ever been to a man, even my father.

I tried to swallow again. To speak. You held a tin cup to my mouth, the other hand cradling my sore head as I gulped.

'Too fast.' You took it away.

The liquid trickled through my chest, cool and fresh. 'Did I do something wrong?'

You shook your head. 'Thought it better if you were out of it for the journey, but the drugs made you restless. Kept on trying to get up and falling. Seen it before, so I thought this would just keep you still for a little while. Do you hurt?'

77

I pulled against the straps. 'Yes. Everything aches.'

'You were lucky.' Your hand slipped behind my head as you offered the cup again. 'Slowly.'

I drank, pulling in cautious sips. As I did, I tried to look up, to see you, but all I saw was a dark head, a shirt that might have been blue once, now grey, with the sleeves rolled up over dirt-brown arms.

You let my head go and it fell back on to the pillow, puffing up the smell of clean linen as the darkness claimed me again.

When I came to, it was morning. My eyelids snapped up. The window was still open but there was an acrid smell in the fresh air. I wriggled, feeling wetness. Beneath me there was a towel and layers of linen on an oilcloth, all wet. Every nerve recoiled. My hands wouldn't reach my face. I couldn't call for you. Was there a woman who could help me? Did you have a wife or a sister? Where was I?

Then you were there. I began to cry hot tears of humiliation. You rubbed a hand through your already tousled hair. 'Had to happen sometime.'

I cried harder. 'Not to me.'

'We all think that. Until it does.' For a few minutes, you disappeared and I lay, distressed at the idea you would leave me like this. Then you returned, the straps gave and you looped my arm over your neck before carrying me outside on to a porch. You dunked me in a wooden tub that stood to the right of the door. I cried out as I hit the cold water, and the white linen dress floated up in the narrow spaces around me.

You straightened, watching me cower from you. 'Ain't gonna get clean sitting like that.'

'What about the others?' I couldn't be alone with you, surely?

'All dead. Just you left.'

'You killed that man, the teamster.'

You ran your fingers down the edge of your jaw. 'He was more broke than a body can take. Figured it was kinder than leaving him to drown.'

'But you shot him. Just like you shot the horse.'

'Yeah, well, I ain't much for watching things suffer.'

'Would you have done that to me?' My teeth were chattering with fear and cold.

There was a silence. 'Lucky for us, we didn't have to decide.' You went inside, leaving me sitting in the water, cold and terrified.

The only sound was the birdsong and the wind. I looked down at myself. My underdress was not only soiled, it was filthy with perspiration and dirt. Leaves and mud clung to it in places. Disgusted, I pulled it over my head, wincing at the pain in my arms as I dropped it into a sopping pile on the planks.

A moment later you returned, silent in your soft boots, with a bar of strong-smelling soap and a bottle of liquid, placing them on a stool by the tub. Surprised by your sudden appearance, I hugged myself away from you.

'There's some fancy hair soap in that. Last tenants left it behind.' With that, you disappeared again, just as quietly.

I blinked, trying to focus. We were on the side of a mountain, grassy tufts rolling away from the front of the cabin down to a thick stand of trees. Beyond was a vast and sparkling lake. As far as I could see were only more rocks, trees and dramatic black and white-capped mountains. I was so far from anything I had ever known.

Picking up the soap I began to wash, arms agony. Shuffling out of my drawers beneath the water, I hesitated, then dropped them on to the wet pile. My concepts of modesty were being abraded rapidly. Naked in the tub, my left thigh was one enormous bruise, black and yellowing. How long had it really been? You came back, clattering loudly by the doorway. I pulled my arms to my chest, crouching over my knees. Mama had told me many times that I should never let anyone see me naked.

You hunkered down by the tub. Your untidy dark hair fell into your face and you hadn't shaved for a few days. But your most remarkable feature was your clear, startling eyes of palest grey, almost silver. You reached over and picked up an enamel jug. 'Eyes closed.'

I obeyed and you tipped the water over my head, your hand against my forehead to guide the stream away from my face. You were trying to be kind. When you handed me the bottle of soap I couldn't even unscrew the thin metal lid, my hands trembling and useless, so you took it from me and did it, pouring some into your palm and starting to wash my hair. I had no choice but to let you. The soap smelt of flowers. Your hands were gentle but I winced as you worked, the bump on my head and strained neck protesting. I drew in a sharp breath and your touch lightened further.

You opened the spigot that sat at the side of the tub and water ran from it. 'Can you get under there?'

I hunched beneath it, yelping in shock at the cold liquid racing down my spine. We rinsed my hair until it was clean. Then you examined the cut on my head. It felt sore and the flesh around it a little spongy. I felt your fingers grazing the scabbed welt beneath my shoulder blade.

'Looks like you've had this one a while.'

I tried to pull away, wanting you to stop touching. It was wrong and my head was too crowded and everything ached so much. The mark on my back seemed trivial. 'It's from the stays. The ends of the bones rub. It became worse with the travelling.'

You made a careful square around the sore with the tip of your finger. 'That contraption did this? You know that ain't right?'

'It's good for posture,' I managed to say.

'Good for nothing now. Had to cut you out of it. Used it for kindling when we got back.' You put thin, creased towels on the stool. 'You can manage?'

I nodded. You left. Truly, I was not sure at all that I could manage for I felt horribly unsteady on my feet as I tried to rise, and sat back with a bump and a splash. Gritting my teeth, I managed to reach the rough bench standing against the cabin wall.

After a painful effort, I was dry and cocooned in the

largest of the towels, covering me almost to my feet. The mountain breeze blew across my bare shoulders as I squeezed the water from my hair as best I could with the square of threadbare cotton. My arms were wretchedly painful and I began to cry. You came back and sat next to me. Then took the towel from my lap.

When you finished rubbing my head you slung the towel over your shoulder and began to comb my hair. 'Well, look at this, I'm finding a use for all these things I have around the place and didn't know why. This comb, for instance. Ain't never had use for one a-them my whole life.'

Your clipped tenor is hard to capture on paper. You rarely finished your words – *talkin'*, *laughin'* – and you placed odd stresses on some of them – *a-gane, no-body, sol-jers*. Sometimes you used French phrases arcane by the standards of even my aged tutor.

I cleared my throat. 'How did you find me?'

'Heard you hollering and saw the coach at the bottom of the river bed.' Silence. 'Were they family?'

I shook my head.

'A girl like you wasn't travelling that trail by herself, surely?'

'No. The tall man and the woman, they were travelling with me.'

You waited.

'They were taking me to my parents. In Oregon.'

'London England to Oregon, that's aways.'

I looked over my shoulder, biting my lip at my sore neck.

'How did you know I was from London?'

'Asked the barkeep at the hotel. In Helena.'

My breath caught, fear tightening my chest. 'Were you following us?'

There was a long, judgemental pause. 'No. Was minding my own business when your team decided to risk that bridge. It's been shaky for a year now. Weren't close enough to stop them.' You finished combing my hair. 'All done.'

'Thank you,' I whispered.

'Come on inside. No point letting you die of pneumonia now, is there?'

Inside the house I looked around, now that my vision had steadied and my feet were a little surer. They looked small and pale on the floorboards, leaving damp toe prints. The house was made up of two rooms. A massive stone fireplace and chimney sat back to back in the centre, the one fire heating both chambers. This room, the kitchen, was sparsely furnished with a big black stove sitting in one corner. There was a scrubbed table with just one chair. And a large, worn armchair by the hearth. Near it was a stool. Besides a few pegs on the wall, holding a rifle hanging by a strap, that was it. You went into the bedroom, which was only partially separated from the other room by the fireplace and chimney – no walls.

From a rough pine cupboard you pulled a shirt. 'Afraid I don't have much in the way of ladywear, and your dress is probably a bit . . . unnecessary here.'

'Where is it?'

'Drying out back.' You held up a pair of trousers. 'I suppose, if we roll these up real good and belt them . . . what do you think?'

No one had ever asked me what I wanted to wear before. My clothes were chosen for me by Mama and planned a week in advance, more for special occasions. And now I stood wrapped in only a towel as a strange man offered me clothes I would expect to see on a London beggar. A man whose intentions weren't clear at all.

'I ain't gonna hurt you,' you said, reading my thoughts. In the clear light, your eyes were icy: dark blue circles ringing Arctic irises. You held the shirt and trousers out, pulling off your belt. The leather was warm from your body. 'Here. It's not pretty, but it'll do.'

I dressed in the bedroom after you left, sitting on the edge of the mattress to pull the trousers on, legs still untrustworthy. The bed had been remade and the oilcloth removed. You'd guessed it would happen . . . Tears prickled behind my eyes. My new clothes smelt of outdoors and soap, drowning me. I belted the trousers by tying the leather back on itself through the buckle as there was no hole far enough in, and bent to roll the legs up several times. Three of me would have fitted inside the shirt; the top button was missing when my cold fingers fumbled for it. I looked like a pauper. I walked to the cabin door, hand hesitant on the brass door knob. Outside, over a small campfire, you had made not the compulsory foul coffee, but tea.

You held out a tin cup. 'Found a box of it that had busted

off the coach before the water got to it. Thought you might like it, being English.'

'Thank you.'

We sat on the bench, but not too close. 'What's your name?'

'Emily. Forsythe.'

You offered your hand. 'Nate.'

I took it but ducked my head, shy of you and your wildness. A thick lock of hair slid in front of my face. You reached over with your other hand and smoothed it back. 'How are you feeling?'

Unsteady from your touch I shrugged; an indelicate gesture.

'Can't work out a thing from that now, can I?'

I took a breath. 'My head aches and everything is humming. I feel like I can't see as well as I should.'

You tipped my chin up on your rough hand, examining my eyes. 'Follow my finger.'

Instead, my gaze settled on tanned cheekbones and sleek, straight eyebrows. 'Are you a doctor?'

'Nope.'

'Then how do you know what to do?'

'Nothing like a war to teach you about what a body will stand.' You let me go.

The American Civil War. I had never met anyone except Papa who had been to war. No one young.

You looked out at the landscape. 'Your parents settling in Oregon?'

'They're arranging my wedding.'

Another silence. 'What's he like?'

'I . . . haven't met him. Yet.'

Standing, you slung your tea into the dirt. 'Sounds just perfect.' You dropped on to the steps, bad leg first. It was a sleight: a trick that allowed you to seem almost sound. I would come to know them. You gestured over your shoulder. 'Make yourself at home, English.'

I returned to the bed and slept almost immediately, despite my anxiety. When I woke, twilight was coming in through the open door and window. I sat up, hair matted from sleeping with it damp, arms and legs cramping.

You were leaning against the stones of the chimney stack, arms folded. 'Want something to eat?'

My stomach growled in response. You stooped to lift me.

'Please don't, I can walk!' I pushed myself up the bed, away from you. Mama had rules about touching. 'Thank you, but I can.'

You straightened up. 'Come on then.'

When I made it outside, stiff and sore, you indicated to the bench and dragged over a small table I'd seen inside earlier. You put down a pot of something brown and meaty with gravy. Then a tin plate of bread and a dish of what looked like yellow, leafy wild flowers. 'I apologize in advance for the cuisine in this establishment.'

'It can't be worse than hotel food,' I said beneath my breath, picking up the spoon.

You laughed. 'Reserve your judgement, Em.'

Em? No one had ever called me Em. The mixture was tasty but my stomach rebelled and I hiccupped, hiding my mouth and looking down the mountain. It was covered with blossom, some like the peppery yellow flowers we were eating, and harebells too. There was a small, high-railed corral – as Mr Goldsmith had called them – with a wide stream, gushing with meltwater. The brown and white mare grazed, free to roam.

'Your horse won't run away?'

You shook your head. 'She stays where I am.' Fetching two tin cups, you filled them with water from the spigot and held one out. 'Morphine powder fair dries a body up.'

I took it. 'Morphine powder?'

'Mixed it with water. I'd preferred you to take it outta my hand, but you weren't in no state to.'

'Your . . . hand?'

You lifted your palm to your face. 'Yeah, you know, lick it. It works quick, but it don't hit you so hard and it lasts longer.'

Lick it out of your hand? The idea was not only incredible, but unacceptable. Mama took laudanum for her headaches, in a crystal glass of cordial. She had given it to me too, the first time my pains had come. I hadn't liked it: the strangeness that weighed so heavily, so I had tipped it away every time since.

I took another draught of the water. The lake glittered in the sunset. Birds settled into the upper branches of the trees, silhouetted black against the bright water. More crows. I shuddered.

'Try some more.'

I ate another spoonful. My stomach whizzed and creaked.

'So, this man you were set to marry? Who is he?'

I bit my lips together, unwilling to say something that might provoke you again. Time passed.

'Rich?'

I said nothing.

'Because no first-water diamond like you is travelling halfway across the world for an ordinary Joe.' You carried on eating, gripping the spoon with weathered fingers. Your manners were better than ninety per cent of Fort Shaw, but Mama would still have been appalled. 'So, I reckon he's rich.'

'My parents love me!' The words came from nowhere: I was not given to rash outbursts.

You snorted. 'Sure they do.'

'They'll pay to get me back.'

Your eyes were suddenly as cold as they were pale. 'You think that's what I want? Money?' Your voice was flat and hard.

I retreated like a tiny creature into a shell. 'I'm sorry.'

Putting down your spoon you sat back, arms folded, shoulders bumping against the planks of the cabin. You rubbed a hand over your face as if you were fatigued. 'No matter. We'll shake down, get to know each other.'

Of course, I knew it was going to take days for anyone to find me, or for you to get me to a trading post. I pushed the spoon into my stew.

'How's the food?' you asked on a grunt, setting to eating again.

'It is very nice,' I said. 'Thank you.'

When night fell, bats slipped through the air, ticking as they flitted past the cabin. I looked into the distance, watching for lights, signs of other people. But there were none. No lights, no smoke, nothing. Only countless swathes of stars. Nearby there was a crunching sound. I started as a pale shape loomed out of the darkness. It was the horse. The crunching was it tearing at the grass. You clicked softly and it raised its head, looking at you.

'That's Tara.'

'It's pretty.'

'Tara. She. Coloured plains horse. The coloureds got the finest temperaments of any horse you'll ever place a saddle on. And Tara is the best of the best. Inch over fifteen hands. Built like a steam locomotive with the heart to match.'

It was the longest speech I had heard you utter so far.

'You look tired. Want to sleep?'

'I . . . I need—'

'Ah, right. OK.' You stood and went inside, returning after a moment with a lantern. You led me off the porch, walking confidently away from the house, slightly downhill, towards the edge of the forest. There was the fast-flowing stream, rushing over rocks. It chattered noisily. Suspended out over it was a small outhouse. You passed me the lantern.

'Can you make it back on your own?'

I nodded quickly and tried to think of Mr Goldsmith's kind words when I had had to request a break on the road: 'Miss Forsythe, ain't nothing to be ashamed of. No matter how high, or how low, when you gotta take your leave, you gotta take it.'

Two minutes later, I was making my way back up to the cabin, my bare feet on the cool grass. Moths battered against the lantern. Inside, you were clearing up the dinner things; you looked up as I came in and smiled. Your face was shadowed in the light from the lantern as I placed it on the table.

'Should I sleep in these things?'

'Unless you want to go naked.' I stepped back in alarm and you put out a hand. 'Just messin' with you.'

'Goodnight then,' I whispered.

You just watched me.

Climbing into bed, I lay down, listening to the clatter as you washed the dishes. Closing my eyes, I fell into the blackness of sleep, tumbling off a cliff edge, shattered.

CHAPTER 6

Hope woke to the light streaming through the open doors on to the balcony. Someone was trying the door handle.

'Hope?' Meredith asked quietly.

Hope curled up in the cool sheet and turned on her side, back to the door.

The handle clicked again. 'I thought we agreed we'd never lock our doors. Never shut each other out.' There was a pause. 'I'll be back later, and we can talk then, before dinner.'

Can't wait.

As her mother's footsteps retreated, Hope rolled over, then groaned at the memory of the previous evening, of coming round on the sofa and being forced to drink sweet tea while Meredith fussed and the Crows stood around awkwardly. Of stubbornly saying nothing and, as soon as she could manage the stairs, going to bed without looking at any of them. She checked her watch. Just before seven.

Climbing out of bed, she padded down the stairs and went into the kitchen. She put the kettle on the stove, trying to work out how to get the gas lit.

'Hey.' Cal came through the glass doors, looking fresh and smelling of the outdoors.

Hope concentrated on the stove. 'How do I—?'

He clicked a button and a ring of blue flame appeared beneath the kettle. Hope put the heels of her hands on the edge of the counter, then realized she was only wearing her sloppy sleep vest and thin cotton shorts, and quickly folded her arms. 'I'm really sorry about last night. You must wonder what you've lumbered yourself with.'

'It's just jet lag. And you should see *my* mom in a temper. Hurricane Elizabeth. Dad hides in the storm shelter.'

Hope managed a weak smile. 'Storm shelter? Want a tenant for the next month?'

'You shouldn't let them put you between them.'

She looked away. 'Easy for you.'

'That was a stupid thing to say. Sorry.' He opened a cupboard. 'What do you want to eat?' Taking out a box of cereal, he put it down near her. 'You eat cereal?'

She shrugged. 'I don't . . . like raisins, sorry.'

'We have types without raisins,' he said, opening the cupboard wider to show off a row of boxes. 'Or . . .' He picked up a frying pan, spinning it in his hand, then pointing it at her. 'There could be raisin-free blueberry pancakes. But only if

92

you're good.'

Hope smiled at his teasing. 'I'm always good,' she said primly, lifting her chin.

'OK.' He passed her a box of tea bags. 'Make the tea, then sit there.' He pointed at the stools beneath the island.

'Tea! Oh, fantastic. We forgot ours.'

'I guessed you might want some, so I looked online, then got Matty to order it into the store.'

'Thanks.' Then she made tea and watched, fascinated, as Cal made American pancakes from scratch, adding frozen blueberries into the batter. 'Who taught you to do this?'

'Mom. She's a great cook. You'll meet her soon. She's due home sometime this week or next – we have a barbecue planned for next weekend and she won't want to miss that. Dad's sister married a rancher near Kalispell and took a fall from a horse last week. So Mom's staying there at the moment. Helping out. There's some strawberries in the fridge. Could you chop them?' He cooked the pancakes and bacon as Hope chopped. Then he served it up and they sat next to each other. The bacon was in a crisp pile on his pancakes, along with the fruit.

Hope stole a piece and bit into it as he poured maple syrup. He stared at her.

'But you're a vegetarian, right?'

'Kind of part-time.' Hope covered her mouth as she spoke. 'After I discovered bacon. Please don't tell Mum.'

He laughed, shaking his head.

After the first mouthful of pancake, she put her fork down.

He eyed her. 'You don't like them?'

She put her fingers to her mouth. 'Bit sick, that's all.'

He bit the inside of his cheek. 'How long since you ate?'

'Last night.'

'You ate last night? I didn't notice. Before then.'

'At home.'

'You got problems with food?'

Hope looked at him, startled. No one had ever asked her that outright. 'No,' she said slowly. 'I . . . can't eat when I'm stressed. I feel like I'm tied in knots in my middle.'

'Yeah, well, you need to get a hold on that.' He stood and fetched a carton of milk from the fridge and two glasses, pouring it out and pushing one towards her. 'Easy on the stomach.'

Hope took a sip.

He carried on eating. 'So, your mom is taking one of the rigs and heading up into the hills today. What are you going to do?'

'Think about the unbelievable lecture I'm going to get later?'

He smiled. 'Through there,' he pointed, 'there's a games room and the library.'

'Library?'

'Yeah, you know,' he teased, 'books. All the classics. Like the Redneck Bible and *1001 Ways with Raccoon*.'

Hope was laughing now.

'And you know about the TV and there's the internet.'

'Thanks. I found a notebook, in a box of the stuff from the

attic. It looks like a diary. An old one.'

He paused in pouring out more tea. 'Please tell me it's not my mom's.'

She smiled, shy. 'No, I mean *old* old. It belonged to an English girl, in Montana in 1867.'

His eyebrows lifted. 'The state was really young then, only three years old. I wonder where it came from, how it got in with our stuff.'

'It was inside a writing box, in one of the crates. The girl, she's my age, well almost, and she's on her way to get married. They've just arrived at a hotel in Helena. I thought I'd read it, if that's OK.'

'Sure.'

They talked as they ate. Hope noticed Cal brought the conversation back to her every time. She wasn't used to talking about herself and his focus was unnerving. They finished eating and cleared away together.

Hope turned from the dishwasher, turning her palms against each other one way and the other. 'Thanks for breakfast. It was really good.'

'Glad you liked it.'

They both hesitated. 'OK, see you later.' She trotted up the stairs. When she looked down from the landing, he was gone.

In her room, Hope retrieved the black book from where she had left it on the desk and went out on to the balcony. The bluff fell away before her, clean-cut and dramatic in the morning light. She sat down on one of the silvery old wooden chairs and turned to where she had left off. *It was then that I saw you . . .*

Only a couple of pages later, Hope's laptop pinged a notification and she ended up in an IM chat with Lauren, who was up late trying to finish an essay. Then she came back downstairs to the smell of coffee slipping through the cool expanse of the Crow house. Hope explored, walking through the games room with its pool table, another TV and easy chairs, into a room lined with books looking out over the meadow at the back of the house. Hearing noises in the kitchen, she peeped from the edge of the living room, and saw Caleb Crow helping himself to coffee.

'Hey there, Miss Hope. How you doing?'

'Good, thank you, Mr Crow.'

'We don't stand on ceremony on these parts, Hope. Caleb is just fine. Deal?'

'Deal.'

'Good girl. Help yourself to any type of breakfast you want. There's all kinds of cereals in that cupboard there, or eggs.' He paused. 'Do vegetarians eat eggs?'

Hope smiled. 'This one quite likes them. But I already ate, thanks. Cal made me breakfast.'

'Ah, great. I'd tell him to take some time to keep you entertained some more but he's got to go upcountry now, to my sister's in Kalispell. Won't be back for a few days.'

'Oh.' Hope's spirits fell.

Caleb poured himself a drop more coffee. 'Elizabeth –

that's my wife – called, said my sister's a whole lot better now, and so he's going to collect her and bring back two of his aunt's horses too, take the load off her some. It's a way away. And he likes to go up through the national park.' He cocked his head to one side, looking remarkably like his son. 'Why don't you go along with him?'

'Oh . . . I'm not . . . I don't think I'd be much help.'

Caleb waved his hand. 'He doesn't need help, but he might like company.' He glanced towards the window at the front of the house. 'He's there now – why don't we ask him?' He strode out of the kitchen straight away, to the open front door. 'Cal!'

Cal was loading a coil of rope into the back of the 250. 'Yep?'

'How's about taking Miss Hope here on your trip?' He turned to Hope. 'He'll be cutting straight through the Glacier National Park. It's some beautiful countryside.'

Cal straightened up slowly, looking at them both.

Hope squirmed. *You don't have to*, she mouthed.

'Are you sure she wants to come?'

'Sure she would!'

Cal resumed shifting things around in the flatbed. 'We'll be sleeping rough, in the back of here.'

Caleb put a hand on Hope's shoulder. 'I bet she's tougher than she looks. And she doesn't want to see our finest scenery from some red tourist bus. You can take her up to Polebridge Mercantile for a lookaround. Get me some of those huckleberry bear claws they make up there.'

'Dad, that'll add on half a day.'

'But it's a fun trip, and you aren't in a hurry.'

'What about your mom?' Cal asked Hope without looking at her.

Hope was getting more and more embarrassed. None of it had been her idea anyway.

'I'll square it away with Ms West.'

Cal put his hands on his hips and looked at his father for a long time. 'You're sure this is a good idea, Dad?'

Something unspoken passed between them, then Caleb patted Hope's shoulder. 'Sure I'm sure! It'll be an adventure.'

Cal glanced up at the sky. 'Can you be ready in an hour?'

An hour later, Hope brought her bag down the stairs, then thought she should probably take the opportunity to use the bathroom one last time. As she came out she heard voices out on the decking. It was Cal and his father. Cal was rubbing a hand through his chaotic hair.

'Jesus Christ. Can you imagine what people would say? What *her mother* would say if she knew?'

Hope crept closer to the doors.

'I don't give a rat's ass for what people say. It'll be good for both of you. I can see you like her, even with your grampa's poker face on.'

'Doesn't make a difference if I *like* her or not, does it?'

'Take a tip from your pa, you don't meet so many women in your life that make you sit up and take real notice the way you've noticed her.' Hope's ears pricked up even further. 'And she shines fit to light a room when you're in it. Should have

98

seen her pretty face when I told her you were going away.'

Hope cringed. *I'm that obvious?*

'She's sixteen. And British.'

'What's that got to do with anything?'

'Three years and four thousand miles?'

'All horseshit if you like each other. Look at me and your mother. The truth? We were crazy about each other, but I didn't know her from a hole in the ground when we got married. That's worked out pretty well.'

'For the love of God, Dad—'

Hope's heart sank. He really didn't want her along. She picked up the diary, intending to sit and read until Cal was gone. Then she heard the single wail of a police siren.

The two policemen they had met in Fort Shaw had pulled up to the front of the house and were getting out of the car. Father and son were already walking forward to meet them.

'What can I do for you, John?' Caleb Crow's voice was harder than Hope had heard it. His relaxed posture had stiffened and suddenly he looked very tall and imposing.

Officer Jones spoke first. 'We've had a report you're employing illegals here.'

Cal stepped forward. 'Says who?'

His father shot him a warning look.

'Now, son, you keep your temper,' the police chief advised.

'How many workers do you have here at the moment, Mr Crow?' the officer asked.

'Twenty-four. All legitimate. As you know.'

'What about that little Mexican I seen in town?'

Caleb Crow rolled his eyes. 'Jesus has been here for four years. He's brought in his papers twice.'

'Yeah, well, maybe he should bring them in again, just to be sure. And that big black fella too, that maintains your vehicles. He's been in the bar some, I'd like to see his credentials. There's a whole raft of illegals coming in here just now for the summer work. Gotta keep on top of it.'

'Cal, go to the office and get the photocopies for Jesus and Sebastian.'

Cal turned on his heel and went off to the far wing of the house, banging into the offices.

'Elizabeth well?' Chief Hart asked, a sly note in his voice.

'As well as ever,' Caleb Crow replied curtly.

'Fine woman.'

'Of that, I am certainly aware.'

'Shame to keep a woman like that hidden away out here, I've always thought.'

Caleb Crow's jaw flickered. 'As opposed to keeping her in a cage and selling tickets? Or what?'

Cal returned with a sheaf of papers in his hand and passed them to the chief. The big man didn't look at them, just carried on looking at Caleb Crow.

'Guess I'll keep these on file at the station. Being as how your men will have the originals, naturally. Tell them to bring them in next time they come to town. Just to be sure.'

Caleb Crow folded his arms and shifted his weight on to one hip, a gesture Hope recognized from Cal.

The two policemen made no effort to move away. 'So you

got two English women guesting with you. Mother and a pretty daughter, about sixteen I'd say.'

'That's right,' Caleb said.

Hope realized they all knew she was there in the doorway.

'Maybe we'll drop by now and again, just to see if she's OK.' The chief turned, pretending to see Hope for the first time. 'Hey, Freckles. How you finding Crow hospitality?'

'I . . . perfect, thank you.'

He saluted with the sheaf of papers. 'Well, you take care now, honeypie, y'hear?'

Freckles? Honeypie? Gross. The two men got back into the police car and it turned in a wide circle, making Cal shift out of the way. Father and son watched it go, then moved towards each other, conducting a low, tense conversation as they walked to the corral, down to where Cal's pick-up was parked.

Hope, feeling awkward, started to walk over to them. Cal was leaning against the side, arms crossed and one ankle over the other, his brown leather workboots dusty. Caleb was standing there with him. They were deep in conversation and Cal looked agitated. Buddy was pressed against his leg as usual.

'Hart is a real curly wolf. Always has been, like his daddy before him, and that son of his.'

Cal took a breath. 'Dan and Steve were in town when we came through on our way back from the airport. They drove by and threw a half-full pop cup at the rig, frightened Hope.'

'Yeah, well, they got no manners either,' Caleb said, his

usually calm voice unexpectedly fierce. 'Which is a well-established fact of public record.'

'There's a few other things that are a matter of public record,' Cal said.

'Son, you did the right thing and you know you did. I know it wasn't easy, walking away from school like that, away from the team, but it was the right thing. We're proud of you.'

'Didn't help Tyler, did it?' Cal muttered bitterly. 'The chief—'

'Ignore anything John Hart says.'

Cal stuck his thumbnail between his front teeth for a second. 'What he says is what everyone else thinks.' He straightened up suddenly when he saw Hope.

Caleb cast him a final look, then smiled at her. 'Well, look at you, all ready for the outdoors.'

Hope looked down at herself, unsure if putting on walking boots and a cardigan was quite outdoors enough.

Caleb strode to the front door and picked up her bag and a long raincoat from the peg. 'Take this slicker, Hope, just in case.'

Hope opened her mouth to say she wasn't going, but he carried on talking, taking her elbow and steering her towards the pick-up.

'I'll tell your mom where you two have gone, and that you'll be back in a few days. Give you both time to see the wood for the trees, I reckon.' He put the bag and the slicker inside the cab on the bench seat. 'Take care of my boy here.'

Hope's skin coloured. Cal looked away and coughed slightly.

'Buddy, hup.' The dog jumped on to the bed of the pick-up.

Caleb embraced his son, and Cal hugged him back. Standing back, Cal opened the passenger door for Hope. Seconds later, he eased himself into the driver's seat. His long fingers caught the key in the ignition and he cranked the engine into life.

They took a track out through the back of the ranch, climbing into the hills. The pick-up was warm and Hope took the cardigan off. The tinny radio crackled with weather news.

'You should put your seat belt on.'

'You haven't got yours on.'

'Yeah, but you should wear yours.' His voice was flat. 'You're my responsibility.'

Hope fastened the seat belt. 'I'm really sorry. Your dad pushed you into this.'

'What do you mean?'

'You don't want me here.'

Without taking his eyes from the road, his hand reached out and touched her bare arm very briefly. 'It's not that.'

Hope swallowed, hoping he hadn't noticed the goosebumps rise instantly on her skin. The woman's voice on the radio read out the temperatures expected in Butte, Great Falls, Missoula and Kalispell.

'The policeman. Why was he being like that?'

It was a long time before he answered. 'Our families have been at odds for generations.'

'Why?'

He lifted one shoulder. 'I don't know. Different folks, I suppose.' For a while it seemed he would say nothing more. Then, 'Truth is, the Harts ain't real nice people. And Chief Hart likes to mess with people's heads. Particularly mine. But you've only got my word on that.'

Hope watched him. 'I don't think they'd let it happen in London.'

Cal's expressive mouth turned down at the corner. 'Like you said, this is nothing like London.'

She didn't know what to say to that, so said nothing. After they'd been driving a while, the silence was heavy, broken only by the crackly radio. The weather report came on again.

'Montana has quite a lot of weather.'

'It's that or the church station.' He glanced at his watch. 'We just might catch the sermon.' He turned off the gravel track, on to two pale channels in the blowing grass. The trailer clattered behind them.

CHAPTER 7

'THE BLOOM OF MODESTY IS
SOON RUBBED OFF, AND CAN
NEVER BE RESTORED.'

When I woke a pink-streaked dawn was filling the windows and, somewhere, a cockerel was crowing. The bed was deliciously warm and comfortable, the mattress well stuffed and the coverlet tucked around me; I hadn't been so comfortable in weeks. I wriggled in a stretch and my naked foot touched something warm. Skin, with a soft crackle of hair. I froze. I could hear breathing, soft and shallow.

I scrambled out of the bed, struggling from the covers and stumbling as my bruised leg protested. You were sprawled on your back on top of the covers, one arm above your head, wearing only a pair of white linen drawers, which ended indecently at mid-thigh, the kind I had seen on camp washing lines. The contours of your stomach were clearly defined above the drawstring tie, the other hand resting on your chest. Your strange pagan necklace hung over the bedpost. A blanket was partly across your hips but your bad leg lay on top of it and I saw then the reason for your lameness: a long, livid scar stretching from just above the knee right down over the top of the foot.

'Glad I don't mind you gawking, English.' You smiled, propping yourself on your elbows.

I lifted my chin, but didn't meet your eyes, face flaming. 'I . . . didn't realize you'd be sleeping with . . . in here.'

'It's my bed.' Getting up, you were suddenly too close.

'Don't touch me,' I said as strongly as I could, then ruined it with a whispered, 'please.'

'You ain't never been around menfolk, have you?' You opened the door, looked out at the weather and stretched, the muscles of your back flexing. The day was fine, the blue sky clear. Tara was waiting for you and you limped down the steps to the grass and scratched her neck, speaking to her softly.

Inside, I sat on the chest at the bottom of the bed in despair. What was to become of me in this place where the rules of my life did not apply? I had, unwittingly, shared a bed with a man whilst engaged to another. I put my head in my hands and almost cried again. But the tears did not come. I thought of Papa, and his advice to me before the journey; the coming weeks would be a trial, but to be brave and do my best at all times. He was right, I should be brave. This was the adventure I had wanted, and afterwards, in the drawing room in Larkin

Street, I would be able to recount it at parties and perhaps even make a joke about how I was a real frontierswoman. Although my beautiful, quiet Mama hated jokes of any kind amongst gathered groups of women.

Fetching the comb I braided my hair as neatly as I could, for I had never dressed my own hair before, but there was nothing to tie it off with. There was a shadow against the sunlight and I looked up in surprise as you held out a bootlace; I hadn't heard you come in.

I tied off the braid, but it slipped immediately from the smooth threads of my hair and fell on to the boards of the chest still coiled. You sighed and sat down next to me, still less than half dressed.

'Won't work if you do it like that now, will it?' With a shake of your head, you threaded the lace through the braid further up, before wrapping it around and around in a thick, neat rope and tying it off. 'Never saw myself as much of a lady's maid, but hell.' You smiled.

My face coloured again. I had heard curses only in the street in London. And once, from Mr Ellis, last year when my staylace snapped in his hand before Papa's annual Christmas party for the other ambassadors. He had apologized to Mama instantly, but I think she was too upset about how long it was going to take to rethread an eight-yard lace to have even noticed.

'You want to wash? There's a place in the stream I can show you. Or I can fill the tub?'

I shook my head, alarmed at the idea of being naked

around you again. 'Not presently. I think I may become chilled. But thank you.'

'Are you cold now?'

I nodded.

'It's warm today, for the time of year.'

'I feel the cold.'

'Ain't surprised. Not enough on your bones.' You picked up a towel from the peg near the door and disappeared up behind the house towards the stream.

When you came back, I was sitting on the bench, looking at the view. Your hair was wet and droplets of water clung to your chest.

I avoided your gaze. 'How far are we from where the coach crashed?'

'Why?'

'I thought . . . that we might try and see if any of my things are still there. My clothes. Some shoes. Before you take me back.'

You looked at me for a long time. 'No, it's too far. And you only had one shoe on when I found you. Didn't think it was much use, one shoe. And the melt was on us.'

'But I can't wear these things. And I have no shoes.' I looked down at my bare, cold feet.

'You've found your voice this morning, ain't you? No one will ever find that coach, smashed up like it was, to splinters. Your stuff is long gone.'

'So . . . well, perhaps that doesn't matter. How far is it to Helena? Or Fort Shaw?'

Inside, the kettle shrieked on the stove and you disappeared. 'Helena? About two hundred miles,' you shouted, clanging about. 'Fort Shaw is about a hundred and thirty, give or take.'

My heart sank. *One hundred and thirty miles?* An impossible distance. When you came back out, you were dressed, and carrying two cups of tea, a tin plate of toasted bread, a bone-handled knife and an earthenware jar tucked beneath your arm. You sat down and took off the lid, digging out a chunk of dripping honeycomb, spreading it on to the toasts.

'So how will I get to Oregon, please?'

You shrugged, passing me the first piece.

I took it. 'Thank you. But you're not being very helpful.'

You raised an eyebrow. 'I pulled you out of a wreck and saved your life. I've doctored you, fed you, clothed you and even acted your maid. And now I'm not being helpful?'

I blushed. 'I'm sorry. And I am grateful. Truly. I'm asking too many questions, I realize.'

'Ask me anything you like. Mayn't have the answer, but you can ask. Eat first though,' you ordered, crunching into your own piece.

I ate.

'Tell me again, why do you need to get to Oregon?'

I breathed out, frustrated, and put the heel of toast down. 'You know why!'

'Yeah, but you don't really want to marry this guy, I mean, do you?'

I folded my hands in my lap. 'That's hardly the point.'

'Crap is what *that* is.'

I gasped.

'I apologize for my language, ma'am,' you said, with a hat-tip gesture.

'Please stop mocking me.'

'Oh, I'm sorry,' you said, sounding not at all sorry, which you never did when that particular word came out of your mouth. That was when you were least sorry of all. You stared, horrified, as the first tear fell. 'Jesus, English . . . don't *cry*.' You looked away, down towards the lake, awkward.

'I can't stay here alone with you, you know I can't.'

You shrugged, still not looking at me. 'Told you, ain't gonna hurt you. You don't believe me?'

'I . . . do believe you, but . . .' Such a discussion was impossible. I pushed the wetness from my cheek, curiosity battling my tears. 'Isn't it terribly lonely here?' Perhaps that was it. Perhaps you were lonely.

You shrugged. 'Had a dog when I first came up here, but he went and got himself killed. Still miss him. I ain't lonely for people though. Or at least, not the kind you find in towns. Ain't much interested in bars. All that noise and getting pestered by whores . . .'

'What are whores, please?'

You looked at me. 'English, I'm getting the feeling you and I are from whole different worlds.'

I frowned, bemused. 'But you were in the hotel bar. In Helena.'

'I'm a railroad scout. And a horse trader. That was what I

was doing in Helena, trading a horse.'

'And you scout for the railway companies?'

'Yep.' You took a sip of your tea, letting your head fall back against the cabin. 'When I'm not up here, that is. Figured this year I'd stay up here for summer again. There's a horse I have my eye on around these parts.'

'A wild horse?'

You smiled, and suddenly it was as if you were lit from within. 'The horse of a lifetime. Maybe more than one lifetime. Been looking for him near on two years. That's what I was doing when I saw your vehicle crash.'

The birds were singing and squabbling rowdily.

'My fiancé . . . Mr Anthony Howard Stanton. His family are the ones who want to build the railway through here.'

You looked at me then, pale eyes taking me in. 'They'll never build the railroad through here.' Waving a hand at the landscape, you pulled a face. 'Look at it. You couldn't.'

'The railways are going to conquer the West, Mr Stanton told me in a letter—'

'*Railways. He told me in a letter,*' you mimicked. 'Has Mr Railroad ever been out West? Does he know what Montana is like?'

I drew back, snubbed, putting down my cup and retreating on the bench. 'Mr Stanton's family are some of America's greatest pioneers.'

'Pioneering in their fancy San Francisco drawing rooms,' you sneered towards the lake as you got up and went to look at something on the porch. It was a butterfly, beautifully coloured, wings spread. After going into the cabin, you came out a few seconds later with a spoon and sat down next to the insect.

I was exasperated. 'Are you trying to catch it?'

'What for?'

'Then what are you doing?'

Your intense eyes were still on the butterfly. 'These little critters rest with their wings up. This one is wings down, all tuckered out. Sometimes you can get them going again with honey.' You pointed to the spoon resting on the boards, the butterfly's tiny sucker in the sugary smear at the end. As we watched, it fed, flexed its wings in the sunshine, and fluttered away.

You weren't inclined to talk more, and went about your chores as if I wasn't there, so I went for a walk. I couldn't go far, because of the lack of shoes, and the brisk breeze outside was cutting me to the bone now I wasn't wearing my many layers of travelling clothes. I found my gown hanging on a line strung between the cabin and the outhouse. The silk was still damp but stiff, shrunken and ruined with watermarks. It was nineteen guineas of useless and I left it where it was. Nearby was a henhouse perched on a post with a strange, comb-like ladder leading up to it, and scrawny roaming chickens strutting in the grass.

The cabin itself was very fetching, for a wilderness hovel. It was organized in an unusual fashion, in that it was almost square. The porch was prettily designed, with rails, and above in the gable, antlers and twisting branches were nailed up. There were eight shuttered sash windows, two in each wall, making the inside as light as outside. And an astonishing luxury in such a place.

As I climbed the porch steps and went into the cabin, you looked up from where you were standing at the kitchen table up to your elbows in flour, kneading bread on the table. I had never seen a man, outside a servant, engage in a domestic task. That must have been written on my face. You straightened up slowly, watching me.

'Well, do you want to do it?' you asked, tone not entirely friendly.

'I don't know how.'

'No time like the present.' Gesturing to the mound of dough, you shook your hair back. 'Come on, English,' you said, with your funny smile. 'Ain't hard.' You reached out with a white-floured hand and took my wrist. Taking my fingers in yours, you placed them on the ball of dough. 'Just do what I did.'

I tried, my fist not making the impression yours had.

'Try again,' you said patiently. You watched over my shoulder, encouraging. 'You'll feel it in a minute. Starts to give. That's when it's getting there.'

I kneaded as you explained the bread recipe, and how it was just a knack to get it right, not a precise science. ''Sides, better enjoy this while you can, as we'll be back on hot water cornbread soon enough.'

I pushed a strand of hair from my face with a floury finger.

'It's harder than I thought.'

You brushed the flour from my cheek with the back of your hand, making me shy away from your touch. 'Everything good always is.' Putting the dough into a greased, blackened tin, you placed it on top of the stove. 'Has to rise a little first, or it'll be like old rocks.' You smiled to yourself in genuine amusement, shaking your head. 'A no mark bachelor like me giving domestic instruction? Don't sit right.'

I couldn't help but smile back, shy in the sudden warmth of your attention. 'Doesn't it?'

'Nope. But Momma taught us how to make stuff with whatever we had. Though she'd be patting out that dough into rounds and frying it in oil. Then we'd eat it with corn and beans and whatever meat there was going.' You beckoned to me to follow and we went outside to the stream, washing our hands in the clear water. As we straightened up, Tara came up, nudging your pockets for a treat. You scratched beneath her thick forelock.

'Your mother? With your first family?'

'Yes. She and my pa came out from the East in forty-three, thinking to settle in Oregon. The government were giving away land to married couples.'

'John Gantt's Wagon Train. I read about it.'

You looked at me, surprised. 'You did? Well, I think things were all right for a while. Momma had a girl, Faith. Then Faith and my pa died while my momma was carrying me.'

'I'm so sorry.'

You shrugged. 'Before I was born. Anyways, she was

frightened of being out there with a new baby and took the first ride she could back East, to her folks. I was born on the road, and she ended up at the trading post what's now Fort Shaw. Then she married an Indian brave when I was a few weeks old.'

I stared at you. 'But your mother was . . .'

You laughed. 'Yes, she was white. Like you. And yes, she married an Indian. Red Feather. He was my father, as far as I remember one.'

'That's why you're so good with horses?'

You shrugged. 'Maybe.'

'Tara dotes on you.'

'Yeah, well. You should-a seen Tara when I first brought her off the plain. As wild as wild. Mainly on account of being frightened, a-course. But we shook down.'

Your meaning wasn't lost on me. I cleared my throat. 'Then what happened? To your family?'

'Momma died, poppin' out one too many babies. Red Feather married again straight away. Same time, my grandaddy put out word that he knew I was still living and he wanted me back East, to my mother's family. They'd made good in Massachusetts. My mother's brother, my grandaddy's heir, had died and I was his only family left. Some gospel sharp convinced him he needed me home and should pay any price to save me from the heathens.' You paused. 'So I was traded, in exchange for a fair number of horses.'

'Traded?' I couldn't keep the rise out of my voice.

You looked down at me. 'Think what you're going into is

115

any better?'

I closed my mouth.

'So I went back, and on account-a me being a savage they cut my hair, put me in breeches and into school, made me sit still and go to church. Sit on my own on a bench up front for sinners, beg forgiveness for my Indian ways.'

I didn't like the sound of that. Papa said it was a cruelty to humiliate anyone. Nor did he go to church. Mama and I went alone. 'And then?'

You took a breath. 'It was more'n I could stand. So I joined up and trailed around with the Union, ended up in Sheridan's cavalry. And then there was the war and near got my leg blown off. Came back here. Lived in Fort Shaw for a while but it weren't for me. Man gets no peace. Or at least, I didn't get none nohow.' Your voice was dark. 'Something bad happened and I figured it was best for me not to be there any more. Came upon this place on the scout two years ago, as if the tenants had walked out and would be back any minute. Decided to stay until they showed up. But they never have.'

I patted Tara's neck with caution. She was totally focused on you, butting her nose into your cupped hand. Her skin was warm and satiny. I could feel the veins beneath her smooth coat.

'Was it terrible, the war?'

'Yes. Saw things I never want to see again, except now they're in my head, so that's just too bad.'

I watched you. The way you narrowed your eyes. It

happened to Papa sometimes. He had fought in the Crimean War when I was a little girl. He said that, as an officer, he'd been far better off than what he called 'the men'. You had been a regular soldier.

'So much chaff,' Papa said, when I overheard him talking about it. I had asked him about the war, once. He was looking out of the library window, at the rain, and I could see he was somewhere else. But he would not talk about it, only patted my cheek and told me it was not the business of a young lady to fill her head with such things.

You slid your fingers under Tara's thick white mane and stroked the length of her neck. The memories my question had roused were bleak, clearly. To voice an apology right then would have been clumsy, so on the next stroke I placed my hand next to yours and copied your movement. You looked at me warily, then limped away. I stood with Tara, both of us staring after you, confused.

We ate a midday meal on the porch. The bread was still warm. A light rain was falling steadily, as it had for most of the morning. All around us, I could hear it pattering, on the roof of the cabin, on the leaves of the trees by the stream.

'What meat is this, please?'

You looked at me for a long second.

I swallowed. 'I don't want to know, do I?'

'Doubt it.'

'When are you taking me back, do you think? Will the weather clear tomorrow?'

You glanced up from your food, out at the drizzle, and shrugged.

'I don't mind getting wet,' I continued, 'so we could travel in this weather anyway.'

Putting down your spoon, you placed your hands flat on the edge of the table. The breeze blew and the rain spattered against the porch. 'I'm not taking you back.'

The words stretched tight between us.

'What do you mean?'

'Ain't taking you back.'

'But . . .' I was entirely at a loss. 'I'm from London.'

'That means about as much to me as saying you're from the moon.'

'I need to get to Portland.'

'Em—'

'Please stop calling me that. My name is Emily.'

'As far as I can see, your name is whatever I choose to call you.' You thought about it. 'Maybe I'll give you one of those old religious settler names. Providence, or Purity. What about Helpless?'

I shrank from you. 'Emily. My name is Emily.'

You got up, stepping off the porch to check on Tara, who we could see sheltering from the rain under a tree.

'My name is Emily and people will be looking for me,' I called from the porch.

You came back and climbed the two steps, the first a big step up from the sloping earth, the second shallow and giving on to the planks. 'They can look. I'd imagine they think you're dead, along with the others.'

'But I'm not dead!'

You went inside, picked up and unpacked a box from beneath the table, scattering bits and pieces of what looked like harness over its surface. My breathing was unsteady and I kept trying to start speaking, but couldn't. You glanced at me, amused.

'What's the matter? Cat got your tongue?'

Having been taught, from an early age, to be gracious and obedient in all things I struggled with my words. 'What's the *matter*?! You're keeping me here, that's what's the matter.'

'I ain't *keeping* you here. You can leave any time you like.' You pointed out towards the mountain. 'Go.'

'But I . . . don't know where I'm going.'

'Oh, really?'

'This isn't fair,' I whispered, eyes wide.

'Life isn't fair. You'll shake down.'

'Stop saying that! I'm not Tara. I'm not a pet,' I said fiercely.

You shrugged, comparing two different buckles against a strip of leather. 'Looks to me like you ain't never been nothing *but* a pet,' you said, almost under your breath.

'I'm not a pet and my name is Emily! Not English, not anything you say. It's Emily!' On the table was a steel bit for a horse, one of the d-shaped rings cracked all the way through. I snatched it up, fingers curling through the ring, and hurled it at you. You ducked, but not quickly enough, and it glanced off your shoulder, clattering to the floor.

'Dammit, Emily!'

I had no idea what I was thinking when I grabbed the rifle hanging by its strap from a peg; I had never even held a gun before. I put my finger on the trigger, aiming unsteadily.

You shook your head at me, rubbing the angle of your shoulder. 'What you gonna do now?' Silence. You gestured beneath your ribs. 'Go for a gut shot. You'll likely hit me at this range, and if it doesn't kill me outright, I'll suffer real good for a few days.'

I faltered, trying not to cry. You lunged for the long barrel and pushed it towards the ceiling, making my finger tighten on the trigger. There was a huge bang and I fell, shocked, as you tore the gun from my grip and fragments of whitewash from the ceiling drifted down around us.

Scrambling up and gathering my legs beneath me, I ran. Down the meadow towards the forest. Not knowing where I was going. Not caring.

CHAPTER 8

'See that bluff up there?' Cal pointed. 'Like the one behind the house? The Indian braves used to drive the bison over the edge of them. They're called buffalo jumps.'

'Great!' Hope said fake-cheerfully, watching the landscape pass. It was beautiful, dramatic. Sharp crags rose up, their grey and black striations contrasting with the blue sky. White clouds dotted the vast ceiling above them. Trees stood in stands and in thick gathers of forest. Every now and then, just off the track, streams, creeks and rivulets trickled and rushed. Sometimes, horses gathered in twos and threes, free to roam. Wild flowers bloomed in carpets by the stands of trees.

'The taxi driver who took us to the airport said people hide away out here. Fugitives and stuff.'

Glancing across at her, he smiled. 'Maybe, but mainly I

think people come out here for space. Less head noise, you know?'

They were silent for a little while.

He spoke again. 'You know, there's a horse up here that people say's been in these parts for ever. A white stallion with glass eyes. Pops used to say he was the sire of the original Crow horse bloodline and little Zach's arrival made me think, but I think it's just wishful.'

'More wishful than a mythical horse?'

He smiled. 'Dad's seen him. Apparently all us Crows get to see him once in our lives.'

Hope remembered the diary and pulled the little book from her bag. 'This is the diary, from the attic.'

Cal glanced across. 'Is it interesting?'

'Yes. She's going to Portland to meet the man she's going to marry. His family firm are building a railway there.'

He thought about it. 'I suppose she'd have come this way to avoid the sickness on the Oregon Trail and then . . . the Sioux Wars maybe.'

'Exactly. She says that. But, the weird thing is, it's almost written like a letter to a different man. A man with pale eyes and a bad limp. I haven't got to who he is yet.'

'And she is?'

'Emily Forsythe. I think her dad's important in London. Like a diplomat or something. Totally Victorian. She's travelling with a woman called Miss Adams, who's supposed to be getting her to Portland for the wedding, and sounds like a proper old bag. And a team of drivers from Chicago.'

'OK . . .'

'OK?'

'Well, read to me then, Hope Cooper!'

Hope hid a shy smile and read on, as Emily and Miss Adams sat in the coach, travelling away from Fort Shaw. Her smile faded. 'Oh God, she's awful.'

'She doesn't sound a lot of fun.'

'Poor Emily. She's going to get married to some guy and she doesn't even know him.'

'Different times.'

Leaning forward, she put the diary on the dashboard.

'Stuff can slide straight out of these windows. I've made that mistake before. Stick it in the jockey box.' He pointed beneath the dashboard on Hope's side.

'Ah, the glove compartment.'

'No gloves in it,' he said with a smile.

Hope opened it and put the diary inside. 'No jockeys either.' She pulled out a strange, ridged object the size of her thumb, dry and fragile. 'What's this?'

He glanced over at her. 'Rattle from a rattlesnake I killed on the road last summer. Bad luck not to take it.'

Hope dropped it back into the glove compartment and shut the door with a snap, wiping her palms on her shorts. 'Gross.'

He laughed.

'So, we're collecting your aunt's horses?'

'Yep. And my mom.'

'Is your mother from around here?'

'Mom? No, she's from back East. Vermont.'

'How did they meet?'

'My mom came out to work as a documentary photographer's assistant during her vacation. Met my dad when they were photographing the rodeo. That was kind of it. She went back for a couple of months and then they decided to get married.'

'Just like that?'

'I was on the way. Probably influenced things a little.'

'Wow.'

He nodded. 'That was when Dad saw the horse. The morning Mom called in tears from Vermont and said she was getting on a bus. Her parents had kicked her out, because of me. Dad drove straight to Chicago and met her. Saw the horse just as he was leaving the ranch. They came back, got married the next week, and that was it. We have to change trails here. We're leaving our property and getting into the national park. It gets rougher from here on in.' He saw her watching the controls with interest. 'You want to drive?'

'Oh, er, no. Thanks.'

'Can you?'

'I live in London. There's public transport.'

He tutted and braked. Popping his door, he got out, then looked back into the cab. 'You should learn.'

'I don't think—'

'C'mon, Cooper. Don't be chicken.'

Hope got out and they crossed in front of the rumbling pick-up. Getting into the driver's seat, she was too far from the pedals.

Cal was already sitting in her seat. 'You'll have to sit forward,' he said. 'Your left foot doesn't do anything, so keep it over against the rest there. Then the pedal on the left is the brake, the gas is on the right. Put your foot on the brake and put the stick behind the wheel into drive.'

'Got it.' Hope nodded.

'Now let your foot off the brake and she'll creep. It'll take a while because of the trailer.'

The pick-up began to move slowly.

'Now press on the gas real gentle.'

They gained speed. Hope steered carefully on the trail.

'This is fun.'

'Told you.'

They were driving at an angle towards a mountain range, but in the near distance the land rose up, covered with trees. Before it there was a deep crack in the landscape, and a bridge towards which it seemed they were heading.

Hope was concentrating on the ten metres in front of the pick-up. 'I'm not sure I could do this in traff—'

'Hope, stop. Stop the truck. *Now.* Do it now.'

Momentarily confused by the pedals, Hope put her left foot on the brake and pressed the accelerator with her right foot at the same time. The pick-up jumped forward and jerked, straining against the brake. Cal reached across her and threw the stick shift into neutral.

'Take your feet off the pedals,' he said sharply.

'Sorry!' Hope held up her hands and drew her knees up.

'Get out.'

She fumbled open the door, unsure what she'd done so wrong. As they passed in front of the pick-up, she mumbled, 'Sorry.'

He caught her arm. 'It's not you, look.'

Hope looked to where he was pointing. On the other side of the bridge, almost on it, was a brilliant and very beautiful white horse. His mane and tail were long and snowy. And he was watching them. They were too far away to see the colour of his eyes.

'Get in.'

Hope scrambled into the passenger seat.

'Buckle up.' Cal was already putting the truck into gear and accelerating.

The pick-up gained the bridge. Hope put her hand out, almost touching Cal's shirt, looking through the windscreen in alarm. 'Wait, is this safe? It looks like it's been here for a hundred years.'

'I've driven over it fifty times.'

The white horse was still standing on the other side of the bridge as they drove on to it. Hope peered out of the window over the virtually empty creek bed, with just a few rivulets of water running through it.

Cal braked hard. 'There's a couple of boards missing. They can't have repaired it after the winter. Damn. Should've checked it. Reversing off will be a nightmare.'

There was a groan from the bridge beneath them. And a distinct sense of unsteadiness.

'Shit,' he said. Silence, then another creak.

Cal accelerated, taking the pick-up over the gap. The trailer clattered behind them, bouncing hard into the open space. There was a terrible crashing sound as the wooden rails broke beneath it and it skewed off to the left. Then, an endless moment of tension as the tow bar bent, but held.

The pick-up jerked backwards, sliding towards the broken hole in the bridge. Hope screamed. Buddy yelped. Cal jammed on all the brakes. Everything caught. For five long seconds, nothing happened. The trailer was still hanging off the bridge. Cal slammed the gear stick into park, boot rammed hard on the brake. The engine was loud in the silence.

'Hope. Pop your door and get out.'

'Only if you come with me.'

'I will, but I want you to get out now. Buddy? Buddy, out!' he yelled to the dog, who had slid to the back of the pick-up's flatbed.

He pushed Hope as she pulled the door lever and struggled with her seat belt at the same time. The door popped open as Buddy hit the planks with a thud. The trailer creaked and swayed. The pick-up slipped a few centimetres.

The white horse turned, and disappeared into the trees.

Hope's side of the vehicle lifted up in the air and the door slammed back into place, sealing them in the cab.

Cal grabbed her hand as, with a hideous shrieking and grinding of metal, the pick-up tipped over the edge.

*

Hope's neck hurt. In fact, everything hurt. She was hanging

127

upside down by her seat belt. *How long have I been out?* She looked over at Cal. He was a crumpled length of whipcord in the roof lining of the upside-down pick-up. She guessed they must be on the creek bed. The front of the truck had dragged against one of the bridge supports, stopping the cab being totally crushed. Rivulets of water were running through the cabin windows, wetting Cal's clothes, streaming through his hair.

Where did that come from? Hope squinted, trying to clear her vision, rubbing her face with wet hands. Somewhere, she could hear urgent barking. She fumbled for the seat-belt clasp, and unclipped it with some effort. She instantly tipped down into the deepening water, bruising her face and shoulder against a ridge in the roof. Her cheek hurt – blood was trickling down her face. Pushing herself on to her hands and knees in the cramped space, she patted Cal's face urgently.

'Cal?'

His blue eyes opened and he shook himself like a dog, swearing. Water droplets from his wet hair spattered on the inside of the broken windscreen. The rivulets were no longer separate streams, but a torrent rushing through the cabin. He reached out and grabbed Hope's T-shirt, fist bunched in material and suddenly wide awake. 'This time, when I tell you to get out, you *go*.' He kicked out the remainder of the wind-screen in three hard slams. It fell back in crackling shards. She felt his boot pushing her as she scrambled out, nuggets of glass cutting into her palms. Her ears were ringing from the roaring. And it was only getting louder. Cal was trying to unstrap the rifle from behind the headrests.

The diary! Hope crawled back to the smashed passenger window and reached inside, pulling open the glove box and fishing out the little book. She shoved it into her pocket. Cal was still struggling with the strap holding the gun in place.

Water was pouring through her hiking boots, up to the ankles, racing through the deformed driver's window. Inside the cab Cal was soaked. 'Come *on*!'

'Coming!'

The noise increased tenfold. Hope looked in the direction of the roar, and saw a wall of water as tall as she was surging down the creek.

'NOW.'

He scrambled from the cab on all fours, rifle over his shoulder. Grabbing Hope's hand, he hauled her to a deep crevasse in the opposite bank. High above them, Buddy ran back and forth, barking frantically. Pushing her in front of him, Cal began to heave her further into the fissure. The water splashed their thighs.

He put his hands under Hope's backside and shoved. 'Get up there!'

'I'm trying!'

A few seconds later, she caught her footing and began to climb, pushing out against the rocky sides of the crevasse. Half a minute after that, she made it on to the grass bank high above. Rolling on to her stomach, she reached back down, catching Cal's hand and bracing herself as Buddy jumped all over her. Her tendons burnt as his boots slipped, but then he gained his hold, boosting himself up the final few metres. They lay next to each other, panting, as the meltwater blasted through the gulch beneath them.

CHAPTER 9

'I AM FAR FROM ASSERTING THAT
THERE ARE NOT INSTANCES OF
NOBLE AND GENEROUS-HEARTED
MEN WHO KNOW HOW TO BE THE
FRIEND OF A WOMAN; THESE
INSTANCES ARE LAMENTABLY RARE.'

By the time I reached the treeline, I was breathless and slowed to a walk. There was no trail. No track. Nothing. The clumps of pine and scrub gathered as the forest thickened. But there was no obvious way through them. I was soaked, even though the rain was light and my feet were getting sore.

Hot, frightened perspiration trickled down inside the cold, wet shirt, making me shiver. What had I done? I knew nothing of how to survive in the wilderness. The ground was springy with moss and pine needles. Something stung my foot. I winced and looked at the red mark, my hand against the rough bark of a tree for balance. The forest was noisy with birds, like a canopy of sound above me. The rain seemed to have stopped and light came down through the trees, glinting off the wings of butterflies, making the undergrowth shine. Twice, I had to backtrack when it proved impassable. I stopped and rested on a fallen tree, thirsty and footsore. Nearby there was the sound of running water and when I had caught my breath, I followed it. But the water looked brown, so I set off again.

When the late afternoon chill set in, I found some sort of trail, or animal track. My feet were a little numb by now. I kept moving to stay warm, but when the light began to fade I found a large rock with a tree growing next to it, and huddled on to it, wrapping my arms around myself. My clothes and hair were still very damp; I wished I'd brought a blanket, or something heavier to wear. I rubbed my sore feet. They were scratched and blotched with red, the right one was smeared with blood from a splinter and they were blue with cold along the edges of my nails.

Soon, it was dark, and I felt the forest had eyes. Something moved in the undergrowth. I choked back a scream as a deer loomed out of the darkness. The fright made me even more sensitive to the cold, although suddenly my skin felt slightly warmer to the touch and my violent shuddering died down. The night-things scuttled and croaked, quietening to barely a murmur. High above, the moon made lacework from the pines.

When I woke with a violent start, it was just before dawn. As soon as there was a bluish-grey light amongst the trees, I set out again, stiff with cold. After a few minutes, I stumbled into a stream. Grateful, I washed my face and hands, and drank a little. An eternity later, or so it seemed, I emerged from the trees on to a grassland.

As the sun rose, I headed what I thought was east. My feet were a mess, toenails rimed with dirt. My empty stomach was complaining and my head ached from lack of water. Sometime after midday, still on the endless grassland, the lake to my right, I stumbled, exhausted, and fell to my knees. I was wiping my face of sweat and a self-indulgent tear when I heard it: a low growl. My head snapped up.

At the edge of the trees, no more than ten yards away was a rock outcrop, perhaps a little taller than me. On it perched a huge tan cat, belly against the stone. An American mountain lion. Its tufted ears were sharply pricked and its tail lashed from side to side. As its muzzle drew back from its teeth, it exhaled a long, low hissing sound, and its back legs pumped in readiness to spring.

A cry escaped me and I fell as I stumbled backwards. The animal gathered to surge from the rock, just as a shot echoed around the mountains, chipping shards of stone by the cat's paws. It coiled back in an instant, snarling, and streaked into the trees.

I could barely breathe. Your hand was hard beneath my arm. 'Up. Get up.' I struggled to my feet, fighting you. You grasped my arms and shook me, hard. 'That's enough.'

'Let me go!' I squirmed, pushing you.

'You want to end up as cat meat?' You were furious as, with one last jolt, you released me.

All the fight left my body in an instant, and a tear streaked down my face. We stood staring at each other, both breathing hard. Finally, you sighed and offered me the water canteen. My instinct was to refuse, but I was so thirsty I took it and drank greedily.

'What have I done to you that's worth dying over?'

I looked at the canteen in my hands and swiped another tear away. 'I just hoped to find people . . . who would help me.'

'Only people you gonna find out here gonna give you the kind of help you don't deserve,' you said fiercely. 'You got any idea what use the miners and trappers out there would have for you? How they would hurt you?'

'Stop! Please!'

'Why? Your ears as prim and proper as the rest of you?'

'Stop it! Stop trying to frighten me.' I was suddenly furious, and threw the canteen into your chest. Before the crash, I could not remember being angry in my life.

You caught the water bottle, holding it to you, the other hand lifted in warning. 'Desist hurling things at me. Ain't never raised a hand to a woman but you are sincerely trying my patience.'

'You promised not to hurt me.'

'That was before you started using me for target practice.' You shook your head. 'Come on. Time to go home.' You caught my shoulder and drew me closer to the horse. 'And seeing as how you're sticking around, you're going to have to get used to how we do things around here. And how we do things is *horses*. Lesson One. Getting on the horse. Her left side is the near side, right side is off side. Always get on the near side—'

I pushed you off, knocking your hand away as hard as I could. 'I can't ride her.'

You scratched your cheek. 'Want to go home hog-tied across the saddle?'

I turned back to Tara.

'One hand on her withers – yep, that ridge there – and one hand behind, on her rump. Yes, *rump*, that's what I said. She don't mind. She's ain't precious like some I could mention.' Stooping, you caught my left shin in your hand, tapping behind my knee with your knuckles. 'Bend your knee. Bounce on your right foot a little and when I say go, let me boost you up and swing your right leg over. Use Tara. It's what she's there for.'

I pulled away from your grip. 'But I can't ride astride, only side-saddle.'

You straightened up. 'Ain't got one on me.'

My lip trembled. 'A gentleman wouldn't make me do this.'

A profanity of the kind I was utterly unfamiliar with split the air. You gestured to yourself. 'Emily, take a good look and tell me which part of this looks like a gentleman.'

I looked you up and down, from your long hair to the ragtag collection of feathers and other things around your neck, to your old clothes and knee-high Indian boots.

With a broken sigh, I turned back to Tara again and placed my hands as you had instructed. The first attempt was useless. You straightened up. 'You gotta slacken up, and just let me lift you. Relax.'

'I'm not feeling very *relaxed*,' I said tearfully.

'Oh Jesus, Emily.' You rubbed your face. 'You can't be this pighead-stubborn and this sorry-ass at the same time. It's just too confusing.' You took my shoulders and turned me back to face the saddle. 'Try again. One, two, three . . . *go*.'

To my surprise, a second later, I was mounted on Tara, who stood still as a stone. Leading her over to a fallen tree, ignoring my frantic grab for her mane, you stood on it, put your right leg over her behind me and eased on to her back. Taking up the reins in one hand, you steadied me with the other. It was all monstrously improper. The idea of me riding astride would have sent Mama into an apoplexy as it was, let alone our current posture, your arm right the way around me, your other wrist on my thigh as you arranged the reins.

'Quit squirming. You ain't an eel and Tara don't like it.'

Tara seemed not to care in the slightest, quiet and biddable as usual. You almost let her lead herself.

'How far did I get?' I asked in dismay.

'Four miles, thereabouts. In the wrong direction.'

We were back in the forest, and whilst the day had brightened around us from a dull start, in the trees it was still dark, though not nearly as forbidding as it had seemed when alone. Only a short time later, we emerged from the forest into the light. I put up a hand to shield my eyes. My bare feet hung down, heels banging against your shins as Tara climbed the grassy slope up the mountain with delicate, certain steps, finally coming to a halt in front of the porch. You dismounted, landing on your good foot, then helped me down. As you set me on my feet, I winced.

'Only yourself to blame.'

I turned to the house, exhausted.

'Ah-ha. What haven't you done?'

I turned back. 'I don't understand.'

You pointed to Tara, standing obediently.

'What?' My voice was sullen, even in my own ears.

'Look, Em, I know you're tired, but you take care of the horse before you look to yourself. Nothing but the work of a few seconds to turn her out. Can't just leave her standing here.'

I lifted my hands to her face, unsure.

'Not the cheek strap. Just undo the throat strap there. The thin one. That's it. Now reach up between her ears and take the crown there. Pull nice and easy.' The bridle came away in my hand and Tara let the bit slip from her mouth, then gave her head a shake and moved off as you slapped her shoulder. Taking the bridle from me, you hung it on a nail in the railing and pointed to the bench on the porch. 'Now, let me have a look at those feet.'

I sat down, stiff, as you made tea. Bringing out two cups, you handed one to me and dropped to your knees, fingers closing on my ankle. You lifted my foot and inspected the sole, making disapproving noises in your throat. 'What am I going to do with you?'

'Nothing. I don't want you to do anything with me.'

You examined the other foot. 'Spider bite.' You felt the

137

skin around it, blackened like a bruise.

Jerking from your grip, I flinched. 'Ouch.'

'Don't be a baby. Do you feel hot? Sick?'

'Cold. Just cold.'

'And no wonder. You ain't strong enough to sleep rough. Didn't even make yourself a shelter.'

'You . . . you followed me?'

'What do you think?' You got up and went over to where the wooden tub sat and turned the tap, filling it with the crystal clear water.

'Why didn't you help me, last night? I was so frightened.' My chin trembled.

You frowned, looking awkward and unhappy. 'Thought you might see sense and come back on your own. Damned if you ain't obstinate.'

'And you had to make your *point*, of course, didn't you?' I said, trying to be both dignified and hurt, like Mama.

Pushing to your feet, you went inside. I buried my head in my hands and cried a few exhausted tears, not feeling you standing over me until you threw a towel into my lap, frustrated. 'For Chrissake, stop crying. It's pitiful.'

I sat up and flung it back at you. 'Stop *making* me cry!' It hit your stomach, then dropped to the boards.

'I told you to *cease* throwing stuff.'

Silence.

'Just get cleaned up, Emily. Everything feels better clean,' you said, weary, and went inside. The door closed behind you.

I swiped a hand beneath my nose, quelling a sob, and

stripping out of my dirty clothes before washing in the chilly water.

As I got out you shouted from behind the door. 'You decent?'

I wrapped myself in the towel, knotted my braid on the crown of my head and sat on the bench, quite a portrait of misery. 'Yes.'

You opened the door. In one hand was an enamel bowl, and in the other a kettle. I could see a pile of dried herbs inside. You put them on the planks and poured the kettle over them, making a fragrant steam rise. You added some water from the tub and tested it.

'Feet in.'

I did as you said, obediently. You handed me a blanket and I wrapped it around my shoulders, huddling up. Kneeling down and pulling my foot from the water, you examined it carefully, pulling thorns and splinters out where necessary with a pair of steel tweezers. I winced.

'Oh no, lady, you've earned every part of this. The bite will bruise for a couple of days, but you've got away lightly, I reckon.'

'I haven't got away at all,' I said quietly. The wind in the trees was the only sound for a few seconds. 'Take me back, Nate. Please.'

You let go of my foot and sat back on your heels, head on one side, strange eyes fixed on mine. 'Ask me anything else in that voice. Say my name like that. And you can have anything you want that I can give you.'

I swallowed. 'I don't understand.'

'Yes you do, Emily, you understand just fine.'

What you were suggesting . . . it was impossible. 'We don't know each other.'

'You don't know the man you were on your way to marry.'

'My parents, they—'

You pushed up on to your feet, hard, towering over me. 'They're selling you. You can't see that? I know how that feels, Emily, and it ain't good.'

It wasn't what you were making out, my marriage. It *was* a good thing. Everyone had told me so. I had to make you understand. Perhaps, that way, you would take me back. 'I *do* know him. Better than you think. We write. They . . . they've shown me photographs. I . . .'

'Photographs?' Your hands clenched into fists. You stalked away, inside the house. When I dared to peep in, you were hunched over the sink, shoulders at an angle.

'I don't belong here,' I said, my voice unsteady as I stood in the doorway, feet wetting the pale floorboards.

You threw your tin cup into the sink in a sudden show of temper, denting it further and making me start back. 'You don't know where you belong. That's your problem.'

Two days passed. You came and went but you barely spoke to me. When I tried to make conversation, you turned away from me so often that I lost my voice, confused by your obstinate silence. But soon I grew to be happy when I saw Tara grazing outside, for I knew you were around. Somewhere.

And the idea of being alone in the wilderness terrified me. Often, you stood near the corral, roping a wooden post, over and over again, snatching down the catch, rope scratching loudly as it tightened. You were clever with it, and sometimes I watched from the porch as you twirled it over your head, sometimes around your body, the noose fluid and ceaseless. On the second afternoon, you stood at a distance from the post and shot arrows from a small, sturdy bow into a deerskin bag filled with dirt. Over and over. Later you told me it was better than wasting ammunition out hunting, because every bullet counts.

I took my courage and walked down the meadow to you. You looked at the bow, not at me, fitting another arrow to it. 'What do you want?'

I took a breath. 'Why won't you talk to me, please?'

'Tried to talk to you and it didn't go so well, did it? Thought I'd just see how it went if we don't.'

'Is this . . . is it because you disapprove of my parents arranging my marriage?'

'Nope.' You let the bow drop a little, then raised it to your eye and fired. It hit the bag with a dull thump. 'But I don't approve of it, no. Since you ask.'

'Well, I don't need your approval, thank you,' I said, chin in the air.

'That you don't,' you agreed, pulling another arrow from the quiver at your bad hip and fitting it to the bow. 'But you do need my help. And because I don't *approve*, I ain't minded to give it.'

'But *please*.'

You shook your head. 'But no.'

'If you make me stay I will never forgive you,' I said, tears flooding my eyes. I turned on my heel and walked back to the cabin.

The arrow speared into the bag. It burst, spilling dirt on to the meadow.

'Never is a long time!' you yelled after me.

I slept in the bed, rose when the cockerel began to crow, and swept every inch of the cabin. I realized that when you said you had inherited the cabin, you hadn't said from whom. The chest in the bedroom gave me some answers. Two blankets, a pretty linen nightgown wrapped in a lace bag. A peculiar little book, which appeared to be pieces of advice for a young woman embarking upon married life, with blank pages for personal observations. There were also a few gold coins stamped in a language I didn't understand, but akin to the German I did know. Bundles of lavender everywhere, falling out of every fold of cloth.

The chest spoke of newlyweds. Of preparation, and perhaps love. The things that I would never see in San Francisco, for I knew in my heart that even if I did manage to meet Mama and Papa and Mr Stanton in Portland, he would never marry me now. And why should he? There was no plausible story for my absence, and the truth – that I had been living alone with a horse trader – would render me worthless.

I explored the kitchen. On shelves were large crocks of

dried beans and peas, which I did not know to soak before cooking and so I boiled and boiled them but they were still inedible. There was also flour, sugar, cornmeal, oats and dried corn kernels. Crates of carefully packed dried herbs were stored under the rough wooden counter. I experimented with cooking and practised breadmaking, though I soon realized I was using stupidly grand quantities, ending up with dough balls like bricks, which was mainly how they turned out. As long as I didn't speak, you let me watch you cook in your simple, economical fashion.

It became apparent I was not much of a modern house-wife, and far less of a pioneer. I cringed at the spiders in the outhouse and shrieked at the poor field mouse that reminded me of Miss Adams. Safe to say, I did not miss her at all, but I was very sorry for the death of Mr Goldsmith, who had been kind to me.

When you were around you said little. Sometimes you sat on the steps and shaved with a straight razor and no mirror, doing it by touch, rinsing the blade under the tap. Once you spent a day chopping wood, the axe a steady thump and crack, the side of the cabin thudding as you placed the logs beneath the shelter there. You did it shirtless and I watched from the shadows at the edge of the cabin window as the muscles of your chest and arms worked like the steel hawsers on the steamship. I had already realized how strong you were from the way you had lifted me with ease, but now I saw it was a strength forged from years of ceaseless labour; a hard life of constant motion had hewn you, rather than raised you.

My gentle life of lessons, reading and sedate walks meant I had less strength than a kitten.

If you'd wanted to hurt me, it would have been easy. Yet . . . wouldn't you have done so by now?

Time dragged. When I saw you in the meadow, so many times I almost went to you, but I was afraid you would dismiss me again. I was bored and lonely. And cold at night.

After that first night when you had slept in your own bed, on top of the covers, you slept in the kitchen in bad weather, and on the porch on fine nights; but in general, you did not sleep much at all and sometimes in the small hours you were troubled by dreams. One night I watched you wake, as usual pale and sweating, on the floor near the stove, blankets pushed aside. I had been listening to your breathing for some time, uneven and laboured, your face half-lit by the red light from the stove door. You hauled in a huge breath and sat up. After a moment you got to your feet, letting yourself out silently.

I hesitated, then got up and went on to the porch. Sitting on the boards, back against the cabin, you glanced up, pale in the moonlight. 'Need something?' Your voice was strained.

'You were dreaming, again.'

'Happens.'

'Mama says laudanum helps her sleep. Perhaps that powder you gave me would—'

'No. Been far enough down that road to know not to walk it again.'

I sat a couple of feet from you, on the step, and looked at

the moon, hands beneath my arms to warm them. I had been using my underdress as a nightgown, but the night air was sharp. 'Might I do anything to help?'

There was a silence. 'What happened to never forgiving me?'

'Never is longer than I thought.'

You huffed your soft laugh.

'I could make tea?'

'Take your rest, Emily. No purpose served by both of us sitting out here.'

I returned to bed and hugged myself as distant wolves began to howl. Dawn was an age in coming.

The following day you acted as if the night had never happened, acknowledging me with nothing more than a hum as you sifted through a bag of nails and stuck a hammer into your waistband before climbing on to the roof, banging a patch over the shingle I'd exploded, and which was now letting the rain inside. Later you made things you called 'biscuits', which weren't like Cook's biscuits but more like soft little cakes, and we ate them with eggs at the kitchen table. The small, speckled eggs were clustered in a dish, still hot from the water.

When I just stared at them, bemused, you picked one up, peeling it deftly, then splitting it on to the biscuit on my plate, hot bright-yellow yolk spilling over the dough. I remembered the many times I sat with Mama, learning how to plan meals and even grand embassy banquets. And all of that time I had been unable to boil an egg.

You folded your elbows on the table and watched me. 'That looks like some deep thinking.'

I shrugged, shy. 'Not much of a cook, am I?'

'No,' you agreed. 'And if you take the lid off my biscuit pan again, I'll make you wish you hadn't.'

Regarding my plate, I began to say, 'I'm sor—'

You shot me a warning look.

I bit my lip, then picked up my knife and fork. 'I was just curious,' I said firmly. 'How was I to know they needed the lid on?'

Just for a second, the backs of your fingers touched mine, the smallest of smiles at the corner of your mouth.

After our meal, you disappeared and I washed some clothes and a sheet in the tub, banging the soap into them with a long-handled wooden contraption. I was becoming accustomed to the constant assault of nature on the mountain, and the work kept me warm. It was never silent, with the endless birdsong during the day, and the noises of the wild things at night.

My laundry skills were improving and I now had a workable system of clothing, which still consisted mainly of your shirts and trousers and a jumble of underclothes. I wondered what Mama would think of my laundressing, our shared things, and my hand-me-down linen. Imagining the look on her face made me smile. Far away, two foxes were playing in the meadow, tumbling over each other again and again as if inside a ball. There were clouds high in the sky and their shadows moved over the blowing, silvery grass. The effect was so peaceful I became much involved in my tasks, and failed to see three men approaching from the forest.

They were all on horseback. The horses were large and dark, not like Tara. The men were large and dark as well, wearing dun- and brown-coloured clothing, the same colour as their tanned and unwashed skins, their duster coats stained and ragged. But they were white men. And I was alone. They took their time in approaching, and the leader, for the leader was obvious, did not speak until they were in front of the porch. I had straightened up to my full height immediately on seeing them, which would not have done anything to impress them, I was sure. Yet it made me feel marginally better.

They pulled their horses to a halt.

'Well well, Nate done got himself a plaything.'

I said nothing to that, for there was no well-bred response.

The man, perhaps as old as Papa, but unshaven and most definitely unwashed, clicked his tongue. 'What is a rose like you doing with a lame savage? You need to get yourself a real man.'

The men chuckled. One spat into the grass in a filthy brown stream. Chewing tobacco. An entirely nauseating habit.

'Nate isn't here,' I said, trying to keep the tremble from my voice. Then I realized my terrible error as their expressions changed.

The leader got down from his horse. 'Then where is he?' He swaggered towards me, big and hard-edged, spurs clinking. He had large, strong features. Near his eye was a small scar and another larger one underneath his jaw which Papa had once told me was what happened when poor people suffered abscessed teeth. At his throat was a dirty kerchief. If he came any closer I was sure I would smell him.

I stood my ground. 'Out. Hunting,' I lied uselessly, 'but he'll be back any moment.'

'You English, ain'tcha? Proper fine English lady.' His eyes narrowed. 'Where'd he find you?'

'None of your business,' I said, in the tone Mama had taught me.

The men all laughed. For a moment, the only movement in all four of us was from the man chewing the tobacco, jaw churning tirelessly.

'What say we come on in?' the leader said.

I took a breath to speak.

'Reckon not, Hart, seeing as it's already paining me hard enough you're breathing the same air.' You limped round the corner of the cabin, rifle over your arm, glaring at the leader. At your hip was a pistol I had never seen before, bullets belting your narrow waist.

My sigh of relief was obvious. Hart winked at me. 'Just wanting to be friendly, Nate.'

You climbed the two porch steps and put yourself between me and Hart. 'State your business.'

'Now, what kind of a greeting is that after the best part of six months? See you ain't made it to the barber since then.'

Silence.

'Got a job in.'

'Ain't taking that kind of work no more.'

Hart shrugged. 'Ain't *that* kind of work. You'll get to keep your hands clean, promise. It's a scout. From the railroad big bugs.'

My heart leapt. Railroad? I could feel the tension radiating from your back, even though your voice was relaxed. You were waiting to see what I did, as much as talking to them.

'Up in savage country. Gotta be done now and we've got business up on the plain to take care of. I'll just take my usual share.'

'Got another mouth to feed. Need more money.'

Hart snorted with laughter, then spat on the porch. 'She don't look like she's eating you out of house nor home. And we can always look in on her while you're gone. Make sure she's taken care of.'

Your boots shifted on the planks.

Hart grinned, teeth yellow. 'Fine, fine. I'll take less. Call it a gesture, for old time's sake. But it's taken the boys and me time to get out here and back, gotta get some compensation for that. Tracking you down ain't been easy. Thought you'd gone back native.' He looked around. 'Heard of this place, hidden away up here. Thought it was a story. Though God alone knows why any sane person would want to live all the way out here.'

You said nothing.

'Two fifty.' Opening his greasy coat, Hart reached into an

inside pocket and pulled out a large paper packet, throwing it on the boards at your feet.

'How long do I have?'

'A month, give or take. We'll be back.'

You ignored the packet. 'I'll come into town.'

'And leave this pretty thing here all alone? And where's that fine mare of yours? The one who looks at you with the cow eyes? Want to sell her now you've traded up to real women?'

'If you don't shut your mouth you can shove your job and I will shoot you when you turn your back.'

'Like the murdering deserter you are,' Hart said mildly.

You took the rifle in both hands.

He backed off the porch. 'No need to be touchy, Nate. I wouldn't leave her alone neither.'

He got back on his horse. The man chewing tobacco spat again, soiling the wild flowers in front of the cabin. Then all three riders wheeled their horses and rode away.

We watched them go. You stood, motionless, for what seemed like an age, pale eyes narrow. When their figures had been eaten by the shadow of the forest, you finally stood down, went inside and hung up the rifle on one of the hooks. I followed.

'Who were they?'

You were looking for something to eat, going through the usual places. 'Trapper scum. Out of Fort Shaw. They take jobs from everyone. They just don't *do* any of them.' Going outside, you took the pail standing near the door and filled it from the spigot. Shifting the packet out of the way with your boot, you swilled Hart's phlegm from the boards, and tipped the rest on to the brown stain on the grass. My mouth twisted with disgust.

You straightened up, collecting the packet on your way back. 'He's a pig. Always has been.' Your voice was sharp. Inside, you pulled out the folded papers and spread them on the table. It was a series of maps. My heart leapt when I saw the largest set were marked with Stanton in the corner. You had both hands on the table, leaning over. 'Is there any tea?'

I went to pour it out. The skin was drawn tight over your cheekbones.

'What did—'

'Just leave it, Emily.'

'I don't understand.'

You linked your hands behind your neck. 'I don't want *him*, Hart, knowing you're here, all right? I don't want him coming *here*. Nothing good will come of it. Nothing. I thought I'd gone far enough they wouldn't find me.'

I stood still and kept quiet.

Then you took a deep breath and blew out. 'Some people foul everything, and he's one of them.'

I bit my lip, understanding I should change the subject as you returned to look at the map. My next effort was another mistake. 'Stanton. The maps are Stanton maps.' I bent over with you, tracing the name at the bottom.

'Stands to reason. If it's his company.' Your tone was abrupt as you followed the path of my finger.

'Stanton Railroad. San Francisco. 1867.'

There was a sealed packet of instructions that had been folded inside, seemingly missed by Mr Hart. You'd pushed them away. I picked them up.

'*Instructions to agent,*' I read on the outside.

'Yeah, yeah.'

'You aren't going to read them?'

'Never do.'

Frowning, I opened the packet and scanned the paper. 'They're quite detailed. About where you should look. Don't you think—'

'No,' you said abruptly. 'I'll go from the map.'

'But they're signed by a Mr Meard, agent for the Stantons. I think they'd want you to read them.'

You took them from me and tore them in half neatly before handing them back, then went on looking at the map. 'Can't. Got as far as learning my ABCs that year at school, before I left. I know *hotel*, and *saloon*, and *telegraph*. Some place names. I can form *Nathaniel* on paper, if I have to.'

I stared at you, my mouth open.

You shook your head in warning. 'Don't dare to pity me, Emily.'

'I'm not,' I said, too quickly.

You went to take the paper from my hand but I stepped back. Putting the two pieces back together, I turned away from you and skimmed it over. I tried not to let you see that I touched the imprinted Stanton letterhead again, with a careful fingertip. 'It's nothing anyway. Just that they expect the job completed as quickly as possible, for the agreed fee, which is five hundred dollars.'

You swore. A long stream of expletives ending with, 'That chiselling bastard. He only paid me two hundred last time, and that was a longer job.'

I was no longer shocked by your casual profanities. Instead, I turned to the table, placed the two pieces of paper on the map and looked up at you, standing closer than I usually would. 'You should renegotiate with Mr Hart. But I think I just made you at least one hundred dollars.'

We looked at each other. I could see you were laughing and hid a smile of my own. Then an awful thought struck me.

'When will you go?'

You raised an eyebrow. 'I think you mean, *we*?'

'But how can I go with you? I can barely ride and I have no shoes.'

'You'll learn and don't need no shoes on horseback. Ain't leaving you here alone now they know where you are.'

Relief flooded my chest. 'But we only have one horse,' I said, a hangnail of anxiety pulling at me.

'Yeah, but we won't be covering big distances at first, and I can get another pretty quickly once we get into Indian country. By then you'll be able to manage Tara just fine. She's a good girl. And she likes you.'

'I think you'll find she likes *you*.'

You grinned your cocky grin. 'Oh no, she *loves* me.'

I took a breath, shy in the sunlight of your attention. 'So, when do *we* go?'

'As soon you can sit a horse on your own.'

The following morning, my second lesson in horsemanship began. When I got up and dressed, Tara was already saddled. You were fiddling with the bridle when you saw me; you beckoned.

I went over to you. You lifted the flap of the saddle. 'Second lesson. Cinches. See this here? It's a cruelty to keep it done up tight when she's just standing around, so we don't. But you need to tighten it before you get back on, or the saddle will slip. Got it?'

'Got it.'

'Good. So this is the cinch ring, see? See this strap here? It goes up here to the ring that sits under the fender, which is there to protect your leg. It needs at least two full passes. You'll struggle to tighten three, so we'll keep it to two. So, it's loose, see? That ain't no good, so take a hold on the inner loop. That's it. Now, when you let out a cinch, the horse will blow itself out. They all do it, and the canny ones like Tara here will do it when you come to tighten them too. So, you gotta knee her in the belly a little.'

I looked up at you.

'Go on, you won't hurt her. Just behind the cinch. And pull as you do it. She knows the drill.'

Doing as I was told, I was surprised by how much the leather gave. I repeated the move with the outer loop.

'Hold on to it there, and now pull the strap through the

ring.' You were holding the fender out of the way to help me. How did anyone do this without three hands?

'That's it. Good job, English.' You checked it with a tug and tied it off. 'Should be just enough to get your fingers between the strap and her belly. You try. See? Now, one hand on the horn, one on the seat. And . . . hup.'

In the saddle, you handed me the reins and took hold of Tara's bridle, leading us down the hill.

'I can ride.'

You glanced over your shoulder at me. 'You can? I hadn't noticed.'

I blushed. 'I rode in London.'

'Some broken-winded old kid's pony?' You made a noise which indicated exactly what you thought of that.

Down in the meadow, you adjusted the stirrups and held the nearest one steady as you showed me how to touch Tara's side with my heels to indicate different commands.

'Will she know? I haven't even got boots on, let alone spurs.'

You glanced up at me from beneath your dark eyelashes, irked. 'If you can't ride without boots and spurs, you ain't no good with 'em. Tara is responding to your legs as much as anything. And that's the way it ought to be.' You looped a rope through the rings of Tara's bit and stepped back, perhaps fifteen feet, holding the other ends. 'Now lead her in a circle and let her move away from your left leg, round towards me. No, no! Jesus, English, don't yank on her mouth like a barbarian. Both reins in one hand, yep just like that, and then take them in the way you want to go over against her neck. She'll move away from the pressure . . . yes. And now you're learning.'

Lesson Two had begun in earnest.

I soon came to learn you were most vocal and communicative when teaching me about horses. Hearing your voice again after so long was very welcome and I enjoyed the long screeds of chatter – *great straight back there, English! Sit down deep when she trots, it's the only way*.

Things almost ended badly on the first afternoon, when you slipped Tara off the rope and told me to walk her down the meadow, then trot her back up to you. In a taller patch of scrubby grass, she flushed a grouse, which flew up directly in her face. She reared back, my foot slipped from the stirrup and I fell to the left with no time to grab for the saddlehorn. I hit the ground, bruising the hand I put out to break my fall. Tara, already recovered, stood over me protectively and as I tried to sit up you skidded into the grass, gathering me up against your chest.

'Emily!'

Rattled, your sudden concern was too much and I burst into tears.

'Where do you hurt? Is it your shoulder?' You felt my collarbone. 'You shouldn't put out your hand like that, just keep your arms in and try and roll with the fall. Dammit, should-a warned you.'

Shaking my head, I was mute as a tear dripped from

my chin.

You put your arms right around me and squeezed re-assuringly. 'There now, ain't nothing. Just a shock to the system.'

I had never been held in my life before: I was over-whelmed by your embrace, and then by your kindness as you examined my bruised fingers.

'Nothing broken.' You touched a fleeting kiss to my knuckles just as dear Tara's face appeared and she blew at us gently, ears pricked. You let go of my hand and petted her cheek. 'Yeah, I know, you didn't mean for Emily to take a fall. She ain't mad at you, are you, Em?'

Tearing my gaze away from your face, I touched my hand to Tara's velvet nose. 'Of course not.'

She snorted and we laughed. I caught the leather lace on your chest, tracing down to the feathers amongst the jumble of articles resting beneath your ribs. Gently, you began to push me away.

Horrified, I realized I had been pressed against you. 'I'm so sorry . . . I—'

You got to your feet with a brush-off gesture. 'This knee ain't good stuck kneeling, is all.'

I stood, and wiped my tear-sticky face on my sleeve. 'You should have said.'

You caught Tara's reins, shrugging, not meeting my eyes. 'Gets me out of church.'

My lessons continued for the next three days, by which time

I was distinctly uncomfortable, but far more capable. My London riding instruction and park hacks had not been in vain and I learnt quickly. Tara was biddable and forgiving; we raced up and, even more exhilarating, down the meadow at a flat-out gallop for most of the final day: *That's it! Lean into it. Knees tight, weight in your heels. Now you're talking! Bring her around sharp now. She turns on a pinhead, so be ready and hang in there!*

And I enjoyed it. Better than that, I *loved* it. And I was coming to love Tara, who dealt with me so kindly, for all my blundering. I slept heavily at night, exhausted, and on the third evening even fell asleep in my supper, rousing briefly as you dumped me on to the bed and cleared away, before going to sleep on the porch.

We muddled along together. I realized I was losing count of the days of my captivity. I had turned sixteen, surely? Sometimes, when I was putting Tara through her paces and you were watching, you'd ask me questions about myself. Sometimes I tried to question you, but you were adept at turning the tables.

On the fifth morning after the men had come to the cabin, we set out. It was only as you finished putting the last pack on to Tara and shut the door that I realized we were leaving the place I had come to feel safe in. Our spare clothes were stowed behind the saddle and I wore what you called a possibles bag across my body. You mounted Tara and helped me up a second later. We settled in the saddle.

'Isn't this too much for her?'

'Nah, she's used to bearing weight. I ain't carrying spare and you don't weigh hardly nothing nohow.'

'What about the chickens?'

'They pretty much take care of themselves. They were here when I got here. And they seem to know how to go on making more little chicks, and surviving up here. How, I have no idea. When I looked at that coop I thought a weasel would be in there before the week was out, but the previous tenants were mighty clever about how they built that ladder.'

I looked at the hens scratching around between the cabin and the stream. 'What happened to the people who lived here?'

'Upped and left. Maybe they got the loneliness. Seen it happen out here. Can kill you if you ain't got the constitution for the place.'

'The loneliness?'

'Yeah. Go a little crazy, stop eating, talking to yourself. Met a guy out on the trail last year, railing about his folks in St Louis. Nothing but a bag of bones and his horse weren't much better. Wouldn't take no help, wanting to go back East. Found his body on the road the next day. Looked like he walked himself to death, horse trailing behind him.'

I frowned, not able to associate such behaviour with our neatly kept little cabin. 'But they put so much effort into building it. They must have brought the bees with them. And the chickens. Because . . .'

'Their loss. Our gain.'

'What if they come back?'

'They ain't coming back.' You shifted the rifle into the sling behind your leg, fussing a little.

'But what if they did? We'd have to give it back to them.'

'And I'm telling you, they ain't. Gone West, I'd imagine.'

We set out. Heading for another adventure that would change who I was, for ever.

CHAPTER 10

Hope and Cal lay on the bank of the creek for a long time, until their breathing had steadied. Buddy licked Cal's face until he was shoved away and flopped on to the grass, whining and trembling. Finally Cal, still flat on his back, pulled his BlackBerry out of his hip pocket and squinted at it in the sun.

'Shit. Dead. The water.' He let his arm drop out to the side, useless phone in his hand.

Hope checked her pockets. Only the diary was in there. 'Mine must have fallen out when we crashed.'

Pushing himself up on his elbows, Cal put a hand to his head and winced. 'Anything broken?'

Hope made a quick check of herself. 'Just bruised, I think. What about you? You were out for a while.'

'Dad says Crows are made of saddle leather. Think he must

be right. Oh Jesus, look at your face.' He put his hand to her cheek. 'You've got one hell of a bruise coming there.'

She began to cry. Then he was holding her tight and talking in his quiet voice. 'Hey, hey, it's OK. We're OK. We got out. And I know this land. There's no need to worry, we'll be fine.'

Hope bit back something that might have been a hiccup or a sob, nodding.

With both hands, he smoothed her hair back from her face. 'We'll be OK. We just need to find some shelter, a little food, and wait it out. They'll realize by nightfall the day after tomorrow that we're really overdue, even if we had gone to the Mercantile. Then they'll raise the alarm and people will come and look for us. Dad knows the trail I took. Come on.' He helped her up, brushing both of them down where the dirt stuck in patches to their wet clothes. Looking around, he got his bearings. 'I think we head out this way and try and hit St Mary Lake by nightfall. We'll overnight there and then somewhere, not too far from the edge of the lake, is an old cabin my grandparents used to visit in the summers. We call it Crow Mountain, though that's not its official name. The cabin is probably a wreck by now, but it might be a roof over our heads until they head out to find us. And there's good water there. Plus, it's the most likely place for Dad to think to look for us. I hope.' He held out his hand.

They set off towards the trees, Buddy at their heels. As they headed into the shaded forest, the air cooled and Hope began to feel cold. She rubbed her arms to keep warm.

'As soon as we get to the lake I'll make a fire, but tonight's

162

going to be pretty cold. There's not much I can do about it.'

Hope trudged after him, bramble stems scratching her legs. The forest was alive with sounds and smells. The creatures among the trees weren't too interested in the humans in their midst. Every now and then, deer froze in the undergrowth, or crashed out in front of them. The first time, Hope shrieked, but after that she managed to bite her lip. Her face ached down the right side. And her shoulder. The trembling that had come on after they had escaped the crash was now only kept under vague control by keeping in motion and her hands jerked when she held them out in front of her. As she was watching them, Cal looked over his shoulder to see if she was keeping up.

He turned, taking her fingers in his warm grip. She could feel a tremor running through his arms.

'It's just shock, Hope. If we keep moving, and keep you as warm as we can, it'll wear off in a couple of hours. I'm shocked too. See? It's natural.'

She nodded. Keeping hold of one of her hands, he led her through the trees. The light began to fail after a little longer. Hope's heart sank at the idea of night. The darkness was closing in around the undergrowth in charcoal smudges. Perhaps her eyes weren't working properly. Her feet and ankles were sore from her wet socks and boots.

'It's not far now,' Cal said, just as Hope stumbled and fell to her knees, knocking her left one badly and scratching her right leg. Instantly his hands were under her arms, lifting her up and holding her tight. 'I promise. Just a little further.'

She nodded, too numb with cold and misery to say anything. It could have been five minutes or an hour later when the trees began to thin, and suddenly they were beside a huge lake ringed by mountains. The whitecaps sparkled in the evening sun. Cal led her down to the lake's edge and sat her down on a rock.

'Stay there. I just need to fetch a few things.'

Hope didn't respond. She was almost comatose with cold and shock. Cal skirted around the water's edge, looking here and there for things, returning, placing them in neat piles and then disappearing again. Buddy never left him. Usually Hope could see Cal's pale shirt in the undergrowth, or Buddy outlined against one of the massive pines, but when she couldn't see them, panic seeped through the shock and she started to shake again. After a little while, he had a good pile of dry wood, what looked like a pile of moss and fungus, and a lot of dried grass and twigs. He dropped to his knees.

On a small rock the size of a fist, he made a pile of the dry fungus and a little of the moss. Pulling a stone from one pocket, and his clasp knife from another, he struck sparks from the rock with the knife. Hope noticed his hands were still shaking.

'Damned flint was the hardest thing to find in this light,' he muttered.

The sparks flew over and over again, but the breeze was carrying them. Hope shook herself, got up and came to kneel by him, cupping her hands around the moss.

A few more tries and the moss caught. Hope cupped it

carefully, protecting it from the wind, as Cal added shred after shred of grass, waiting until they had a small pile burning before adding the thinnest twigs and brush. Even Buddy had drawn close and was staring, trying to understand why the flames were the centre of such attention. Cal chanced adding the first of the larger sticks. It took almost straight away and he breathed a sigh of relief.

'Once it's really going, it'll be fine.' The breeze was helping now, rather than killing it, and soon the fire was crackling merrily. Hope was still bone cold. She sat back on the rock. Cal came to sit next to her, shoving his boots off. 'Yours too,' he said. 'They need to come off. And the sweater. Better get as much dry as we can.'

Hope obeyed, handing over her things without a word. Although the cardigan had still been damp, exposing her chilled arms to the air made her shudder. On the other side of the fire were more rocks, sticking straight up from the bank, forming a shelter of some kind.

'Here. It's out of the wind.'

Hope picked her way carefully over the stony ground and sat, her back to the rock, knees pulled up.

'Buddy, come.' Cal ordered the dog to lie on Hope's cold feet like a furry blanket, and then hugged her against his side, a long arm around her. She looked at the fire and their wet things spread in front of it. The gun was in easy reach of his left hand.

'Hope we don't need that,' she said.

'So do I. Only two rounds in it,' he muttered.

Night had fallen around them. Periodically Cal got up to feed the fire. Once, he disappeared into the undergrowth and Hope heard him take a pee. They were both stiffening up, cold and wrenched from the accident. The fire cracked and, all around, the forest shifted and stirred. Then, from somewhere far off, there came an eerie howl, drifting across the water before fading out. Hope sat bolt upright. So did Buddy. From the other side of the lake, their side, the howl was answered. Then again, and again, until it seemed they were surrounded by the noise. Hope put her hands over her ears with a pained cry, desperate to block out the sound.

'Hope? Hope, listen to me.' Kneeling in front of her, Cal tried to lift her chin, putting his arms around her head when she shied away. 'They won't come near the fire. Really they won't. *Listen* to them, it's beautiful.'

Eventually she nodded, taking a deep breath, breathing in his reassuring warmth. 'OK,' she said, as another burst of echoing howls rang out around them. It was another hour or so before the wolves became quiet. Hope finally dozed against Cal, and after what seemed like a lifetime, dawn began to creep over the ridge at the eastern end of the lake, striping the shifting surface of the water with red and gold.

The fire was still flickering. Cal got up slowly and went around checking all their things. He handed Hope her socks and boots. The boots were damp, but nothing compared to the blistering wetness of the day before. She pulled on the socks for warmth and put the boots back by the fire for the last few minutes.

'There should be water around here and I don't want you to get dehydrated. I'll be back in a minute, OK?'

'Can't we drink the lake water?'

'I prefer it running. Back soon.' He went off along the lake's edge.

Hope sat, watching the sun rise. She pulled the diary from her pocket and checked it. It had survived the crash without any damage and didn't feel damp. To pass the time, she opened it and turned to where she'd left off.

Soon, Cal was back with Buddy, kicking out the fire. 'I found water.'

His arrival made her jump, startling her out of the diary. She got up. 'Cal?'

'What?'

'I . . . this diary . . .'

'What about it?'

'The stagecoach has just crashed into a gulch, which is filling with meltwater. The bridge gave way beneath it.'

She held it open on the page of the crash description. He read the passage and then returned it to her, silent, walking off back the way he'd come. Hope followed him to a small tributary and drank, feeling gritty and clammy, and splashed water on her face. Still in silence, they made their way back along the edge of the lake.

'What do you think?' she asked finally.

He stopped to look at the landscape, and avoided an answer. 'I think . . . that at the moment we need to get on the other side of these trees, higher up, so that I can see the ridgeline. Pops used to tell me to look for the crag above the cabin. It's distinctive. If we find that, we'll find the cabin. Are you up to a climb through the forest?'

'Do I have a choice?'

He didn't answer, but led her along an animal track of some kind, through the undergrowth that was sometimes as high as her shoulders. After an hour or so, they came to a small clearing, where a stream had formed a pond. It was full of bright green plants with spear-shaped leaves.

'Look,' he said, 'breakfast.'

He reached into the mud beneath the water. Sleeve pushed above his elbow, he rummaged around, pulling out a small piece of plant that looked like a cross between a potato and a cocktail sausage. He dumped it, muddy, on the bank while he fetched more. When he had a pile, he rinsed them off in the pond water, then held one out to Hope.

'What is it?'

'Duck potatoes.' He bit into another with a snap, crunching it like a radish.

Hope laughed. 'I'm good, thanks.'

'They're starchy and they'll give you energy.' He kept on holding it out. Taking it, Hope studied it for a while before taking a cautious bite from the edge. It tasted like raw potato, which wasn't great, but it wasn't bad either.

'Want more? There's plenty,' he said when they'd finished them.

Hope shook her head and scratched Buddy's ears. 'What's he going to eat?'

Cal rolled his eyes. 'Anything, given half the chance – I'm not worried about him.' He looked through the forest again. 'Push on?'

She steeled herself, and got to her feet.

Two hours later, they broke the cover of the forest and found themselves on a scrubby hillside full of shale and patches of grass and flowers. After a dramatic rise, a mountain ridge towered above them, crags and peaks forming a black and grey, horizontally striped range. Cal led them west, rifle slung over his shoulder, studying the range all the time. After a few minutes, he pointed. 'See, there? The square one with the black cap? That's where we're heading.'

Hope's heart sank. 'Got it,' she said as brightly as she could manage.

They set out.

'We'll find some water and take a rest. Then, if I'm right, we'll be able to cut in a littleways and hit something called the Loop Trail. That'll take us within a few hundred metres of the cabin. And the walking will be easier. Maybe we'll even run into some hikers or a ranger, though it's a little early in the season.'

'How far have we walked, do you think?'

'Seven miles perhaps?'

They found a stream not long after, and sat to drink and rest. The sun was directly overhead and the day was warm. Hope lay on her back, looking up into the blue. Cal lay down next to her. They were quiet. High above them, a huge bird wheeled, emitting a screeching cry, like a ping of sonar bouncing through the mountains.

'Bald eagle,' Cal said.

'This isn't much like Hackney, you know that, don't you?'

'Hackney? Thought you lived in London.'

'Hackney is in East London. It's busy and dirty and it has great coffee, cafés and people. It has a lot of people. And bicycles. And parks. There are squirrels. Oh, and there's Hackney Marshes. That's more birds though. Small birds. Like the size of my hand.' She held up her hand, palm up against the sky. 'Not ones like flying doors.'

He laughed and jumped up, muscles loose again after the walking. 'Let's go. Maybe we can be there by late afternoon.'

They found the Loop Trail without too much trouble, and the walking was easier. Occasionally Hope flagged, before she roused herself to pick her feet up. Butterflies and bees dipped and hovered over the wild flowers and once something Cal identified as a weasel scampered across their path. Buddy shot after it but was easily beaten and returned, tongue hanging. The sun was dropping and a cooler breeze picking up, bringing down the air from the glacier, by the time Cal turned off the trail.

'It's up here, I'm sure it is,' he said, almost to himself.

'Have you been here often?'

'Yeah, when I was young. Not after Pops and Gramma died. After that, it made my parents sad to be here. We talk about coming back a lot – we just never seem to get around to it.'

The mountainside wasn't that steep, but steep enough for Hope to lose her breath. They entered a thick stand of trees, the undergrowth scraping Hope's legs.

'Ouch!' she gasped.

Taking her hand, he pulled her on. 'C'mon, I promise,' he said, voice urgent. 'We're almost there.'

They emerged on the other side just as the sun hit the mountain.

There stood a ramshackle cabin. High above it was the crag. In front of it, like a vast green carpet, was a hillside meadow, strewn with wild flowers. Hope let go of Cal's hand and flung her arms around his neck, forgetting her shyness as a tiny sob of exhaustion and relief rose in her throat. He lifted her off her feet for a second, holding her so tightly it betrayed his own relief. They broke apart and headed up to the cabin with stronger steps.

Closer to, it became clear that time had taken its toll on the little house. One of the two front windows had fallen in and some boards were missing from the porch, on which stood something that had once been a cross between a small bathtub and a washing tub, split and cracked. Cal climbed the two steps and tried the door. The iron knob squealed, but it turned and he pushed open the door with a creak. Hope followed and peered around him.

'Wow.'

Cal pushed the door further, and walked in, dust motes swirling around them. 'Yeah. Wow.'

Inside, there were odd signs of habitation – hikers had

used the cabin at some stage. In one corner was a stove and next to it some kindling, a couple of logs and, even more precious, on top was a box of matches with one sticking out, ready to be struck. A badly torn blue windbreaker was draped over an old wooden chair and on the table was a small jar of instant coffee, half full.

By the door a row of hooks and pegs stood empty. The main hearth, designed to heat both rooms, was full of ashes that had been rained on many times down the chimney, the water running in inky lines down the stones to the floor-boards. There was a shallow stone sink, a counter and, through in the bedroom, a rough pine cupboard and a chest. A very old bed with a rope-strung base had been dismantled and propped against the far wall. Hope went to check the chest. It was locked. But inside the cupboard were some old clothes. There was a heavy canvas smock, large.

'That belonged to Pops, I think.'

Hope pulled out a plaid shirt, which was little more than rags clinging together with thread. There was also a thick knitted jersey.

'May I wear this, please?'

'You really don't need to ask,' he said, distracted by laying a fire in the stove.

Hope pulled it on, her hair springing tousled from the collar. The jersey came way past her hands and almost covered her shorts.

Cal was already putting a match to the kindling. 'Let's hope this thing isn't coked all to hell and gone.'

It seemed it wasn't, and was soon burning merrily, door open. Hope came to stand next to Cal, who was sitting on the wooden chair and watching the flames.

'You said this place was in your family?'

'I think we did own it, once, but we gave up everything this side of the river when the national park was created a hundred years ago. Pops certainly *felt* he owned it. It's all a bit lost in the mists of time, to be honest.' He reached out and picked up the jar of coffee, twisting off the top and sniffing it. 'That's not even that old.' He looked around, then got up and fetched a small pan from the side. 'I'll get some water from that stream out there and take a look around. You look for something to drink out of.'

He went out and Hope began to search for cups. There were some enamel ones in a cupboard. Right at the back were two very battered tin cups, one of them almost deformed. Hope pulled them all out and put them on the counter by the sink. As she took out one of the tin cups, it rattled. Shaking it out, a key fell on to the counter. She picked it up, and looked over her shoulder, through to the bedroom and the chest that stood there. She knelt and pushed the key into the lock. For a second it bit but refused to turn further. Then it gave.

Hope pushed up the lid and peeped inside. She almost cheered. Neatly folded inside was a large patchwork quilt, delicate and faded. Carefully she lifted it out. Beneath were blankets, all carefully interleaved with pieces of cedar wood and lavender bundles, so old all the fragrance was gone. At the bottom was a huge, finely tanned animal hide that looked alarmingly similar to Chuck's. It was dotted with small holes and she wondered if perhaps moths had eaten it over the years. There was a satchel covered in beadwork and worn with use. Taking up the coverlet, she went out to the porch and took the diary from her pocket, stripping off her still-damp boots and socks, huddling up and sitting cross-legged, finally feeling warmer.

She opened the diary and began to read. A few minutes later she got to her feet, shouting, 'Cal! Cal!'

He appeared, Buddy on his heels. 'What? Are you OK?'

'They're here!'

'Already? Someone must have found the rig wreck almost straightaway.'

'No, Emily and the man who found her in the river bed after the crash. She's just woken up and is describing where she is.' Hope stepped down from the porch to him, reading as she went. *We were on the side of a mountain, grassy tufts rolling away from the front of the cabin down to a thick stand of trees. Beyond was a vast and sparkling lake . . .* ' She looked up into his confused gaze, then turned, pointing down the mountain. 'It's this cabin. *This* lake. It just must be.' Glancing back at the cabin, she looked down at the diary. 'It's like they're still here.' A bird cried, far away over the water. They both looked towards the sound. When Hope spoke again, neither of them knew if a second or a minute had passed.

'No, it's as if we've just missed them.'

CHAPTER 11

'ABOVE EVERY OTHER FEATURE
WHICH ADORNS THE FEMALE
CHARACTER, DELICACY STANDS
FOREMOST WITHIN THE PROVINCE
OF GOOD TASTE.'

We made slow progress down from the mountain, and began to head east, along the edge of the lake. Just before nightfall, you decided to strike camp on the bank at the very eastern edge of the lake, from which we would trek down into the plains. The water was glowing gold as the sun disappeared over the mountain and our campfire took hold. I stretched my legs out and rubbed my chafed thighs together.

'You OK?'

'Yes,' I said instantly, blushing in the darkness.

You watched me, suspicious.

We ate bread and honey you conjured from the pack. You fetched water from a tributary and we drank and cleaned our teeth with salt and a washcloth. I hid my face as I spat in the dirt, making you smile. I had noticed before that you had very fine teeth and that you cleaned them religiously. When I'd asked you about it, you'd launched into a surprisingly vocal, for you, rant about how people should look after their teeth more and a man with no teeth might as well just 'give up and die' because he 'weren't gonna be no good to nobody. Fact'. The salt had taken a little time to become accustomed to, but already I found it better than the gritty, astringent tooth-powder Mama had always given me.

Soon, it was completely dark. I started at every crack of the fire. An owl hooted too close and I almost jumped out of my skin. You packed things away and put things out, hanging the food up a tree, away from us.

'Won't stop the bears or the big cats, but at least they might not eat us too,' you grinned.

I shuddered, hating that you even joked about it. I watched as you lay out what Mr Goldsmith had described as a 'bedroll', when I'd seen soldiers sleeping on them in Fort Shaw. You settled down, holding an edge of the blanket up.

'Come on then.'

I stared at you.

You sighed. 'Em, we established you ain't any use at sleep-ing in the wild. And I got only the one roll. In the Army they taught us to keep warm by sharing. This ain't no romantic proposal. I know you're saving yourself for Railroad.'

Mama would have taken a fit if she had seen what I did next. Cautiously I got up and walked over to where you lay. Arranging myself next to you in the narrow bedroll, I turned awkwardly on my side and you wrapped us up in a cocoon.

The ground was hard and I realized I'd be bruised in the morning. Beneath our heads was Tara's saddle blanket, with its horsey reek.

We settled ourselves. 'You slept like this with other soldiers?'

'Often enough.' You yawned. 'This is an improvement.'

I didn't know how to answer that, but a question had been niggling me for days, and in the forced intimacy of our situation I suddenly felt I could ask it. 'That man. Hart. He called you a deserter.'

'Better a deserter than a shitheel,' you said behind me.

I ignored that. 'What did he mean?'

For a while you said nothing; I wondered if you were asleep. Then you spoke. 'He means that at the Battle of the Wilderness, I caught a big piece of shell debris in the leg and I was left for dead with all the other carrion, 'cause being with a cavalry regiment in that terrain was a death sentence. Lost our position, and the road. A scavenger found me as she was cutting off my buttons. The battalion I had fought for was almost entirely wiped out. I ended up in a godforsaken filthy field hospital I knew would kill me, with a sawbones desperate to take my leg off.'

I shifted on to my back so I could see your face. You propped your head on your fist and rearranged the blanket over me before putting your hand in the dip of my waist over the thick wool. It was surprisingly heavy.

'Knew enough doctoring from the tribe to know that if I could just get away and get cleaned up, I could probably save my leg. So I splinted myself, stole a big old dose of morphine powder, got a horse from the line and got outta there.'

I watched the firelight flicker on your face. 'You deserted?'

'Temporarily. Was always coming back, just wanted to come back with two legs.'

'Then what happened?'

'Caught up with the Army when I could stand upright again, and they were going to shoot me as a deserter. So *then* I deserted.'

'How did you get away?'

'Couple of the guys broke me out just before dawn. Jeb Mullins and Al Donaghy. Said they didn't have no interest in putting a bullet in me after all those years. I got into the river and let it carry me a few miles downstream, then headed back to Montana.'

'So what Hart said was true?'

'Yep. I'm a deserter. A coward. What do you think of that, Emily Forsythe?'

'Papa says deserters should be shot. As an example to the other men.'

'Ain't interested in what your daddy says. I asked what you think.'

I studied your face, your eyes. 'They would have discharged you anyway, I imagine, with your leg as it is.'

'They wanted to make an example of me, as a coward.'

'But how does Hart know?'

'Army puts out notice of deserters in each state. And Hart, unfortunately, through long and sorry association is one of the few people to know me by all three of my names. My mother's family's. My father's. And the name of the tribe I was raised in.'

'Why is that?'

'His family have been out here as long as anyone. Fur trappers originally, with their coonskin hats and their three teeth apiece.' The scorn in your voice was clear.

I sensed there was more to the story. 'And?'

'And when Momma was in Fort Shaw with me at her breast, Hart took a shine to her. Could see she was having trouble keeping herself together and food in her mouth.' You were warming to your subject. 'So the days pass and he's not taking no for an answer 'cause he thinks he owns the place, and anyway she makes a scene. He knocks me outta her arms and makes a real bad mess of her. Red Feather is in camp. Fierce-looking, big scar right the way down his cheek, off his chin and clear on to his chest from a spear strike. Still, had a strange sense of fair play, particularly where women were concerned and he never liked to see them getting beat on, whatever the colour of their skin. So while the rest of the camp, whites and Indians both, looks on, he steps in. Gives Hart the beating of his life. And that was that. Red Feather had just lost his wife through some fever, and he takes me and Momma home.'

I frowned. 'But . . . what about your mother? Did she want to go with him?'

You shrugged. 'She never said. But she liked being part of the village and she was always laughing, never seemed

179

unhappy. Unlike Hart. He ain't never got over being bested by an Indian. Felt Momma was his woman. Made her life hard when we came into camp as little ones.'

I was silent, listening.

'Anyways, forget that. The Army only knew my father's name, but word got back to Fort Shaw. Hart put two and two together, and now he holds it over me whenever he thinks he can score a point.'

'But he wouldn't tell anyone, would he? He wouldn't get you into trouble?'

With a groan you let your head flop onto the blanket. 'He already tried.'

You were easily close enough to have kissed me. Looking back, I wish you had, because I think that would have saved us a great deal of trouble, in the long run. But you didn't.

'When I came back to Fort Shaw, he sees me there, thinks on making me look like a trouble-causer so I won't get work. Pays a man to pick a fight with me in the street.'

'What happened?'

You shrugged. 'Killed him.'

'But why?'

'To stop him running his fool mouth as much as anything.'

I gasped.

Your eyes met mine. 'Still got too much of the war in me, huh? Then after that, had to leave. And now I gotta take every job Hart gives me or it'll just be more of the same and a price on my head before long.'

'Did . . . did you like the Army?'

'Didn't mind it, before the war. I was mainly with the horses, being as how I have the knack and all. And I'm proud of fighting to free the coloureds. Slavery ain't right. People ain't property.'

We looked at each other for a long moment, words unspoken in the narrow space between us.

'But still, the Army don't seem that fair to me now.'

'Why not?'

You picked at a slub on the coarse blanket. 'Because it puts men together in ways that mean they become fastest friends, makes them rely on each other. Then it sends them to war and blows that all to hell and gone.' The distant look had come into your eyes again.

'Were the things you saw so very bad?'

'Yes. Seen a lot killed. Done a lot of killing. Don't seem to be able to get away from it. Got the knack for that too.' Lifting your hand, slowly and carefully, as if trying not to spook me, you drew your finger down the side of my face. 'You scared of me again now?'

The wolves and coyotes began to howl. I shivered and turned away from you, folding my hands beneath my cheek and watching the flames.

Your voice from behind me was quiet, resigned. 'Pay them no mind. They ain't coming anywhere near this fire.'

I was up and had just finished washing in the lake when you returned the following morning. I'd woken alone in the bedroll, the blankets drawn around me, face damp with dew.

The fire had been built up and water was just coming to the boil in a can; you hadn't been gone long. By the cups was a pile of green shoots. I picked one up and smelt it. Mint.

After making the tea I washed in the cold lake water, looking at the speckled greens, reds and greys of the stones beneath the astonishingly clear surface. When you returned with Tara a few minutes later, the tips of your hair were wet and your shirt was sticking to you a little. I realized you'd gone elsewhere to perform your morning rituals, giving us both privacy. You took the mug I held out and we sat together on the blankets, awkward. You were looking down, at both your hands holding the tin mug, strange eyes shaded. Your question still hung in the air. Was I scared of you? Truly? You glanced at me sideways and I saw, all at once, the child growing up at the edges of two societies, the boy who went to war, and the man trying to make a life at the margins of civilization.

I took a breath. 'No,' I said. 'The answer is no. I'm not scared of you. Not any more.'

You sprang into action so suddenly I was surprised. 'So,' you handed me the last of the loaf and pulled from the pack what looked like a small square of ancient leather for yourself, 'the weather looks set fair and I reckon we can reach Indian territory by this afternoon, but we'll have to push it.' You chewed on the leather and sipped at the mint tea, as if our conversation of the previous night had not happened.

'What's that, please?'

You looked at me. 'What?'

'That.' I pointed to what you were chewing.

'Pemmican. It's buffalo meat. Trail food for the Indians. I make it sometimes, if I get some meat. But I ain't killing a whole buffalo just for me, so usually I trade something for it. And mine isn't great, to be honest. You need the kidney fat to make it real good.' You held it out. 'Try it. It's got dried huckleberries.'

Taking it gingerly, I bit off a tiny piece. I had to almost tear it with my teeth. It was all very unladylike. I tasted salt and fat and the slight sweetness of the berries.

You cocked an eyebrow, head on one side. 'Whatcha think?'

I touched my lips as I chewed industriously. 'Not as bad as I thought. Very . . . savoury.'

'Yeah, saved my sorry ass on the scout more than once. I'll get some laid by for the winter, just in case.'

I'm not sure that at that moment I even registered your reference to the future or anything else you were saying. Something strange had happened: for the first time in my life I lived only in the moment I occupied. I was no longer in a perpetual state of preparation for a day that would not come. I did not need to change or control my person in order to please anyone but myself. As you spread out the map and examined it, pale eyes intent, talking half to me and half to yourself, I understood, with a physical jolt, that I didn't have to change myself to please you either.

I realized you'd stopped talking and that I hadn't heard a word you'd said. 'Em? I didn't mean it about the ravine. Ain't dangerous. Melt's over.'

I stared at you, trying to form something coherent.

'Em?'

'It's OK,' I said. 'I was just thinking.'

You stared back at me for a long moment. 'It's OK? Did I just hear English say *o-kay*? Wait a second, I think I got water in my ears or something.' Making a show of clearing your head, you looked at me again, full of mischief.

I blushed.

Still laughing, you bumped your shoulder into mine. 'Look. We're here.' You pointed to a spot on the map.

I saw how very far away Helena and Fort Shaw were. You tapped the map with a knuckle, northwest. 'This is where we're headed. Railroad thinks he wants to go over the top, through Blackfoot country and just touching the Flatheads and the Kootenai.'

'And what do you think?'

You shrugged. 'I think he doesn't know shit about mountains or Indians. But I ain't paid to offer my opinion on that, so I'll just scope the land.'

'But it'll take us days to get there at this pace.'

'I told you, we'll get another horse.'

'From whom?'

You pulled the map into your lap. 'Something will turn up. Always does in Indian territory.'

Boosting me into Tara's saddle when we'd broken camp, you must have seen me wince. After five days of riding, one with no stirrups and all my weight in the saddle, I was more than uncomfortable. Reaching up, you caught me around the waist, and pulled me down. It had taken me a while to become used to such casual physicality and I stood, confused, as you unfastened one of the blankets from behind the saddle, folded it and placed it over the seat. You adjusted the stirrups on both sides.

'Why didn't you say something?' Your voice, accusing. 'Jesus, Emily. You gotta tell me. Ain't no magician on a stage, can't see inside your head.' You flicked my temple and I batted away your hand. 'Maybe you should decide which is more delicate, your ass or your pride.' Boosting yourself into the saddle you tucked the blanket down in front of you. Then you lifted me up. 'Sit square on that. Yep. Feet in the stirrups. Should-a done this yesterday. Wasn't thinking, like a fool. If you get uncomfortable, stand up and stretch yourself out.'

'What about you?'

'Em, I been in the saddle since I could walk, my backside is tougher than pemmican.'

Unable to help myself, I had to stifle a laugh. It was what my mother said was a giggle and only practised amongst scullery maids.

You gathered up the reins in one hand, the other around me. 'And that is definitely the sweetest sound I've heard in a while.'

We rode for hours, leaving our mountain territory behind and skirting the edge of the plains to the east. You were right, the stirrups and the blanket made things much easier. It also meant my feet didn't go numb from hanging there in the air. Sometimes you stole the right stirrup from me to stretch your leg.

'Does it hurt?' I asked, as you pushed the stirrup back to me.

'It's a real pain in the behind.'

'Oh, I . . .' It hurt *there*?

You put your arm about me, laughing. 'No, Emily, no hurt. Only in snow season. Mostly it's just a little numb and useless, but I'd rather have it than not. Anyway, don't need talking about. Can't be helped or changed. It's just what it is.'

We were quiet for a while.

'Tell me about you,' you said, after we'd stopped to let Tara drink at a stream and were on our way again, splashing through the water and gaining the opposite bank.

'Me?'

'Yes, you.'

I faltered. 'I've told you everything already, I think.'

'Yeah, everything about what you *must* do, and *should* do, but what did you *like* to do? Before we met.'

I thought about it. No one had ever asked me before. 'Reading. Writing letters. Language lessons. I had a lot of tutors. I had a little dog called Tippet, a spaniel.'

You brushed my hair to one side, out of your face. 'You loved her?'

'I loved her so very much. But Mama thought she was a distraction and gave her away.'

You were silent.

'And I read a lot of poetry. Milton and Dryden and Shakespeare.'

That seemed hollow too, now. I leant back against you, my shoulders against your chest; you liked it when I did that, I thought. I held my hands out over Tara's neck in position one for the keys. 'And I play the piano. Mozart, Beethoven, all sorts.'

You transferred the reins to the other hand and put your arm back around me. 'So when the railroad scouting is done, I can put you in a saloon on the piano?'

This time I giggled out loud. 'Maybe. Because I don't think I'm ever going to be able to make an honest living in a bakery.'

You laughed and dropped your face into the exposed side of my neck, running the tip of your nose up the tendon there, breathing in beneath my ear. Your hand was only just resting on my waist but suddenly it was as if there was nothing but you and where our bodies touched. I couldn't breathe, feeling as if I were back in the corset. I stiffened. Your hold on me loosened instantly and you sat up. Tara walked on, and order was restored to our little world.

Late that afternoon, we were crossing a plain. I did not much care for it after the mountain, although it had a thrown-open quality I had become used to from the train. The plains were also strangely silent after the birdsong and fauna of the cabin. There was a dry ridge to our west, the land in front of us rolled in shallow waves, a patchy green and tan. You had told me, perhaps an hour before, that we were starting to enter Blackfoot country. I could feel something was wrong from the tension in you. After our jokes, we had been quiet, our bodies slackening into Tara's rhythm. Yet you kept looking up at flocks of birds wheeling, far away.

'What is it?'

'This plain should be covered with buffalo at the moment. And pronghorns . . . the antelope. They should be here too. And we should have seen people by now. Indians.'

'I don't understand.'

You chewed the inside of your lip.

We continued on.

'Can you smell that?'

'Smell what, please?'

You didn't respond immediately, pulling Tara to a halt and surveying the landscape. 'I do not like this. Not one bit.' You pointed. 'See that butte? I want to get up there and take a looksee.' You put my hands on the saddlehorn. 'Hang on. Tight.'

Tara surged into a sure-footed gallop. We covered the ground at breakneck speed, the plain flashing beneath us. She raced with economic grace towards the crags ahead, neck stretched, fluid, joyous. As the ground began to rise, we slowed and you reined to a halt. 'Em, are you up to some walking?'

I looked down at the ground. 'I think so.'

You jumped down and brought me down to stand by you. Throwing the reins over Tara's head, you pointed to the nearest bluff. 'Even with only three good legs, we'll be faster on foot now.'

We began to climb, leaving Tara by a rock shelf. Soon I was perspiring a little. That is to say, sweating, Mama. You helped me on to ledges my legs were too short for, but my pride soon got the best of me and I scrambled up unaided. After making it on to a larger step I turned and held out my hands without thinking. You thought about it for a moment, then your hands caught my forearms, we both pulled and you came up next to me.

Hopping up on to the plateau, you walked to the far edge, looking out on three compass points of the plain – west, north and east. You froze. I came up behind you, the plains wind blowing strands of hair from my face and cooling the sweat on my forehead and upper lip. Far below us, and as far as the eye could see, lay many dozens of buffalo, their mammoth bodies pitched into the dust. Above wheeled flocks of scavengers on the wing.

I stared, feeling nauseated and overwhelmed. 'Did they become sick?'

'Worst kind of sickness. Mankind sickness.'

I looked more carefully at the dead bodies. 'But . . . I . . . they've skinned them. That's it?'

'That's it.' Your voice was bitter.

'There's so many.' My voice was leaden and stupid. Mama and Papa would have disapproved of it.

'Looks like at least a hundred head to me. Lotta calves too.'

A sudden voice startled me and I spun. There, in front of me, was an enormous Indian. His chest was bare apart from a rifle strap, the barrel sticking up over his shoulder. He wore only white leggings with beads in a stripe on the outside, a deerskin loincloth and long, soft boots. On either side of his face was a red streak and through his eyebrows and over his hooded eyelids was smeared a canary yellow paste. His nose was high and fine and his forehead broad. His hair, which was as black as mine and almost as long, was braided into two pigtails.

I moved to stand behind you.

'What did he say?' I whispered. For surely, in my ignorance, all Indian languages were the same.

'He said, all white men are bastards.'

I stood back, eyes wide, as the two of you embraced, laughing. You held each other's arms and looked each other up and down. You were taller but you lacked the Indian's muscular bulk. The two of you spoke in a language I could not comprehend even the sound of, it was so alien: like dice being rattled in a shaker and the sanding of wood at the same time. Stepping back, you took my hand and stooped to my ear, whispering.

'After he speaks to you, just say *ka-hay*. Nothing else.'

You spoke to the Indian again. He looked at me with interest for so long it would have been considered beyond rude and into insolent in any polite drawing room. From my dirty bare feet to the top of my unruly head.

He nodded, and spoke.

'*Ka-hay,*' I replied.

His eyes flicked to you. You shrugged and spoke, putting your hand on my shoulder. I recognized only one word: *English*.

The Indian tried it out. 'English.'

You pulled me into your side. 'Em. This is my brother, Little Elk. Momma always spoke to me in our own language, and I was just learning to talk when he was born, so I always called him Lucky.'

I looked up at him. 'Your brother?'

'Momma and Red Feather's son.'

The Indian, Lucky, was still regarding me with interest. I realized I too was staring.

You spoke again, gesturing out to the plains. 'Lucky only got here this morning. Looks as though this was done yesterday. Maybe the day before. Big operation too. Many hands. The corpses, they're fresh. Only a couple of days old at most. And they're not that spread out. That means surprise. Lot of repeating rifles, and a lot of knives to get the hides off quick smart. See the wagon trails? This many white men way up here, that's new. Gonna cause all kinds of ructions.'

The anger in the Indian's controlled, measured voice was clear, although I did not know what he was saying.

'Rose?' you said suddenly.

Lucky nodded, once.

'Rose?' I asked.

'My sister. Half-sister. I haven't seen her in almost a year.' Your face was animated. I looked up at you as you spoke to your brother. I could see no resemblance between the two of you. I wondered what your sister would look like.

I did not have to wait long to find out. Lucky spotted her first, a figure on a grey horse, trotting through the buffalo massacre. We climbed down from the crag. He and I exchanged a glance when you landed awkwardly on a ledge and had to recover yourself as your knee gave way, before turning to help me down. The Indian's face was expression-less, but we had communicated all the same. By the time we reached the bottom of the crag and collected Tara where she waited with Lucky's horse, the rider was only a minute away.

If I had an idea of an Indian woman before Rose, it was of the squaws coming and going from Fort Shaw on their ponies, sometimes with a baby in a cradleboard. Rose was not that woman. She sat on her horse with the same ease you did, long legs dangling free from the stirrups, which were crossed over the pommel. She had a high, fine nose and forehead. Her hair was collar-length, worn loose with a centre parting, exaggerating her cheekbones and strong jaw. Like you, she had a wide, expressive mouth. She was dressed in deerskin leggings and a tunic decorated with beads. Over her shoulder was a rifle. She looked me up and down before dismounting. She was shorter than her brothers, but not by much. I have read since that the people of your tribe are all tall, and most of the men over six feet.

You embraced and she grinned, the same wolfish, joyous grin as you. The same white teeth. I realized she wasn't so very much older than me, but she was strong and robust-looking, with corded red-brown forearms. You tousled her hair, the tone of your voice teasing, and she punched you smartly in the chest. You told me later that hair is sacred to the people of your tribe and that touching the hair of another was intimate.

We went through the same process of introduction. She was as reserved as her brother, but not unfriendly, though she questioned you extensively, looking at me as she did so. She even walked right around me, looking me up and down. Though you had laughed every now and again, you didn't tell me what her questions were. Finally the three of you discussed the buffalo for a long time, your gestures becoming ever more exaggerated. Lucky didn't raise his voice – he never did – but you and Rose were almost shouting at each other at one point. Rose kept holding up the index finger on one hand, then on the other. I stood with Tara, stroking her nose and feeling superfluous.

The shouting died down. Rose fiddled with the strap on her rifle and looked annoyed. The tone of the conversation changed. Suddenly I was aware you were all talking about me. I put my head down. With a final comment flung over your shoulder, you walked over and took my hand, pulling me towards the saddle. A second later, you were mounted. You spun me, catching me beneath the arms from behind and lifting me right up. I am not, quite, that gossamer, but you were right about your toughness and I had become accustomed to you hauling me on and off Tara. I drew my leg over the horn and dropped down into the saddle with a jolt. You gathered the reins and looked at the others, waiting. They mounted up.

We headed west, trotting towards the lowering sun.

'What's happening, please?'

'They're coming with us. We can get the scout done in a third of the time.'

'Where are we going now?'

'Their camp.'

'Oh.' A thousand questions burnt on the tip of my tongue.

'What is it?' You sounded amused.

'What was Rose saying?'

You were suddenly serious. 'One for one. The death of one buffalo, like that, all that waste, will cost the life of one Indian, come winter.'

'Is that true?'

'Maybe. It's worked for the government against the Navajo for the last few years. And that was only sheep.'

I plucked up some courage. 'But what was she saying about me?'

'Wanted to know how much you'd cost me.'

Turning to see your face, I frowned at the smile in your voice. 'I hope you told her the truth.'

''Course. Told her you ain't cost me a penny, only my peace of mind, and my own bed.'

I huffed and settled back against you, sitting into Tara's easy gait and playing with the strap of the rein dangling from your hand where it rested on the saddlehorn.

'How old is she?' I asked, risking a shy glance across at her.

'Couldn't say. But she's youngest of us still living. Momma doted on her, but Red Feather wasn't much interested in girl-children. Hence her being called Rose by Momma. Said she always wanted a little girl called Rose.'

At that moment Tara, usually so sure-footed, tripped, and pecked the ground with her nose. You hauled on the reins and held on to me as she skittered to the side to regain her feet, almost colliding with the glistening, fly-blown carcass of a buffalo, raising a buzzing cloud. We flinched in unison and you steered Tara away quickly. I tugged the shirt cuff over my hand and held it over my nose and mouth until we were clear of the swarm.

Waiting until we were closer to the others, I dropped my hand. 'There are more?'

The angry tension had returned to your body. 'One. He Who Walks. He was the cripple of the family, before me. Younger than Rose. Twisted pelvis so could never sit a horse. He died soon after I went East. Some problem in his guts.'

'I'm sorry. Did you miss them, when you left?' I looked over my shoulder at you, seeing you bite the inside of your cheek.

'Always.'

'Then why enlist? Why not just come back?'

'I truly do not know the answer to that. Felt like maybe I didn't fit here either, being as how they'd let me go for a few horses. Thought maybe I should try to make a life with my own people. But turns out I ain't a great fan of most of them.'

'I'm sorry,' I said again.

You roped my hair around my neck like a collar and nudged my head with your chin. 'Some of you ain't so bad.'

I pushed your hand away, full of bees in my middle. We were still skirting the edge of the massacre. Thankfully we were upwind, but I still kept my face turned away from the horror of the huge bodies sprawled on the grassy plain. We were close enough to see the flies buzzing and the smell of the flesh beginning to spoil gusted towards us as we reached the other side.

I swallowed, revolted. 'This is all such a horrible waste.'

You made a sound of disgust. 'Welcome to the white man. And the railroad is only making it worse. Divides the herds, stops them moving across the plains. The more railroads, the more divided, the more people and the more hunters. Those trains will end their way of life. Probably even wipe them out. And the Plains Indian along with them.'

'So why are you helping them? The railroad people.'

'I'm not helping. I'm telling them, honestly, where they can't hope to build. I may be poor but I ain't a liar.'

'But you're taking their money. Isn't that hypocritical?'

'Em, in case you hadn't noticed, I'm a cripple. The life I got now is pretty much the only one I'm fit for out here. I could trap for fur, but I ain't a fan of killing anything I ain't gonna eat. I can break one, maybe two horses at a time. And I'm picky about it. The horses and the buyers. It ain't a gold claim.' Your voice was patient and laced with your pioneer practicality. 'And there's you to think about.'

'Me?' I looked up over my shoulder at you.

'You need things. Clothes. Shoes. Pretty hair soap. More stuff than you got now, anyways. And taking money from Railroad to buy it for you seems fair enough.'

Anthony Howard Stanton had become so distant to me that your connection to him, even through such sketchy employment, seemed more real than mine had only a short time ago. The marriage was now utterly doomed, of course, but strangely it did not tear my heart. The thought of Mama and Papa being displeased with me made me unhappy, but here on the plain, even that seemed very far away.

Ahead of us, out of the haze, appeared what looked like a camp. There were three more horses and, on the ground, a pile of packs and blankets. A woman sporting the same long braids as Lucky, but in a white deerskin dress over her leggings, was tending a fire, cooking bread on flat stones surrounding it.

'Who's that?'

'That's Lucky's new wife . . . Clear Water.'

'You sound surprised.'

You laughed. 'I am. He did nothing but tease her when we were kids.'

I glanced across at the forbidding brave, his painted face unreadable. 'Teasing? He doesn't seem the sort.'

'Ah, that's 'cause he's fixing to be a chief one day. He's a real joker when you get to know him.'

I said nothing.

You leant to the side to see my face. 'You don't believe me?'

'Yes, of course. If you say so. It's just that he doesn't . . . look very humorous.'

'Nor do you.'

I twisted, indignant. You were laughing and pulling Tara to a halt, getting down and bringing me to stand next to you. Clear Water came up and smiled, happy to see you. She was tall and handsome but seemed shy – far less assertive than Rose – as you spoke. Her eyes were wide as she looked at me. You didn't touch her, and after a brief greeting and introduction to me, you went to look at Lucky's horses with Rose, running your hands over their legs, looking in their mouths. You were particularly interested in a leggy red horse with a fine face and nervy movements, and seemed to have forgotten I was even there.

I waited awkwardly. Clear Water hadn't gone back to her fire but was watching me, seeming equally ill at ease. After a minute, she beckoned and went to the fire, where she crouched, flipping the hot bread with deft hands. I knelt next to her and watched, nodding in what I thought was the right place.

You came over. 'We'll spend the night here and break camp in the morning. You and I'll head into Flathead territory, Lucky and Rose can cover the Kootenais. They speak the language a little.'

'You don't?'

'Kootenai? Not at all. It's not like ours. Not like any other Indian language.'

The only shelter provided near the camp was a stand of

rocks, climbing to a small butte. That evening, we all sat around the fire. Me and you, Lucky and Clear Water and then Rose, a small distance apart. Rose liked to sit alone. You all talked. From the tone, I could tell you were sharing news, telling stories. At that moment you were one of them, and the Nate I had come to know on the mountain was a stranger, his face shadowed by the firelight and alien words on his lips. It unsettled me; a moment later, mid-story and without looking at me, you reached over and smoothed a lock of hair behind my ear.

After sharing our tin plate of nondescript brown gravy with some corn in it, and the delicious baked bread, we repaired to bed. Returning from the stream, our bedroll suddenly seemed a sanctuary and I nestled down like an animal inside a den, in the waxed cotton smock of yours I wore on cool evenings. A few minutes later, you appeared out of the dark, unfastening your gun belt and putting it on the ground near our blanket pillow. Under the blankets, you slung an arm around me.

'You OK?'

'Yes. Thank you.'

You squeezed me a little. 'Yes but what?'

'But you all talk a lot.'

'We're family is all. And we ain't seen each other in a while. Don't you talk to your family?'

'Mama says frivolous talk is unattractive. And I speak several languages, but now I don't speak the right one. I don't like not understanding things.'

'Plenty in the world I don't understand. Sometimes you just gotta accept things as they are. Not let it make you unhappy.' You tucked the blanket around me more tightly and settled down to sleep.

The fire sparked, sending tiny fireflies of orange up into the night. On the edge of it I could see Rose. She looked asleep already, hair over her face and one hand flung on to the grass. On the other side, opposite us, Lucky and Clear Water were bundled in their blankets. From where I lay, I could see them clearly. They were talking in whispers. Then they kissed, mouths open. I saw Lucky's hand slip inside her dress, tugging it open. I gasped and recoiled.

'Em?' Your voice was drowsy and uncertain.

I turned over within the confines of our bedding, hiding my face in my hands against your chest. 'Nate—'

The sleep disappeared from your voice and you shifted, ready to get up. 'What?'

'They . . . I—'

You looked over me, arm over my shoulder, before letting yourself drop back on to Tara's blanket with a grunt. 'Jesus, Emily, they're just fooling around.'

I was shocked. Shocked that they would do it, and that you wouldn't care. Had you behaved that way? I couldn't catch my breath, rigid beneath the blankets.

You shifted on to your back and held me against your chest. 'Ain't worth fussing over. Just try to sleep.'

The fire cracked again behind me and I flinched as if I'd been shot. Your touch was making me feel strange. *Everything* was making me feel strange. I couldn't bear it. Struggling up, I pulled the top blanket away and, wrapping it around my shoulders, I stamped away towards the rocky butte. The night was dark, the moon just a slip, and I didn't know where I was heading so blindly until I walked straight into a rock, bruising my knee. Feeling my way, I huddled down against an upright, tucking my feet beneath me and putting my head against the stone. Many yards away, the fire still burnt. I closed my eyes, not wanting to see anything. Not them. And not you.

The morning came, and I woke with the dawn. Stretching my cramped limbs, I looked up at the watery sun, then at the camp. The fire smoked and Clear Water crouched beside it. Rose was gone, with her horse. You were with Tara and the other horses and Lucky was swinging his arms in the cold morning light. I was shy, and conscious that I had made a fool of myself. I chewed my lip, a habit Mama had always castigated me for. Finally I got down from the rocks and walked to where you stood, talking to the horses. As I approached, Lucky called over to you and gestured towards me with his head. You replied, not looking at him, picking up the hoof of the red horse.

I gave Tara a pat. You'd already saddled her, so I went through the motions of checking her cinch. Finally the words burst from me. 'I couldn't bear it!'

'Bear what now?' You dropped the red horse's rear hoof and straightened.

'That. Last night.'

You watched me for what seemed like an age. 'That's just nature.'

Pushing the drifting strands of hair from my face, I huffed. 'Not *my* nature.'

'No,' you said placidly, fashioning a bridle and reins from one long piece of thin rope around your elbow with practised ease. 'Not *your* nature.'

The others ate the bread, toasted, for breakfast. I stood stubbornly with Tara, stroking her white face.

As we mounted up, you handed me the water canteen. 'Gotta drink if you won't eat.'

I drank and handed it back, refusing to look at you. With a swift movement, you were suddenly mounted on the red horse without a saddle, for Lucky did not have a spare. You gathered the reins. 'C'mon, English. Mount up. We got work to do.' You wheeled your horse around, leaving me standing next to Tara. I climbed into the saddle as quickly as I could.

We rode out. Lucky streaked away to what I thought was northwest. You and I went west, steadily.

'Where are we going?' I said sullenly.

'To a place on the railroad map. Check it out. Look at the rocks and see if they can be blasted. Or not. See about water. Elevations. Landscape.'

'Oh.' Something else I didn't understand. I sighed and looked down at my hands on the saddlehorn. Mama would be aghast at how tanned I was becoming. You leant over and caught Tara's reins and hauled on yours, pulling us to a halt.

'Em? What's the matter?'

I said nothing.

You sighed audibly. 'Remember what I said, about accepting things?'

I nodded, but still didn't look at you, so you reached across and tucked the persistent stray strand of hair behind my ear, pulling on the lock. A tiny mischief. 'The people I grew up with ain't like you.'

'So I see,' I said stiffly.

'Don't make them wrong, just makes them different.'

I turned my head away.

'They ain't savages, neither. And you're dreadful pretty when you sulk, but I don't hold with sulkers.'

I bit my bottom lip. You were right, sulking wasn't nice. 'But they . . . that wasn't proper,' I said, voice small.

You responded immediately. 'I do get that you wouldn't understand. I do. But they weren't doing nothing wrong. You think soldiers are any different with the women they engage with on the march?'

'Engage . . . ? W-wait, have *you* done that?' I asked, shocked and petty.

You took a deep breath. 'Look, I'd rather Lucky'd waited until we were asleep, but they're newly married. What do you expect? He's having a hard time working out why you'd rather sleep up on the butte – if you slept at all – keeps asking me if I've forgotten how to please a woman now I'm living like a white man.'

You ducked and caught my eye, teasing. I turned my head so you couldn't see my face.

'Oh . . . come on, it ain't like he was hurting her, is it? She—' There was silence as the penny dropped. 'Emily? What do you *think* they were doing?'

I wanted the ground to swallow me, fiddling with Tara's reins. She shifted, picking up on my unease.

Your hand came beneath my chin, lifting my face in a way that brooked no argument. 'Look at you, all fine and dandy, with your Mozart and your Milton and your pretty manners. You don't know nothing about nothing, do you? And your momma, selling you into wedlock on a foreign continent without even . . . Shameful is what it is.' You broke off, disgusted, and let me go.

Shameful. You thought my ignorance was something to be ashamed of.

Far off, there was a gathering noise: Rose, galloping across the plain. She was magnificent. Tall in the saddle, hair flying. Powerful, strong, capable. Everything I wasn't. She crashed to a halt between us, voice clattering.

You and she talked, your red horse increasingly skittish. Sitting down hard, bareback, you settled him, keeping up a constant conversation with Rose. Suddenly she wheeled away and was gone, leaning into her mare's neck, barely moving in the saddle.

I cleared my throat. 'Is she always so dramatic?'

You glanced at me, calculating, before allowing our previous subject to drop. 'Pretty much.'

'What did she say?'

'That the buffalo hunters are in Blackfoot territory.'

I took a breath, and my courage. 'What are we going to do?'

You shrugged angrily. 'Nothing we can do. Rose is up for rallying the Blackfoot, but that's dangerous, pitting the Indian against the white man.'

'Will they listen to her?'

'Well, traditionally our tribe and the Blackfoot ain't the greatest of friends. But they do like nothing better than a good scrap and it don't take much to rile them. And Rose and Lucky have roamed around this territory all their grown lives, got friends everywhere, on account-a Rose being Rose.' She was a speck in the distance now.

'What does that mean, please?'

'You noticed Rose's clothes?'

'Yes.'

'Who do you think she looks more like, Lucky or Clear Water?'

I thought about it. 'Lucky. She dresses like a man.'

You nodded. 'Fights like a man too. Tough as hell. They say she's two spirits in one body, a brave and a woman. It's a sacred thing out here. Rose gotta lot of respect around these parts.'

'Rose fights? With men?'

You grinned. 'When we were kids she fought with the boys like a Kilkenny cat. Rode out in her first skirmish party, the year Momma died. All the old vets were laughing at her, noisy little thing that she was. Weren't laughing so hard when she came back with a scalp on her saddle.' You watched her disappear, suddenly serious. 'But these days, Rose goes to war. Which is what I'm worried about.'

'Aren't we going with her?'

'Nope. Ain't getting involved. I got enough on my plate as it is. Got a home to look to now. You and Tara and this fella here to take care of. Ain't putting my ass out on the line again because Rose is itching for a scrap, 'cause trust me, that ain't no irregular occurrence.'

'But if the killing goes on, won't the Blackfoot die in the winter without the buffalo?'

Glancing over at me, you raised an eyebrow. 'You sound like you want to go with her.'

I thought about it. I never wanted to see another buffalo massacre. And I was worried for Rose. Papa said that women had no place on the battlefield. Yet he had always told me I should try to do the right thing and behave with integrity.

'We should try and help,' I said, into the silence of the plain.

'Why, Emily? Why would you want to go parley with Indians over the fate of some dumb animals?'

It took me a moment to speak, wanting to answer carefully. 'Because this is wrong. It's needless killing, and it doesn't matter if it's animals or men. And in this case it's both. Papa would think we should attempt to help.' I lifted my chin and tried to sound certain.

'It won't be safe.'

I shrugged, trying to seem nonchalant. 'Safe seems like a long time ago.'

You looked into the distance, eyes narrowed. 'OK, English, if this is what you want.' The red horse sprang forward under your heels and Tara raced to catch up. We tore over the rolling plain.

When we finally caught up with Rose, she was with Lucky and Clear Water, who had broken the camp but not made it far. Clear Water was sitting quietly on her roan pony, but Rose and Lucky were talking. You reined to a halt next to them and added your voice to the mix.

I was still catching my breath when your discussion finished.

'Well, it's settled then, we're going to the Blackfoot.'

'How far is it?'

'I don't know. We'll have to find the band nearest the hunters. When I was up here last year there was one about two hours' ride from here. Should be close enough. Just gotta hope all their braves are in camp.'

We set out, arriving after some hours at the camp over a bluff giving on to a large, spread-out settlement of buffalo-hide tents of varying size. Small campfires burnt, some with pots hung over them, some just smoking. Women walked around, in long sleeveless dresses, carrying large wooden bowls on their hips or talking; children played at their feet. There were dogs everywhere, many of them at the heels of children. As we rode in, the camp stirred and young men on horses came toward us. Most of them were wearing simple deerskin shirts and their hair was different from Lucky's, worn in varying styles. They were not quite as tall either, and very slender. Most of them looked about my age and they crowded together, blocking our way.

'Quit gawking, Emily,' you said out of the corner of your mouth. 'Ain't mannerly.'

I dropped my eyes. A thin, older man approached on foot. You all began to dismount straight away and I slid down from Tara, landing awkwardly on feet that had lost their circulation. It was clear the chief knew you from the way you all spoke together. Almost instantly he called you away into one of the lodges, closing the door flap behind you.

I stood with Clear Water, loosening the cinches on all the horses between us. Other women came up. They were particularly interested in my pale skin and in my eyes, and talked amongst each other as they examined me minutely. When they began to touch my face and clothes, Clear Water intervened. She handed me two of the water canteens and I followed her to the stream which flowed behind the camp. One boy, my age, was standing waist-height in the water, throwing it over himself. Shaking water from his hair like Tippet used to, he turned and waded out of the river. Naked. I stared, eyes wide, as he grabbed a loincloth from the bank and began to dry himself. Clear Water stifled a laugh at my gawping. I started and glanced at her, embarrassed, then concentrated on filling the canteen.

Clear Water and I sat on the bank for a while, watching the camp. It was a beautiful day and we were warm in the sun. Clear Water produced a piece of hard, biscuit-like tack from her bag and passed it to me, making an eating motion. I thanked her gratefully. Then I got up and went to check on the horses, who were standing, docile, by the large tents. I saw you standing with Rose, sharing a machine-made cigarette. Rose looked at me, the corner of her mouth kinking up, and said something to you.

You shook your head, stole the cigarette from her and offered it to me, eyebrow raised in challenge. I rolled my eyes, another habit Mama loathed, and took Tara and your red horse to the river to drink. Listening to them suck up the water with satisfied grunts, I didn't notice the boy from earlier standing behind me. He was wearing leggings and a tunic and his hair, still damp, was in a thick, sleek ponytail. He smiled.

'Hello.'

My eyes widened. 'Hello.'

'You are surprised I speak your language.'

'A little, yes.'

He patted the red horse, stroking a hand down his flank.

'I am often in Fort Shaw, with my father, Two Tails. He is the chief here.'

'Oh.' I tried to think. Finding common ground was important. 'My father is a chief too, amongst our people.' It wasn't a lie, after all.

He looked pleased. 'You are called English, yes? Like your tongue.'

I couldn't see the point in correcting him. 'Yes.'

'They are curious.' He gestured to the camp. 'They have

heard you belong to Pale Eye and want to see his wife.'

'I'm not his wife,' I said stoutly, surprised at my own voice.

His expression changed. 'But he has the agreement of your family?'

'I . . . er . . .' My voice petered out.

He looked at me, his copper-coloured skin smooth in the sun. 'But Pale Eye claimed you. Before my father. I heard him say it.'

Claimed me? *Claimed?*

'Dog Child? You trying to get me into trouble?' You loped up behind him, elbowing Tara out of the way and putting a large, flat saddle on the red horse.

The boy shrugged, unperturbed. 'I only told her our customs. If you have not the agreement of her father, have made no offering, you are not married and she does not belong to you.'

You ducked beneath the horse to grab the cinch and straightened, threading it through the rings. 'Run along now and play with your little toy bow and arrow.'

'Maybe that arrow will not feel so small if it is lodged in your chest, Pale Eye.'

You snorted with laughter, finishing the knot. 'You in the market for a suitor now, English? I missed this news.'

The remark confused the young brave. He looked at me, eyes dark, one last time, then walked away.

You shook your head. 'I leave you alone for a solitary minute and you're playing truant with the chief's son.'

'I was not!' I said, indignant. 'He came to speak to me.'

'Which is against the rules and he knows it.'

'Rules? Oh yes, you've *claimed* me, apparently,' I retorted sharply, my mettle thoroughly tested. 'I wasn't aware that the Indians raffled off their women. Did they ask to see a winning ticket?'

You laughed, pretending to stumble and clutching your heart. 'Nice shot, English. Didn't stop him trying his luck though, did it?'

'What *luck*? I don't understand,' I said, thoroughly confused by the whole exchange.

'I gotta explain every last thing to you, Emily?' You tutted, chucking me under the chin. 'Looking up at him with those blue eyes as if he's the only man in this world, the poor boy don't know where he is.'

'What on earth do you—'

You talked over me. 'Your momma did a fine job of raising you up to make a man drunk just talking with you and you know it.'

'Mama did no such thing and I don't know it. You mustn't say so, because I don't. She and Papa raised me to be good, and kind, and to try my best.'

You adjusted the saddle, pulling on it. 'They did such a good job maybe even *you* don't know you're doing it.' You glanced at me. 'Maybe.'

'If you don't stop I'll . . .'

'What'll you do?' you teased. 'Take me over your knee?' You made a show of patting your pockets. 'Ain't got a spare horse bit for you to practise your aim with this time. You feel up to trying the rifle again?'

'Shut up,' I said, then covered my mouth in shock at my bad manners.

You were buckling the throat strap on your red horse, and you laughed out loud at that. 'I only *claimed* you 'cause we're moving out. You'll be safe here until we get back, if they think you're mine. OK?'

'Oh.'

'But the chief's son probably got more sway, and he's definitely got more than one good leg, so maybe it's time to switch your allegiance.' You turned back to the red horse.

'Do stop. Such humour is in very poor taste.'

You mimicked me in silence, still checking and rechecking the kit behind the saddle. I looked around and saw signs of the camp galvanizing. Women were carrying saddles to horses, braves talked in small groups. Two thin, wiry warriors painted each other's faces with white and black stripes across their eyes. Clear Water and Lucky stood close together by his horse, barely touching, yet Clear Water's adoration of her husband was plain on her face. I looked away, feeling as if I were intruding, and the reality of my situation set in. 'How . . . how long will you be gone?' I asked your back.

You shrugged, still not looking at me. 'Don't know.'

'What are you going to do?'

'Make a stand against the killing party. Probably start a state-wide war. Bring down the wrath of the *people's* government upon these fool Indians' heads. Get my own shot off.'

You sighed without turning around. 'Leave you all alone.'

'No!'

You flung the reins over the horse's neck. 'You wanted this, remember?'

'But I—'

At that moment, Rose rode up and barked out a question without looking at me. I stood holding Tara's bridle in a slack hand, staring up at her as you answered, then turned to me.

'Well, Emily, it's been a pleasure.' Stooping, you touched your lips to my forehead, ignoring my startled intake of breath. 'Give my regards to Railroad. And don't worry yourself none whatever happens.'

Across the camp, braves were mounting their horses. You swung into the saddle. What if you were shot and I never saw you again? And to sit in a camp where I would be stared at and poked like a butterfly on a collector's pin? No, that held no appeal. Yet if there was to be a battle, I had no place in it. Yet I could not stay here alone without you. No. It wouldn't do. It wouldn't do at all. Besides, Rose wasn't staying behind. I tightened Tara's cinch and stuck my foot in the stirrup. Grabbing the saddlehorn, a second later I dropped into the seat. You both stopped talking and turned to stare at me.

Gathering the reins, I looked at you. 'Well, I seem to remember this was all my idea anyway.'

'Em—'

My insides trembled with fear, but I tried to make my voice steady. 'Why not?'

'Won't be no place for a woman.'

I fed the leather through my fingers, not looking at you. 'Rose will be there.'

'Like I said, Rose can take care of Rose. And she'll probably take care of about five of them too. I don't want to have to worry about you.'

I thought back, listening to my father's interminable diplomatic conversations, and the red flock wallpaper and the bright green ferns of our drawing room. 'Well then, Pale Eye, you should have left me in that river bed, shouldn't you?'

Rose looked between us, and raised a soot-black eyebrow.

You set your jaw. 'Well then, Emily Forsythe, let's go.'

Setting our heels to our horses, we left the camp at a brisk trot and headed out towards the east.

The camp, you told me later, was large for the Blackfoot, numbering perhaps two hundred souls, of which there were thirty braves. You and Lucky rode to one side of Two Tails, his sons, including Dog Child, to the other. Rose rode slightly separately. I stayed at the back, the only other woman. The men ignored me. Tara kept up easily and, at that moment, I was pleased with my decision to come. Then the band halted and there was a brief conversation. We were exposed as a large group, that much even I could see. Dog Child had dismounted and was examining the ground. I looked down, seeing rutted wheel tracks running through the grass. The hunters had passed this way.

As the group split into three, wheeling away north and south, you dropped back and fell in with me and Tara.

'Likely we won't have much time when we get upon them, ain't much element of surprise out here. You stay back when I tell you, and if it all goes to shit, you turn Tara around and you get back to that camp as fast as you can. Yes?'

I nodded. You carried on speaking, to yourself as much as me.

'We're coming at them from three angles and we got a two-part plan. The first is to scatter the herd. The second is to drop as many of the hunters as possible. It ain't going to be pretty, you know that, don't you?'

'Yes,' I said, my voice as firm as I could make it.

'And, worse comes to worst? If something happens to me, and getting away isn't possible, you get near Rose and she'll take care a-you. Lucky, the same. OK?'

'Nothing's going to happen to you, is it?'

'Hope not, but when it's your time, it's your time.'

I shifted in the saddle, uneasy. The scout returned. They had found the wagons, which had halted – for reasons of surprise – some distance from the herd. There were three young men driving the wagons, but it looked as if they were preparing to follow the main hunting party. Rose favoured taking them out immediately, by stealth if possible, so as not to alert the main hunting party, who were half a mile further on, approaching the herd. As you relayed the information, I stared at her. She meant killing them. People were going to die.

Rose and two braves rode away. Soon afterwards, one of them returned. The men with the wagons were dead, two by

Rose's knife. We went forward; my hands were shaking and I wound them around the saddlehorn, holding tight even though I looked like a child on a seaside donkey. Arriving over the hill, I looked down on the scene before me. Three wagons, each drawn by two horses, stood below us. On the ground were three bodies, one at a distance – clearly he'd been trying to run. An arrow stuck from his body at an awkward angle. One of the braves was quieting the horses at the head of a wagon; Rose was stooping to pull an arrow from one of the bodies, tugging when it wouldn't come easily. My stomach rebelled and I fought not to gag. As we approached, she knelt and took out her knife. Grasping a lock of hair at the crown of the man's head, she slit a small disc of scalp from his head and pushed it into the bag at her waist. I swallowed a cry.

You held out a warning hand. 'You wanted this. You. So you just sit there and you take it, Emily.'

Rose straightened, high cheekbones flushed. They remounted, taking their horses from the scout, and we continued, scout at the head. We were climbing steadily. To our right was a high ridge, another to our left, and a river meandered at the base of the valley.

Little did I know, the herd was just over the next rise. Suddenly there was the distant boom of a buffalo gun. Then the air rang with them. You cursed and jabbed a finger at the ground.

'Wait here. Here! Not an inch in any direction, Emily, or I will tan your hide blue.' Unshouldering your rifle, you

216

clapped your heels to the red horse, a feral yell breaking from your throat. You and the braves soared over the hill in a phalanx of screaming, yelling warriors, guns and bows held aloft.

As you disappeared, my heart raced. The first of the buffalo were cresting the rise coming in the opposite direction and heading straight for us. You'd told me that the bulls weighed over a ton. Tara stood immobile, a teacup of courage, as they thundered towards us, ground shaking beneath them. I gripped the saddlehorn. Perhaps twenty, of all sizes, from vast adults to calves, streamed past in a sweating, snorting, stinking charge. I found I was gripping Tara's mane, sweat prickling inside my shirt, as their hoof beats died away behind us.

Then I was sitting on Tara alone, in the middle of an empty hillside over which I could hear the racket of tribal war. Something screamed.

I squeezed Tara into a walk. We crested the rise seconds later and saw the battle spread out before us. Buffalo still fled in all directions, but centred below us was the most extraordinary scene. My eyes sought you. I didn't know, at that time, that the rifle which never left your side held six shots in a revolving chamber, like a pistol with a long, wicked barrel. With it you were deadly: a fact the hunters quickly recognized, and you were soon the focus of their attention. All of them had been employed for their skill with a gun. There were almost twenty of them, armed with what you told me later were powerful Sharps rifles. In the dirt lay the bodies of at least seven buffalo. Men and horses clashed everywhere and I watched as the horses played as much a part in the battle as the men, ramming into their opponents, shoulder to shoulder – riding off, you told me later. You sat on the red horse, a short distance away, calmly reloading, lifting the weapon to your eye, taking shots as they came. But you did it totally exposed, as if inviting a bullet.

I wanted to shout to you, to urge you to seek some cover, but all I could do was watch. I saw you kill three of the hunters before one of them, breaking contact with a brave, galloped towards you. Instantly I regretted that I was there; had I not been, you would have been mounted on Tara. The young, nervy red horse shied violently as the other rode down on him, throwing your weight on to your weak leg. Both hands on the gun, you fell from the saddle, hitting the dirt, rifle discharging. The rider circled and returned. My heart was in my mouth: on the ground you were lame and slow.

Quite how what happened next came to pass I am still, all this time later, unsure.

Tara hurtled on to the plain, my face by her neck, legs tight, reins caught only by a thread. She knew what was required of her, always, and speared straight for the hunter's large bay gelding. Her hooves darted into the dirt and we arrowed towards them just as you gained your feet and the hunter levelled his rifle at you. He had taken his time, gloating, halting his horse and preparing to shoot you from little over ten feet away as you stood and waited for it to come.

What Tara did not have in weight, we made up for in speed, smashing into the gelding's shoulder with a force that made my teeth rattle, bruising my right leg, flinging me against the saddlehorn and down over Tara's flank.

I kept my seat only just, but I had been ready. Righting myself, I looked up at the hunter . . . Hart. His face was full of rage, rifle in the dirt. I felt winded from the impact and the saddlehorn in my stomach. Tara wheeled away instantly in a prancing gallop as I grasped the reins I'd dropped and urged her back around as you rescued your rifle. But I misjudged Tara's line, wanting to come between Hart and you until you had time to get back in the saddle, and then the bay gelding was alongside us. Hart reached over and grabbed my long braid, yanking me towards him. Broaching the distance, he caught me and hauled me on to the pommel of his saddle. Using my body to shield his chest he turned. His horse halted, shifting restlessly on the spot. Tara skidded to a halt a few yards away, watching.

Hart was breathing hard, the rank stench of his breath against my cheek. 'Go on, do it. You'll blow a hole in her like a lead bucket.'

I squirmed, terrified, but he held me tightly. You lifted the gun to your eye.

Hart dragged a knife from his belt and put it to my throat. 'Think you're good enough?'

You said nothing, squinting down the barrel. I closed my eyes, feeling the blade press to my neck. There was a sting and blood trickled into the sweating hollow at the base of my throat. Around us, battle raged.

The gunshot reverberated across the plain.

Hart was thrown from the saddle, taking me with him. We hit the ground, hard, his body on top of mine, knocking every ounce of air from my lungs. He was heavy, stinking lumber. A moment later, you hauled him off and hurled me to the ground behind the warm bulk of a felled buffalo. Dropping to your knees, you pushed the rifle into my hands and opened the action.

'Shake out the chamber. Reload from the left side of my belt. And stay low.' Drawing your pistol from the right, you took aim at a hunter getting back on his horse near where Rose was wrestling on the ground with another.

Reaching around you, I pulled a bullet from your belt and stuck it in the chamber, then another. Then an incoming bullet met its mark. You spun, sitting down hard against the buffalo's side, a bloody rip in the sleeve of your shirt.

'Ow! Damnation!'

'You're shot!' I cried in horror.

Scowling at me, you checked the rip, before turning and taking aim, quickly letting off a bullet that felled the guilty party. 'Scratched,' you corrected, as the man hit the dirt.

You swapped weapons with me, revolver chamber open and spinning, spent cartridges clinking on to the dirt. 'Right side.' I began to reload as you raised the rifle and took careful aim at the hunter locked in a deadly tussle with Two Tails, guns knocked aside and knives flashing. I felt you breathe in and hold it. Your finger tightened on the trigger, and with a thundering crack the hunter fell from the saddle. Two Tails looked up and saw you, raising his knife over his head in salute, before circling to find his son.

I do not know how long it was before the battle was over; the sun had moved. The buffalo were long gone, apart from the bodies in the dirt. Scattered amongst them were all seventeen hunters and six dead horses but, miraculously, no braves. Rose had three scalps in her bag and a deep cut on her arm. Lucky's chest was bruised and scraped from a fall when his horse had been killed beneath him, but he remained as unperturbed as ever, and one of the braves was shot in the shoulder. Two Tails gave orders and two of the younger braves gathered up the hunters' surviving horses, who had spread themselves across the plain. The scout, on the band's fastest pony, disappeared over the rise.

'What's happening now?' I asked you, feeling juddery and uncertain.

You holstered the pistol and shouldered the rifle. 'The men will butcher the animals and the women will come for the meat.'

As you spoke, the buffalo that had sheltered us, face in the dirt and legs buckled beneath it, groaned. You crouched by its head as its wet nostrils flexed, blowing into the grass. Blood ran from a series of bullet wounds across its flank – so many of them had been sustained in protecting us.

'Come here, English.'

I knelt by you as you pulled the knife from the sheath that hung by your shoulder. Rose appeared, hunched over one

221

knee on the other side of the animal's thick neck.

'Give me your hand.' You grabbed my wrist and folded my fingers around the haft of the knife, yours on top. Your free hand felt for the animal's throat. I recoiled but you held me, hard, and stuck the buffalo straight in the jugular vein. Blood spurted, spraying my clothes, splattering your thigh. The animal groaned a long exhalation, blood bubbling through the wound around the knife still deep in its neck. Awareness faded from its large brown eye. You touched its head and said something I couldn't understand as Rose leant forward and placed her hand in the gore and dragged her fingers down my face. I started back.

'Let her do it, it's tradition.' You held my arms.

The air smelt of iron, salt and dung as we got to our feet. Two Tails approached, his thin face unreadable as he looked me up and down. His eyes flickered to the carnage around us, then back to me. Your hand rested at the base of my spine. A fly landed on the blood on my cheek, but I held his gaze. He looked at you and there was the slightest lift in his eyebrow. Then he said something and smiled. Raising his rifle above his head, he let out a pealing cry, echoed by the braves all around us as they worked. Finally the chief turned away and I could breathe again.

You looked down at my bloody face. 'Jesus. Christ. Emily.'

'What did I do wrong?' Tara nudged my shoulder and I took her reins.

'Nearly got yourself killed, that's what.'

Behind you, two men hauled the liver out of the buffalo,

up to their elbows in intestines. The others were working further afield on the other carcasses.

'I'm fine,' I said quietly, fiddling with Tara's bridle, stroking her flat cheek.

The others, Rose included, were now busy hacking soft hunks off the quivering mass of liver and stuffing it into their mouths.

I shuddered. 'Please tell me I don't have to do that.'

Your bark of laughter filled the air, high up to where the scavengers were already circling.

By the time the women arrived, dragging sleds behind their ponies for the spoils, I was flagging and thirsty. Even some children helped, their dogs carting smaller sleds. I sat on the hillside, drinking from your canteen and watching. The corpses of the hunters were gathering flies. You limped up the slope and collapsed next to me on your elbows, bad leg stretched out.

I passed you the canteen. 'Did we do the right thing?'

You took a drink and thought about it. 'I don't know, Em. Hart . . . I ain't sorry that bastard is dead, nor most of the others, but those on the wagons were just men needing work, probably struggling after this last winter. Getting their throats cut out here for a few dollars.' You lay back on the grass. 'I'm sick to the back teeth of killing, that much I do know. And it's like every time I come down off that mountain, I get my hands in the mire. Again.' You held out a calloused, dusty hand, bloody palm up, to prove your point.

I looked at it, then placed my own on top of it, not

meeting your look of surprise. 'So what happens now?'

We gathered the horses. You caught Hart's horse and handed her reins to me. 'Take this one back into the village. Then it's your coup.'

'Coup? From the French?'

You nodded, then settled into the saddle of the red horse. As it turned out, he hadn't fled far and had trailed back as we were getting ready to move out. 'Getting the enemy's horse, getting a scalp, engaging in battle and coming out the other side, they're all coups. More coups you got, the more respect.'

'How many have you got?' I asked, intrigued.

'My share.'

Riding back to the Blackfoot camp, we were accompanied by perhaps ten men, Rose and the wagons. My face felt by turns sticky and crackly. Dusk was falling and I had to catch myself awake like Tippet as a puppy, slumping over the saddlehorn then jerking upright, the reins of Hart's horse clutched tightly in my hand.

Back at the camp, all was activity. You helped me down and we took Tara and the others to drink. I tugged off her saddle as she sucked at the river water. You slapped her sweat-stiff neck and talked to her. Her blanket was damp as I shook it out and rubbed her down, then I pressed my cheek against hers in gratitude, kissing her white and tan face. She huffed over my shoulder, muzzle dripping water down my back.

Next to us, you stripped to the waist and used your shirt to wash your dirty face and hands, wiping the back of your neck. You examined the blackened and bloody streak on your bicep.

'Looks painful.'

'Smarts some but ain't nothing. Had worse.'

Clear Water appeared next to us with a wadded cloth and an earthenware pot of salve. She gave them to me with her kind smile, gesturing to your arm, and you thanked her.

I wet the cloth and took your elbow in my hand, fingers against the soft inside. It truly was only a graze cutting across the smooth curve of your bicep, with almost no blood lost at all; I applied the salve.

'Well, Dr English, what do you think?'

I flushed, letting go and stepping back, embarrassed. 'Should we bind it?'

'Nah, let it dry. I'll just try and keep it clean is all.' You were already donning a fresh shirt from our pack.

The dark was deepening by the river and I jumped as we heard the first drums. The camp was littered with small bonfires – *feux de joie*, you called them – and a little distance from it, a larger one burnt fiercely. Over fire pits huge hunks of buffalo meat were roasting. The smell of the buffalo cooking filled the air and children sat at the edge of the light, eating fry-bread sopped in meat juices. Rose was sitting in a circle with the men. In groups around them the women gathered. I saw Clear Water, but she wasn't looking at me.

We sat in the ring with the warriors, cross-legged. The brave to your left passed a canteen and you drank, sucking in a breath through your teeth and wiping your mouth on the back of your wrist. Handing it over, you coughed. I took a sip and almost choked then, still spluttering, offered it back to you.

'No, no. Take another. A proper mouthful this time. Then pass it on.'

I steeled myself and took a gulp, handing the canteen on to the brave next to me. Rose was laughing as I swiped my fingers across my lips and gasped, eyes watering.

My head was spinning with fatigue and hunger, and when you fetched a wooden platter of roasted meat and fried bread for us to share as the singing started, I was very grateful. Blackfoot music is unique, you explained, passing me a neat fold of soft, crispy-edged cornbread and meat. Beautiful, haunting loops of repeated phrases. I listened, fascinated. And I ate like a savage, with my hands and my teeth, face bloody, watching them whoop and holler and dance to the pounding of the drums.

It was always like this, you said, after a battle. I drank more water. And more firewater, offered to me by a drunk young brave and tipped over my upturned face when I couldn't swallow any more, my throat like razors. You laughed as I spluttered. I watched Dog Child dancing with a girl, stamping around each other in circles, bells on their knees, as I sat cradled between your bent legs, feeling safe, protected from the strange world I had found myself in. And I liked lounging against you, after so many years sitting bolt upright and alone in my cages of whalebone and steel. Sometime later, the tiny son of Two Tails's second wife crept up and touched me, leaving a long brown feather in my lap.

'Coup-feather. For your first battle,' you said.

I caught the leather lace around your neck and examined its ornaments. The feathers, the shell casings, a silver button and a regimental badge; the knife you never used.

'These are *your* coups?'

'Yeah, Emily. They're my coups.'

I let the shell casings clink in my palm. 'You didn't tell me.'

You pushed my tangled and bedecked hair aside and spoke into my ear. 'I told you if you moved one step on that hillside, I'd tan you blue.'

I watched the flames and the dancers, content and sleepy, liking the closeness of your voice. 'I've been blue for days. And I saved your life.'

Laughing, you crossed your arms in front of me. 'You did.'

I don't remember falling asleep on you but I do remember waking as you laid me on a pile of buffalo hides and buckled me against your side in the lodge they loaned us at the edge of the camp. Your breath was warm against the back of my neck. The doorflap was open and the last thing I saw, high in the heavens, was a star shooting across the glittering ceiling of the sky.

CHAPTER 12

Hope read aloud as Cal worked to make the cabin
more comfortable.

'I'll find something to eat in the morning.' He
shook out the blankets and started to make up a bed in front
of the fire he'd lit in the hearth. The little house, despite the
cool night air coming in through the broken window, was
tolerably warm, with the stove and a log fire burning. Hope
came and sat on the bedding, cross-legged. Buddy sat with
her.

'He's not taking her back.'

Cal sat next to them, rubbing Buddy's ears. 'Well, it is a
long way, and he's just done the journey.'

'That's not the point and you know it,' Hope said.

He sighed. 'I'm trying to give the guy the benefit of the
doubt. Like he says, he could have done anything he wanted

to her by now, but he hasn't.'

Hope smothered a yawn. 'Hmm.'

'Tired?'

'Yes. I wish I had a toothbrush.'

He got up and went to the kitchen cupboard, looking inside and opening things. When he found what he wanted, he returned with one of the cups.

'Old backwoods trick. Salt and a wet cloth. Scrub your teeth and rinse your mouth.'

They spat the salty water off the porch, looking up at the moon.

'Gross.' Hope winced.

'Gross but effective,' Cal corrected, wiping his mouth.

Back inside, they huddled down in their clothes beneath the quilt and the blankets. After their night in the open, sleeping next to each other didn't seem a big deal. Their empty stomachs growled and Hope shivered, tugging the rolled-up smock beneath her head.

'You're cold?'

'Freezing.'

He put his arm around her, her back to his chest, and pulled the coverlet tighter. 'Better?'

'Much, thank you.'

It wasn't warmer, because Cal was almost as cold as she was, but it was definitely much better than him not having his arm around her, so Hope reasoned with herself that it wasn't really a lie. Buddy lay down at their feet as she fell asleep, exhausted, one hand on the cover of the diary, the other slipping inside Cal's on the quilt.

Soon after dawn, Cal nudged her. 'Cooper? You're on me. And I need to get up.'

'Sorry,' she mumbled, sleepy, and realizing she was sprawled across him. Pulling away, she curled in on herself into the covers.

Cal and Buddy went out immediately. Hope rubbed her eyes and sat up; it was another beautiful day. Going outside, she took a pee in the woods behind the house and washed her hands and face in the stream. When Cal returned, he brought more foraged duck potatoes, as well as water. His hair was wet and his shirt stuck to the definition of his chest.

Cal broke the silence as they finished eating, setting some aside for later. 'I was thinking that they must have been in Fort Shaw pretty much the first year it existed officially. It was just a military outpost called Camp Reynolds before then.' He checked on the water, which was finally coming to the boil. 'Wish I could have seen it. Read some more to me?'

By the time the coffee was made, Hope was breathless with excitement. They picked up their cups and went outside to the porch, sitting on the step.

'*Hot, frightened perspiration trickled down inside the cold, wet shirt, making me shiver. What had I done? I knew nothing of how to survive in the wilderness—*' Hope broke off, looking out at the meadow. 'I'm frightened for her.'

'As long as *you* don't run off down the mountain, everything will be fine. Let's find something to eat.' He took the diary from her hands and put it on the porch, pulling her to her feet.

'Where would I go?' Hope looked at the vast wilderness around her. 'And what will we find?'

'You'll see.' He picked up the rifle and slung it over his shoulder.

'Wait.' Hope went inside, taking the diary and returning with the satchel, looping it around her neck. 'We might be able to use this.'

'Good thinking.'

They walked down the mountainside, Cal scanning the ground.

'What are you looking for?'

'A lot of these flowers are edible. I'll pick some later. They won't give us calories, but they might make things more interesting.'

Through the forest, they walked to the lake. Hope was hot by the time they reached the shoreline. She splashed some water on her face and yelped at the chill.

He grinned. 'It does stay pretty cold. But you know what that means?'

She shook her head.

'It means the fish are good eating. Trout, mainly.'

'But how are we going to catch fish?'

He held up his hand and waved his fingers. 'With these.'

She wrinkled her nose. 'People can't really do that, it's just in films.'

'O ye of little faith,' he mocked, walking along the shoreline to where the stream from the cabin let out. It was wide and more powerful this far down, and looked about waist-deep. The banks were made up of scrubby grass and plants. Cal lay down on his stomach, looking into the clear water and Hope lay down next to him, resting on her elbows. Buddy lay down too, then crawled to lay his belly over Cal's lower back.

Cal glanced over his shoulder. 'Jeez, Buddy, you're a real help.'

The dog's face was split in a wide, panting grin. Hope stifled a giggle. A stiff breeze gusted from the lake and far out, towards a small island covered with dense pine, white-capped waves bounced. All around them, huge crags rose up and the pine trees shifted. The stream ran swiftly.

'There, do you see?' Cal pointed, moving to his left a little.

Hope wriggled up next to him, watching. 'No . . .'

'Big trout, about six inches below the surface, facing into the stream. Just under that rock ledge.' He slipped his hand into the water, approaching the fish slowly. With his hand underneath its belly, he touched it carefully.

'How long does it take?' Hope whispered.

'Hard to tell. You don't know if it's going to work until you try to land it,' he whispered back. She watched, fascinated. A few minutes later, Cal tensed. 'Buddy, get up, you great lump.' Buddy stood instantly and retreated a couple of paces. 'Well, here goes nothing.'

He sat up, flinging the fish on to the grass then picking up the rifle, and hit the trout once, hard, on the head with the butt. Hope flinched.

'Sorry, should have warned you,' he panted, more from

adrenalin than exertion.

The fish lay, inert and glistening on the bank. It took an hour to catch another one, during which time Hope dozed in the sun next to Cal's warm shoulder, head on her folded arms. When he was finished they walked back up the mountain in companionable silence. Butterflies flocked around them to the spring flowers and birds sang.

'I can't stop thinking about them. I mean' – Hope gestured to the mountain – 'this place has hardly changed since they were here.'

Cal nodded, thinking. 'Look, up there. To the left of the cabin. See it? All those broken rails? I guess that's the corral.'

Hope followed his finger. 'I see it.'

Back at the cabin, Cal went down to the stream to prepare the fish. It didn't take him long and he came back with both of them threaded on to a stick. Hope was sitting on the porch, reading the diary, Buddy at her feet.

'Hey, you can't read it without me,' Cal protested. Taking the fish inside and resting the stick over the sink, he came back out and sat next to her. 'Well, what's happening?'

'Nate's not speaking to her. He kind of told her he loves her, I think, and she didn't understand, or pretended not to. And she can't survive out here without him, so she's stuck. Like a prisoner.'

'Worse prisons to be in.'

Hope looked out at the view, hunched over her knees. 'How come he was there to rescue her when there was no one else for miles?'

'You think he was following them?'

'Maybe. Maybe he caused the accident.'

'Why would he? *How* could he? It was only by a fluke she survived. If he wants her, why take that chance? It'd be like me deliberately crashing the rig to get you up here.'

Hope laughed. 'Was that why you kept insisting on the seat belt?'

He smiled and shook his head. 'Know what, Cooper? With that imagination you *should* be a writer.'

For much of that day, they sat, absorbed in the diary and watching the clouds throw shadows across the mountain.

Hope broke off for a second, voice a little hoarse. 'So, you think they'll know we should have arrived by now?'

Cal nodded. 'About now. Problem is, they're used to me taking my time, so they probably won't start to worry until nightfall when I'm not answering my phone. Or you yours. Second problem is, there's not much reception up here anyway, miles and miles without it. Only kicks back in when you drop out of the national park. Might not cause them to think anything's wrong.'

'So when will they start looking, do you think?'

He thought about it. 'Tomorrow, maybe.'

'So they'll find us tomorrow?'

'Maybe, if they start looking during the day. Mom's pretty laid back. She may even wait until nightfall. I reckon we've got maximum another forty-eight hours before someone gets here.'

Hope sighed. 'OK.' She smoothed her hands over the front cover of the diary. 'At least we have this to keep us occupied.'

He nodded, running a hand over Buddy's coat. The dog panted in the sun. She picked at a splinter on the edge of the step, diary on her knees.

Cal spoke first. 'Tell me about your friends.'

'My friends? Well, there's Lauren. She and I have lived on the same road for ever and we hang out a lot when I'm home. She goes to normal school and she's great. But she's got lots of other friends, obviously, and she invites me to stuff but I get shy in big groups. And Scott's a genius and the funniest person I know. We spend the weekends together mostly.'

'Scott?'

'Yeah. He's another home-schooler, but that's because he's too clever for ordinary school and on the autism spectrum and his dad's some sort of professor of quantum mechanics or something. I met him on a Spanish conversation course last year.'

Cal studied Buddy's ears. 'So why not date Scott?'

'Well, I could . . . I suppose, if I wanted to play third fiddle to gaming and extremely freaky Japanese comics.'

They laughed for a long time. The afternoon was cooling and Cal got to his feet. 'I'm going to check the stove's still alight, then rig up a spit out here for these fish.'

With a flat stone he scraped a small pit, then created a fire with a burning log from the stove. Hope searched for forked sticks that would support a spit and they banged them into the earth with the stone. It took a couple of hours to get up to heat, but by the time the sun went down it was burning bright orange in the centre. The sunset was beautiful, spreading a reddish glow over the meadow and the lake. Hope wound her hair into a loose knot at the back of her head.

'How do you get it to do that?' Cal asked.

'What?' she asked, surprised.

'Stay up like that, without pins.'

'Oh, I don't know,' she said, both blithe and uncertain under his scrutiny. 'It just kind of does.' She went inside and fetched a pan of water to boil the duck potatoes. By the time they were ready, Cal had gathered some greenery.

'Fireweed. It's good. I eat it sometimes on the ranch if I see it.'

Hope put down the tin plates. Her stomach growled ferociously. Cal began to ease pieces of fish off with his knife, checking it was cooked. He put a couple on her plate, next to the duck potatoes. He helped himself to more. Hope sat down, cross-legged, next to him and picked up her plate.

They didn't speak, both too hungry to do anything other than concentrate on the food. Hope ate everything, including the fireweed. 'This really is tasty.'

They took their empty plates and washed them and their greasy hands in the creek before coming back to sit close to the fire.

'Can I ask you something?' Hope said.

'Sure.' He banked the flames.

'Why didn't you finish high school? Because it looks from the stuff in the crates in the barn that you're like . . . clever and everything. And you were good at football.'

He was silent for a while. 'Not that clever. And not that good. I made a big mistake.'

Hope waited.

He took a breath. 'There was this guy, Tyler Cross, we were on the team. He was getting hazed, real bad. You know what hazing is, right?'

Hope nodded. 'Bullying.'

'Yeah, well, for some reason, the guys just had it in for him. And I didn't like it, but I said nothing. Coach said nothing, no one said anything at all. Then we were up for a few big games in our class. Tyler just couldn't keep it together, kept missing easy passes. Had a lot to do with what was going on, I thought. Anyway, Dan and Steve Hart, the idiots with the plastic cup? Dan's the chief's son, Steve's Dan's cousin. They were at the centre of it all, ragging on Tyler the whole time. Then one day, we'd lost at home to Billings. I mean, *Billings*.' He looked at Hope. She shrugged. 'Never mind. And then in the locker room, they're really going for Tyler. I was rushing to get home because I had chores, and then I see they've got him on the floor, stripping him off, and they've got a gallon pack of glue, and this sack of feathers. So then I knew it wouldn't have mattered if we'd won or lost, because they were going to do it anyway.'

'Do what?'

'Feather him up and handcuff him to his car in the parking lot.'

Hope pulled a face.

237

'Yeah. Exactly.'

'So what did you do?'

He shifted. 'This is where I'm not so proud of myself.' Taking a breath, he went on. 'Dan's the leader of all that stuff, always has been. So I hauled him off and, well, I lost my temper. Really lost it. Got *him* down, covered him in glue and tipped the whole lot of those feathers right over him. The others just watched, like they couldn't believe it. Except Steve, but he wasn't in a hurry to do a thing after I put Dan down.' He rubbed his face. 'Then I dragged Dan out to the parking lot and handcuffed him to the door of that truck of his. Threw the key in the bushes and left him there, everyone still leaving the stadium.'

Hope put her hands over her face. 'Oh God.'

'Yep. I mean, we hated each other before that, but that was the icing on the cake. And it made no difference anyway. In fact, probably made things worse.'

'How?'

'Ty took his own life that night.'

Hope gasped. 'I'm so sorry . . .' she stammered.

The sound of the wind and the birds was the only noise on the mountain.

Cal nodded. 'After that, things just . . . I just couldn't be there any more. It was so messed up. Tyler had left this note, not naming any names, and because I'd done that to Dan, pretty much everyone outside the team thought I was the ringleader.'

'That's not fair.'

He shrugged. 'Tyler's dead. Fair doesn't mean much in the face of that. And I don't care, because it's not going to bring him back, is it? And what I did was wrong.'

'But Dan had it coming.'

'Oh yeah, he had it coming. But I should have stuck up for Tyler a long time before that.' He narrowed his eyes, looking into the distance. 'And I didn't.'

The silence became intolerable. 'We should read some more,' Hope said abruptly, getting to her feet. She fetched the book and a blanket from the cabin and came back, dropping to the ground and tucking her legs beneath her. Opening the diary, she began to read aloud, Cal pointing out the last leaning and rotten corral post when Hope read of Nate and Em's argument there. He leant back on his elbows, watching the last of the light bounce off the lake, as Hope read on, reaching the arrival of the men from Fort Shaw.

'Wait,' he said, stopping her. 'Hart?'

Hope looked back at the diary. 'You think he's an ancestor of the police chief?'

'Think he has to be. The Harts have been around here as long as we have, well, Fort Shaw anyway. There's been bad blood between us for as long as anyone remembers, although no one really knows why. What happened with the team made it all a hundred times worse. And the chief seems more than happy to carry it on too. Grudges of all kinds, with all kinds of people. He hates Native Americans, says they've got blood on their hands as far as his family's concerned. Though he won't be drawn on it.'

Hope chewed her lip. 'Shall I keep reading?'

He nodded, thinking.

Sometime later, during the riding lessons with Tara, she stopped. It was dark and Emily's writing wasn't always easy to work out, full of old-fashioned loops and swirls. 'Nate's such a mixture of all the things I think of when I think of America. He's a cowboy *and* he's an Indian. And he fought in the Civil War, which is incredible, even though it's awful about his leg and the nightmares.'

Cal put his elbows on his bent knees and nodded.

Drawn into the story, Hope went on, 'He really loves her. I mean, I'm not even sure he wants to, but he can't help it. That's why he'd never hurt her.'

Somewhere nearby, a lone cricket chirped.

'Maybe he just wouldn't hurt her because he's not that sort of guy,' Cal said, voice clipped.

Hope nodded. 'Yes. But it was love at first sight too. For both of them.' He said nothing so she stumbled on, 'At least, that's what I think.'

He flicked a pebble off the porch, irritated.

'Sorry, I've said something wrong.'

'No, you haven't. Forget it.' He took a breath. 'Look, Hope, I really like you but . . .'

She pushed to her feet, blanket abandoned, diary in her hand. He stood too. Buddy looked between them, confused.

'How have we got to that from . . . I wasn't being . . . I mean, that's not what I was saying. And I never said *I* was interested in *you*.'

'And I never said *I wasn't* interested in *you*.'

'Oh.'

He scrubbed a hand through his hair. 'I'm trying to be realistic. You live in another country, for Chrissake! And you're sixteen! How can I be involved with a sixteen-year-old after—'

'I can't help the age I am. Being sixteen isn't a crime.'

'Of course it isn't. Look, I . . . I've got problems. After what happened to Tyler, things got crazy.'

Hope took a step back. 'We're miles from anywhere and you're telling me you've got *problems*?' She hugged her arms to her chest, diary tucked inside them. 'You're scaring me.'

He took a deep breath. 'Don't be scared. This is just something I have to deal with alone, that's all.'

There were only the sounds of the mountain. Finally Hope spoke. 'Alone is hard. Maybe I could help.'

'I'm not sure anyone can. I made a big mistake. Huge. Stuff happened and . . .' Buddy whined. Cal bent down to him, wrapping his hand around the dog's muzzle. 'It's OK, boy.'

There was a long silence.

'It probably isn't that bad,' Hope said, uncertain.

'You really don't know that.' His voice was as dark as the night around them.

CHAPTER 13

'THE VERY EXPRESSION – FALLING IN
LOVE – HAS DONE AN INCALCULABLE
AMOUNT OF MISCHIEF, BY CONVEYING
AN IDEA THAT IT IS A THING WHICH
CANNOT BE RESISTED, AND WHICH
MUST BE GIVEN WAY TO, EITHER
WITH OR WITHOUT REASON.'

We left early the next morning and spent the following two weeks scouting for the Stanton railway, the five of us: you, me, Lucky, Clear Water and Rose. A more unlikely team cannot be imagined. During daylight hours, our group separated, coming back at night to Clear Water and the camp, which changed every couple of days. Sometimes, when there was work to do, I stayed behind with Clear Water and the extra horses. Lucky had acquired another two after the battle, bringing the surplus mounts to five, although you said Hart's bay gelding's mouth was ruined from bad handling, and you'd sell him on as soon as possible. I would rather have been with you but it didn't seem right to leave Clear Water on her own all the time, even though there was precious little conversation to be had.

Clear Water was, however, intuitive: she knew before I did that I was about to be inconvenienced as women are, for I had never established any reliable notion in that department. Liza my maid had said it would most likely come after I had a child of my own, as if an infant were a magic watchmaker within my body, *tick-tock*. Clear Water took great care of me and showed me, with dignity, how Indian women dealt with such indelicate issues, making me bark tea for the discomfort and wrapping a fire-warmed flat stone in a leather cloth for me to hold against my middle. She also gave me one of her and Lucky's blankets and made me a bed on the ground away from you – I found out later that native women live separately at that time.

You affected not to notice, and returned the blanket to Clear Water as we prepared to retire, ignoring both her surprise and then my over-heated and restless jolting in the night. Soon though, my time passed, and I wanted to be back on Tara. And with you. A few mornings later I came back from the river after an early start and fetched my saddle and bridle. You said nothing, just watched me tack up in silence, drinking the hot herbal tea Clear Water made each morning and smoking a cigarette.

'Long ride today. Up to it?'

Instead of replying, I flipped the worn leather fender off my shoulder, straightening the stirrup and buckling the throat strap of Tara's plain bridle. The pack I fastened behind the saddle now contained the hide of the buffalo who had sheltered us, presented to me as a gift when we left the

Blackfoot. In the soft, thick skin were thirty-eight thumbnail-sized holes. Clear Water had spent much time and a huge effort in curing and smoking it over the past days, for which I was unable to express my gratitude. But I had asked you to thank her, and she had smiled her beautiful smile to me the previous evening.

You watched me finish. 'Reckon we should be done by nightfall.'

I kissed Tara's nose and scratched beneath her forelock. 'And then?'

You stood and threw out the dregs of your tea. 'Home.'

Soon, we were leaving camp. Lucky and Rose were coming out with us, as their portion of the scouting was done. We rode due west to look at the mountain range indicated on the map in your possibles bag. You and Rose spoke occasionally, but Lucky was mainly silent. The weather was clear and bright, and far away to the north a herd of buffalo dotted the landscape. By midday, we had reached the foothills of the range. You sat, leaning back in the saddle, looking at it for what seemed like an age. You got down and kicked at the earth with your bad foot. Looking up again, you bit the inside of your cheek.

'What do you think?' I'd let the reins slacken and Tara pointed her near-side hoof like a ballerina and scratched her nose against her leg, one side then the other.

'Ain't nothing coming through here, blasting or no blasting.'

I thought of the Stantons' broker – the paymaster for this

job. 'Is that what you're going to tell Mr Meard?'

'Yep. Maybe Railroad can go further north, across the border into the British Possessions – your name for Canada – maybe further south, towards Missoula, but it ain't coming through here to Spokane.'

'Spokane?' I asked. 'That's where we're scouting?'

You nodded and gestured to the mountains. 'Keep going dead west through them hills and you'll get there.'

'How long would it take?'

You looked up at me. 'Why, English, fancy making another run for it?'

I said nothing.

You shrugged. 'Well, you got Tara now, and all our food, so you'd probably make it.'

Looking out at the mountains, I still said nothing.

'Rose goes as far as Spokane sometimes. Knows the trail. Could ask her to take you,' you said slowly.

'Stop it.'

'Stop what?' You adjusted the red horse's bridle needlessly.

'Trying to make me go.'

'I thought you wanted to go. You could deliver your report to Railroad in person. Big romantic reunion. Wait, no, for a reunion you'd have to have met already.'

I could have kicked you. I might have, if the others hadn't been there. But instead I decided to play you at your own game. For it was a game, Nate, I knew you well enough by then.

I lifted my chin. 'I cannot possibly go anywhere looking

like this. We'll have to wait until you've been paid and there's money for decent clothing and shoes.'

'And then I'll ask Rose to take you?' You put your hand on the horn of the red horse's saddle, not looking at me.

The die was cast; we both knew it. This was my life now. You, Tara and your family, for as long as they chose to stay with us. A family that would defend me to the death, though we could not even speak to one another.

I had thought to spin out my life in West Coast drawing rooms and the society pages, yet here I was, a player on a different stage in the theatre of a new America. I looked back towards the mountains and for the first time in my life felt a profound sense of belonging.

'Then I may think about it,' I said at last.

You hid a smile and lifted a hand to the back of your neck, as if you had been about to reach out to me and stopped yourself. Then you froze. I followed your gaze, but couldn't see what you were looking at. Lucky had though, his far-seeing eyes like slits. You spoke without looking at each other. Rose turned her grey, black-freckled mare to see too.

'See that, English?'

'No, I don't see anything. Buffalo?'

'Closer than the buffalo. He's here.'

There was wonder in your voice. Then I saw him.

It was a horse. *The* horse. He was beautiful: astonishingly white, heavy with muscle, a deeply crested neck, broad chest and fine conformation. His mane and tail were long, blowing in the breeze, forelock covering one eye. Before you I had seen all horses as the same, simply a means to an end. Now I knew them for themselves: their strengths, weaknesses, and how they could show us the best of who we are. Only the wind moved on the plain as we, all five of us, watched him.

The horse of a lifetime.

You mounted up and your hand went to the coil of rope on your saddlehorn. 'Big riding, Em. Be ready.'

I sat deeper into the saddle and waited, Tara tense beneath me. You and Lucky were talking, voices low, but not looking away from the horse. Rose was unfastening a rope from behind her saddle, slinging the loops around her neck.

'Do you want Tara?'

'No, this kid's faster on the flat even if he is a little jumpy. And this'll be all about the running.' I could see, already, that you were anticipating the chase. You licked your lip, catching it in your teeth as your chest settled on a deep breath.

We set out, slow and easy at first, spreading out across the plain, trying to get as close as possible. The white horse wasn't spooky though, and when the band split – me with you, Lucky and Rose to east and west – he carried on grazing, mane flowing over his neck with each snatch at the grass. You ignored me, in the main, your focus with the stallion, but at last, when we were no more than forty yards away, you spoke.

'Em, when we go, we go. If you lose us don't fret none, I'll be back. OK?'

'OK.' I nodded, threading my reins.

'And don't tire Tara out trying to chase us. I don't want

247

her leg in some prairie dog hole and your necks broke for the sake of it.'

'Yes.'

You lifted the rope from your saddlehorn and began to feed it out. Lucky was watching you, waiting for the signal. Rose was letting out her rope too. You unlooped the canteen and passed it to me. I put it over my shoulder.

The stallion raised his head, wary. He lifted his muzzle into the wind, scenting our approach. He watched, alert, as you and Lucky began to close in on him, Rose at the rear. Suddenly he wheeled and took flight across the plain, heading straight for the buffalo herd. Lucky let out a cry as you all bolted after him. I followed, Tara surging into her skating gallop as we drove the stallion and the herd ahead of us. The sun was hot on my face and the wind blew as I sat deep in the saddle, urging Tara on, reins over her neck. The combination of the herd's presence and my lighter weight meant that we had no trouble keeping up with all of you, and I felt soaring pride as our little mare ran neck and neck with Rose's magnificent grey. She looked across and grinned, all hair and teeth and russet skin, whooping with joy at life.

In the end, it was the stallion's decision to flee into the herd that led to his capture. The buffalo were fast, but not nearly as fast as we, and their delay in reacting meant he was hampered considerably, although the dust storm they created as they began to stampede was quick to blight the air. Lucky rode him off, steering him directly into your path. There was a moment when I feared, desperately, that he would barge

248

your red horse, throwing all your weight on to your weaker leg. But it didn't happen and then your noose was dropping over his head in the cloud of dust raised by the buffalo.

Rose rode in from the other side, rope falling over the stallion's crested neck. For a few seconds, I lost sight of you all, the dust was so thick. I reined Tara to a quick halt, coughing. We sat, immobile, in the fog. A buffalo calf cried out for his mother and she lowed in return. Tara and I moved away from the sound, not wanting to come between them. We shifted out of the dust, back the way we'd come. Cresting a small rise, we sat and waited, watching for you. It was only a few minutes before you appeared, leading the white stallion like a pony.

Your face was filthy and you were sweating, your shirt sticking to you in patches. Rose appeared, sneezing roundly, and then Lucky, his face as deadpan as ever but dust clinging to the sweat and clay on his chest. Tara and I fell in with you. Your eyes never left the white horse as we headed back across the plain. You'd given him plenty of rope, but he did not seem to be averse to being led. I could see you were frowning.

'What's the matter?'

'Ain't supposed to be this easy is what's the matter. This horse, supposedly uncatchable, is acting like he wanted to be caught.'

We walked on steadily. 'But how is that a bad thing?'

You shrugged, still worried. 'Don't know. Maybe he's sick or something.'

The horse followed on behind us all day, as we rode

southeast. Ultimately we were heading for our mountain, but it would take us time to get there, perhaps as long as four days. You were confident the scout was done.

'Told you, ain't nothing coming through there.' I could hear the satisfaction in your voice.

That night we struck camp by a shallow creek threading its way through the plain and ate a spare meal of pemmican and water. You had spent an hour or so getting close to the stallion, purely so you could restrain him by tying him to a tree. Yet the white horse remained perfectly still. Finally you stood at his head, speaking to him but not touching. His ears flicked backwards and forwards alternately, listening. Tara edged her way closer to him as she cropped the grass content-edly, and by the time we were preparing to bed down, they were standing together, blowing into each other's noses.

You lay down next to me at the edge of the fire. Rose was nowhere to be seen, but Lucky and Clear Water were follow-ing our lead. Propping your head on your hand, you watched the stallion and Tara.

'Your horse is a flirt, know that?'

I craned my neck on the blanket to see them. 'A flirt?'

'She sure is. Give it another day, she'll have him eating out of her hand.'

We watched them in silence as Tara turned abruptly and walked off, leaving the stallion unable to follow. You shook your head, settling down. 'Women.'

I elbowed you in the stomach but we were so close together in the bedroll there was no force behind it. You huffed a laugh.

'Tara's my horse now?' I asked, settling my head on her blanket.

'Guess so, English. Don't girlfriends gang together?' You said, drowsy, laying your hand against my face. Just for a second, your fingers touched my mouth before they moved to rest on the blanket.

'I don't know,' I said some minutes later when I could breathe again, but you were already asleep.

It took us exactly four days to reach home, by which time I was considerably tougher, although very bruised and sore. It seemed to mean little to me now when it rained occasionally as we crossed the plain, or at night when we lay beneath our large oilcloth sheet, talking in the dark as the raindrops bounced and popped from the material above us, tented by the saddles. I no longer felt the cold, nor minded sleeping on the ground.

As we broke from the forest and the cabin appeared high on the mountainside, my heart lifted. It was mid-afternoon and the sun was full on the meadow, lighting up the shingle roof and the wild flowers. We rode up to it and you led the stallion into the corral. Rose and Lucky put the rails in place behind you, almost six feet high, then you ducked out between them with your peculiar slight of shifting your weight so your right leg didn't buckle.

I untacked Tara at the porch rail, rubbing her down and thanking her for her service. As I slipped her bridle, she blew at me, then moved off towards the corral and the stallion.

Dropping the saddle over the rail, I hung up her bridle and eyed the washtub. It had never looked so inviting, yet I couldn't take advantage of it with your family so close by. Clear Water was already making camp near the stream, just down from the cabin, setting up a fire pit and moving purposefully from one task to another. Lucky was sitting, cross-legged, looking at the view and smoking. Rose was watering the horses and preparing to tether them where they could rest and graze. You were already inside the house, getting the stove and the fire lit. Coming on to the porch, you saw me looking at the washtub.

'Want to take a bath?'

'More than *anything*,' I said, like a tired child. 'But how can I with everyone here?'

You studied me for a few seconds. Disappearing inside, you returned with the quilt from the bed. Shifting Tara's saddle, you draped it over the porch rail. You put her saddle blanket over the side rail, effectively creating a screened area. Filling the tub, you studied me over your shoulder.

'Never say I do nothing for you.'

'Have I ever said that?' I asked honestly, shoulders slumping.

You straightened up, shaking off your hand. 'Guess not.'

Going inside, I stripped and wrapped myself in a towel, taking the soap and the bottle of hair wash. I ached to be clean. On the porch I crouched behind my screen, yanking the lace from my braid and shaking out the thick, dirty hanks.

I clambered into the tub, sat down with a bump and threw water on my face. It was wonderfully cold and refreshing. I realized I'd forgotten the jug. I hesitated.

'Nate?'

'Yep?' you called from somewhere behind the cabin, near the woodpile.

'I forgot the jug.'

There was a pause. 'What use are you?'

I smiled against my bruise-spattered knees. 'No use at all.'

You appeared on the step half a minute later, a piece of cut wood in either hand. I sat in the tub, hugging my shins. You shook your head, laughing. Returning with the jug, you made as if to pass it to me, then pulled it out of my reach as I was about to thank you. You put your free hand to your ear.

'What did you say? I didn't hear . . .' You were teasing.

'I said thank you!'

'You did? Maybe I'm going deaf.'

I looked at you primly. 'Maybe you are.'

Grinning, you stooped, filled the jug in the tub by my legs and tipped it straight over my head. I shrieked with surprise and laughter.

'Nate!' I tried to wipe my face and maintain my modesty: it wasn't easy.

You dropped to your knees and rubbed my head with soap from the bottle, rough and gentle at the same time. 'Do I have to do everything for you, English?' you teased, laughing.

'No!' I spluttered.

Your hands stilled instantly. 'You don't like this?'

'No. No, I—' I had said something wrong.

You knelt in front of me and rested your wrists on the edge of the tub, watching for a long time. I sat in your captivating pale gaze, blinking as water trickled into my eyes. Reaching up, you hesitated before running the backs of your fingers over the line of my collarbone to my shoulder and down my arm. My breath snatched and I sat back, away from you, hands crossed over my chest.

You crouched back on your heels, very slowly. 'Emily, you need to work out what you like and what you don't.' Pushing to your feet, you dropped down from the porch steps and went to talk to the others.

I sat in the chill water, my hair a sodden sheet, eyes stinging with soap. And my fingertips tracing the path of yours across my skin.

I barely saw you for the rest of the day, busy in our homecoming chores as we were, and that night I felt awkward. We ate with the others but I wasn't hungry and didn't eat much of the rabbit Lucky had snared. You rarely looked at me and you all spoke in your scratchy talk. Getting to my feet, I went back to the cabin. Tara was by the corral again, flirting you said, so I ignored her, annoyed. Climbing into the armchair, I wrapped myself in the quilted coverlet and watched the fire as I gnawed on your words. Yet I was too exhausted to do so for long and soon I was fast asleep.

I woke, at dawn, in our bed, still swaddled in the coverlet, spine against your chest where the pigeon-feather mattress pushed us together in the centre. One of your arms was beneath my neck, hand slack on the sheet in front of my face, and now and then one of your fingers twitched in your sleep. The other arm was around my ribs. It felt wrong without the cramped bedroll; we weren't on the plain any more. Yet it was so perfectly warm and comfortable after our weeks on the hard earth, my body was unwilling to move. I lay for a long time, reassured by the steady movement of your chest as you breathed, though agitated by it at the same time. But I didn't know why. Full of confusion, I pushed your arm away as if it were burning me, and got to my feet.

'You all right?' you asked, no sleep in your voice.

No, I wasn't all right at all. I opened my mouth to speak, but the truth stuck in my throat. 'Perfectly, thank you.' I roused the embers of the stove, then fetched some water to boil.

You were soon up and out, first to the stream, then to the corral. I washed and dressed and walked down to where you stood, bad foot on the rail and a blade of grass in the corner of your mouth. You were watching the white horse.

I settled my hands on a rail, unsure of my reception. 'What's going to happen with him?'

It was a long time before you replied, but when you did your tone was friendly. 'Well . . . well, English. It's like this. It'd be a damnable shame to back a horse like that one there. He ain't never gonna be no riding animal. I like the horses I break to lie down and play dead if I ask them to, and he ain't ever gonna be that biddable. Wouldn't want him to be.

Though he's making a pretty good pretence of it now.'

'He's pretending?'

You were bemused. 'I ain't real sure, Emily. I mean, entires can be real placid around a mare, but . . .'

'Entire what, please?'

You put the back of your hand to your cheekbone and rubbed it down your jaw, looking away. I realize now, of course, that it was in a sterling effort not to laugh.

The silence confused me. 'So what will you do with him?'

'My meaning was, he's a breeder. So, I'm thinking, we should put him to a mare.'

Aware of my shameful ignorance, I said nothing.

'Problem is, which one? Rose's grey is one hell of an animal, but she's been in season just a few weeks ago. And Rose ain't one to stick in a place for that to come around again and, besides, she ain't got no time for a birthing mare nohow. And I ain't kept track of what Tara's up to, when it's just the two of us up here.'

As far as I was concerned, your words were nonsense. I had no idea.

You slapped the rail. 'Problems for another day.' Your knuckle touched my chin so briefly I half started and half wondered if it had happened as you turned and walked away to talk to the others, who were stirring in their camp by the stream.

The following days passed quickly. At night I pretended to be asleep when you turned in. And we slept in our bed as we had on the plain: companionably enough. Other than that, you didn't touch me again.

I worked hard to restore the cabin to order, Clear Water ordered her camp by the stream and you, Lucky and Rose spent interminable hours with the horses. Often, you all rode out together to find food. Once, you brought back the carcass of a deer, which kept us going for some time. Apparently Rose had shot it with her bow from the saddle. In your absence, Clear Water and I had been surprised by a gigantic, cream-coloured animal in the meadow, looking like a cross between a colossal goat and a sheep. It grazed for a few hours, then moved off. When I mentioned it to you, you laughed.

'You mean we rode five miles for a deer when we could-a had a mountain goat just here?'

'Is that what it was?'

You nodded, still laughing to yourself as you hung up the red horse's bridle, while below us in the meadow, Clear Water butchered the deer.

'I've never seen a goat that big. It was the size of a small buffalo!'

'Impressive, ain't they? They're coming down from the heights for breeding season.' You took the cup of tea I was holding out and we sat on the steps and watched the others.

'Do you have a headache?'

You looked at me. 'Why?'

'The way you keep almost closing your eyes.'

'It's just the weather changing. Always get it when there's a big storm coming.'

Hesitating, I bit my lip. 'Mama asks me to rub her temples when she has the headache. She says I have magic hands. I . . . I could try, if you'd like.'

'Be my guest.'

I knelt behind you, sitting on my feet. You shifted on to the bottom step obligingly. I smoothed your untidy hair out of the way, surprised by how soft it was. It brushed your shoulders and was streaked with lighter shades from your time outside, and even glints of auburn here and there. I pressed on your temples, gentle at first, then with more pressure. Mama said it was good to build up to it. After some minutes, the tension leaked from your shoulders.

'I wasn't sure I could ever have something in common with your momma, English, but she's right. You do have magic hands.'

I smiled, threading my fingers into your hair and pulling in sections, as Mama had taught me. You groaned.

'You have more in common with Papa, I think,' I said.

'I do?'

'Yes. He fought in a war too. In Crimea. That's why he went into the diplomatic service, to try and prevent wars before they happen, so that men's lives would be saved. Papa speaks very calmly, but once I heard him say at a dinner that he would spend his life in service gladly if it meant one more boy didn't freeze to death in one more godforsaken foxhole on one more godforsaken battleground.'

'Perhaps your daddy ain't as bad as I've had him painted,' you said after a while. 'Do you miss them?'

I played with your hair, enjoying its glossy softness. 'Sometimes,' I said, as honestly as I could. 'I wouldn't have seen them again after the wedding, not for years anyway, so I think I had accustomed myself to that.' I drifted in thought, and saw Clear Water standing by her smoking campfire, watching us. You noticed too. Reaching up, you took my hand and kissed the palm.

'Thank you to your magic fingers, English. Much better now.' Pushing yourself off the step you went to see the white horse, Tara still lingering by the railings.

Later that afternoon, I visited Clear Water. She had some white deerskin in her lap as I approached and appeared to be sewing, but when she saw me she put it away in a hurry. I halted, not wanting to intrude, but she got up, smiling, then pointed to the cabin. I looked at her questioningly, then realized – she had never been inside.

'Oh, do come!' I said at once, starting up the hill.

On the porch she hesitated, peering inside the open door.

I beckoned. 'Come in, please.'

She took a step inside, staring around her. The stove and our cupboards were examined thoroughly. She opened everything, including the chest at the bottom of the bed, looking inside. I stifled a laugh at her impolite curiosity. When everything had been investigated to her satisfaction, she turned to me and nodded in approval. Then she went back down the meadow to her fireside, and carried on with whatever she had been doing. I watched her go and wished I knew how to talk to her for I felt in my heart we could have been true friends, and I had never had a friend.

The afternoon grew humid as it wore on. I washed some clothes in the tub, including two of your shirts. Before I put them in the water I held them to my face, inhaling sweat, horse and pine, blushing when I saw Lucky ducking out of the corral, his eyes on me. Looking back, it must have been obvious to everyone that I was bewitched by you. I snatched the shirts from my face and dunked them in the tub. Lucky straightened up slowly and watched me for a few moments, before striding back down the meadow.

I was hanging the shirts to dry when you and Rose returned from a brief hunting trip. You had some sort of dead fowl hanging from your saddlehorn, head bouncing limply. I had spied two eggs from the roaming hens whilst hanging up the washing and brought them to show you, warm in my hands, as you untacked the red horse.

'Good work.' You glanced up at the sky. 'If this weather holds we'll eat well tonight.' Unstringing the fowl, you went to give it and the eggs to Clear Water.

I watched as she took it with a smile and immediately went to work on it. Lucky sat, smoking. When you came back, I was standing on the porch.

'Clear Water is always working, and Lucky and Rose are always sitting and smoking. Why?'

You glanced back at them over your shoulder and shrugged. 'Just the way it is with Indians.'

'It's not very fair on Clear Water.'

'Maybe not. But she ain't riding into battle nor hunting

neither, so I guess it evens out.'

My voice was doubtful. 'But what will happen when Rose gets a husband? They can't both sit and smoke or they'll starve.'

You laughed.

'What's so funny?' I asked, bemused.

But you only gave me a peculiar look and put a cigarette in the corner of your mouth, striking a match on the porch rail.

'That is a truly filthy habit.'

You sighed, shaking out the match and putting the cigarette behind your ear. 'They think I shouldn't do no domestic stuff on account-a having you now.'

'You haven't been, I've been doing it.'

You gave me a cocksure grin and a wink. 'Exactly.'

'Oh,' I said, in realization.

'They'll move off pretty soon. Rose is already restless. Thought I'd pick up any slack on the chores when they'd gone, but there don't seem to be none. You're becoming a real frontierswoman, English.' You were still laughing.

I shook my head at you as sternly as I could, and went inside.

As the sun set over the western reaches of the lake, I saw Clear Water had banked up the campfire and the flames were much higher than usual. Rose lay on her back, watching the clouds gathering in the sky and smoking, cigarette hanging loosely from her lips, hands behind her head. You were in the cabin stitching together a new bridle from all the scrap pieces of harness, working the thick needle through the ready-made holes in the stiff leather with an occasional curse. I saw the map on the corner of the kitchen table, sitting beneath the steel bit.

'When will you go to Fort Shaw to tell them what you've found?'

You shrugged. 'Meard is based in Helena, may have to go there if he ain't in camp.'

I took a deep breath. 'So how long will you be gone?'

The needle stilled. You were looking at me, pale eyes intent. Trying to work out why I wasn't asking you to take me with you. 'Maybe a week, maybe more.'

Nodding, I got up and tidied the map away into the chest.

'Want me to ask them to stay while I'm gone? So you ain't alone?'

I returned to the table, relieved. 'Yes, please. That would be very kind if they would.'

Rising, you moved to stand in front of me and put the tip of one finger beneath my chin, your beautiful eyes searching mine. 'You ain't gonna ask me to take you back?'

I shook my head.

You stooped and, after a slight check, pressed your lips to mine in the most gentle of kisses. We hesitated. Your cool hair fell against my cheek. And against the backs of my fingers as I lifted them to your face. You kissed me again, so lightly our lips barely touched. I should have been doing something, or you should, but I didn't know what. I stood on my toes, pressing my mouth to yours, clumsy and uncertain. You pulled away, and when I opened my eyes I could see you were smiling.

You were laughing at me. Again. Shame flooded my chest. I snatched my hand back and put my head down, turning away. I wanted to cry in humiliation, at everything I didn't know. You caught my wrist.

'Emily, I wasn't—'

A shadow fell across us from the open doorway. It was Rose, watching and laughing her silent laugh.

I wrenched my wrist away and walked into the bedroom, hurt and flustered. I heard you leave with her, your voice talking over hers, irritated, as she very clearly teased you about what she'd witnessed.

Down in the meadow, the others were planning what looked like a feast of fireweed, wild flowers, stewed venison and the fowl, roasted. I made a large loaf of bread to keep myself occupied, unable to rid myself of the feel of your lips on mine. Twice I had to splash cold water on my face and wrists to calm myself. What did it mean? What if you touched me like that again? What if you touched me as Lucky touched Clear Water? At that thought, strange, tingling waves flooded my skin.

Did you *want* to touch me like that? The thought stopped me as I folded the stove cloth, breath catching. Did *I* want you to?

Intolerably confused, I wished for the hundredth time that there was someone I could ask.

The cloud-bruised sky was darkening by the time the food

was ready, my stomach growling at the smells drifting up to the cabin from the campfire. Pulling my bread from the stove's pocket oven, I turned it out and looked at it. Perhaps I could make an honest living in a bakery after all. I wrapped it in a cloth and went out to where you and the others were already gathered. I offered the bread to Clear Water and she took it graciously, smiling between me and you. I couldn't look at you as I sat down next to where you perched on a rock, the booted ankle of your bad leg hooked behind the good one, arms folded and shoulders hunched, looking down.

Clear Water distributed the food and we shared a delicious plateful as the others sat on the ground. The stew was perfectly savoury and I wished I were the cook Clear Water was. The conversation around the fire was light, and Lucky was clearly recounting a story, with interjections from Rose.

'He's telling me a story about some battle with the Pikuni. Gotta big grudge going on with them. Rose thinks he's over-doing it. Just called him a blowhard.'

We had barely looked at each other, despite our proximity. You were awkward and ill at ease, unlike your usual calm self. Perhaps your head was aching again. The pressure in the air was almost unbearable, and the wind was picking up. When the storm broke, we'd have to repair to the cabin. Then there would be no avoiding what had happened. Perhaps you would kiss me again, if I could make it clear I wouldn't mind. But how? I saw you watching me, your eyes dark for once, in the firelight.

When we had finished eating, everyone became silent. Clear Water got up and went to her packs. With some small ceremony, she drew out a piece of folded cloth and presented it to me. I took it in both hands cautiously. Holding it up, folds falling, I saw it was a white deerskin tunic-dress covered on the top half with blue beads and elk teeth, stitched in neat chevron patterns. It was the shirt she had put away so hurriedly when I had surprised her that afternoon. With it was a pair of white deerskin leggings, the blue bead pattern echoed down the outside seams.

Clear Water was talking to me. You cleared your throat. Rose was watching us, waiting for something. Clear Water gestured to you and then me, urging you to translate for her.

You took a breath. 'It's for you.'

'It's so beautiful, thank you,' I said sincerely, looking up at her. 'Please tell her how beautiful it is,' I asked you.

Your shoulders became even more hunched as you stared resolutely down the mountain, saying nothing. Rose smirked.

'What's the matter?' I asked you, bewildered.

You gritted your teeth, not looking at me, and took a long time to answer. 'It's a marriage outfit.'

I stared at it, then put it down. Thunder rumbled above the lake. Clear Water looked terribly disappointed.

'It's so very kind, but did you explain that I'm not getting married now?'

My stupidity is obvious, of course, and with hindsight I can scarcely believe I put us all through such a pantomime. Your jaw was quilted with tiny muscles as you clenched your teeth hard enough to break them. Rose said something and you snapped at her. She made a rude hand gesture and Lucky admonished her with a single word, his eyes fixed on you.

I stared at them, looking from face to face. I was anxious because I didn't understand and I truly didn't want to offend anyone. Papa had taught me to say nothing in such situations at the embassy parties. A sheet of lightning lit us all up for a second, and stilled the swirling confusion in my brain.

'Oh,' I said.

'Yeah, oh,' you said.

I looked at the foods laid out, so beautifully, close to us, and at the plentiful, expensively salted roasted meat and stew, more food than I had seen the Indians make for one occasion. Unless it was a very special occasion. I stood, turning on you. There was an almighty clap of thunder and I raised my voice.

'I am at my own wedding and you didn't even tell me? Or ask me? Or *anything*?'

You stood, looking helpless. 'I didn't know they were planning it! They wanted to do it for us as a surprise. I just thought we'd let them celebrate and it would be a party. That's all. It doesn't have to mean anything.'

'How can you say that?' I gestured to the food, to the clothes. 'Look at all the effort Clear Water has gone to!' The wind gusted, chill, into my face, bringing with it the first drop of rain but I was too upset to care.

You were trying to find words to placate me, then Lucky spoke, a long string of harsh consonants. You looked as if someone had struck you. Even Rose looked abashed, fiddling with the tie on her knee-high boot. Clear Water was close to tears.

'What did he say?' I asked over the rising wind.

Silence.

'What did he *say*?'

There was a long pause before you replied, but you didn't look at me. 'He wants to know why you won't be my wife. He wants you to tell him, to his face, if it's because I'm a cripple, and you think I won't be able to provide for you.'

I stared at you, astonished. Your infirmity meant less than nothing to me. I was so surprised at Lucky's logic that I couldn't speak, and blinked stupidly. Why would they think that?

Rain began to fall around us in earnest. Wounded, Clear Water darted forward and gathered up the dress and leggings, wrapping them back up in their oilcloth. Lucky was staring at me, his eyes like granite. Rose gave a hard, cynical laugh. I felt small and friendless.

'Fuck this,' you said suddenly. The worst of all your bad words.

'Nate!'

'Fuck this and fuck you,' you muttered, walking away as quickly as you could.

I turned to Lucky and shook my head furiously, eyes stinging with tears as the rain soaked through my shirt. He watched me through his narrow eyes, face unreadable in the firelight. I bolted after you, bare feet slipping on the wet grass.

'Nate! Wait! I would never—'

You spun and I cannoned into you, your hands already in my hair, holding me still as your mouth stopped my apology, thunder cracking all around us. You were so angry I could taste it as you kissed and kissed me, all your gentle caution gone. I stood, passive in your grip, hoping you would understand it was the only way I had of trying to say I was so very sorry for my stupidity. Tolerance, the pamphlet had said. Now, I realize of course, that such passivity was the very worst thing I could have done; you needed reassurance that Lucky was wrong, not mere tolerance. The rain fell hard, soaking our hair and clothes.

You let me go abruptly, as if you could not bear me. We stared at each other.

'Just go away, Emily.'

You pushed me in the chest, harder than you perhaps meant to, and I stepped back to keep my balance, raising my hands. I took a breath to speak but you turned and walked away into the rain-soaked dark without looking back. I stared after you, mouth bruised, face scraped by your stubble, scalp stinging from your fingers in my hair.

And then I knew: I had never been the captive.

CHAPTER 14

The night passed awkwardly. Hope swaddled herself in the blanket and the fragile quilt, leaving the other blanket and the buffalo hide for Cal. She'd pretended to be asleep when he'd come into the cabin but perhaps the stress of their situation had tired her, because she slept soundly until sunup. When she woke, the door was open and Cal was sitting outside with Buddy, scratching the dog's ears.

She came out, still wrapped in the blanket against the morning chill.

Cal glanced up at her. 'You OK?'

She shrugged.

'I'll go and try and find us something to eat. Didn't want you to think I'd abandoned you.' He got to his feet and shouldered the rifle. 'Stick around the cabin, OK?'

She nodded and watched him go, Buddy at his heels. It

was going to be another beautiful day. After attending to Nature she huddled back up in the quilt, the diary in her lap. She examined it as an object, the worn leather that spoke of years of handling. The pages were so fine, the writing closely packed. In places, the ink changed slightly, indicating a break. She turned to where she had left off.

So deep in thought was she that she didn't hear Cal and Buddy return sometime later. She was staring down the mountain at the dozens of shades of blue and green radiating from the lake and trees when he arrived at the side railing by the tub, surprising her. In his hands was a selection of plants and greenery.

'Well, we're a little heavy on the salad,' he said, 'but I guess you're used to that.' He came to the front steps. 'Reading again?'

She didn't look at him. 'The satchel, the beaded one we used for the fish, it's in here. I think.' She lifted the diary. 'A possibles bag?'

He nodded. 'That's what they're called. They come in different sizes for travelling, or for hanging up inside. Anything else?'

'There are hunters massacring the buffalo on the plains. But Nate's Indian family have turned up.'

'Yeah? What are they like?'

'A half-brother he calls Lucky but is really Little Elk, his half-sister Rose, who sounds totally insane, but good insane, and Lucky's wife, Clear Water. Rose is furious about the massacre and wants to go to a tribe called the Blackfoot to ask them for help to stop the hunting.'

Cal hesitated, then climbed the steps and sat down next to her. 'The Blackfoot? They're the tribe that used to be north of here. There's still a pretty big rez. And the buffalo massacre was real.'

Buddy slumped across Hope's feet.

'It's so sad.'

He nodded, rubbing the dog's head. 'Yeah. You know they killed something like twenty-five million of them in less than twenty years?'

'But *why*?' Curiosity was overcoming her reserve.

'Three main reasons. First, the hides were in demand back East; and second, they were there, in such numbers it probably seemed like they could never push them to the edge of extinction; and third, Rose is right, the government wanted to drive them, the Indians, off the plains and on to the reservations. Montana was a new state, only three years old in 1867. Country was getting divided up, settled. Government didn't want nomadic tribes.' He snorted. 'But unregulated hunting of millions of animals to the brink of extinction, hell, that's *fine*.'

'It's rubbish,' Hope said inadequately.

He glanced across at her. 'Here we are and I'm running on about environmental issues.'

'Tell me, I'd like to hear.'

So they sat by the fire pit and prepared a scanty breakfast of cold, smoky trout and some flowers, and Cal told Hope about the near-extinction of the American Plains bison. Buddy disappeared and arrived back on the porch with

271

bloody chops and some sort of fur clinging to his snout. Hope grimaced and shoved him away when he wanted to lick her face. 'Buddy, gross.'

'Our ranch was one of the original five to become a sanctuary for the buffalo. In 1871, there were less than seven hundred head left in the wild. Ten years later, it was less than a hundred. We divided them up and bred between the ranches until the thirties, when there was enough to start putting back into the wild. There's about four thousand buffalo in Yellowstone now.' There was an unmistakable note of pride in Cal's voice.

Hope crossed her legs beneath her. 'That's amazing.'

'Yeah. So many others didn't make it though. The Passenger pigeons Emily saw from the train? Went from billions to just one, called Martha. Died in captivity in 1914. River otters, nearly lost them too, to the fur trappers.' He shook his head. 'Ignorance is all it is. Ignorance and greed.'

She looked at the mountain range and the lake, at its vast beauty, teeming with life despite its savageness. 'I kind of see now why you love this place so much.'

He glanced across at her. 'Only kind of?'

She ducked her head. 'I see. Now.'

Elbowing her gently, he looked over at her. 'Friends?'

She nodded. 'Friends.'

He stood and held out his hand. 'Then let's take a walk.'

Hope put her fingers in his, letting him pull her to her feet, leaving the diary on the boards as they passed the porch. He swung their hands. Buddy paced after them. They came to the log shelter leaning brokenly against the cabin's back wall.

'Great. Look at that!' He picked up what looked like a net cage, the green nylon webbing clinging to a rusted wire frame. 'We might be able to eat something good today after all.'

'What is it?'

'Crawfish cage. Pops probably brought it up here – I remember catching crawfish with him. It'll do the fishing for us. Easy one-pot supper.'

Cal showed Hope how to set the trap in the stream, anchoring it firmly and placing it to face upstream.

'See? This way they get washed in and can't get back out.'

They continued exploring the area around the cabin. Hope surveyed the landscape. 'It must have been really nice here, with chickens and everything working.'

'The people who built it sure knew what they were doing.' He ruffed up the fur on Buddy's neck.

'I wish we knew who they were and what happened to them. I mean, why did they leave here after putting so much effort into it?'

Cal shrugged. 'Like thousands of other frontier people, I guess, it just didn't work out and they moved on.'

'Maybe they got sick.'

'Maybe. Or maybe they just got lonely, like Nate said.'

'He talks about loneliness like it's a disease.'

'Yeah. I've heard old-timers talk about it like that. Apparently it happened a lot in the Depression, especially in remote places.'

Buddy sunbathed in front of them.

'What do you want from your life, Hope?' Cal asked after a while.

She thought, and shrugged. 'Probably the same as you.'

'You want to breed buffalo and rare cattle?' He raised an eyebrow. 'And the very finest American horses?'

'That's it?' she teased. 'That's *all* you want to do?'

He took a breath. 'Be happy?'

Hope smiled. 'Yeah, being happy would be nice.'

'So . . . what will make you happy?'

Hugging her elbows in tight, Hope pressed her fingers to her lips. 'I want to write books.' She stretched out her arms as wide as she could. 'Tell stories, big ones, that stay with people.' She stopped, embarrassed, and hugged herself again. Wrists on his thighs, he watched her but said nothing.

'You're not going to tell me it's a stupid thing to want? That it won't work out and I should have a *real* plan instead?'

'Why would I? But you gotta tell your mom, not let her make your plans for you.'

Hope sighed. 'I'm not brave enough.'

He squinted into the sunshine. 'Yeah, you are. Just hard to find the words sometimes.'

When she tucked her hair behind her ears, pulling her knees up, he kept his eyes on her, even though she was too shy to look at him. 'We're going to stay in touch, aren't we? After this.' She played with the laces on her boots, poking the tips into the lappet eyes.

'I think we probably are, yes,' he said at last.

Unable to read his tone, Hope shrugged. 'Yeah, that's right,

Crow. Play it cool, I would. We've only known each other less than a week and you've nearly killed me already, we're lost in the wilderness and we're almost starving to death. Now is definitely the time to be cool.'

'Don't exaggerate,' he said severely. 'We are *not* starving.'

Hope pushed him, then dodged off the rock as he grabbed for her and broke into a run. She was already shrieking with laughter before he caught her around the waist and swung her in a circle.

Seconds later she was breathless. 'Stop! Stop!'

They collapsed on the ground in front of the cabin, winded, Cal breaking her fall. She lay on him, laughing, hair hanging in curtains around them. His eyes searched hers and his hands tightened slightly on her ribs.

Hope chickened out. 'I . . . I should . . .' She pushed herself up quickly. 'Natural break.'

Cal said nothing, just put his hands behind his head and closed his eyes. Buddy padded after Hope. *Great, because I need an audience.*

She returned less than a minute later and halted by the cabin, fear clenching her gut. Cal lay, frozen on the grass. Scrabbling at the leftover breakfast fish in the fire pit was the biggest bear ever. Hope's knees weakened. Buddy's hackles rose and he began to growl.

Cal spoke, voice clear but quiet. 'It's OK, he's just hungry. He's been in hibernation. Look, the pads of his paws are shedding and he's disoriented. Don't panic. You need to get my rifle from the porch.'

Hope grabbed the side rail and climbed under it, stepping through the broken washtub. She picked up the rifle where it lay against the planks.

'Got it.'

'I'm going to try and get back to you without attracting his attention. Everything's going to be fine, but I want you to look at the gun and slip the safety. The small catch by—'

'Got it.' Hope clicked it with trembling fingers. He pushed up on his elbows a little more and edged backwards.

'Good. Now hold it tight by your side and point it towards him, finger on the trigger. Don't put it near your shoulder – if you have to fire the recoil will hurt you. Pull the trigger slowly until it tenses.'

Hope did as she was told. The bear was shoving the fish scraps into its mouth clumsily. Its coat was patchy dark and light and it seemed unfocused. Suddenly Buddy paced forwards, shoulders dropped and hackles high.

'Buddy, you stay back. Now, damn you.' Cal tried to pull his feet beneath him. The action alerted the bear. It dropped to all fours and began to lumber towards Cal, covering the ground at astonishing speed.

'RUN!' Hope yelled, terrified.

Cal scrambled backwards. The bear charged. Buddy launched himself at the massive animal, tearing at its face. The bear swiped the puppy away and Buddy hit the ground with a yelp. There was a huge crack as Hope pulled the trigger, the sound rebounding across the mountain, the single shot sounding like a dozen. The bear bellowed and sheared off, towards the stream. It bounded through it, water splashing, and disappeared into the forest behind.

Hope almost dropped the gun in shock, running with Cal to where Buddy lay, limp, on his side.

'No!' Cal's voice was broken. He skidded to his knees in the grass and dirt. 'Oh no.'

Hope knelt next to him, putting the rifle down. Buddy's flank was raked with blood. The puppy's breathing was shallow, thin ribs pumping with the effort to stay alive.

'What can we do?' Hope held his head.

Cal's expression was raw. 'Nothing.'

'Don't say that. He's just a baby.'

'Fucking look at him! I can see his insides!'

Hope stroked his head, kissing his grey and white muzzle. He tried to lick her tears. 'Oh, Buddy.'

They stroked him very carefully. He died a few long minutes later, his last breaths almost inaudible.

Hope was sobbing. 'But the bear was just hungry.'

'Stupid,' Cal chastised himself. 'Idiotic. I've been taught better than leaving evidence of food around. I don't know what I was thinking.' Carefully they gathered Buddy up, cradled against Cal's chest. 'We have to bury him. Somewhere. Leaving him out for the scavengers would be wrong.'

Hope nodded.

'There, if we take him over there by that tree, and get two good stones, I think we could dig a grave deep enough so it won't be disturbed.'

Slowly they walked to a wind-blown and stunted tree at

the edge of the forest. It was a good spot. By the time they were there, Hope had found two flat, sharp stones that could be held in two hands. The earth was hard, but soon they began to make progress, hacking away grass roots and lumps of soil. It took them hours. Buddy was going cold beside them, his limpness stiffening into rigor. Cal refused to look, working as if on a chain gang. Sweat gathered across his forehead and bunched in his shirt beneath the arms.

By midday they had dug a pit almost a metre deep, their hands sore and bleeding. Placing Buddy inside, they began to throw earth on his body with shaky fingers, piling it in until there was just a small mound in front of them. Their hands and knees were filthy. Hope began to cry again.

'Poor Buddy.' She choked on a sob.

He hooked her head against his chest with a brown elbow. 'Hope, please. Don't keep crying. You're breaking my heart. We'll have to be more careful, is all.' He put his lips to her forehead. 'Thank you. You saved my life.'

Hope scrubbed her wet cheek with the cuff of the jersey miserably. 'But not Buddy's. Will the bear come back?' she asked into his shirt.

'Hopefully not, but I'm not sure you got a clean shot and an injured grizzly is dangerous so let's just play it safe, OK? We'll be safe enough if we just stay with the cabin, get the fire going and keep our eyes open.'

They sat on the porch, sometimes talking, sometimes not, watching the fire Cal had reignited in the fire pit. Finally the silence got too much for Hope.

'Should we read some more?'

He eyed it. 'I don't know.'

'Why?'

Cal shrugged, settling his back against the boards of the cabin. 'Forget it. Sure. That would be good.'

Hope read aloud the visit to the Blackfoot camp. 'Pale Eye. It suits him.'

Cal spoke after thinking. 'It would have marked him out. Blue eyes were prized among the Indians at that stage. Grey ones even more so.'

He was sitting, feet apart, back propped against the cabin wall, wrists resting on his knees. She sat next to him, their shoulders touching, and twisted her hair into its messy knot.

'. . . and the last thing I saw, high in the heavens, was a star shooting across the glittering ceiling of the sky.' Hope closed the diary. The leather cover was starting to feel like home beneath her fingers. She rubbed her hand over the front of it and looked out at the view. It was hard to imagine something so different to her London life. And it was beautiful.

Cal let his head drop back against the wooden boards. 'Keep reading. I'm hoping they're wondering where we are about now and I need the distraction.'

Hope returned to the diary, and to the sighting of the white horse on the plain. 'It's the white horse!' she said, breathless. '*Your* white horse! It can't be the same one,' she added quickly and rubbed her nose. 'That would be mental.'

'Yeah. Crazy.' Cal's voice was strange and distant. He stood and picked up the gun. 'I'm going to check that crawfish pot. Can you put some more wood in the stove and some water on to boil?'

Hope watched him go. 'Be careful,' she called after him.

He raised the rifle in acknowledgement, not looking back.

CHAPTER 15

'TO KNOW HOW TO DO EVERYTHING
WHICH CAN PROPERLY COME WITHIN
A WOMAN'S SPHERE OF DUTY OUGHT
TO BE THE AMBITION OF
EVERY FEMALE MIND.'

When you didn't come back that night or the next day, and the red horse was nowhere to be seen, I guessed you had gone to find Mr Meard. You had taken Red and the bay horse with you.

Summer was coming, although the cool breeze came up from the lake in late afternoon, as always. The Indians sat in their camp and I stayed by the cabin. One afternoon, a couple of days after your departure, I was washing some clothes in the tub when I saw Rose standing some yards away, watching me. Her eyes were as unreadable as ever, a trait she shared with her brothers. I carried on working, getting hot and sticky as I scrubbed. When the clothes were finished, I went to hang them, dripping, on the line.

Rose was stripping off upstream, down to her thin loin-cloth and the band of soft deerskin she wore to bind her chest. Clear Water had made one for me on the scout and I must confess it was an excellent arrangement, and far more comfortable than a corset. In the shade of the trees there was a pool deep enough to bathe in, and even to swim a few strokes, you told me. You used it often. I hadn't ventured in so far, for I had never learnt to swim. Rose had a long body and carried little flesh, although she had a distinctly feminine curve to her breast and hip, which was not apparent in her man's garb. Her coppery skin was paler on her body than on her face and arms, but she still glowed in the afternoon sun, turning her face up, burnished like a polished penny. She saw me staring. I felt my cheeks redden and carried on hanging the clothes. I caught myself, and was caught, staring at Rose quite often. She fascinated me: I had read about so many different cultures and never come across anyone like her. In the books I had been given, women were supposed to be tractable and obedient. The idea of Rose doing as she was told was practically laughable.

Suddenly a wet shirt moved aside and she stood in front of me. She was still smiling as she took my hand and tugged me up the hillside to the shade of the trees. She gestured to my clothes, indicating that I take them off. I shook my head, pushing her hand away when it went to the button of my shirt. She retaliated and pushed me, hard. And I fell straight into the cold water! Surfacing, shocked and spluttering, I wiped the water from my face. My braid hung like a wet rope over my shoulder and everything stuck to me. The water came to the bottom of my ribs, cold and raising gooseflesh across my skin. Rose joined me in the stream and splashed at me playfully, laughing at my splutters.

'Stop!' I protested, but couldn't help laughing. 'Rose!'

She threw more water into my face and I splashed back, soaking her. I liked this Rose, full of mischief as ever, but light-hearted. We stood: laughing but wary.

I thought I had become accustomed to unexpected happenings in my new life, but what occurred next was a considerable surprise: Rose placed her hands on my shoulders, leant down and kissed me full on the mouth.

I think, often, of that time, and the many things it taught me. I was no longer the girl who had left Portman Square all those months ago. That girl had vanished and in her place was someone I barely recognized, someone my family would not know at all. The work of simply surviving both on the plain and at the cabin had forged muscle and sinew where none had been before. I could lift Tara's large saddle on and off her now without a thought, and could even tack up your tall red horse without much effort. I had gained a healthy appetite and some weight, despite our spare diet. My hands and forearms were tanned, and I knew my face was similarly tinted by the sun, although I had not seen my reflection since Fort Shaw. My fingers were becoming a little calloused from Tara's reins and the lye soap of our laundry. It was a body that dictated its requirements in ways that were new and surprising to its owner. It *wanted* food, sleep, sunlight and sensation.

In the dark I lay in our bed and longed for you to return.

After a week, I found myself scanning the mountainside

throughout the day. Lucky, sick of Tara's mooning over the white stallion, had put her in the corral with him and they stood together most of the day. Lucky hunted and Clear Water cooked, always offering me food. She still talked on mysteriously about her domestic arrangements and Lucky still pretended I didn't exist, or watched me with his clever, knowing eyes. Rose brought me a small gift each time she drew me from the cabin: a necklace decorated with teeth, a small braided bracelet in bright blues and yellows, and a little knife of my own amongst them.

As the week rolled over, I sensed a change in the little camp down the hill, and one morning there was no smoke from their campfire. Rose pulled me out of our house, crossing the threshold for the first time, long fingers locking around my wrist, and I understood. They were leaving.

Rose's last gift was her possibles bag, looped around my neck. I wanted to ask her to stay, but I didn't know how. And, truthfully, I knew Rose would do as she pleased. She tugged my braid to turn my face up, and scrutinized my features for a long time. Then she pushed the back of her hand to her suddenly bright eye. And shoved me in the shoulder.

Tara and the white horse were in the corral as the Indians packed up their camp. I busied myself with small jobs, not wanting to give in to my growing fear of being left alone. I was finishing the washing-up when Clear Water came to say goodbye. I stood, shaking the wet from my hands, then walked back with her to Lucky, Rose and the horses.

Lucky looked at me for a moment, his dark eyes serious.

Rose was already in the saddle. Clear Water squeezed me tightly, smiling her gentle smile, and handed over the marriage outfit. Then she was up on her little roan pony. Lucky spoke and I heard your name. I shook my head, and gestured around, for I knew no better when you were likely to return than they did. His eyes narrowed, troubled. Then he nodded, once, and vaulted into the saddle. They rode out, not looking back.

You didn't come home that night.

For a time, I faced the idea that you would not come home at all. The days were warm and our mountain sang with life. You finally appeared on the afternoon of the eleventh day.

I was sitting on our porch when your red horse paced into the meadow. Gaining my feet, I walked to the edge of the double step. You vaulted to the ground, graceful as ever, without looking at me. Slinging Red's reins over his head, you led him up to our house. I stood, hands fisted against my thighs. You avoided my eyes until the last possible moment. Red halted.

I ran. Hurtling into your embrace, I slammed up against you, joined from chest to hip, arms around your neck, legs around your waist. You caught me, holding tight, face in my throat.

The door to the cabin was still open as twilight drew in. I lay in our tumbled sheets, stretched on my stomach. You lay next to me, head propped on your hand, fingers ghostly on my spine. There was so much to say it was hard to know where to start, although you seemed content not to talk.

'You went to Helena?'

You made a yes noise, watching your hand as it drew patterns on my skin.

'And saw Mr Meard?'

'Yep.'

'What did you tell him?'

'No railroad is what I told him. Take it through Missoula. Or someplace else. Not here.'

'And nobody mentioned me?'

You lay back, putting a hand behind your head and looking up at the ceiling. 'It was business matters, no social event. Rumour in town is, you all been killed by Indians and the wagon burnt.'

I let my forehead drop into the pillow. 'My parents will have heard by now.'

'Reckon so.'

'I hope they're not too sad. They went to such a lot of trouble arranging the wedding.'

You rolled your eyes at the whitewashed planks above us.

'I was thinking, while you were away,' I said, hesitating.

You met my gaze. 'Thinking what?'

'That I'd never chosen anything for myself before.'

'Meaning, exactly?' Reaching over, you caught the end of my braid and stroked your cheek with it.

I curled my feet up, heels kicking myself as I thought. 'Not food, not clothes, not when I did things, or what I did. Or even who I married. Not anything.' I stretched. Outside, the birds sang their early evening goodnights. 'And you've let me choose.'

As I talked you tugged the lace free and began to unplait my hair, combing your fingers through the heavy locks.

'I can choose when I get up, what I wear, from slim pickings admittedly, but still. To do things or not do them. To save things, to make them better. Go to war.' My voice hitched as you trailed the back of your hand down my body.

You laughed. 'Looks like I found myself a real pocket tyrant.'

I moved closer and you settled me on your chest, stroking my sliding hair back. 'Nate?' I asked uncertainly. 'Have you ever had someone like me?'

Your pale eyes sought mine and you touched my face like something precious. 'Emily, there's never been anyone like you.'

CHAPTER 16

By the time Cal returned to the cabin, Hope's pan of water was coming to a slow boil. He put the crawfish pot in the sink, where they scratched and flopped as they crawled over each other as he banged around in the cupboards, searching for something.

'What are you looking for?'

For a minute he didn't reply, then drew something from the back of the pine cupboard and held it up. It was a half-bottle of bourbon, cap intact. 'Knew there'd be something here if my grampa had anything to do with it. We should drink to Buddy.'

Ten minutes later they were sitting at the table eating the boiled crawfish and toasting Buddy's life from the battered tin cups. Cal cracked a tail in his long fingers, removing the flesh in one piece. He held it out to Hope.

She took it. 'The eighteen-sixties must have been an amazing time to be here, with all this stuff going on.'

He nodded, swallowing his own mouthful before speaking. 'But it was the beginning of the end for the Indian tribes here, with the buffalo massacres and everything. A whole way of life, wiped out in twenty years. And then you had the pioneers.'

'Like Nate.'

'Like Nate.'

'He makes me think of the Puritans.'

'Reckon he comes from that kind of stock originally. With the grandfather sounding like a zealot and everything.'

'It's not so much that. There's a . . . certainty to him . . . I can't think, a sureness, yes, that's what I mean. He just *knows*.'

Cal smiled. 'Yeah, he does. Perhaps because he's pretty much got it mastered. And scouting paid well, precisely because the railroad people didn't know the land and had to trust those who lived on it. Growing up on this terrain, he knows it. He doesn't want to trap, and he couldn't pan for gold, standing in cold water all day long with his leg the way it is. The generations before him, most of them were just clinging on by their fingernails.'

'And I didn't realize that the Indians and the settlers married.'

'Quite a bit, I think. White women were high-status wives and a lot of the railroad and trapping scouts took Indian wives because they already knew the territory. Saved them a lot of time and trouble, and they knew how to live on the move, so they were an asset.'

They piled shells into a dish on the table between them.

'Do you think they'll be looking for us yet?'

'Maybe. They'll know something's up by now.'

Hope sighed. 'Good.' She put another shell into the dish. 'I think I'm full.' Getting up, she washed her hands from the container standing in the sink. Outside, a light rain had begun to fall, even though the sun was still shining. The remnants of the campfire smoked and there were the beginnings of a rainbow shimmering overhead. 'It's so lovely here.'

He glanced over at her for a second, then picked at the surface of the table. 'You really think so?'

She nodded and came back to the table, picking up her tin cup, looking at the dash of alcohol still in the bottom. 'Do you think these are theirs?'

Cal looked at his own. 'Maybe. Strange to think it.'

Hope lifted her cup. 'To Buddy. Again.'

He tapped the bent rim of his mug against hers. 'To Buddy.'

They drank, and returned to the diary. 'More?'

Sitting at the table, they learnt of Nate and Em's Indian wedding party.

'Amazing. And awful,' Hope said in wonder. 'Poor Nate.'

'Yep,' Cal agreed.

'And poor Emily. He should have warned her about it being a wedding.'

Cal shrugged. 'I think he thought he'd probably get away without telling her. Indian weddings weren't such a big deal back then, just a feast and then you moved in together. Not much fuss.'

'Apart from the outfit.'

'Oh, yeah, you were supposed to have one of those.'

She sighed. 'And she's decided she doesn't really want to leave him.'

He nodded. 'It's a real kicker.'

'*Rose* is a shit-kicker.'

Cal barked a laugh. 'She is. But I like her.'

Hope rested her head on her hand. 'Were there lots of women like her?'

He sat back. 'I wouldn't say lots. But the Indians recognize more genders than we do. So someone like Rose wasn't out of the ordinary for them.'

She picked up the diary and read on a few pages. 'I did not see that coming with Rose.'

Cal laughed. 'Nor did I, but I'm not sure anything Rose does would surprise me. I think she's making it up as she goes along. And she's given me an idea.' He jumped up and held out his hands. 'Come on, let's swim.'

'But . . . what about the bear?'

He shrugged. 'I don't know, but I'm not sitting trapped in here. I'll go stir-crazy.'

On the porch Cal stripped quickly, down to his jersey trunks. Hope hesitated, then undressed to her pants and T-shirt as he hopped, pulling off his socks.

'Ready?' He glanced across at her.

She nodded.

'Go!' They ran to the stream in the pattering rain and jumped in with a huge splash. Swimming quickly to keep themselves warm, they scrubbed their sore hands and Hope washed her dirty knees. Cal ducked beneath the surface and then stood up, shaking the water from his hair and gasping. Hope floated on her back for a few seconds, looking up at the sky. High above them, a jet leaked a contrail. She pointed.

'Look at that. All that way up there. And they have no idea we're here, even if they were looking. Like Emily's family.'

Cal boosted himself on to the side of the pool, just leaving his legs in the water. Hope got up to sit next to him, her hair sopping wet and running. The sun was still shining and out of the water it felt warm. The air was damp but it was no longer drizzling. High, fine clouds streaked the blue sky in mares' tails. Light bounced off the lake, making the treeline a dark silhouette. There were more wild flowers than ever in the meadow.

'Cooper?'

'Yes?'

'You're pretty great, you know that, don't you?'

Hope ducked her head. 'You're not so bad yourself.'

'I'm going to take that as . . . awesome, incredible, or something.'

She laughed.

Getting up, he picked up the rifle and held out his hand to her. 'C'mon. Thought we'd take a tip from Nate.'

Hope let him pull her to her feet. 'What's that?'

'You'll see.'

At the edge of the forest, they found a patch of wild mint.

'Oh, yes please,' said Hope. 'That coffee's a bit rank, to be honest.'

A short time later, they sat on the porch, drinking the mint tea and talking. Hope was wearing an old shirt she'd found in the cupboard inside, and her shorts. Cal was back in his jeans and shirt. Their wet things were hanging over the porch rail.

Hope scanned the hillside. Dusk was coming down. 'How much longer do you think?'

He shrugged. 'No idea. I was hoping Dad would have thought of this place pretty quickly. Tomorrow?'

Hope rubbed her arms, nodding. 'I'm not sure how many more crawfish I can boil alive.'

He smiled. He was sitting with his back to the cabin wall, a blanket like a shroud around him, knees bent, watching the fire in front of the little house. Hope fetched the diary and sat down next to him, shoulders touching.

She opened the book. Soon she paused, breathless, as Nate returned to the cabin. 'He's back!'

'Go on then. What happens next?'

Hope read on, her voice faltering slightly. After Em's recounting of Nate's return, Hope closed the book. They both looked down at the meadow.

'They—'

The kiss surprised her, his hand against her hair. Sweet and gentle, it was a gesture to a moment in time, an honouring of the story that had unfolded in the same place one hundred and fifty years before. And it was the perfect first kiss.

A flock of butterflies settled in Hope's stomach. She had always imagined kissing someone properly would be weird and awkward at first. But it wasn't. Her fingers slid into the thick, soft hair at the back of his neck as she leant against him. He covered her hand with his own and broke away slightly, touching his forehead to hers and closing his eyes. Neither of them were breathing steadily.

'Hope, there's something I need to tell you.' He shifted away a little. 'You remember Chief Hart?'

'Yes. Like the Hart in the book. Dan's father?'

'Yes. They have a daughter, Carrie, too.'

Hope said nothing.

'So, anyway. She was sweet on me, always, since we were little kids. Year younger. And the chief's a real piece of work inside the home, if you get my meaning. Carrie's mom's one of those women who walks into a lot of doors. And everyone knows, and no one says anything. And so he just gets away with it. That police officer, the one at the store. She does a lot up on the rez – she's big on issues like men beating up on women, and tried to speak to Carrie once, but even she can't do anything about it. I mean, who's going to prosecute a police chief for domestic violence in a place like this?' He struggled to speak through his teeth, then went on, 'Anyway, she – Carrie . . . well it got a little crazy.' He pushed a hand through his untidy hair. 'We started seeing each other, after Tyler died. Mom and Dad knew, sort of. They didn't know we were seeing so much of each other. I don't even know why I was doing it really. To make a point?' He took a deep breath.

'So, a friend of Matty's has this great cabin upcounty. There's two of them on the edge of a trout lake. I told my parents I was going to stay over with Matty. But Carrie and I drove to the cabin. It was a Saturday.' He hesitated. 'Then there was a banging on the door and Dan and Steve were there. They'd followed us, seeing as how my rig isn't exactly the least distinctive vehicle around, and they'd been drinking. Anyway, due to the situation being as it was, they got a drop on me, and I got pretty broken up. Carrie's screaming at them. And then her father arrives, with what feels like half the county police.'

His face was unreadable. There was a pause before he went on.

'Carrie had chickened out of telling her parents she was spending the night away. Her dad's real strict and she just hadn't . . . so they were looking for her. She'd never even mentioned she was going anywhere. I mean, you can under-stand how they were worried. And when we'd arrived . . . I . . . I threw her over my shoulder and carried her into the cabin and she was shouting and beating me on the ass. This woman, she was staying at the other cabin and she'd seen that, and at the time she thought it was just in fun, which it was, but when the police arrived she must've kinda got caught up in the story. And she told them that, and made it sound bad. They thought I'd . . . made her go there.' He breathed out in a rush, shaking his head at the memory. 'Carrie was always so scared of him and when they came through the door yelling and hollering at me to get down on my knees and put my hands behind my head and all that stuff, she started to cry and . . . let them believe that it was true—'

'She did *what*?' Hope whispered.

He waited for a second, trying to stem the tide of words threatening to flow out of him. 'Yeah, I know. And I kinda understand why she did it, but—'

'What happened then?'

'They broke my face some more and a few ribs, my throwing arm. Hauled me into the station. And over the coals.'

Hope stared at him.

He shrugged in answer to her silent questions. 'No, it wasn't the most fun I've ever had.'

'And then?'

'And then my dad came and they talked and Carrie's dad said he was going to prosecute me for rape.' He dropped his head. 'And then Carrie begged him not to, told them she couldn't stand it if people knew what had happened to her. That this was a small community and that everyone knew our families. But of course, Fort Shaw is a small town, so the whole place knew within twenty-four hours. It was in every local paper, my name. *Our* name. Then the chief put word out he was dropping charges for Carrie's sake.' His voice was bitter. 'I still have a criminal record.'

'But if you didn't do it and the charges were dropped, how—'

'Sex crime arrests aren't expunged. Even if the charges are dropped.'

Hope rubbed her face. 'Oh God. Is she still here?'

'Yeah. They live just outside Fort Shaw.'

'Do you see her around?'

'Not really. I don't want to see her. She tries to call me sometimes, usually late at night, but I just let it ring out. Look, I just needed to tell you. When we get back. Back from here. Well, I didn't want anyone telling you anything that might freak you out . . . I thought I should just tell you my version of the story. And now Chief Hart's made it his business to persecute my family. Even the people who work for us end up getting a parking ticket every time they go into town.'

Hope folded her arms across her chest. 'Can't you complain to someone? He can't harass your family like that.'

He shook his head. 'The police are like God around here, Hope. Dad went to Helena to lodge a formal complaint but he was pretty much told I'd brought it on myself. And who could possibly want a relationship with someone when there's that hanging over them?'

'Maybe you should give someone the chance to decide.'

'You look at me as if I can fix everything. Just by existing.' He touched her cheek with the back of his fingers. 'But I can't. The only place I'll ever get a job is here at home. Imagine everyone in your hometown either looking at you with pity, or like the worst kind of scum.' He buried his head in his hands.

Cautiously Hope put her hand on his shoulder. 'It's . . . not your fault.'

Taking her hand, curling her fingers closed and pushing it away, he shook his head. 'It *is* my fault though, isn't it? Tyler, Carrie, us lost out here? Buddy? Jesus Christ, Buddy. All of it

297

is because of my bad decisions.' Then, suddenly, anger overcame the sadness. 'I've ruined *everything*,' he exploded, pushing to his feet. He walked into the dusk, shoulders hunched.

Hope sat on the porch as the dusk came down. She kept the fires going and wrapped herself in the blanket. The ragged old plaid shirt beneath it was warm. She lapped the blanket over her toes and watched the bats swoop around the cabin. Beyond the forest, the water glowed silver in the moonlight. The light from the fire spilt orange through the open cabin door.

Finally, when the air began to chill, Hope saw a figure walking up the meadow. Cal's pale shirt took shape as he got closer. Hope got to her feet and let the blanket drop. He halted a little way away, watching her. She took a step forward. Then another. Stepping on to the bottom step of the porch, she waited. For a long time they just looked at each other.

Cal closed the distance between them and shoved a hand through his hair, gnawing his lip. 'I yelled and I shouldn't have. Crow temper.' A rueful laugh escaped him. '*My* temper. Forgive me?'

She took his fingers and placed them over the button of the shirt, near her heart, which she was pretty sure he must be able to feel beating hard enough to break out of her chest. Reaching up, she hesitated, then touched her lips to his.

By the time they made it to the buffalo hide they were breathless and half-naked, helping each other to struggle out of their things. Cal lay on her, his weight strange and reassuring at the same time. He kissed down her neck.

'Say stop and we'll stop,' he said against her skin.

She arched her back and gasped. 'Don't stop doing that, please.'

'But you'd better stop doing *that*,' he said, taking her hand as she tugged the buttons of his jeans. 'I didn't exactly come prepared.'

'Oh . . .' She felt herself redden. 'But there's other stuff, isn't there? I mean . . .'

He laughed, threaded his fingers through hers and kissed her again. 'Oh yeah, there's other stuff.'

Hope was worried she'd get it wrong or do something stupid, but there wasn't really time for that. Not that it was over quickly, it was just that one thing led to another and there was no room for thinking. Cal was every bit as good to touch as he was to look at, and Hope had no intention of stopping. And then it was too late to stop anyway and all the good, sensible choices Hope had been taught to make got lost.

Afterwards, when the only sounds were their breathing and the distant white noise of the wind over the lake, Hope lay cuddled against Cal's chest, their skin sticking. He kissed her hair and trailed his fingers down her shoulder blade.

'How you doing there?'

Hope nodded, tucking her cheekbone against his flat chest, shy again.

He hesitated before speaking. 'So, that got . . . out of hand.'

'Sorry,' Hope said instantly, starting to move away from him.

'Hey! That's not what I meant.' He hauled her back. 'I'm not sorry at all, as long as you're not.' Night had come in and his eyes were dark in the light from the fire, examining hers.

Hope shook her head.

His arms tightened and he kissed her forehead. 'We took a risk. It'll be fine, I promise. Whatever happens, I'm not sorry. I am sorry I hurt you though.'

'It wasn't as bad as people make out.'

'Right.' He sounded deflated.

'But I was wondering . . .' Hope bit her lip.

'. . . About?'

She hid a smile at the anxiety in his voice. Full of mischief, she traced the vein that stood up slightly on the inside of his arm with a careful fingertip. 'Are you this good at *everything* you do?'

He let her go, looking shocked. 'Good, Cooper? *Good?*'

Hope burst out laughing and he grinned, shaking his head as he pulled her into his arms again.

'Oh, of course!' she said, between kisses. 'I meant awesome, incred—'

CHAPTER 17

'TO LOVE IS A VERY DIFFERENT THING
FROM THE DESIRE TO BE LOVED.
TO LOVE IS A WOMAN'S DUTY. TO BE
BELOVED IS HER REWARD.'

The next seven weeks on our mountain were blissful. Our life settled into a rhythm of chores, horses, talking and not talking. You taught me to shoot, and the basics of hunting, skinning and preparing what we caught. And swimming, at which I am a natural! I learnt the basics of your Indian language, and some of their plant remedies. We talked and laughed and loved each other with an intense curiosity. I adored the way your hair fell across your face as we walked home with stained hands and a dish of berries; how you checked your pockets for your knife as we were talking. I had so much to discover about you; the things I had associated with love – loyalty, duty and family – were discarded as I learnt to love you with everything I was.

Often, you stood by the corral and watched the white horse with Tara. They too remained obsessed with each other and their behaviour made you smile. But as time went on, you became increasingly interested in the stallion, who remained, so patiently, corralled on our mountain. Inside the rails, you spoke to him, roped him, even slapped him down gently with a blanket and put it over his back. To all of this he looked vaguely bemused but stood, quiet. I watched you pull his ears in fun, then clap his neck in friendship.

'I don't understand him,' you said one evening as we sat with plates in our laps and talked about the horses. 'I'd be expecting him to be restless, but he's like a kitten. Ain't right. Horses like that ain't walkovers. But it's like he knows what I'm thinking. Like he and I have always been meant.'

'Perhaps you can work with him then,' I offered, spooning up my stew. It had been a long day and I was keen to take the edge from my hunger.

'Maybe. Still ain't sure I want to keep him. And he ain't no horse to be sold, ever. Not sure if it weren't just the challenge of bringing him in that had me so wrapped up.'

'Perhaps you'll feel like that about me soon,' I teased, sure of myself.

'Yeah, maybe I will,' you said.

I took a breath and pouted. You laughed and leant across and kissed my neck before straightening up. 'But most likely my love for you will be in this wind when I'm dust. And probably long after that.' You put down your spoon and took my hand. 'Come on, I want to try something.'

I let you lead me to the corral. As you began to take out one of the rails from the gateway, I frowned. 'You're setting him free?'

You grunted a laugh. 'No chance, yet. Can you get through there?'

I looked at the gap, and the white horse and Tara grazing. Slipping through, I stood up.

'Go see him. He ain't no good if only I can work him. So just walk right up nice and easy. And the second he backs off, or you're scared, just turn around and put your back to him. Don't need to touch him, just get near him. One day at a time.'

I walked up slowly to the white horse. He lifted his head and watched me. I came closer; we looked at each other and his weight shifted away from me. I turned my back. That way, I was facing you, and I saw you watching, bad foot on the bottom rail, wrists crossed over each other on an upper rail. As ever, I couldn't read your eyes. Then I felt a nudge and the white horse's nose appeared over my shoulder. I daren't move and we stood like that, together, watching you. I turned my head and kissed his face, lifting my left hand to his sharply pricked ear and stroking its soft back. He blew at me, like your huffing laugh. I smiled. You shook your head and turned from the corral, dismissing us with a wave.

'You got a real future as a horsewoman, English,' you called as you walked back up to the cabin. 'With that and the saloon piano I'll soon be a tycoon.'

A few days later, you decided to back the white horse. You were still adamant he wasn't a riding animal, but such was your friendship with him, you thought it was possible.

'Emily, we know he seems real placid but he may kick me to hell and gone. And on the ground I'm not real fast, so . . .'

'Then don't do it,' I said, alarmed.

'Life ain't nothing without a risk, and it'll be worth it. Even if I only get to sit up there once in this lifetime.'

I pulled a face.

You kissed me. 'Don't sulk. If I ain't here, you and Tara're more than capable of getting yourselves out of trouble now. Get down on to the plain, head south and find my family's people, like I told you.'

I frowned, unsettled that you were even talking about it. 'Are we really going to them for the winter?'

'Yep. You're not cut out for the snow up here, let alone—' You broke off and shook your head. 'You'll want more company than me by then.'

'I won't. I—' My protest was cut short as you put your fingers to my lips.

'Trust me. And I can't take him to them without at least putting a few manners on him, can I? What would they think of me? Besides,' you grinned, 'I want to do it.'

Your reasoning got the better of me every time. 'Fine. But don't get yourself killed.'

You grinned. 'Got no intention. Too much other stuff going on I want to be a part of.'

We spent a couple of days accustoming the white horse to a rope bridle. He didn't like it much, but his expression was more one of disdain than outright objection.

The morning you finally backed him was sullen and over-cast. I was tired, and you made the tea as I lazed in our bed and you fussed over me. You had done the same the previous morning; not like you at all.

But you were intent on your purpose and went down to the corral as soon as I was drinking from my cup, knees drawn up beneath the coverlet, cheek branded with your kiss. After that I dozed for what I thought was a few more minutes, and woke suddenly on my stomach, cup on the floor and my fingers on the floorboards. I sat up, momentarily confused about where I was.

'Emily?' you called from somewhere.

'Yes?'

'Come outside?'

'Coming.' I pushed the covers aside and stumbled out on to the porch in my inherited nightgown, rubbing my eyes as it billowed around me in the breeze. There you sat, on the back of the white horse, one hand holding a section of his mane. The corral gate-rails were down and the rope bridle still hung from the post. Both of you were looking at me: the muscular white stallion with his big, crested neck arched, and you, completely at ease on his back. The white horse pawed the ground as if impatient for my praise.

'You did it!'

You grinned. 'Weren't nothing to it. Maybe I was wrong when I said he ain't a riding animal. Maybe someone already broke him. Can't work out how else he'd be this calm.' You eased him into a walk, circling him in front of the cabin. I came down to you. He stopped in front of me and I stroked his face.

'You didn't use the bridle?'

You shrugged. 'Nah.'

'Can I try?' I asked, studying the horse's level glass-eyed gaze.

'Nope,' you said with certainty.

'That's not fair,' I protested. 'You can't just keep him to yourself. You said that before.'

'Yeah, well, I can. Ain't interested in you taking a fall for the sake of it.'

'You didn't care when I was learning.'

You pulled a face at me. 'I care now. No.'

The white horse nudged me in the middle, as if agreeing with you. I stroked his nose. 'I think both of you are most uncharitable,' I told him in a half-hearted scold.

Moving off, back towards the corral, you laughed. 'Then I'd better return him to Tara, before I try his charity any more.'

After that we spent a lot of time with the horses – Tara, the stallion and Red, who was turning into such a good riding animal you said you 'would be sorry to sell him'. We never ventured far, for everything we needed was in the cabin, or to be found on the mountain. Except perhaps a pair of shoes, but it had been a long time since I had missed them.

One night, I woke in the dark, finding myself alone. I got up and went to the porch. You were sitting against the cabin wall, shrouded by a blanket, watching reds, yellows and greens streak across the star-splattered sky. I stared at the heavens, astonished.

You held out a wool-draped arm like a wing and I hunkered down against you. 'They call it the Northern Lights.' You wrapped us up. 'Closest I've ever come to God.'

We made tea and watched for hours, waking on the porch the following morning in a tumble of tin cups and blankets, the horses staring at us from the corral like disapproving Latin masters.

The days were warm, and sometimes I wandered the mountain only in Clear Water's chest band and the deerskin leggings, my feet now immune to the ground beneath them. I had become a wild thing, as interested in the plants and animals of our home as I once had been in Milton and Dryden. My shoulders and stomach soon tanned and my contrasting pale skin fascinated you.

You watched me. Sometimes I caught you staring, a strange expression on your face as you sat smoking your rare cigarettes on the porch.

I asked you, once, if other people felt as we did.

You were slow to answer. 'I guess they do. Guess that's why there's so much fuss talked about love.'

I twined my wrists around your neck. 'I hope they do. I hope everyone gets to feel this way, with someone.'

'As long as they don't get to *feel* it with you, I don't care,' you laughed.

'When did you know?'

'In Helena.'

'Oh, but I loved you for a long time before you went to see Mr Meard, even if I didn't know how to show you!' I said indignantly. 'I tried, the night you left but it didn't work.'

You talked over me. 'Helena the first time.'

'Oh!' That revelation took a few moments to sink in.

Almost reluctantly, you went on. 'Asked the barkeep about the beautiful girl in the dark dress, upstairs.' You took a breath. 'Thought maybe . . .'

I stared at you. 'What?'

You shrugged. 'Thought maybe if there was a chance I could get to talk to you, maybe . . . the way you looked at me . . . then he told me you were some rich English thing with a full Chicago team and that was that, I thought. Might as well have told me you were a fairy princess in a golden chariot. Sold my horse, sat on the stoop outside with a half pint of whiskey and felt sorry for myself. A dirt-poor, half-wild, crippled deserter.'

It took a few moments for that to sink in. 'You're not so wild,' I said softly, shy again.

You laughed beneath your breath, just as shy in your own way. 'Tamed by a creature that ain't nothing but a handful of thistledown.'

'A creature you saved from a wreck.'

'Yeah, well. Maybe there is a God. But I am sorry I'll never be able to give you fine things.'

I pulled you down for a quick kiss, then gestured out to the mountain. 'But look at all the fine things you've given me.'

'There's another I've a mind to give you, right now.' You hauled me up against your hips.

'You have no calling as a diplomat,' I laughed.

You teased me like that, often, and sometimes you said things in the darkness that bring colour to my face even now: an ambush of memory. Shocking me amused you, and I soon learnt not to rise to the bait. Sometimes I indulged in my own teasings, with pleasingly predictable results.

My growing confidence and the clear satisfaction you took in it made me realize how unremittingly patient you had been, both before and after your return. We were sitting inside because it was raining. You were lounging in the armchair and I was sitting at your feet, watching the fire spit and hiss as the raindrops came down the chimney. The door was open and the three horses stood stoic in the rain, resting a rear hoof, drenched. White-tailed deer browsed along the edge of the forest.

I looked at our entwined fingers resting on my shoulder, and kissed the hollow dip of the tendon at the base of your thumb. 'Thank you.'

'For what?'

I shrugged. 'For everything.'

You huffed a laugh. 'Ain't no one ever thanked me for *that* before.'

Rolling my eyes, I said, 'I didn't mean *that*. I meant for being so kind to me.'

With a slight tut, you brushed your thumb against my chin. 'What else was I going to do with you? I ain't an animal.'

'That's not what I meant either.'

'So what did you mean?'

I gathered my courage and explained, falteringly, about the pamphlet. About its advice. About 'tolerance'.

You watched me, expressionless, until I finished speaking. After a few moments your chest rose on a deep breath. 'Sorry state of affairs.' You blew out slowly.

I nodded, touching my cheek to our woven fingers. 'And that was why I . . . the night of the storm. I thought it was the right thing to do.'

You were thinking, stroking the edge of my jaw.

'And I'm so sorry,' I finished.

'Nothing for you to be sorry for.'

I looked up at you. 'You were hurt. I hated it.'

'Can't say as I enjoyed it neither.' But there was a hint of amusement in your voice.

I rose from the floor and knelt across your lap. One knee, and then the other. Your hands rested on my waist and you smiled at my silly swagger. I leant forward and whispered in your ear. Laughter hummed in your chest, your arms closing around me as the rain fell outside.

Looking back it had to end, I suppose. Perhaps the universe has a system of checks and balances that prevent such extraordinary joy from destroying the order of the world.

We were at the cabin, early one morning. You were cleaning your rifle and I was putting wood into the stove. I was wearing my deerskin leggings and a shirt. My hair was braided and tied off with the lace.

Dismantling the gun, you laid out all the pieces with care, in an orderly pattern. Then you handed me your pistol and pointed to the other end of the table. 'Might as well learn. Now you know how to shoot, gotta know how to take care a-your weapon. And this one here, she's easy.' You released the action and pointed. 'That's it. Lift the chamber out and set it down on the table.' Within a minute, I had the revolver stripped on the rough wooden surface.

'Now—' you began.

'Wait.' I tugged the diary from my pocket and opened it, pointing. 'What's this letter?'

You glanced at it. 'It's an "e", as in Emily.' Leaning down, you went to take your usual reward. The reward that stopped your lessons progressing perhaps faster than they may have otherwise.

I turned my cheek and held up the diary. 'This one?'

Straightening up, you raised an eyebrow. 'A "t" . . . as in tease.'

Laughing, I pointed at another letter.

You smiled. '"K" as in kiss.'

I held my face up. You obliged. Then you pulled away, frowned and turned, going to the door of the cabin and look-ing down the meadow.

'What is it?'

'We got guests.'

I put the diary back into my pocket and came to you, look-ing out of the door. Before my eyes, and I couldn't quite believe it, were six men on horseback. One of them was Hart, wearing the same filthy getup but now also sporting a dull sheriff's badge. He was clearly very much alive. One sleeve of his coat was empty, his arm in a sling inside it. Another of the men was Papa. And, unmistakably, with him was the Anthony Howard Stanton I remembered from the photographs.

Papa and I stared at each other.

After a long moment, he said, 'Emily?' almost as if he doubted the tanned, barefoot creature before him could be his daughter.

You put your hand on my shoulder.

'Get away from her, you murdering piece of shit,' Hart said.

'Why couldn't you just stay dead?' you responded with venom.

I moved in front of you, instinctively. Papa got down from his horse. 'Come here, Emily.'

I shook my head.

'Emily,' he said, 'come here. Sheriff Hart has told us what happened, with the coach. How this man arranged for his Indian family to ambush it and dispose of it. Everything will be fine, darling. But you must come to me now.'

'No, Papa,' I insisted. 'That's not what happened. It's not what happened at all. The bridge broke. He saved me. I would have died.'

'And he just happened to be there to save you?' It was Mr Stanton who spoke. 'A man with desertion and murder in his past.'

We stood side by side, my feet braced on the boards. 'He only deserted to save his leg and he isn't a murderer. Mr Hart paid that man to—'

'Sheriff Hart now, lady.' Hart spat in the dirt.

Papa looked at him, uncertainty in his face for the first time.

You shook your head. 'He was nothing but some young idiot needing – what? What did you pay him? Fifty dollars to run his mouth at me until he got his brains spread over the chapel wall in Fort Shaw?'

'Shame he can't talk about that now, ain't it?' Hart spat in the dirt again.

I narrowed my eyes, wishing I had the rifle from the table so I could shoot him with it. The thought must have gone through your head too, as you glanced over your shoulder through the cabin door.

Anthony Stanton cleared his throat, raising his voice slightly. 'At what point was he going to go through with his plan and hold you to ransom, I wonder?'

'Ransom?' You turned on Hart. 'This is you, you lying scumbag. This must be your dream come true.'

Hart said nothing, just looked faintly smug.

I shook my head furiously, taking your hand. 'You don't understand.'

'Emily, come to me now, or the sheriff's men will have to intervene,' Papa beckoned.

Your pale eyes were tight, but your expression was impassive, as if you didn't care at all.

I was convinced that only I could save you, for you were too proud to save yourself. I rounded on them. 'I won't let you hurt him.'

'Emily! Come here, darling,' Papa beckoned. 'Now!'

'No,' I cried. 'You're going to hurt him, I know you are!'

There was a deafening bang.

Hart's buffalo gun smoked, supported by the hand in the sling. And you dropped like a stone on to the porch, slamming back against the wall as the massive bullet ripped through you, red blooming across your chest.

I fell to my knees, clutching your shoulders. 'Please, Nate! *No!*'

Papa was climbing the steps of the porch. I crouched over you like an animal. 'You stay away, just stay away from us,' I warned him, palm out.

He offered his hand cautiously. 'Emily—'

I touched your chest, helpless, as the dark pool spread around us, soaking my leggings, smearing my hands. So I held your face and spoke to you, a stricken babble of how much I loved you.

You spoke with huge effort. Your teeth were bloody. It was everywhere. I was covered in it. 'Guess this is my time.'

'No!'

You managed to touch my cheek. 'Em, hush. No tears. You know I can't stand it when you cry.' Your laugh was a choking cough. Struggling, you tried to focus off the porch, eyes searching. 'Stanton?'

Anthony Stanton was down from his horse. He stepped

forward, his handsome face pale as he pulled his hat from his head. 'Yes.'

'You take care a-her, or I'll be seeing you.'

It took Mr Stanton a few moments to speak. He nodded, face set. 'I give you my word.'

'No!' I sobbed brokenly.

You hushed me again. 'Go now. Be happy. For me.'

'But how can I . . . without you?' I held your fingers to my tear-streaked face.

You pulled me down for our last kiss. 'I'll be with you. Always.'

And you died.

CHAPTER 18

I t was a few hours after dawn. Hope lay on the buffalo hide by the fireplace, watching the sunshine spilling into the cabin, over discarded clothing, blankets, the diary. Cal's back was tense as he sat, elbows on his bent knees, looking out of the open door at the smoke drifting from the campfire. The birdsong was loud outside.

'People are going to think I took advantage,' he said, not looking at her.

She sat up. 'You didn't.'

He didn't say anything for a while. Then, 'Jesus Christ, Cooper. This is crazy.'

Hope blinked back a tear, glad he was looking away from her. 'I understand, and I don't expect any—'

Shoving his hair back, he set his shoulders and blew out. 'Come back for the summer.' He looked at her over his shoulder.

Wait, what? 'You . . . you might have had enough of me being around by then,' she said uncertainly.

He raised an eyebrow. 'Yeah, somehow I doubt that. Seeing as how I haven't been able to get enough of you being around since the airport.'

She blushed. 'Really?'

He shrugged and looked towards the open door again. 'Wouldn't say it if I didn't mean it.'

Hope's heart soared. She wrapped her arms around his chest and kissed his cheek, hugging his warm back. Yet she couldn't stop her doubts surfacing. 'But will it be OK with your parents?'

'Well, seeing as how you've got my dad wound round your pinky finger in two days flat, and Mom would go crazy for a girl around the place, I think they'll be fine. Your mom might not be so keen though. Let alone when she finds out about . . .'

Hope wrinkled her nose. 'No.'

'Can she stop you?'

'I don't *think* so, now I'm sixteen. Dad's lawyer wrote a letter saying she couldn't stop me seeing him if I wanted to, so I guess it's the same. But I'm not sure I have enough money.'

He shrugged. 'I can pay.'

'No. I have to pay for stuff I want,' Hope said proudly. 'Rules.'

'Yeah, well, I think we've broken a few in the last few days. And some really big ones in the last few hours. I'll pay.'

'You mean it?'

'I have to bribe you, obviously. *So*, will you come back for

317

summer if I promise I will teach you to ride, drive, and maybe . . . swim a little better?'

A grin of uncontained joy replaced Hope's shy smile. She kissed him, laughing at his teasing. 'Yes. Yes! Please. If you're sure.'

'Yeah, I'm sure. Your swimming needs work.'

Hope pushed him.

He grinned and then was serious. 'One condition.'

'What?' She hesitated.

'When we get out of here, you call your dad.'

'But . . .'

'He's your father. You should know each other.'

Hope thought about it. 'OK, deal.'

He leant across the boards, picked up the diary and handed it to her. 'So, Cooper, what happens next?'

The brief account of Nate's death left them both in silence, just as the dull thud of a helicopter reached their ears.

'Quick, up!' Cal urged.

Hope scrambled to her feet, pulling on her clothes. 'I just want to get out of here.'

He kissed her forehead in a quick bump. 'Yeah, me too. We'll be home soon. Everything will be OK, I promise.'

Pushing the diary into her pocket, Hope ran to the door of the cabin and hurtled into the meadow. A rescue helicopter was cutting over the lake, straight towards the cabin and the still-smoking campfire. She jumped up and down and waved, flinging her arms in wide movements. The helicopter raced in, then slowed above her, hovering.

A movement at the edge of the trees across the stream caught her eye –

And the bear broke cover, charging into the water.

Cal was coming out on to the porch, hauling his shirt on, still buttoned.

Hope screamed his name, pointing towards the bear.

He grabbed the rifle and raised it, yelling something at her she couldn't hear over the sound of the helicopter. He raised the rifle as the bear emerged from the stream, water running from its shaggy coat. It looked disoriented, chest stained dark and matted with blood, but was heading straight for Hope. The helicopter was deafening, hovering only ten metres above the ground, the downdraught blowing her clothes and hair flat against her. Then she saw, in the side door of the aircraft, a man with a rifle.

Hart. He raised the gun and took aim.

But not at the bear.

Hope flung both her arms out, shaking her head and screaming at the police chief not to shoot, as the bear bore down on her.

Cal pulled the trigger.

And at the same time another rifle shot rang out. From the helicopter.

Cal hit the porch as the bear fell into the meadow, three metres away from Hope.

Already running, Hope hurled herself up the porch steps, seeing the huge red stain across Cal's shirt.

'NO!' *Not like Nate, please, not like Nate.*

Hope dropped to her knees beside Cal, as the helicopter landed behind them. Out of it spilled Chief Hart, Officer Jones, and the mountain rescue team. Hope shoved open Cal's shirt. His hands lifted, uncertain.

'I'm OK. Really, I—'

She bit down on her reply, placing both hands over the wound in his chest, blood spilling between her fingers as she pressed down.

He flinched, cried out and coughed all at once, blood flecking his chin. 'This is really getting to know each other, huh?'

'Don't joke,' Hope said, 'Just—' The noise from the helicopter was deafening.

Cal coughed again, his blue eyes losing their clarity. 'Maybe this was meant to happen . . .'

She shook her head, pressing on his chest, but realized the pool was already spreading beneath him, from his back; she was kneeling in it. Trying to get her hair out of the way she streaked it, and her face and neck, with red.

'Help us!' she yelled over her shoulder, and when she looked back, Cal was no longer conscious.

The mountain rescue team were already racing up with a stretcher, taking over, pushing her out of the way. Behind them came the police.

Hope got to her feet and turned on the police chief. Fury such as she'd never felt before boiled through her: fury that someone would hurt Cal. 'You SHOT HIM.'

Chief Hart stood, looking down at Cal's body, no expression on his face. He took his sunglasses from his shirt pocket and put them on. Hope launched herself at him. Officer Jones pushed her back, restraining her, arm hooked around her waist like a field tackle. 'We thought he was aiming at you, miss.'

'Me?!' Hope stepped back, holding up her bloody hands for him not to touch her. 'Why would he shoot *me*?'

'Miss Cooper, look at you. You're hurt and in distress. He was aiming a gun at you.'

'But he wasn't! He shot the bear!' She pointed down the mountain, at the huge, still carcass.

Chief Hart squared his shoulders. 'The boy has a history of offending—'

Hope held up a finger. 'One. And I know exactly what—'

The slap caught her hard across the face and stunned her, knocking her against the side of the cabin, banging her head and opening up the cut on her cheek. She sat into a defensive crouch then straightened up slowly, hand to her face, staring up at Chief Hart. The paramedics stopped talking amongst themselves, latex-gloved hands tapping Cal's jaw, trying to get a response.

One of the medics looked up as Hope righted herself and faced up to the police chief, fists clenched. He got between them, one bloody glove on each of their chests. 'I'd say you two are about even. So why don't you try helping this guy. He's losing blood fast. It's the best part of an hour to Helena and they're gearing up the surgeon.'

*

The journey in the helicopter was the longest of Hope's life. Cal showed no signs of a response as she sat with him and held his hand. The two mountain rescue paramedics had donned headsets and spoke to each other through them without Hope being able to hear what they were saying over the thudding of the helicopter. They'd stripped Cal to the waist and he was covered in electrodes. The bullet had gone straight through his lung, and the gauze dressing pads beneath him were soaked within minutes. It didn't look that bad from the front, just a thumbnail-sized red and black hole on the left side, but his back was a mess. And all the blood so dark.

Hart and Jones sat on the other side of the helicopter, not speaking.

As the mountain receded behind them, Hope felt the diary in her pocket like a lead weight.

As they landed on the tarmac in front of St Peter's Hospital, the surgeon and a medical team were already waiting for them. Hart and Jones went into a huddle, walking away from the racket of the helicopter.

Hope ran alongside the trolley as Cal was wheeled through the doors of the huge, square building. People stared at her bare feet and her tear-streaked face but she didn't let go of Cal's hand until he was taken into surgery, the nurse barring her way as inside the theatre the surgical team descended on him like vultures.

She stood, staring at the door, unable to take in what had happened. The ordinary noises of a hospital intruded on her.

A nurse led her to a seating area and offered her a cone of water from the dispenser. The swing doors opened and a familiar voice spoke.

Meredith touched her arm. 'Hope?'

It was a few seconds before Hope responded, blinking and looking at her mother.

'Oh dear God, look at you,' Meredith said, shocked. Hope saw over Meredith's shoulder Caleb Crow asking at the nurses' station to speak to a doctor. Dazed, she looked down at herself, seeing her bloody legs and clothing, patches of her hair in clotted strings. Cal's blood had dried in the webbing of her fingers. It was everywhere.

Her mother was examining Hope's bruised cheek. 'Did he do this to you?'

Hope flinched away. 'We were in an accident. The rig crashed.'

'I was out of my mind with worry. I brought you some clean things. I didn't think to bring different shoes,' she said, looking at Hope's filthy bare feet. 'But I'm sure there's somewhere here you could shower.'

Hope stared at the bag, bewildered. 'I—'

Caleb Crow's voice interrupted them. 'We'll know nothing for a couple of hours. He's lost a lot of blood.' His voice cracked slightly on the words as he looked at Hope.

'I'm so sorry,' she said, gesturing to her appearance and sniffing back a tear. 'I haven't had a chance to—'

He put a hand on her shoulder. 'It's OK, Hope. But you should probably get cleaned up, Cal's mother's on her way.'

'Hurricane Elizabeth.'

'You'd better believe that,' he said, patting her. 'And some-one should look at that cheek, honey. It's one hell of a bruise.'

Hope shrugged. 'I'm fine. I hit it on the roof of the truck, that's all. In the crash. On the bridge. When—' She was stuttering, teeth chattering. 'Maybe I'll take that shower now.'

Meredith decided Hope needed to eat and went out to find a store, describing the offerings at the hospital as inedible and unhealthy, so when Hope came out of the shower her mother was nowhere to be seen.

Hope was sitting on her own in the nurses' station, where one of the nurses had taken pity on her and given her a hot coffee. But the nurse had to go, leaving Hope feeling deso-late. Then a friendly female police officer with her brown hair in a bun came to the desk.

'Hi, Hope Cooper? My name's Officer Langton.'

Officer Langton began to ask her about what had happened. Hope almost didn't know where to start, and it took some time to explain that the truck wasn't, as the officer continued to imply, hidden somewhere near the lake, but miles away at the bottom of a river bed under millions of gallons of meltwater.

'And we'd like a doctor to give you a medical exam.'

Hope frowned. 'Why? It's only my face. I bruised it in the car accident.'

'What about your hands? They look sore. How did that happen?'

'I . . . we had to bury Buddy—'

Officer Langton smiled sympathetically. 'Is there anything you would like to tell me, Hope? Anything Cal Crow did or said to you that you might have felt was inappropriate?'

'I have no idea what you mean.'

'Nothing physical happened?'

Hope lifted her chin. 'We were in a car accident together – I'm not sure how much more physical there is.'

Officer Langton persisted. 'Still, we'd like a doctor to conduct the exam, just to rule out any difficulties in establishing your story.'

'I haven't got a story, it's the truth. We were in a car accident and we were waiting at the cabin to be rescued.' Hope's voice was rising now.

'Easy, Hope. No one can hurt you now . . .' She put out a hand.

Hope backed up. 'No one *has* hurt me!'

Officer Jones came up and beckoned. The female officer excused herself and they talked in the corner for a few seconds. When she came back, she smiled. 'The clothes you came in wearing, we'll need them.'

'What for?'

'Where are the clothes?'

'I don't know, maybe my mother has them,' Hope lied. Her bag was, in fact, behind the nurses' station by her feet. 'I need to go to the bathroom. May . . . may I have another coffee please?' She drained the mug and held it out.

The officer nodded and smiled, taking it. 'Sure, honey. I'll be here when you get back. Where has your mother gone, did you say?'

Hope shrugged and the officer turned away, heading for the coffee machine. Grabbing her nylon bag, Hope carried it against her front, arms tight, to the bathrooms. Inside the stall, she unpacked the bag, thanking her mother silently all the time for the extra set of clothes she had brought to the hospital and for the fact she always made Hope put plastic sacks in the side pockets. Pulling one out, she put in the extra-clean shorts, underwear and a T-shirt. Into another, she put everything from the mountain except the plaid shirt and the diary, which she replaced into the holdall. Leaving the bathroom, she put her mountain clothes in a yellow bin marked 'Hospital Waste' and stowed her bag back behind the nurses' station. Walking back to the coffee area, she handed the female officer the bag of clean clothes.

'Here, I forgot I'd left them in the bathroom.'

The officer smiled, taking the plastic sack, almost holding it at arm's length. 'That's understandable, with everything that's happened to you. Now, explain to me again how the vehicle crashed.'

Hope saw, with relief, Meredith stalking towards them. She let her bottom lip tremble. 'Mum,' she called out, 'they're asking me questions, and I—'

'Officer! What on earth are you doing? I cannot believe you are questioning my daughter after the ordeal she's had!'

The officer stood up, offering her hand. 'Officer Langton, ma'am. We're just trying to establish the facts, ma'am.'

Meredith put her arm around Hope. 'Are you all right?'

Hope nodded, feeling genuinely tearful. Just then, a doctor came up, a woman in her late thirties.

'Ms West? I'm Doctor Ellison. I was wondering if I could just look Hope over, make sure she's doing OK?'

Meredith got to her feet. 'Should I be there? Hope?'

'It's not necessary,' the doctor said, shepherding Hope away.

In an examination room, the doctor asked Hope to hop up on the bed and lay back. She examined Hope's cheek, then took a photograph of it.

Hope winced in the flash. 'Why do you need a photograph?'

'It's for evidence, Hope. That's all.' She put her hand on Hope's arm, reassuring.

Pushing herself up on her elbows, Hope shook her head. 'Evidence of what?'

'They've asked me to catalogue your injuries, that's all.'

'Is no one listening to me? I'm *fine*.'

The doctor turned aside. 'The police officers noted you have bruising to one of your thighs, so, if you could just take off your things and slip into this gown for me.'

Hope jumped down from the table. 'No way.'

Turning back, the doctor looked at her, face kind. 'Hope, you can tell us anything, you know.'

Pulling on her cardigan, Hope pulled her hair out of the back of it. 'There's nothing to tell. And I don't want to be *examined* any more than I already have been, thank you.' She walked back out to the waiting area and sat down next to

327

Meredith and Caleb Crow, folding her arms and staring stubbornly into space.

Four hours later, Cal was out of surgery and in the ICU. He had not regained consciousness and the surgeon had decided to induce coma to see if it helped him stabilize. Hope sat by his bed with Caleb until Elizabeth Crow arrived.

Cal's mother was tall, dark-haired and impressive in her fury. Coming in, she walked straight over to her son's still form in the bed and kissed his forehead, stroking away a stray lock of hair that Hope had been too afraid to touch. After a long moment of gazing at her son, her eyes fixed on Hope.

'Hope Cooper?'

'Yes.'

Elizabeth Crow nodded. 'What happened?'

'The bridge gave out beneath the truck and trailer. We made it to the cabin and waited to be rescued. But I shot a bear—'

'You shot a *bear*?'

Hope nodded miserably. 'It was going to hurt Cal. It killed Buddy. But it came back. It must have . . . been disoriented by the helicopter or something. Flushed out. Cal thought it was coming for me and raised his gun and Chief Hart *shot* him.' *And this whole thing is history repeating itself and I can't tell you because why would you believe me?* 'They keep asking me questions, and I think they're trying to twist things.'

Cal's mother looked at her, gaze steady. 'And what did you tell them?'

Hope tried to hold her stare. 'That we crashed and that Cal took care of me. And . . . I know he didn't do anything to Carrie.'

Elizabeth nodded and squeezed Hope's hand briefly. 'Carrie's sweet, but she's weak. Getting involved with her was a mistake. The feud between the Crows and the Harts is as old as Montana and that just made it worse. Hart was looking for an excuse.'

Caleb Crow was letting himself back into the room, looking out of place in his plaid shirt and jeans. Hope stepped away, not wanting to intrude. The monitors beeped and droned fitfully. A nurse hovered.

Elizabeth Crow held out her hand to her husband. He took it.

Hope took a deep breath. 'Mr and Mrs Crow, can I ask, have you ever heard of a girl called Emily Forsythe?'

They both looked at her, blank. Elizabeth Crow frowned. 'Is she a friend of Cal's?'

'No . . . she . . .' Hope shook her head. 'Don't worry, forget I asked.'

Outside, in the waiting area, Meredith came around the corner from the nurses' station, with a brown bag from a sandwich store. Hope had never felt less hungry, but she took the bag.

'Thanks,' she said listlessly. She was feeling cold in the over-heated hospital, despite being dressed in jeans, a camisole and a shirt, more clothes than she'd worn in days.

'Would you like to eat it here or in the car on the way back to the ranch? Jesus will drive us.'

Hope looked up at Meredith, mystified. 'I'm not going anywhere.'

'Hope, you need a good meal and rest. And I need to work.'

'You go and work then, I'm not stopping you.' The tense silence that followed made Hope's fingers tighten on the bag. 'But thanks for the food, and everything.'

'You need to rest.'

'I'm fine here.' Hope stood her ground.

Meredith's lips thinned, then she stalked out towards the nurses' station, to where Jesus hovered anxiously by the door, hat in his hands, disliking the hospital atmosphere intensely.

Hope looked inside the paper bag: a salad in a plastic tray and some rolls. Just then, the elevator opened and four policemen walked out, including Chief Hart and Officer Jones. They were heading towards the ICU, where Cal was.

Hart and Jones went inside while the two others took up positions outside the door. The nurse rushed past Hope, who followed on her heels. Caleb was holding Elizabeth back as Officer Jones handcuffed Cal's unresisting arm to the bed railing.

'None of this is helpful for the patient!' the nurse was saying urgently, checking Cal's monitors as she looked back at the officers.

'It's procedure, ma'am, is all.'

'I'm going to call a doctor,' the nurse muttered, and left.

'Procedure, my ass,' Caleb ground out.

Officer Jones turned and Hope dodged between them

towards the bed, taking Cal's free hand, careful of the cannula.

'Miss Cooper, we're advising you to stay away from Mr Crow at this time,' the police officer said. Chief Hart folded his arms and looked at her.

Hope lifted her chin. 'Why?'

'Because he's the subject of an investigation, and we advise it.'

'What investigation?' Caleb asked.

'We're still considering the charges based on the collection of evidence.'

'He didn't abduct me,' Hope said clearly. 'He saved my life.'

'Miss, we're not sure you're in a position to make a judgement on that at this stage. Mr Crow's record indicates—'

The room erupted as Caleb, Elizabeth and Hope spoke over the officer all at once.

A second later, the nurse pushed back into the unit. 'All of you! Leave, now! Get out before I call security. This is *not* the place. He can probably hear you and this will be distressing him.'

Hart spoke briefly with one of the police guards by the door and then strode away, shiny boots squeaking on the linoleum.

As the elevator door closed, the door to the stairwell opened a little, and a pretty brunette girl put her head through the gap. 'Have they gone?' she whispered.

Hope nodded. The girl slipped through the doorway, clutching the strap of her bag. She had very straight hair, with a thick fringe, and dark-brown eyes.

'I . . . had to come. Is he OK?' She struggled to speak.

'Cal? No. He's just out of surgery and he's been handcuffed to the bed.' Hope watched her, and then realized suddenly who she was. 'You're Carrie, aren't you?'

She nodded. 'I don't know if Cal told you . . .' And as Hope nodded, her face crumpled. 'I should . . . I know I should have told the truth, but my father . . . I came to say, and just let me say it, that my father doesn't have any evidence, not really. The rig and the trailer have been found in the creek bed. But my dad's real clever at making things look different than the truth, and I heard him say he was going to make this hard on Cal when you were found.'

'Hard? He shot him!' Hope exclaimed.

Carrie winced. 'He's . . . I don't know why he's taken it so far this time. Our families have never gotten along, but this is . . . What happened up there? It's not . . . what my dad says, is it?'

Hope thought of the diary, of the rerunning of another story, but there was no way to explain.

Taking a deep breath, Carrie went on. 'There's a lady, in the Helena police department. She's called Margaret Redfeather. She's . . . helping me and my mom with some stuff. You should speak to her. She gave me a ride here.'

Redfeather? Hope pressed her knuckles into her forehead. 'OK. Where is she?'

'In the parking lot.' Carrie nodded towards the stairwell.

Hope took a deep breath. 'Come on then, let's go.'

They headed downstairs, not speaking, and walked out into the bright spring sunshine. Leaning against a faded green convertible was the tall woman from the Black Eagle Stores, wearing a sharp black suit with a white shirt, and stubbing out a cigarette.

Carrie was nervous, looking around. 'I'd better go. If my daddy finds me here, he'll get you fired,' she muttered to the tall woman. And with that, she was gone, fear driving her feet.

As Carrie left, Hope turned to the tall woman. 'You're a policewoman! Why couldn't you stop Hart harassing Cal and his family? Make Carrie tell the truth?'

Margaret Redfeather looked at her for a long time. 'Cal has told you his side of the story?'

'You mean the truth,' Hope said, stubbornly.

Margaret sighed. 'You know, all this is as old as the hills. But Hope – may I call you Hope? – Carrie is a victim too in this. And she is the only person who can make the choice to defy her father. I'm tryin' to help her and her momma make that choice. Maybe when you get a few more years on you, you'll understand that—'

Hope closed her eyes, hands clenched, and took a breath. 'Cal is lying in there in a coma! He might die. Because of some stupid feud.'

'If he survives, the Crows have more than enough to press charges against Chief Hart. I looked into it since the incident at the store the other day. Too much harassment, too much to ignore.'

'That won't help Cal if he's dead, will it?' Hope said, furious.

'Hope?' Meredith's voice cut across the car park.

'This is my mum. She—'

'Hope? I told you, Jesus is going to drive us back to the ranch,' Meredith said, standing a little apart from them, ignoring the other woman completely. She looked down at Hope's feet. 'Oh dear, I wish I'd thought about shoes . . .'

Sitting in the back of the jeep, Hope stared out at the landscape. Streetlights and stop signs passed. Boulevards and fast-food restaurants.

'Mum? This isn't the way home.'

'Home? Yes, darling, it is.'

'No . . . this is the way we came. From the airport.'

Meredith said nothing.

'Mum?'

'The policeman called the hospital and says we are advised to leave now. There are things about that boy you probably don't know, Hope, and if we stay around it could make things worse for everyone. Worse for *him.* Or' – and her voice broke a little – 'for you. Especially if you're not planning on saying anything against him . . .' She sighed. 'I brought our passports with me when they called because I was worried about our health insurance policy, and there's a flight to Salt Lake City in an hour. The police chief just organized everything – they'll send our things on – and it really is the sensible thing to do.' She checked her watch.

'I—'

'I'm sorry, Hope. I know you like this boy, but it'll take him months to recover . . .' She paused. 'And I . . . need to keep you safe.'

Hope stared at her mother. 'I can't leave. It's running away!'

'The flight is already booked.'

'Mum, I'm asking you, please. Don't do this.'

Meredith's lips thinned, and Hope could almost see her mother's feminist instincts fighting against her mother instincts. The mother side won for once. 'You're not thinking straight, that's all. This is the best thing to do right at this minute. We can talk more when we get home. Away from this mess.' She stared out of the window of the jeep, refusing to say any more.

CHAPTER 19

'THE FACT THAT NO SINGLE MOMENT OF
OUR LIVES, WHETHER EXULTANT OR
DESPAIRING, CAN EVER BE RECALLED,
IS OF ITSELF ONE OF THE MOST
MOMENTOUS TRUTHS WITH WHICH WE
ARE ACQUAINTED. EACH MOMENT OF
OUR PAST IS GONE FOR EVER AND
NEITHER INGENUITY, NOR EFFORT,
NOR PURCHASE, NOR PRAYER
CAN CALL IT BACK.'

So, my dearest Nate, here I am. Back on our mountain. It took some effort to persuade my husband that I should return, particularly as I am with child again.

Five years have passed since our adventure, and still I think of all the things you mean to me. This little book has become my harbour and our son is my life's joy. Of course, now that I look back, I realize you knew I was carrying your child. The way you cared for me was a giveaway, but also the way you took to laying in our bed in the morning, your head near my middle; and the manner in which your hands rested there when we sat on the porch in the evenings. How you talked of us going to your family for the winter. I wonder when you would have told me. I was not at all sick until we reached

Portland, and I thought it was only that my body had broken along with my heart.

The only time I roused at all on the journey was when I heard of the plan to separate me from Tara. Hart, leaving us at the first trading post, had offered to buy her. I stood in the thoroughfare, gripping her noseband as he took her reins and announced to the whole settlement that if Tara were sold to him, or if any attempt at all were made to separate me from her, that they would find me dead at the first opportunity I could affect it.

I was entirely sincere and Mr Stanton intervened immediately, his hands held out in an honest promise that no one would try to take Tara away. He pledged to see to her welfare himself.

Hart laughed at his attempts to pacify me, but accepted the money my future husband produced from his soft leather wallet; then he spat in the dirt at my feet and called me the cripple's whore. Mr Stanton dismissed him sharply and Hart laughed in his face.

The subsequent journey to Oregon was harsh. The days were long and dry, the trail hard. Our pattering showers were gone. It was four days to Spokane. I was mute and recoiled from anyone's attempts to touch me, even in assistance. Spokane was a settlement of fur trappers who had eyed my blood-soaked leggings and rough shirt with interest when we arrived that baking afternoon. The first night there, my clothes were taken in my sleep and replaced with a cheap cotton muslin gown, purchased in the hardware store. I sobbed in silence, and refused to dress. Papa was distressed, but told me I must wear it for it was time to leave and my other clothes were beyond ruined and had been burnt. The gown itched and the seams chafed. I refused to wear the shoes they had bought me.

It took us another ten days to reach Portland, Tara trotting behind the coach Papa had hired. After the first two days, Mr Stanton sat opposite me. Papa preferred to ride after I told him I would not remain in an enclosed space with him. He had, after all, been the cause of what had happened to you.

To Mr Stanton I said nothing, and stared out of the window. He remembered our letters, and how I had told him of my wish to continue playing the piano and working on my writing. He asked if I had seen anything of the landscape during my time in the Montana wilderness and if I could describe it. I struggled to look at him, but his relentless attempts at conversation were, I see now, admirable in the face of my desolation. And by the time we reached Portland, Mr Stanton had arranged with Papa for the wedding to go ahead.

It was done quickly, with no fuss. I cannot remember saying my vows and I suspect Mama had put something in the tea she urged me to drink that morning. She had been horrified by my appearance when I stumbled into the house in Portland, and had me scrubbed raw, then covered in creams to whiten my skin. I barely noticed, for I was little more than undead at the time.

I want you to know that Anthony has been a very kind

husband. He is a truly honourable man, and says he never considered that the marriage would not go ahead. He had kept all my letters and read them, so many times. And he had made plans; created a life for us in Larkin Street.

He was disappointed, naturally, when it became apparent on our honeymoon that I really was more than just heartsick. I was delivered of your son seven and a half months after the wedding, at a pretty boarding house by the sea in a place called Heaven's Anchorage: a child with pale eyes and the most astonishingly powerful lungs.

Anthony has supported me, as he said he would, in my own interests. And in addition, we have built a glasshouse garden here in San Francisco not far from our house. Many people visit it. They must apply for a ticket but it costs them nothing, because I think you would have liked that. The garden is filled with plants and flowers from Montana and the Rocky Mountains. I go there early in the mornings and sit by myself.

Tara, who bore me from the mountain with the same stoicism she always displayed, brought forward a stunning glass-eyed colt the month after I gave birth. He is destined to be the finest breeding stallion in the Western States, apart from his sire, who has not been seen since he kicked his way out of the corral as Hart attempted to catch him. Hart was thrown to the ground by a blow from the stallion's head and the man who chewed tobacco caught a kick in the chest and didn't get back up. I watched as the white horse galloped into the forest, Papa's hand at my elbow.

A man stayed behind to bury you; he was already digging beneath the old tree by the corral as they took me away.

But I cannot think of you in the ground or my heart would shatter again, and leave me as it did for so long, clutching a door handle or a fire mantle, as the reality of a world without you in it crashed upon me. Instead, I imagine you here, following the life you made for us. I like to think that the white horse visits you, from time to time, in this place.

I have not seen Mama since my wedding day. On the day they left for England, Papa came to tell me he was so very proud of my courage and wished me every success and happiness in my new life. I neither looked at him, nor spoke. He put his hand on my hair and told me he had only been trying to do the right thing. It was the closest I have ever known my father come to an apology and I cried, then.

He pulled up a chair and began to tell me a story. The story of a father who saw only a life of confinement and unhappiness for his beloved daughter in London: the laudanum, Papa said, had long had the upper hand over Mama, and when he had seen me that day the year before, blank and glazed, his decision had been made. He had lost a wife, but he would not lose a daughter. So he had made a bargain with a good man, the best he could find, and sent his child, alone, across the world to a new life, only to think he had lost her altogether.

My eyes asked the questions I could not voice, and Papa explained, in a few sentences, how Mama's troubles had begun before I was born. The doctors had thought a child would help; I had not. And now that I was ruined – despite my subsequent marriage – she did not want me near her.

She did not come to say goodbye.

These are but small sadnesses, and I tell you them only so that you will know how my life is now.

Our son is a fine, strong boy with your looks and what I think will be your height. Anthony made over my dowry to me for his upkeep. Our boy is, to all good intents and purposes, raised with genuine affection as my husband's own child, yet Anthony insisted that your name was on the official paperwork for he wished, at some stage, for a legal heir of his own. More money was given over for this purpose, largely for the purpose of keeping it private, I suspect, but I did not object to it. In fact, it made me very happy and I think it would have made you proud, though it did pose me one small problem, which I shall come to.

After much thought, I have purchased a large farm out here to be our son's inheritance, a ranch for the breeding of horses. The very finest American horses. I have also set aside some of the land as a reserve for the plains buffalo, and have employed a man to oversee it.

One Michael Calton. He is a true cowboy, pioneer-stock. I think you would like him. He came all the way to San Francisco on a ticket I mailed to Wyoming, so that I might meet him regarding the position. And he reminded me a little of how you might have been, in our fancy drawing room: a spooky yearling. He ran his hat brim through his hands as I stifled a laugh and begged him to sit to take tea. And he knows these lands. He is familiar with the reservation set up for your people two years ago, somewhat to the south of our ranch, and can scratch through in their language. His writing is rough, but he sends regular updates as the homestead down in the hills takes shape.

Lucky is now Chief Little Elk, as you predicted, and at war with the Pikuni. I know nothing of Clear Water, but live in hope of news. Rose was seen in Fort Shaw the day before Sheriff Hart was found hanged from the cell bars in the jailhouse with his own knife in his back, his sheriff's star smashed into a mess of tin. On closer examination, they saw he had been scalped. I send his widow a modest pension for the care of their son, though I am uncertain of my motives.

Soon after that day, Mr Calton wrote to me of a small incident on the ranch. It is necessary, for now, to keep our buffalo corralled close to where the barn sits and the main house is being built. They are precious, now that so few remain. The house lies in the shelter of trees and a high bluff, from which there is a fine view of our land. The bluff is an ancient buffalo jump, but no more will die there, and it will be, in time, a home. Mr Calton went out at dawn one morning to check on a cow and calf and high on the ridge, against the jump and the dawn, sat an Indian brave on a grey mare, smoking a cigarette, rifle sticking up over one shoulder. The Indians have been no threat to the homestead, and I had written with instruction that no Indian camping party should be displaced or turned away: a pax. Mr Calton returned to work. When he looked up again from the calf, horse and rider were gone.

Rose, for I believe it *was* Rose, has not been seen near a

white settlement since. She roams the plains, and makes war against the hunters who come to Montana in ever greater numbers. She has, on two occasions, made the San Francisco newspapers, at the head of a band of braves. I read aloud her endeavours to my tea parties with a fierce and secret pride. They gasp and sip at their china cups. And they will never know.

As you predicted, the white man is determined to drive the buffalo into the dust. I read often of further massacres. But not here, Nate. Not on our land. When he is of age, our son will inherit this ranch to do with as he sees fit; I hope he will see it as your legacy. A legacy of your love of this place, its animals and its people. For I will tell him of you, when the time comes.

We are on our way there now. I am bringing Tara home. It will hurt me sorely to part with her, for she is my truest friend and without her I would have grieved to death. But neither she nor her son, the young white plains stallion, Isaac, belong in San Francisco with its leafy parks and its wide enamelled roads.

And nor do I. But there I will stay. Anthony simply oversees the railroad now; it is thought he will be a senator by his thirtieth year. And you were right: the tracks will not come through your mountains. The story of my 'rescue' never reached the newspapers, although heaven knows how much Papa and Anthony had to pay to keep it out.

Thought we speak of it rarely, my time with you is woven through the fabric of our lives, colouring them with sun

343

showers. Anthony is much accustomed to my continuing fascination with the new America, and he remains devoted to the medium of the photograph. Last year he hit upon a capital idea. He asked me to find a photographer, to document the people and landscapes of my West, his gift to me.

Mr Edgar Carson, who was born in Wisconsin, was the ideal candidate; we engaged him to document the native way of life and the buffalo, while they remain. He roams east of the Rocky Mountains with his photographic equipment and an assistant, returning to San Francisco every few months. I stood in the dark room with him as he developed his last set of plates, and watched as a familiar face emerged from the solution. Dog Child. Mr Carson told me Two Tails's son now has ties to the US Army, as a scout. I was pleased to see the young Blackfoot warrior once more. But it was a cruel reminder that no camera will ever capture the face I would give everything to see again.

Yet, onward. I spend my days on charitable works and furthering my husband's political career. Larkin Street is a happy home, and likely to be even more so in a few months' time. I found a nurse, from Virginia. She is fat and black and full of joy, and she sings when she thinks she's alone. I told her, on a quiet afternoon, that I'd once had a friend who'd fought for the Union Army. She put her hand on my arm and told me that you and she would be introduced in her Promised Land. Hattie adores your son, and she is making plans for these babies. For they think, Nate, that I am bearing twins.

I am sitting on our porch as I write this. Our son is playing in the meadow, making friends with every living thing. When he is still, which is rarely, he watches the world with eyes that see everything, as if time moves around him, not he through it. In those moments I see the man he will become and I feel my soul tear with love.

And the loss of you.

Our cabin is largely unchanged and I shall pay a man to come up from the ranch and make sure it survives the winters, for my lifetime at least. With him this year, he is bringing a stone to be placed here for you. I had to think hard about what I should put on it. To me you are simply *Nate*. Yet that wouldn't do for a memorial, would it? And when our son was placed in my arms I had to think about what you might like me to name him, and how we should remember you. It was a problem for but a few moments: I named you for your tribe, the Apsáalooke, although I have given you their English title. It is the name our son also bears.

Now I must go. Back to a life of *must*, of *should*. And one enormous maybe.

After I write these final words on this last blank page, I shall put this strange little book away; to start this tale from the beginning would be to live our story again. And those who are left behind must guard what remains of our hearts. Perhaps, one day, someone will find it and read how you once told me your love for me would be in this wind long after you were dead. They will learn how I sit on this porch and feel it still. I hope they will inherit the extraordinary love we found here, and that they have the time to live it, as we did not.

One day I'll return again, for the last time. But not yet, Nate, not now. Now, our boy and I will join the wagon that waits for us in the meadow. I recalled often, whilst carrying him, the stories you told me as we sat on this porch. Quiet hours and tales not only of your Indian family, but of a different American people: the settlers who came to this land two centuries ago to make a better life.

And so I named him for the very first of your pioneer ancestors.

His name is Caleb.

CHAPTER 20

People stared at the two police officers escorting a scruffy, barefoot, wild-looking teenage girl, pushing her when she halted, uncertain and desperate in the gathering bustle of the terminal. A squad car had been waiting at the airport.

'I will never, ever forgive you for this,' Hope turned and said to Meredith, a policeman's fist bunched in the back of her shirt. 'This is everything you're supposed to be against.'

Meredith's mouth tightened as she took Hope's arm, pulling her out of the police officer's grip. 'It's for the best.'

'Not for Cal. Not for me. How could you *do* this? You're going back on everything you've ever taught me.'

'They're calling your flight, ladies,' Chief Hart said. 'We'll take you to the plane.'

Hope looked at him with murder in her eyes. Their things

had already been checked, and in Meredith's hands were passports and boarding passes. As they were escorted to the gate, Hope's heart and mind raced. She pulled the diary from her pocket and clutched it to her middle for comfort. There had to be a way to stop them taking her away, like Emily had been. There had to be.

The large doors were open ahead of them and as their documents were checked Hope could see they were to be the last people on the plane. She looked around. Life continued as normal in Helena's small airport. Hope felt as if hers was ending.

As they walked out on to the tarmac, Hope's feet became more leaden with every step. Her hand trembled when she reached for the handrail of the metal steps and she wasn't sure she could make it.

'We'll be home soon, Hope,' Meredith said. 'Here, take these.' She passed Hope her passport and boarding pass, ready for the flight.

The attendant was waiting at the top of the stairs, smiling and holding out a welcoming hand.

'Let me take that for you though,' Meredith said, reaching for the diary.

Hope jerked back.

'Hope? Hope!' Margaret Redfeather was sprinting across the tarmac as the plane's engines wound up, badge clutched in her hand. Behind her were two security guards and what looked like a porter. They skidded to a halt, breathing hard.

Margaret shook her head. 'John Hart, who the *hell* do you

think you are?'

Hart folded his arms. 'Just making sure Miss Cooper here doesn't miss her flight.'

'You are not border control and you have no right to do this.' Margaret's voice was clear and strong. 'You can't just deport people.'

Hart stared at Margaret. 'You interfere, I'll get you fired.'

'Try it. One more reason on a long list for me to find a way to kick your ass, eventually. And who knows when that day will come?' A hint of a smile crossed her face.

He snorted. 'You people. You've been beat for a hundred and fifty years and you still can't see it.'

Meredith hoisted her bag a little higher on her shoulder. 'I want to take my daughter home. She's not thinking clearly.'

'*I am,*' Hope objected. She looked at the police chief, then at her mother. 'This is about you, Mum. You're trying to control me. I don't *want* to go home.'

Margaret turned to her, taking her shoulders. 'Hope. You're sixteen, right?'

'Yes.'

'And you're on your own passport with a tourist visa, yes?'

Hope nodded.

'And you want to stay here. I need you to say it aloud, if that's what you want.'

Hope looked at her mother, at all of them. 'I want to stay,' she said in a level voice. She clutched her passport firmly to her chest with the diary.

'Hope—' Meredith began.

'No, Mum, personal agency, remember? I'm choosing this. *Me.*'

Margaret nodded, once. 'Good enough for me. You can stay. You've done nothing wrong and no one can make you go.'

'I say she goes,' Hart snapped, leaning over Margaret.

She eyed him, only an inch or so shorter, not backing down. 'This is your life, isn't it? Endless little abuses of your power to make yourself feel like the big man. Hating on my people, fitting up others for things they didn't do because of some grudge you imagine you got. And that's only the tip of it. I know, 'cause I've looked. Well, I've called Internal Affairs.'

'You called IA on me?' Chief Hart began to go purple in the face and drew back his arm, fist clenched.

Margaret took a step away, pulling out her gun from under her black jacket, pointing it directly into his face. 'You strike me and it'll be the last thing you do. For a hundred and fifty years the Harts have been lying and cheating their way into Montana law enforcement. No more.'

He spat on the tarmac at her feet. 'Dirt-worshipping *bitch*. You've gotten above yourself with this one.'

Margaret laughed. A wild, joyous laugh that battled the plane's engines. 'Call me all the names you want, shitheel, but you won't touch me and you won't make that girl go anywhere she doesn't want to go.' She turned to Hope. 'When you're ready, the car's parked out front.'

Hope looked over her shoulder at her mother, standing on

the metal steps of the plane. Then she ran back to the terminal, bare feet pounding the tarmac.

In the old convertible, more grey than silver, Hope held the
diary on her lap and waited as the wiry policewoman slid into
the driver's seat. Margaret turned the engine over and pulled
away from the front of the terminal. Hope felt awkward in the
silence.

'Thanks, and everything. Although I don't really know what
I'll do now.'

Margaret pulled on to the slip road from the airport. 'The
Crows are good people – they'll make sure you have somewhere to stay. And there won't be any trouble, that was just
Chief Hart scaring your mom. I'm going to take you back to
the ranch now, get you some shoes and some warmer clothes,
and then I'll take you to the hospital. OK?'

'Thanks.'

'You English are real polite, aren't you?' The corner of her
mouth turned up. 'But the best way you can thank me is by
telling me what happened out there.'

Hope opened her mouth to speak.

'Wait, I think I need a cigarette. Pass me one from . . . yeah,
perfect.' Margaret put the cigarette between her lips. 'I know,
I know,' she said, to Hope's unspoken words. 'It's a filthy habit.'
She looked surprised as Hope burst out laughing. 'What?'

'Nothing. I can't explain.'

'Yeah, well, you'd better try, because it sounds as if I'm
going to have to call in a favour or two and I want to know the

reasons why. Start with the crash and go from there.'

As quickly and clearly as she could, Hope began to explain about finding the diary, about the crash, and about how things had happened on the mountain. It was a long story, mixing together both the tale of Emily and Nate and that of herself and Cal, and it all came tumbling out, a story of the sort any writer would be proud. They were some distance from the town, heading out on the road to the Broken Bit by the time she finished.

Margaret Redfeather said nothing, but paid attention to the road and smoked another cigarette.

'So,' she asked, when Hope ground to a halt, 'what happens in the end?'

Hope looked at the diary on her lap. 'I don't know. I haven't had time to read to the end.'

'Then read, Cooper.'

A few short minutes later, Emily's story drew to a close. '. . . *His name is Caleb*.' Hope's voice cracked as they approached the outskirts of Helena.

Margaret gripped the steering wheel. 'Hope?'

'Yes?'

'The Apsáalooke. Nate's people? That's *my* tribe. We're the Crow Nation. Rose Redfeather was the head of my family. Emily's son is Caleb Crow. The Crows have owned that ranch since what, 1871, right?'

'That's how it began, with Nate and Emily. And the cabin.'

'Holy shit,' Margaret said. 'I thought I knew everything there was to know about Rose. You know she's a legend, right?'

Hope shoved her hand under her nose, trying to stop the tears from falling. 'No, but how can we stop what's happening to Cal and his family?'

'What if . . .' Margaret drummed the wheel. 'What . . . if—'

The car leapt forward from the lights and Margaret executed a sharp U-turn as Hope clung on to the seat. 'What?!'

Margaret took her eyes from the road for a second to grab her phone. She put it into Hope's hand. 'I think we may have halted it already, just by stopping you leaving.'

'I—'

'Think about it, Hope. It went wrong for Nate and Emily when his Crow family left. If they'd been there, the outcome would have been real different. Dial this number.'

Putting in the number Margaret dictated, Hope heard it dial, then ring.

'Put it on speaker,' Margaret said, just as a voice answered.

'Davis.'

'Andrew?'

'Margaret?'

'Remember that favour?'

'Yes,' the man said warily.

'I'm calling it in. I'm going to call out some names and I need you to look at the records and meet us at St Peter's as soon as you can. Like, now.' Margaret hit the accelerator and the old Mustang shot through the stop light, dust spinning in its wake.

Back at the hospital, they ran through the ward to the ICU.

A man in a suit was waiting outside the unit, a police badge displayed over the breast pocket.

'I've been calling you back,' he said to Margaret.

She felt for her phone. 'I was driving. There's been a lot going on.' She turned to Hope. 'This here's Commissioner Andrew Davis. Hope Cooper.'

The dark-haired man offered his hand to Hope, his expression serious. They shook.

'OK, I've been looking, very quickly, at the history of police harassment against the Crow family by John Hart over the past decade and particularly the last couple of years,' the commissioner said to Margaret. 'It's all way out of line. There are other things too, other cases, with witnesses who've come forward, but we don't need to get into that now. I understand, Margaret, that you have a statement from Carrie Hart to confirm that there should be no outstanding accusation against this boy. I have no reason to disbelieve you, although we will obviously need to check this, but I can state clearly now that there are no official charges against Cal Crow and there won't be. His record is also clean.'

Margaret turned to the police officers still sitting outside the ICU. 'You can go now,' she said abruptly. 'Cal Crow is a patient here, nothing more.'

The commissioner showed his badge and handed the officers a piece of paper. One of them took it, surprised, getting to his feet.

The commissioner turned to Margaret. 'And I wanted to tell Mr and Mrs Crow in person, apologize to them on behalf of

354

the force. They should have come forward with this a long time ago.'

'Yeah, well,' Margaret said, 'I think you'll find they ain't complaining people.'

Suddenly Hope felt the deep silence from within the unit. She turned and stared through the window. Then she saw Elizabeth sitting silently, tears running down her face.

'I'm so sorry—' The nurse who had been so kind began, coming out from behind the station. She put her hand on Hope's arm.

'What?' Hope's voice was faint. She burst into the room, even as the nurse tried to hold her back. 'What's happening?'

'Hope,' the young doctor said gently, taking her arms. 'We've done all we can to stabilize him, but his vital signs went into decline just after you left.'

'You have to let me talk to him. I need to speak to him – there's things he needs to know. It doesn't matter how many people are in the room now, does it?' Hope said urgently as Margaret Redfeather and the commissioner came in behind her.

Margaret nodded to Cal's parents and pulled a key from her pocket, unfastening the handcuff from Cal's wrist, the metal bracelet falling on to the webbed blanket.

As they all looked on, Hope took his hand. 'Cal? Cal, it's me. It's Hope. The police are here. But it's not what you think. They're here to tell you they know what happened. You're in the clear!' She rubbed his cold knuckles. 'You have to help him now!' Hope pleaded with the gathering medical staff who watched her, awkward and unsure. 'Please!'

An unwilling audience in a tiny theatre.

She fumbled in her hip pocket with the other, pulling out the diary. Pressing her forehead to his, she touched a quick kiss to his mouth, distorted by the intubation tube, the ventilator pumping air in and out of his patched-up chest. 'Listen. What if Emily was right, that the universe does have a system of checks and balances? What if the white horse led us on to the bridge so that we could put things right?' She held the diary close between them, against her heart. 'Nate and Emily didn't get to choose, but we do. She came back to the mountain and wished for someone to inherit their story. And she wished that we'd have the time they didn't get. So you were right, this is crazy. But it's beautiful, and it's only just beginning.'

She took a deep breath, her voice breaking as the heart monitor flatlined . . .

'I love you.'

CHAPTER 21

ope sat on the hospital fire escape. In her hand, she held Elizabeth Crow's phone. Far away, clouds gathered over the mountains. There was an afternoon storm coming.

Behind her the door opened and Margaret Redfeather bunked down on the step, patting her pockets for a cigarette. 'You OK?'

Hope said nothing.

'Dumb question.' Margaret stuck the cigarette in the corner of her mouth and cracked the lighter. It flared and she breathed in quick then blew out slow. 'This Crow–Hart mess goes back a long way. I think a lot on this, you know, Hope. I think about who we are and if we can escape our pasts. But in the end, all we can do is our best. And you did it. You really did.'

'I'm not brave like you, or Rose. Or Emily.'

'Yes you are, even if you don't think it. Took real courage to stand up like that, amongst strangers in a strange place. To tell someone what you really feel.'

Hope hugged her hollow, aching chest. 'I'm not sure it made any difference, in the end.'

'Guess we'll never know.' Margaret picked a shred of tobacco from her tongue, looking out towards the mountains. 'But you know, when my tribe used to go to war we had this system—'

'Coups. Like Emily won.'

Margaret raised an eyebrow. 'So then you know what "Redfeather" really means?'

Hope shook her head. No, this she hadn't learnt from Emily.

'For my people, if you took a clean coup, you got an eagle feather to wear in your hair. But if you won a coup against the enemy and it cost you real bad, but you survived to fight another day, you dyed that feather red and you wore it with pride.' Margaret ground out the tab beneath her heel and stood, putting her hand on Hope's shoulder. 'Why don't you come on inside now? Everyone's worried about you out here all alone.'

Hope shook her head, looking at the sky. 'No, there's something I promised Cal I'd do.'

For a moment, Margaret said nothing. Then, 'You earned yourself one hell of a red feather today, Hope Cooper. Be proud. Own it.' She walked away, throwing her final words over her shoulder. 'And remember, call me if you need anything.'

The fire door banged and Margaret Redfeather was gone into the stormy Montana sunset.

Hope looked at the time on the phone in her hand and then entered the number she knew by heart but had never actually dialled. It rang for what seemed like a long time.

'Hello?' a voice said, a little blurry with sleep. Then again, after a pause. 'Hello?'

Hope took a deep breath. 'Dad?'

On finally returning to England, Hope stepped off the red-eye flight, took the Tube to Marble Arch and walked to Portman Square. There, she sat on a bench in the London rain and looked at the house where Emily had grown up, the square's garden green and wet around her.

She went home and, after some discussion with Meredith, she became a student at a local school. In the times Meredith worked away, Hope began staying with her father's family in their noisy, echoing Hampstead house, which was still falling down around their ears. She had a tiny bedroom there in the eaves, with an old metal single bed and a view over the jungle-like garden. Everyone talked at once as they sat around the dinner table and they welcomed Hope into their chaotic midst as if she had been part of their lives all along.

She helped her father learn his lines outside the kitchen door, as he strode around the yard, clutching his silver hair and a glass of wine. She watched with her half-brothers –

James and Tom – three sets of elbows on the timber balcony, as her father took the stage at The Globe theatre; they visited him on the set of his detective series. She formed a tentative, honest friendship with her father's wife, although Mags could never be a real stepmother to her. Affectionate and tactile, her father and Mags however encouraged Hope to follow her heart: she wrote continually, and sent off her work to magazines and journals as often as she could.

Over in Montana, it had taken almost two years for Hart to be dismissed, officially, from his post. Although there was never any real chance it would get to trial, Hope had been glad to see him punished. The ex-chief still lived on the outskirts of Fort Shaw and spent a lot of time in the town bar apparently. There was nothing for him to go home to, after all, as Carrie and her mother had disappeared that summer.

A year after her time there, Hope had received, via Margaret Redfeather, an unsigned postcard from Denver. It featured a picture of the city and across it in large yellow letters it said, 'Hello from beautiful Denver!' Margaret kept in touch, always, and was working full-time now with victims of domestic violence. Still wearing sharp suits, still smoking untipped cigarettes, still driving her silver Mustang.

At university, Hope studied English literature as she had planned – something Meredith had finally accepted – and made a large group of friends, although she saw Lauren and Scott often. Caleb and Elizabeth came to London for two weeks and on a Sunday morning ate ranchers' salad outside an East London hipster café, as babies in buggies cried and dogs lay under every table and nobody cared. Caleb Crow declared himself a big fan of London, and wondered how Chuck was faring back home.

In her final year at university, Hope had a book published. A novel, set in Montana.

The diary accompanied her everywhere, although sometimes she did not look inside it for months. She found out all she could about Emily Howard Stanton, contacted her descendants, still living in San Francisco, and emailed them a transcript of Emily's account of that summer. She researched Nate's second family, and discovered the history of Little Elk's long reign as chief, the early death of his wife Clear Water from influenza, and the extraordinary life of Rose Redfeather, who bore a daughter to an unknown father some ten years after Emily's summer. Of Nate's first family, Hope never found a trace.

Cal was constantly in her thoughts. Often, she missed him so much she could barely breathe, finding herself lost and confused in a coffee shop, or reprimanded in a lecture for inattention.

She never stayed away from Montana for long – how could she? – and the Broken Bit was another home. Then, as time passed, she realized part of her had never left the mountain above Upper St Mary Lake, and that ingenious pioneer cabin, where she and Cal had been tenants for such short, precarious days.

Over the years, the pull to return to the cabin became stronger and stronger until it was impossible to resist . . .

Montana. Now.

Hope is on the porch. Before her the expanse of St Mary Lake stretches for miles in both directions. The cabin is restored, and the window replaced. On the wreck of the old corral by the wind-stunted tree sits a battered red Ford pick-up. A few deer move in and out of the treeline. The diary is at her side and she has retrieved from the dark corners of the chest a ragged eagle feather, a brittle blue and yellow bracelet, some elk teeth and a broken D-ring snaffle bit. And the possibles bag. Wild flowers carpet the meadow.

The untethered days up here putting the place to rights have been perfect. So much of who she is was forged on this mountain, and in such a short time. Emily's diary has become a touchstone, and Hope's life has taken roads she never could have imagined on that first flight to Helena.

She stands and walks to where Cal is loading the rig, ready for the drive home.

'Dearest Buddy.' Hope puts her hand over the shirt in the small of Cal's back, warm and damp from work, and looks at the spot near the tree where they once buried the funny, brave young puppy.

'He was a good little guy.' Cal wipes his face on his sleeve, and stoops to ruffle the white, grey-tipped ears of the wolf-dog lolling on the ground next to him. Another dumpster baby.

Hope crouches and kisses the dog's head, laughing as he

licks her cheek in a rough swipe. 'Yes, Jake, almost as good as you,' she tells the huge puppy. She stands. 'How's the shoulder?'

'Not bad. Only a twinge.' Cal pushes his fingers into his chest. 'Can it really be five years now?'

'What, five years since you died?'

He tucks a strand of hair behind her ear. 'Only for a minute.'

'Might only have felt like a minute to you,' Hope retorts.

'Anyone would think you cared. Cared enough to try and restart my heart by yourself. Railing on the hospital staff the whole while.'

'You don't remember that,' Hope says, accusing.

He smiles. 'Mom and Dad paint a pretty good picture.' He looks into the distance, towards the whitecaps, suddenly serious. 'So, do I get my answer?'

She says nothing, for a while.

'C'mon, y'know it makes sense. All this messing about with visas is getting to be a nightmare. And now you've graduated you said you wanted to take some time off anyway, with the new book. The plans for the house are finished. Mom and Dad are happy for us to start building whenever we like. And Zach will be the most incredible wedding gift!'

'Stop saying the W-word,' she interrupts. 'I think I have an allergy. And I'm still too young.'

'And *that* argument won't wash for so much longer.'

Hope laughs, tugging on his shirt. 'I want it in the vows that you'll make sure I have the internet. I've agreed to live off grid, not in the Stone Age.'

He hides a smile, sensing victory. 'I promised you, didn't I?'

'I really don't see why we can't keep living in the barn loft.'

'Oh yeah? If we start now, we don't have to share a shower block with two dozen hands all summer.' He pulls a face. 'And my folks are just about dying over the idea of us living on the ranch for good.'

Hope shakes her head. 'Your dad. I swear, if he cracks one more grandpa or baby joke, I'll . . .' she threatens, undermining it by laughing as he wraps his arms around her waist.

'I told him straight, we've got a few more years of practising before we start work on Cal Junior—'

'What if *he's* a girl?!'

He raises an eyebrow.

She sighs, conceding defeat on that one. 'But what about Mum? She does her nut about settling down so early every time I see her.'

'I thought we agreed we weren't going to let Meredith tell us how to live our lives quite a few years ago?'

'I know. But if it wasn't for her, we'd never have met.' Hope frowns. 'I can't even imagine what that would have been like. And she's definitely chilling out a bit, don't you think?'

'I'm not sure I'm ever going to think of your mom as chilled, but yeah, she's better. Since she got it that this isn't like her and your dad. This – you and me – is for ever.'

Hope shakes her head but she's laughing, forehead against his chest. 'For ever. That's a crazy concept, cowboy.'

'So let's just do it,' he says, keeping his voice deliberately light.

'Excuse me while I die of romance.'

'Oh, I'll romance you, Cooper, don't you worry, but I want you to say yes first. And mean it.'

She sits on the tailgate of the rig and loops her arms around his neck. 'Where would we have it?'

'At home.'

'When?'

'As soon as we can get it organized.'

'Where will we put everyone?'

'There's thousands of acres to put them in.'

'Dad will want to come. And James and Tom. And I can't invite them without Mags. What a mess that'll be.'

'Nah, we'll keep them corralled. I'll put Matty on segregation duty.'

The breeze is coming up from the lake, gathering pace as the day recedes.

'You're not happy. What's wrong?'

Hope takes a breath. 'I am – you know I am. It's just, I've been thinking, a lot, about coming up here. About them.'

'You think a lot, you know that?'

'Yes. Probably too much, but I keep coming back to the minute you were gone. Emily lived a lifetime of that minute.'

For a while, he's lost in thought, fingers tangling in the shreds of her hair. Finally the words come. 'Emily lived a fine life. She knew love. Real love. And she loved. Stanton adored her. She was a great woman, an activist who devoted her life to making things better. She raised children who went on to be pioneers in their fields. A surgeon, a politician, a rancher.

Maybe it wasn't the life she would have chosen, but she made the best of it. And maybe that's all we can do.'

Hope shivers. 'Then to die in the San Francisco earthquake.'

'Did she die? They never found her body. Only his. And sometimes, I wonder . . . if somehow, she made her way back. Like she promised. Those things we found – the shawl, the reading glasses, I just wonder. Maybe she lived out her days here in Montana.'

Hope glances back at the cabin. 'They feel so close.'

'Always. And I'm grateful to them. To Emily, for being the woman she was, starting everything here, making us who we are. But to Nate too, for . . . being Nate. Although, you know,' Cal takes a deep breath, 'he's a lot to live up to.'

'You're not doing so bad,' Hope teases.

He points to the rig. 'We should get going.'

With a last look around, she nods. 'Yes.'

'Home by nightfall.'

Jake is scratching over in the dirt of the old corral, near an ancient tree.

'Hey, boy, what is it?' Cal walks over and bends to see what treasure the dog has unearthed. Half-buried in the dirt, moss and lichen is the corner of an old black slate stone. 'Hope?'

Sliding down from the truck bed, Hope comes over. 'What is it?'

Cal is already pulling the stone from the dirt, shoving it upright against the withered tree. The dirty black surface is etched with words and dates. No ceremony, no celebration, no sentiment.

NATE CROW
1867
and
EMILY
1923

For a long time, only the sounds of the mountain can be heard.

'She did it,' says Cal at last. 'She came back.'

When Hope speaks, it isn't to Cal, but to the stone itself. 'OK, you two, I give in.' She looks at Cal. 'As soon as we can get it organized?'

He watches her. 'You mean it?'

'Yes. How can we argue with them? I stopped trying to on that porch five years ago.'

Cal's yell of triumph echoes round the meadow as he lifts Hope clear off the ground and spins her around. Setting her back on her feet he kisses her. 'Come on, let's go home. We've got people to tell.'

Hope pops the driver's door as Cal hups Jake into the back of the rig, fastening the tailgate. The sun is behind him, gilding his hair and skin. Everything is gold and silver. For a fleeting second her heart hurts, with love and pride, and with what she almost lost for ever

Then a movement near the cabin catches her eye. 'Cal?'

The white horse stands in the meadow, studying them through pale eyes. His hooves are four square in the wild flowers as his mane and tail are caught by the wind.

The world continues to turn, but on the Montana mountain where the tale of one American family began and so nearly ended, time is once more irrelevant and immeasurable. Radiant in the lowering sun, the stallion turns his head and looks west: the horse of a lifetime.

Maybe more than one lifetime.

And all the birds, singing.

ACKNOWLEDGEMENTS

'The Montana Book', as *Crow Mountain* is known by my family and friends, has had a fast journey to publication and my head is still spinning. The story was initially sparked more than a decade ago by a book called *Bury My Heart at Wounded Knee*, introducing me to the history of the Native Americans. And by a lovely stranger on a long Miami Beach afternoon who laughed and told me the tattoo on the inside of her wrist was the state outline of Montana, 'the most beautiful place in the world. Home.'

I worked in America for some time after that meeting and adored it: the sense of potential spinning across a continent, yet also that sense that no one is ever far from the edge of disaster. I read about settler marriages. And divorces. The stunning alpine wilderness of Montana, and in particular the Glacier National Park and St Mary Lake. I read about the railroads. The American Civil War. The terrible subjugation of the Native American people as the US government fought a hypocritical war to free the Southern slaves. But the story that stuck in my marrow was the near-extinction of the plains bison. Twenty-five million deaths in fewer than two decades. This story lies at the heart of the book.

How to tell it? That was the problem: I just didn't know. Then in February 2014 I visited an Amish craft store in Ohio. I was lecturing on eighteenth-century childbirth in Cleveland and we were taking a day out. My host went to the restroom so I loitered, looking at the frying pans, washtubs and wood-fired stoves. There were also cute but complicated oil lanterns, ingenious wooden spoons, spatulas with hook handles for pulling out hot tins and a wall of pretty cookie cutters in the shape of every state. I picked up Montana immediately: an automatic reaction. Two dollars, I thought, who cares? Then I hesitated. Why should I clutter my already crammed kitchen drawer with it? Because of a beautiful girl with a now-outdated tattoo? Because since then I'd read dozens of academic articles and books on people who abandoned everything they knew to make a new life on the edge of a new world? The horror of exterminating a species? I put it back. Yet as I looked at it, I saw Nate and Emily, Hope and Cal. Just like that, I knew what they looked like and who they were, their voices crowding my head. My host returned. I grabbed Montana and paid. We walked into the car park and the cool sunshine of a new American Spring. In the car, I watched as we passed horse-drawn carriages, rolling hills, homesteads and barns, people still living in another century. I came home and wrote the book. Still haven't made the biscuits.

As a historian, I wanted to make this book true to the remote young states of the second half of the nineteenth century, and as such the events – such as the Battle of the Wilderness, John Gantt's wagon train and the construction of Fort Shaw from what was Camp Reynolds – are all real events. I've tried to do justice to the varied tribes of Montana, although I deliberately robbed them of a voice, apart from Dog Child, who is one of the only documented and photographed Blackfoot braves of the time. I can't speak for them, and I wouldn't pretend to: it was not my remit here.

But the writing of this book has been such a joy, and I thank everyone involved in it. Imogen Cooper, Barry Cunningham, Rachel Hickman and the wonderful team at Chicken House have supported the cast of *Crow Mountain* like friends. Thanks too, as ever, to Kirsty McLachlan and all at David Godwin Associates. Big thank yous must also go to Lucy Fisher, Essie Fox, Brigid Coady and Sally Harris for being early and such encouraging readers. To Richard, Mr Inglis, for his constant love and support, and for ignoring the tears streaming down my face during the days it took to write the end of Nate's life and Emily's final letter to him.

And thank *you* for reading to the end. This has been a wonderful part of *my* story, but if you take one thing from this book, take the last words my beloved Emily left in my head:

All our lives will be, in time, just stories. Live the best story you can.

CITY OF HALVES

London. Present day. Girls are disappearing. And strange creatures are on the streets.

When Lily is attacked by a two-headed dog, she's saved by hot, tattooed and not-quite-human Regan. As Guardian of the Gates it's his job to protect both halves of the City, new and old, from a world of restless creatures that threaten its very existence.

As the City spins out of control, Lily and Regan race to find the girls, discover the truth, and expose a terrible conspiracy.

Paperback, ISBN 978-1-909489-09-7, £6.99 • ebook, ISBN 978-1-909489-53-0, £6.99

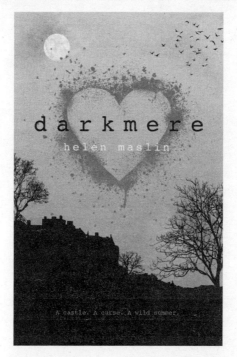

DARKMERE by HELEN MASLIN

Outsider Kate has a crush on the coolest boy in school, Leo. He's inherited a castle, a menacing ruin on the rugged English coast. When he invites her along for the summer, she finally feels part of the gang.

But Darkmere's empty halls are haunted by dark ghosts. Two centuries ago, Elinor – the young wife of the castle's brooding master – uncovered a dreadful truth.

As past and present entwine, Kate and Elinor find themselves fighting for their lives – and for the ones they love.

Paperback, ISBN 978-1-910002-34-6, £7.99 • ebook, ISBN 978-1-910002-75-9, £7.99